THE VAMPIRE'S CAPTIVE

KAY ELLE PARKER

THE VAMPIRE'S CAPTIVE

Vienna

In the space of one night, my world is thrown into the air and dropkicked into a new dimension. Sounds dramatic, right? Probably because it is. I'm no stranger to drama, but this... this takes the award for Best Dramatic Bombshell.

It all starts with a carjacking on a dusty highway twenty miles outside Tucson, Arizona.

That's the normal part of that night, I guess.

What happens after that...well, let's just say I'll never be the same again.

Colt

The moment I sense her spying on me, I know I can't let her go. She isn't what I was expecting to find. She isn't like the rest of the mortals. So I steal her and make her my captive.

No one knows she's been taken. No one knows where she's gone. No one knows what her future holds, except that she belongs to me...

Until death do us part.

1

*ienna*

It's so goddamn hot.

It's two a.m. so why is it *so goddamn hot?*

I don't like the heat; I hate the way it makes me sweat and feel as though I'm about to pop out of my skin. I can deal with it through the day because it's expected, right? The sun shines its bountiful rays down on the earth and hey presto, we bake in its blessed goodness.

But these temps at this time in the morning?

God is surely laughing at everyone as they toss and turn in their beds, restless and antsy, begging their air-con units to take the edge off. For some relief from the heatwave dogging the region, with no end in sight.

God and I, we're not on the best of terms right now. I figure I'm the tiniest ant in the colony called Earth, and He's taking too much pleasure in frying me in the beam of His magnifying glass. Relentlessly—no mercy to be had for little old me.

Trudging along in my battered flip-flops with stones poking through the flimsy soles into the bottoms of my feet, I scowl as a truck blows past without stopping. Jesus, can these assholes not *see* my thumb waggling around like it's possessed? That's the fourteenth one in the last hour that hasn't even tapped the brakes.

It displaces the hot air around me, kicking it back in my face and making me choke on heat and dust. I stumble, flip the truck the bird, then curse as the blast of an airhorn and my own pained shout echo in the desert. Stupid stones!

Trekking down Route 19 is possibly the stupidest thing I've ever done, and hitchhiking the most dangerous, but fate —that persnickety, devious bitch—has had her fingers in my pie yet again, and is apparently not going to stop until I'm literally begging on my knees for a reprieve from the shit she keeps dumping on my head.

I mean, come on. A flat tire in the middle of nowhere is bad luck. It sucks beyond belief, especially in the eerie darkness with coyotes calling in every direction. I'm not weak and I don't scare easily, but hell, I was willing to crawl back into my banged-up Chevrolet, lock the doors, and cower in the footwell until dawn.

But no. Being as I'm supposed to be a strong, independent, fearless woman who can change the tire while lifting the damn truck with one hand, I did the dutiful thing and got to work with the spare and the jack. I thought I was doing just fine until a car pulled up beside me, music thumping and the smell of pot wafting from open windows.

The faces in the car were friendly enough, I recall sourly. I'd felt better after counting two females on the younger side of twenty and the driver—a young man who probably wasn't quite of drinking age—as the only occupants.

High as kites, they'd stumbled from the car and the boy gallantly offered to replace my tire, an offer I couldn't refuse. In hindsight, I could damn well have said no. Should have done.

Didn't.

Like an idiot, betraying my supposed intelligence, I let my guard down as the kids' whacked-out chatter made me mellow... or maybe it was the passive smoke from the joint in the boy's hand. All I know for sure is, one minute I was waiting for Ricardo to finish changing the tire, and the next...

Well, we'll just say watching my only mode of transportation—along with my bag, wallet, and phone—drive away without me, was not my finest moment.

So now I'm stuck trying to hitch a lift in the middle of the night with no phone or money, and it's hot as freaking Hades. Sweat runs down my back and between my breasts, and I'm wishing for some sign of civilization other than the assholes driving past me without slowing down.

The next signpost I see tells me—no word of a lie—it's eighteen miles to Tucson. Eighteen. Freaking. Miles. Pretty sure I'll be dead and vulture bait before I make it another three. I kick listlessly at a small rock before I remember I'm only in these damn flip-flops, then hop around cursing God, life, the universe... anyone and anything that comes to mind.

I almost miss the smaller sign tacked beneath the main one, declaring a rest area only a little further ahead. I could sit, I muse as I flex my bruised toes. Maybe there'll be somewhere I can sleep until morning, when things might look brighter in all respects.

Tucson isn't my original destination, but if it saves me

from dehydration and vulture-related death, I'm happy to give it a shot. I'm a bit of a drifter, don't really spend much time in any one area, and my job goes where I go. Everything in my little world isn't perfect but it's comfortable.

By the time I drag my sorry ass to the *rest area*—which is little more than a twenty-foot track down to a small clearing big enough for half a dozen cars, surrounded by a handful of ginormous boulders—my feet are blistered, my tank top is several shades darker than its original color, and there's more dust in my throat than there is in the Sahara.

I hobble to the boulders for somewhere to sit, and on the far side of one hulking rock, I find a series of ledges—some deep, some shallow—which make perfect benches. I climb up onto a deeper one, smoothed out by weather or multiple butts perching in this same place, and finally relax.

The stone has maintained some of the heat from yesterday, but it's still cooler than the air around me. I settle into it, closing my eyes and banishing thoughts of stolen cars and forgotten dreams, ravenous hunger, and an insane need to glug down three gallons of water in one go.

I think I must drift for a little while because I know I'm not asleep, but I'm certainly not fully awake. It's that weird state of consciousness where the body sleeps but the brain still has a gear ticking over slowly, a watchdog that doesn't rest.

The growl of an engine sounds close but doesn't seep into my reality. It's followed by two more before the engines shut off. The slamming of several doors has me jolting fully awake and I think, *Yes! Thank God, there's people.*

As I scramble to lurch off the ledge, common sense tuts at me and stops me before I give away my presence. It's still dark, with only a couple hours before dawn. We're eighteen miles outside of a large city, tucked away from seeing eyes.

Why would three vehicles pull over here together at this time of night?

A lot of things spring to mind, none of them I want any part of, ever. Human trafficking, sex trafficking, drug trafficking—you know, the three T's you never want to become involved with, particularly as a female alone in the desert.

I freeze in place as voices carry in the still air. I count three different male voices as terse greetings are offered and, in my mind's eye, I add another six silent guards into the equation. If books and films have taught me anything, it's that no traffickers of any ranking would meet with fellow badass criminals without backup.

"Is this really necessary, Oberon?" Voice One sounds disgruntled, a hard Russian accent biting off the words. "Meeting all the way out here when we all have secure places for this kind of rendezvous?"

"Anywhere within the city has ears," comes the bitter reply. Voice Two's owner is not a happy man. "Someone tipped Lucius off to the ring. He doesn't know who or how yet, but he's resourceful. It is for all our benefit to take precautions—*better* precautions—from this point. One of us has a leak, gentlemen, and Lucius enjoys... plugging dams."

There's a quick barrage of curses, more impressive than mine, and I'm sure something growls. Viciously, like a rabid wolf. I'm hoping I'm mistaken and that one of these lawbreaking individuals hasn't brought along their pet murder hound for a ride out.

I smell bad enough, *I* can smell me.

"Can't be much of a leak if he doesn't know who or how," the third voice drawls. It's lazy, almost careless, as though being discovered by this Lucius doesn't really hold much concern. "We'd all be ash by now if he had enough info to act. Lucius isn't king because he lets things slide by the wayside. You break his laws, he breaks you. It's that simple."

King? I frown. I've never heard of a King of Tucson before. What the actual fuck have I landed myself in? I ease back against the boulder, bringing my legs in so I can wrap my arms around them. It's doubtful the men will have a reason to come scouting around here, but I'm not taking any risks.

"I have a shipment ready to go," the Russian says bluntly. "Fifty head of mobile blood bags ready to be dispatched. Are you trying to tell me it is not safe to ship them, Oberon? This would be very bad for our working relationship."

Mobile blood bags? I think I gasp, but I'm too busy twisting those three little words around in my head until they make sense. Which they don't. Hell, how can they? That makes it sound like they're ferrying people around for their blood. Hospitals? No, surely no self-respecting or law-abiding establishment would *buy* innocent people for what kept them alive.

"We just need to be more cautious for a few weeks," Oberon stutters, and I swear I can smell his fear drifting this way. Whoever he is, he isn't as high up the food chain as he thinks—and he knows it. "Fifty is wishful thinking, Vadim. Holding a large amount of product is risky if Lucius has gotten our scent. We should only ship what we can redistribute immediately."

"So you are telling me, what? I should lose money on the product *you* requested, that I have spent time, effort, and cash sourcing for you, because you are scared of the big, bad vampire? You disappoint me, Oberon."

"You'll get your money back, Vadim." That slow-as-molasses voice speaks again, just as implacable as before. "Down to the last ruble. Lucius doesn't welcome strangers into his den with open arms, and his reputation for dealing with those who defy his rule is legendary. Oberon may have a point."

The Russian scoffs. "The Vampire King can die as easily as any of us, Colt. He hides behind his minions and his club, distracted by that sexy little piece of ass. Easily removable from his throne of power and replaced with someone more deserving."

Now I know I'm dreaming. I pinch myself, hard, but the nip of pain calls me a liar. I'm wide awake and trapped in a nightmare where, if all indications are correct, vampires exist. Like, for real. For *real*, real.

"Seeing as you're not from around here, I'll excuse your ignorance this once. Lucius is king for a reason, and with the years he's got behind him, he won't die *as easily as any of us*. We have nothing on him, Vadim. He can crush a skull in his hand faster than you can blink. Speaking of treason—even all the way out in this godforsaken hell—isn't wise." Colt of the wonderful voice is starting to get riled, if his tone is anything to go by. "If you want to try, go ahead. I'm not risking my neck on a suicide mission—I like my head exactly where it is now."

"So what do you propose? I lose money every day I have to feed the whining creatures in my care."

"I can take the fifty. My buyers can probably take a few extra each, as long as the merchandise is as described. After this shipment, we need to cut down the amount of head sent our way. Smaller numbers, more deliveries. Not quite as cost effective as I'd like, but until we know for sure that Lucius isn't already on our trail, it will have to suffice."

There's silence for several ominous moments and all I can hear is the boom of my heart beating erratically in my chest. My body is cold now, whether from shock or fear, I don't know. I just want them to leave so I can get the hell away from here.

"I will give the order. They will arrive on Friday. Eight p.m. at the usual drop-off. I intend to return to Moscow tomorrow night. Fix this issue, Colt, or no more of my product will feed your hungry mouths. They'll have to fend for themselves if Lucius is not brought to heel."

Three car doors crack shut like gunshots, making me jump, then an engine revs and tires spin, kicking up gravel as the car turns in a fast circle and speeds away.

"Told you bringing that Russian asshat was going to give us nothing but trouble, Obe." Colt's tone is disapproving. "No way in hell I'm taking a shot at assassinating Lucius. It's been tried before, and I've seen the faces of those who witnessed the repercussions—they were scared as much as they were awed. He's not someone to mess with."

"What other choice do we have? Vadim can source the rarest of bloodlines, the blood-type that's going to make us richer than Midas."

Colt laughed. "I can guarantee we won't be getting pure Rhonull donors, Obe. He just said he's got fifty head waiting to go. We'll be lucky if we get *one* Rhonull in that batch. There's less than fifty Rhonulls documented in the world; the only way to get that many would be if he's breeding them."

"Maybe he is."

"Wouldn't put it past him."

"Fuck. If he sends mediocre quality goods, we're in so much shit."

"I'll put the word out. I can find buyers for whatever comes. Food is food, however discriminating the palate."

"Goddamn him. Why are Russian vamps such assholes?"

"Bet he's thinking the same about us."

"Probably. Look, I've got to go do some damage control. I'll talk later. See what you can find out about what Lucius knows, will you? You know people close to him, maybe wheedle some data from them, and make sure we haven't got an axe hanging over our necks."

"Sure thing."

Only two doors close this time, and the car drives away at a more sedate pace than the Russian's. Shortly afterward, another two doors crack shut, and the last car disappears back up the short track toward the highway.

Thank God.

I take my first full breath in twenty minutes, resting my head back against the rock as I begin to shake. This is too much freaky shit for me to handle. What am I supposed to do now?

I could carry on my merry way and pretend I haven't just been privy to a conversation that's rearranged my world. I could probably erase any thoughts of vampires and Rhonulls, whatever the fuck they are, with enough alcohol to sink the Titanic. But I'll always *know*, and that... it shakes the foundation of everything.

Suddenly, being outside at night doesn't seem to be the smartest idea.

But what else can I do? I don't know this Lucius. I hardly think a mortal walking up to the *Vampire King* would go down very well. I have three names and a conversation, not much of a lead for him to follow. No physical descriptions or car license plate numbers. For all I know, the men used aliases to meet up with.

I don't want to move from my spot, but then again, I can't stay here with the echoes of three very bad men—vampires, sorry—haunting me the longer I tremble in place. I have to move, to burn off the shock and the restless energy beginning to build inside me. Prey instinct.

Run and hide.

Pushing myself off the ledge is the hardest thing I can remember ever making myself do. Something inside me is physically rebelling at the thought of stepping out into the big, dark world with what I now know is out there.

I want lights, lots and lots of lights, and a door with a lock.

Several locks.

Nausea turns my stomach as I limp gingerly into the clearing, thinking of the eighteen miles of darkness I need to make it through to get to shelter. There's no way I'm hitching a freaking lift now—vampires are sitting pretty above serial killers and rapists at the top of my no-fucking-way list.

The hairs on the back of my neck and my arms rise, a subtle warning, an instant before a warm, lazy voice floats around the ring of boulders.

"Thought I could smell an eavesdropper. Didn't expect one quite so pretty."

I whip around, eyes scanning for the source, unable to find it. My heart is hurtling around inside my chest, bouncing off my ribs until I can hardly breathe.

"You're incredibly lucky my associate didn't clock you. You'd have been sucked dry and tossed aside for the coyotes by now." A soft chuckle. "Bet you're glad you landed yourself with me, huh?"

Glad is not the word I'd use, no. How the hell did he pull this off? His car *drove away*. I heard it; I know I did. I try to school my breathing back to normal, turning in a slower circle as my eyes scour every inch of rock and shadow. "Where are you, you bastard?"

A rich, vibrant laugh I would never have expected from a freaking *dead man walking* bounces around me and hits me square in the ovaries. "Feisty little eavesdropper, throwing down the gauntlet." His tone is mocking, teasing, and it's making me mad. He's like a hyena calling a hapless tourist's name in the middle of the desert, drawing his victim away from the safety of camp into the jaws of death. "Tell me what you overheard, and you might live to see dawn."

"If we stay out here, you're the one who'll see dawn," I retort, inwardly cursing myself for this surge of nervous bravado. Taunting him isn't the best decision but without so much as a hairpin to defend myself, words are all I've got. "Your last, I'd guess. Not big on tanning, are you? And I'm thinking shaving is gonna be difficult."

Something whispers past me, spinning me around before I can brace myself, but there's no one there. This guy's either a prankster or a sadist, and I can guess which. If he thinks he can make me run, screaming... he might be right, I admit to myself as I'm knocked back in the other direction.

"Such a shame," a voice croons in my ear—I mean, *in* my ear, as though he's stood right behind me. "I really can't let you wander around with all our secrets in your head. Who knows who you might tell..." It feels like a cool fingertip is skimming down my back from nape to butt, but I'm locked in position, unable to move. "Who you might divulge my secrets to..." Something sharp nips the lobe of my ear. "Who you might go running to and get me killed."

"You mean Lucius?" I throw the name out into the open confidently, as though I know exactly who he is. "You *really* should be more careful about where you discuss your super top-secret, nefarious plans, *Colt*."

A low growl follows the path of his finger, but when I

thrust my elbow back to hammer his ribs, I meet nothing but empty space. I'm flung around again—this time, I feel his fingers gripping my arm as he spins me. It's only for the briefest instant, but it's enough to burn my skin with the connection.

Not hot like a human, not cold like a dead guy.

He's a strange, oddly compelling temperature. Like something you'd want to cuddle up to on one of those nights when the bed's freezing cold, with enough coolness to make snuggling possible all through the night, not just until you get too hot and double-barrel his ass off the edge of the bed.

Until you remember he's one of the undead and has sharp, pointy teeth.

I'm getting a bit pissed off at being manhandled by this dead guy. It's one thing playing with your food, and then there's just being a fucking asshat with a really sexy voice whom I shouldn't be letting get under my skin.

"What. To. Do. With. You." He almost hums the words in a sing-song fashion, and I know he's toying with me. He didn't sound this insane when he was hashing out the details of shipping human beings into the country, destined to be snack packs for his kind. "Evidently, my dear girl, you heard everything. Well, I suppose the kindest thing to do would be to snap your neck, but all that blood pumping fearfully through your veins smells deliciously enticing. It would be despicably rude to waste it, wouldn't it?"

Restraining myself from bolting takes effort. Icy prickles of fear are spreading under my skin like some kind of rash because his voice is changing. The casual, lazy edge is gaining a predatory finish, razor-sharp and deadly. Running is only going to solidify the impression I'm prey, and I'm not dying tonight.

Carjacking, I can deal with.

Dying is a huge no-no.

I only have one weapon at my disposal and I'm going to use it. I don't have anything else left to bargain with. "You know, Lucius isn't going to be happy if you kill his newest employee. I'm figuring something along those lines will get you beheaded even if he never finds out about the smuggling."

Colt snorts. "You? Lucius's employee? Pull the other one, sweetheart. What possible use would the Tucson King have for the likes of you? No car, no bag. Dressed in... what is that? Beachwear gone wrong?" He's moving around me faster than I can keep up with him, staying constantly out of my line of sight. "Tank top, Daisy Duke shorts and flip-flops? Is he out of low-class strippers now?"

My lip curls at the insult. "For an old dead guy, you're rude!"

"For a woman with seconds to live, you're sassy. I like that. But please, let's not get distracted with insults. Tell me more about this *employment contract* you have with good King Lucius."

Shit. What do I have that a vampire would want other than my blood? I have skills, a few that come in handy, but so do a lot of people. More than likely, any who are required on a regular basis become... permanent members of Lucius's domain.

"Not that it is any of your business," I state primly, standing still as all the spinning goes to my head, "but I'm an artist."

For a few seconds, the world keeps on whirling past, then I get my first good look at a combined creature—the man who's tormented me for what seems like an age, and my first vampire.

No wonder I couldn't see him in the darkness, I think sourly. He's dressed all in black, fading into the shadows easily. The only thing that makes him stand out is the paleness of his hands and face, but that's not exactly as stark as I assumed. He could fit in with anyone off the street, in a crowd. Hell, you could stand next to him in a bar and not know the devil waited beside you.

At well over six feet, he dwarfs me without effort. I'm a good five-nine without heels and he's... well, I have to tip my head back to keep my eyes on his. Strong, thick arms are crossed impatiently over a broad chest straining the material of his black suit. He really does fill it out nicely, which I'm guessing is how he lures in his victims.

Any woman gets a look at this guy in attire like this, she'd better have her last will and testament written because she's going to follow him wherever he beckons. Add in the dangerous aura, arrogant smirk, and primal understanding he'll ride you hard and put you away still wet and wanting... yeah, he's lethal.

Broad shouldered, deep chested, muscular of limb... and none of that compares to his face. While his body is that of a warrior's, his face is part artist's dream and partly ethereal in the shadows. I can't see it as well as I would like, despite my eyes being adjusted to the darkness, but what I can see excites me.

Bad, bad girl.

He has dark hair that almost brushes his suit, with shorter strands hanging over his right eye to the middle of his cheek. It's almost straight except for the subtle wave that makes it not-quite perfect. His beard is just as dark but nowhere near as long, neatly trimmed to barely an inch—I think a magazine I read called it *long stubble*. It suits him, much to my disgust.

His eyes are too eclipsed by the night for me to read their color properly, but their intent is unmistakable. They're boring into me right now, hard enough I wonder if he can read my thoughts, but his eyebrows are drawing together slowly as though annoyed he can't access my head.

Yay for me.

"An artist?" he asks dubiously, raking that gaze down my body, and back up again with blatant suspicion. "I'm supposed to believe Lucius hired an artist to... what, decorate the inside of his chambers?"

"I wasn't given details. I was contacted, offered a sum of money large enough to drag me all the way out here, and here I damn well am. Stuck out in the middle of freaking nowhere, with a raging lunatic who *eats* people. As if being carjacked and robbed wasn't bad enough!" I shout at him and lose my temper enough to shove my hands against his chest. Not that I budge him an inch, but boy, does it feel good. "You believe what you want, I don't care. Just do what you're going to do before you bore me to death!"

The only thing breaking the deathly silence falling over us is my labored breathing. I'm mad enough to spit feathers, and if I had some tar to hand, I'd damn well tar and feather his no doubt glorious ass and kick it into next week.

"Pretty sure I'm not the lunatic here," he murmurs in that lazy drawl, letting his arms drop to his sides. "What kind of artist are you?"

I glare at him. Apparently, he can switch from bloodsucking fiend to easygoing jackass in a smooth transition. I'd admire that but I'm still in my feather-spitting mood, and easygoing isn't going to calm me down. "Oh, so *now* you're interested. Not in my name, of course, because that might create a personal connection you don't want when you rip my fucking throat out." His chest is a much better target now without those arms in my way. "First opportunity I get, pal, I'm making a replica of you in clay and then I'm gonna —" I stomp my foot on the ground to demonstrate exactly what I'll do to his clay image.

Colt checks his watch, rolls his eyes toward the sky, then simply sighs. "I haven't got time for hysterics, vixen." He bites his bottom lip and shrugs nonchalantly. "Well, if in doubt..."

He moves so quickly, I'm up and hanging over his shoulder before I can scream. Blood rushes to my head as he bands one of those cable-strong arms around my legs and strides away, whistling. *Whistling*. With every note, my anger becomes more volatile until I'm vibrating with fury hot enough to singe.

Hammering my fists on his back does nothing but bruise them. He's built like a rock, damn him. If I try and bite him, I'm pretty sure I'll break my teeth. "If you don't put me down, I swear I'll stake you to death with a cocktail stick!"

He just saunters along, giving me a quick pat on the ass. "Now, now. You should be thankful I'm not drinking the life from you. At least this way, we can get to know each other a little better before I decide whether eating you is the most profitable decision."

"I—profitable?" My mouth drops open as I think of the *mobile blood bags* he trades in. "I swear to God, I will end your existence if you even think about selling me to the highest bloodsucker!"

"First attempt's free," he tells me without concern.

I snarl, slightly breathless now, and dig my nails into the sensitive skin of his sides. Of course, they're buffered by that damn suit, so it's not nearly as effective as I need. "Take me to Lucius. Get me there safely, and we'll forget any of this ever happened."

"I could wipe every last memory from that pretty head in under two minutes," is his reply. "Forgetting isn't the issue. There are other things in motion now, and I just need to figure out where you fit into them. Giving you to Lucius isn't a card I hold in my hand, sorry."

"Sorry? Oh, you will be."

Ahead, I hear a car bleep and catch the quick flash of alarm lights flashing in the dark. My struggles increase, but with all the blood drowning my poor brain, things aren't working as well as they should. If he gets me in that car, I'm fairly sure things won't look rosy when the sun rises.

"You went to all that effort to con me?" I demand, slurring slightly. I think my tongue is swelling.

"Effort? No effort required," Colt answers cheerfully. "Slam the car door a couple times, drive away, and run back to wait for you to emerge from your hidey hole. I knew someone was there—I kept catching whiffs of fear. Waited for Vadim and Oberon to do the same, but you were lucky. I think they both thought the smell was coming off Obe. That little gasp of horror capped it, though."

Damn it, I wasn't sure I'd made a noise. Maybe I'd convinced myself I hadn't. I should've taken off across the wilderness while I had the chance.

"I'd let you ride up front, but I don't trust you not to try kill us both while I'm driving. I don't have any restraints on me tonight so I'm not willing to take that chance."

Something clunks softly, then I'm flipped over his shoulder, flying backwards and falling into a small, confined space. As I flail, my faculties not entirely in order, I stare up at the vampire as he braces both hands on the raised trunk lid. "You'll be pleased we're not taking a long trip. Thirty minutes, maximum. Now, you make a peep, you try kicking my rear lights out, you'll end up somewhere you really won't like."

"No!" If there's one thing I fear, it's being trapped in a small space. It's my worst nightmare. Claustrophobia is not only mentally destructive, it's physically debilitating. Thirty minutes is going to blow my head into a blubbering, screaming wreck. "Please, not the trunk. I can't stand confined areas, Colt, I—"

The fucker slams the lid down without saying a word, leaving me in this dark prison by myself. Frantic, I slap my hands around the edges of hell, squirming in an effort to discover some little crack, a chink I can pry open to fresh air or light. The car rocks gently as Colt settles his ass into the driver's seat, then vibrates lightly when he turns on the engine. Within seconds, he's got his foot to the gas while I'm bouncing and yelping in the trunk as the tires hit potholes and rocks, before he hits the highway, and everything smooths out.

I don't know what kind of car this is, but the trunk is surprisingly roomy, not that it helps. I scream at Colt, using my feet and hands to pummel every surface I can find. The sides are closing in on me, oppressive, and threatening to crush me.

Something crunches in my left foot as pain spikes up my leg, but I'm finding it hard to draw in a full breath. My lungs are working in shallow movements, offering little sips of air that aren't aiding necessary bodily functions like keeping my heart beating but are just fueling the titanic surge of panic bearing down on me.

My face is wet, and I can't pull any oxygen in through my nose. Great, they'll find me suffocated in my own bodily secretions.

Vienna Mulrooney, daughter of multimillionaires Tyson and

Moira Mulrooney, found dead at the age of twenty-eight. Drowned in her own panic snot, discovered in ratty flip-flops, sweat-soaked tank top and shorts. With no signs of foul play involved, police believe she was her usual irresponsible, flighty self, and have dismissed the case as an unfortunate accident.

I laugh hysterically until it becomes shrieking, hiccupping sobs and wheezing breaths. That's probably going to be the damn write-up of my life in the *Chicago Tribune*—one paragraph that doesn't come close to summing up who I am at the heart of me.

I scream Colt's name furiously, clawing at the back of the trunk until I dig through what feels like nice carpet and hit metal. I press my hands to the coolness, then to my head until my skin loses several degrees of heat. It's so goddamn hot in here, I sympathize with every poor dog ever left in a car on a hot day.

If I thought I was uncomfortable in my skin before, this is torture.

Music fires up in the car. An attempt to drown me out, I realize. Colt is a vampire, right? And as such, he has really sensitive hearing. He can hear me devolving in here, is listening to me suffer with an honest phobia, and he wants to block me out.

I wonder if he can hear my heartbeat.

Flopping onto my back in what little space I have, I close my eyes and pretend I'm not being kidnapped, that I'm not locked in a small metal box awaiting execution, and manage to slow my breathing. I start to *think*.

When I engage my brain, I'm dangerous.

It doesn't happen often, it does take some effort to get the gears moving in the right direction, but once those gears start rumbling and working as a machine...a lot of people believe I'm three beers short of a six-pack, but they believe wrong.

I may look and act like my ditzy mother, but I have my father's smarts.

Any self-respecting vampire driving a high-end car like this—the quality of the carpet in the trunk gives it away—doesn't keep his greasy, soiled tools in the footwell of the backseats. That's what this piece of hell is for. Which means, logically, somewhere in here with me is a weapon.

All I need to do is find it.

Obviously, there's nothing on the insides or floor of the trunk, but that doesn't mean there's nothing *underneath* it. I know some older car models have the spare wheels stored in a special area under the floor, and all I can do is hope this is the same.

Maneuvering onto my side takes some wriggling, and more than once I yelp as my injured foot knocks against something, but I finally end up with my back to the rear of the car and stretch out in the dark for the section of metal I revealed earlier. When my fingers touch it, I start digging to get them under the carpet, pulling and yanking, ripping the damn stuff up until it peels off whatever adhesive the manufacturers tack it down with.

I think I'm making more noise than when I was struggling with the anxiety attack, throwing myself around so I can shove and kick the numb material out of my way. There's a door set into the floor; I can feel the faintest crack where it rests.

Where there's a crack, there's a catch.

Sweat drips into my eyes, and off my nose. Seriously, I'm torn between wanting Colt to let me out of here so I don't sweat to death, and facing him again without a weapon in my hands. I really want to wipe that smug grin off his face, I decide with a huff.

I discover a tiny swivel catch along one edge, along with a finger-sized hole, and fiddle with it until I've lined the catch up enough that I can pry the hatch open. Only a couple inches, just enough to force my wrist painfully through the narrow gap and grope around for a weapon.

Everything feels delightfully cold. There's less space in there than there is in here, and things are starting to cramp as I contort myself to open the lid just a little more. I pat rubber, following the curve of the spare tire, then smile as my fingertips brush over the stiff leather of a tool pouch.

My father has one like this. Rigid, hard-wearing, and they literally last for decades if stored this way. Some go unused for years, just waiting for a tire to pop so they can see the light of day.

I work the zip and slip my fingers inside, searching for what has to be in there. When I find it, I know Colt's future just took a really bad turn.

2

Colt

My fingers drum on the steering wheel as I cruise into predawn Tucson, my thoughts preoccupied with the high-strung brunette stashed in the trunk.

She's gone quiet, thank fuck, but I'm not surprised after all the kicking and screaming she was doing when I set off. While her frantic struggles might have been muffled to a human's ears, she almost shattered my eardrums several times. I really don't need that kind of attention while driving through my home city—it may be early, but there is always a set of eyes and ears to take in everything that goes on.

I shouldn't have taken her. I know that. Going back to the meeting spot to catch the sneaky little eavesdropper was the right decision, *that* I know without a doubt. Oberon and I do not need an audience with Lucius, and she is the only one who can tie us to Operation Rhonull.

Vadim is likely to be furious if he finds out we weren't alone for the meet, and probably apoplectic enough to rip my head off should he discover she's not dead yet.

As the head of the operation, he is not a vampire I want to annoy.

As the Avtoritet of the vampiric Bratva in Russia, he's not someone I want to cross unless I really have to. His connections are legendary, stretching out globally. Vampires and mortals alike are not safe from him and his organization.

I got myself tangled up with the asshole when Oberon pulled the wrong shit with the wrong guys and, like the idiot I am, I stepped in to pull his ass out of the fire before it got too badly singed. Unfortunately, there were witnesses to my heroic rescue, and word got back to Vadim.

Resourceful and *methodical* were two of the words Vadim used to describe me at our first meeting, and I'd nearly laughed at the idea of me being either. I roll with the punches, shit slides off me like water off a duck's ass, and I've pulled bullets from myself with my bare fingers, but I'm a wild card.

Methodical is not my style.

For almost fifty years, I've been snagged under Vadim's thumb. Bitch boy, errand boy, you name it, I've done it. I don't approve of much of what he does, and there are things I've done for him that don't sit well in my gut, but surviving is the curse of all of us.

We do what we have to.

Operation Rhonull is Vadim's baby. An expensive, wasteful baby. Millions of dollars' worth of global currencies have been poured into the project from greedy vampires based all over the world. Top geneticists and hematologists are locked in a secure medical facility under one of the

Russian mountains—with some snooping, I've narrowed it down to either Elbrus or Dykh-Tau.

From every corner of the world, mortals are snatched from their lives, their families, to keep Vadim's dwindling stock of original Golden Blood donors alive. Reports say that there are only forty-three known, but there were a great deal more before the mad Russian got the idea in his head to kidnap and breed the poor bastards, raise and drain them for the blood in their veins.

Now he's moved on to selling them. And my part in this? I'm the fucking moron who's been given the debatable honor of distributing them to their new owners. Of selling them like cattle to fat, greedy vampires who want a taste of the rarest blood in existence.

Rumor has it, Vadim is keeping all the humans with any variation of the Rh type, experimenting with them, playing with them to see if breeding them will produce what he really wants.

The ones who don't produce the goods... well, my sources say he has more than a few vampires in his employ who lack the morals to turn down a baby-sized meal.

A hard shudder seizes me as I take a left turn into the parking lot of an old warehouse. I've been a vampire for hundreds of years, sometimes I forget how many. I've eaten men who were dying in battle, done my share of raping and pillaging in villages across Europe, scavenged off the survivors of catastrophic disasters. But babies... I'm a monster, undeniably, but babies are my hard limit food.

Thoughts swirl in my head as I stop the car between the faded white lines of a parking space—ridiculous, really, considering I'm the only one who comes here, for the most part—and switch off the engine. It ticks as it cools and, without the aircon blowing gently, the interior of the car rises in temperature.

Silence surrounds me and I wonder if the little female has passed out after all her exertion. I can hear her heartbeat chugging in thick, liquid beats, so I know she's still alive. Bonus for me if she's unconscious—it'll make carrying her inside, partaking of a quick snack, and finding somewhere secure to lock her down so much easier.

Dawn is already sending out alarm bells to my kind, warning of its arrival. I have some time, but not much. I don't bring people here—not vampires, not meals—and I'm not prepared to hold a captive. Especially not when she'll be unsupervised all day.

I open the door and step out onto cracked asphalt, shutting the door behind me as I round the back of the car. Something inside me quivers in excitement as I pop the trunk and prepare to greet my pretty captive.

It's been a long time since I had interesting company to keep me occupied.

Pain hits me square in the dick. For a second, I think the crazy bitch has shot me. As ball-busting agony radiates outward from the single pinpoint of contact, I wheeze out a string of curse words and fight not to drop to my knees and retch.

I catch a glimpse of a slim length of iron sliding back into the trunk and realize she just slammed me in the crotch with the end of a fucking tire iron. That same damn iron hurtles back at my face, propelled by a tiny hand at each end, and smashes into my mouth and cheekbone.

Motherfucking *ow*.

It's enough to knock me on my ass. Sprawled on my back, my own blood filling my mouth as pain devours my face and my poor defenseless dick, I watch with reluctant admiration as my captive clambers unsteadily from the trunk. Tire iron in one hand, she holds onto the car with the other as she sways in place.

"Picked the wrong woman to kidnap, Colt," she tells me, her voice rasping. All that screaming won't have done her throat any good, but right now, I want to rip it out and throttle her for the discomfort I'm in. "But thanks for the lift. Saved me hiking eighteen miles in these goddamn flip-flops."

My mouth is already healed, but she must have fractured my cheekbone. I can feel it knitting back together slowly. I turn my head and spit blood onto the ground, gathering myself for an attack she isn't going to see coming.

She thinks she's done the impossible and taken down a vamp. No doubt she's read books and seen movies about my kind. That trash is everywhere, and not one of them has hit what we can truly do on the head. Because while humanity paints us all with the same brush, each vampire is an infinitesimally different shade to all the others.

"Gonna have to finish me off, little girl. I'm coming after you if you don't."

Five feet and nine inches of angry female straightens through force of will. My bruised cock jerks with consideration as I take note of the curve of her hips and waist, the length of her legs. Her breasts lift attractively as she swings the iron onto her shoulder, and I imagine how they'll taste in my mouth before my fangs sink into the supple flesh.

"That can be arranged. I'm not the dumb blonde girl in a horror movie, Colt. I learned a long time ago you don't just knock the bad guy out and wait for him to come after you. When it's life or death, you take the kill when you can." She has the most glorious colored eyes I've ever seen, especially when they're backlit with such a ruthless glow.

Heavy on cerulean, with an almost stone-gray tint. I want to see how many shades of both they can make. "I'm thinking beating your head into a pulp won't kill you, right? But it'll keep you down long enough for the sun to finish you off."

Hmmm, that could work in theory. It's not something I've ever thought about, if I'm honest, nor an experiment I want to be the guinea pig for. If I don't regenerate fast enough, I will definitely be a crispy critter in short order. "Make damned sure," I warn her. "I won't be merciful when I catch you again."

Her lips press together tightly as she processes that, and I wouldn't mind dipping into her brain and scanning her thoughts for entertainment purposes. I have a feeling ten seconds inside that mind would be better than any movie ever made. But she just lifts her shoulder and steps closer.

Stopping just out of my reach, she raises the tire iron. Those stunning eyes glimmer with a mix of emotions and, in the same moment as she brings the iron down at my head, I make my move.

My body spins away on the hard ground and I'm back on my feet in front of her before the business end of the iron cracks into asphalt. I wrest it easily from her delicate hand and fling it across the parking lot, listening to it clatter noisily and thud to an abrupt halt against the warehouse wall.

I grin, my fangs on full display, and deflect the neat uppercut she aims at my chin. There's shock written on her face, nervous energy buzzing through her veins as it dawns on her she's just been bested by a vampire. "Now then, where were we, little one? Oh, I know. No mercy."

"Fuck," she breathes, and then inhales deeply. I slam my palm over her mouth and encircle her throat with my free hand to encourage her *not* to let rip with that eardrum-destroying scream.

"Make a sound, say a word, and this ends right here," I say quietly, leaning down so my eyes meet hers. Compelling her would be safer, easier, but I like sparring with this fierce creature. "You're in my territory now, and you'll behave or you will die. That trunk you're so scared of will be your final resting place, I promise you. Understand me?"

The way her eyes widen and her heart kicks tells me she's heard the dominant tone and respects it. Maybe it's wishful thinking, but I get the impression she'll be just as inclined to obey it when she's naked and cuffed to my bed.

I sniff lightly at her hair, her throat.

The smell of sweat and fear almost masks the delectable sweetness of submissive scent, but I detect it, nonetheless. Mortals are rarely capable of concealing their true natures and have no idea how much they give away through scent.

Murderers? Rich and bitter.

Rapists? Strong and sour.

Optimists? Sweeter than cotton candy.

Submissives? Fucking divine.

When she nods slowly, I remove my hand from her mouth but leave her collared with the other. She wants to play with fire, I'm happy to oblige. Slamming the trunk shut, I lock the car. I've seen how she's decimated the interior of her temporary holding cell—I'm not happy, but at least I know she's not concealing weapons in fascinating places.

"Took guts, dismantling everything in there to get to the tire iron," I tell her in a displeased tone. She trembles as I slide my grip around to the back of her neck, and I know we're both thinking how easy it would be to snap it. "Luckily for you, it's a retractable one. I'm surprised I didn't hear you snapping it into position."

She snorts as I march her forward, her hair tickling the back of my hand as she moves. The simple vanilla of her shampoo is kicking my lust into gear, and I yank my libido under control before I do something stupid, like fuck her against the wall. "I'm shocked you hear anything but your own ego talking back to you, asshole. God, this is so fucked up!"

My lips twitch. I've lived through times where women were killed for speaking out of turn, never mind using the kind of language she comes out with. This one spouts obscenities for fun. Testing the waters, I crack my hand across the rounded curve of her ass, first one cheek and then the other to keep things even. "Mind the mouth, little one."

She has the audacity to snarl. God, she is phenomenal. I really need to figure out what my options are before Vadim or Obe discover her existence. "This is how I talk. If you'd let me go, you wouldn't have to deal with it, would you?"

"Keep it up. I have several ways of *dealing* with you." I push her around the side of the warehouse to the entrance I use most often. "You won't like most of them... or maybe you're the kind of girl who will."

She stiffens in silent protest as I shove her face first against the door and hold her still while I deal with the security. Palm plate and voice recognition, six-digit pin and thumb print scanner. Overkill for some, but when you're a vampire, you need assurances your nest is safe while you sleep.

The warehouse is ten thousand square feet of space, hemmed in by solid metal walls. No skylights in the roof, and no windows. After I bought it, I made some massive adjustments, the first of which was to seal the loading doors with the same security as the entrance we just used.

Unless someone blows them with a large amount of C4,

my enemies will have to crack the security on the door I'm now locking behind us or use exceptional force.

I feel my prisoner shudder as the darkness surrounds us, and I take pity on her. I can see perfectly but she obviously becomes distressed when her sight is taken from her. Ever the gentleman, I reach out and switch on the lights, waiting for them to flicker to life before I release her.

"This is my home. The only exit is the one we've just come through; the loading doors will not provide you with a viable escape route." I don't waste my time telling her she won't be able to leave here without me by her side. "I'm afraid I don't have much in the way of food suitable for humans. You'll have to go hungry until tonight. I think there is a case of water in the back somewhere, I'll find it once I have you secured."

She wraps her arms around herself. "Secured?"

I laugh. "I'm nocturnal. I sleep heavily through the day, and I don't trust you not to stake me or make a run for it while I'm under."

She's looking around with a blank expression. "You have a living room set up in an empty warehouse," she murmurs. "No bedroom, no kitchen, nothing but a living room. Where the hell do you sleep? Hanging from the rafters?" She glances up as though expecting others of my kind to be dangling like bats.

It is an odd arrangement; I can't deny it. I have a TV, couch and coffee table set randomly in the middle of the warehouse, merely for aesthetic purposes. It's not like I get much company, but it offers an illusion of life.

My real home is several feet below us, but my guest will need to be on her best behavior before she's allowed to reap the benefits of what lies beneath. After all, if I ever let her go, she will be party to knowledge no one else on earth possesses, and that opens a lot of doors for dangerous people.

"You and I—for today, at least—will be sleeping downstairs." I lift an eyebrow when she gapes at me. "What, you want to sleep in the car? Might be uncomfortable in that trunk now it's trashed."

Those eyes flash daggers at me before she stomps away and throws herself onto the couch. She kicks off the ugly flip-flops, settles back and huffs to herself, seemingly content to make herself at home. Where does she keep those steel balls of hers, because I am dying to find out.

I walk over and sit on the coffee table in front of her. Her curled lip doesn't deter me in the slightest. "Might as well get used to me being in charge. I want some answers from you, and how you respond will make a huge difference as to whether or not you see the moon rise. You got me?"

She shows me white teeth in reply, and I respond in kind.

"What's your name?" It's the question I've been putting off asking.

"Oh, *now* you want to know." The bitterness in her voice is new. "My name is Vienna. I'm twenty-eight, I come from Chicago, and I'm an artist. I can kick your ass from here to fucking Montana and, given the opportunity, I'm going to dance on your ashes. Now fuck off and leave me alone. Go hibernate or something."

While she's offered a great deal of information of her own accord, her tone is disrespectful, and I can't allow that. My hands lash out and snag her ankles, yanking her down the seat. She cries out in pain and I scowl, sure my grip isn't tight enough to warrant that reaction from so tough a woman.

She's kicking at me with her right foot but keeping her

left strangely still. Carefully, I study the immobile foot and notice signs of bruising boiling beneath the skin. Her appendage will be black and purple by tonight. I press gently with my thumb and she recoils with another sharp cry.

"You weren't limping when we walked to the warehouse," I accuse her suspiciously, "or when you marched yourself to the couch."

"Adrenaline masks pain," she snaps back, leaning forward to try and pry her foot from my grasp. I reward her with a quick slap on the hand. "It's nothing, just leave it. Consider it a handicap for when I murder you."

Dropping both her feet to the floor, I watch her struggle to push herself back into a sitting position. By the time she's comfortable again, I have a plan of action in mind, and act accordingly. I launch myself at her before she can react, shoving my knees between hers and insinuating myself between her legs, forcing them to drape over my thighs.

Alarm races over her face as I bracelet her wrists in one hand. "I've had enough of the attitude, Vienna. My intention was to spank you and send you to bed, and pick up this conversation tonight, but although you know what I am, you have no realistic concept of *what* I am capable of. I'm going to change that now, then perhaps we will start on more respectful footing by the time this evening comes around."

"You can't just—"

"No concept," I repeat darkly, and reach around the back of her head to gather her hair into a sleek tail in my hand. I drape it down one shoulder, leaving her neck bare on the other side. "I am death, make no mistake. You seem to think you can toy with me, taunt me, without repercussions."

"Colt!"

My name sounds like a plea in that breathy, frightened

tone, and my cock surges to attention. Sex will have to wait for now. My eyes fixate on the pulse in her throat, bounding erratically, beckoning my fangs to come play. "If you'd been a good girl, you'd have been coming around my cock as I did this, Vienna. But you pushed all the wrong buttons, and bad girls don't get orgasms when I feed."

Blood erupts into my mouth when I strike—sweet, fragrant blood unlike any I've ever tasted before. It's heavily spiked with fear and, oh fuck yes, arousal. But the substance itself is heavenly, addictive in a way I know will be dangerous for me, and for her. I could drain her in seconds and still be desperate for more.

Her hips are trying to rise, to grind against my cock for relief, but I deny her any semblance of release. If she'd given me less lip, I might have been persuaded to slip my hand into those shorts and fingerfuck that slick pussy until she came, but as I said, bad girls don't get orgasms.

I'm lost in her mewling cries, the tug of her fingers in my hair, the scrape of her nails across my back. She doesn't know what to do with herself, with the sudden surge of pleasure rising inside her. The bite brings ecstasy as much as it gives pain—it's one of the few things I remember about my own siring.

Fire scorching my throat, ejaculating hard enough to wrench my soul from my body, then a flood of thick, coppery blood flowing down to my belly and my heart thudding one... last... time...

Jerking out of the memory, I release Vienna's neck with reluctance, lapping gently at the puncture wounds to clean them, then nip my lower lip. I kiss the wounds, sealing them with my blood. A quick study of her face reveals she's blissed out—her eyes are half-closed, but from what I can see, her pupils have eclipsed the irises.

Her body is limp, her hands sliding off my back slowly until they thump gently onto the couch. For the first time in our acquaintance, she doesn't have a word to say.

Excellent. It would be so easy to finish her off now, to empty her of that incomparable blood. My demon is in full agreement—we're greedy, and we want to gorge on her. But I resist, with difficulty. Something tells me I need to.

I bite into the pad of my thumb with one fang, then shove it into her mouth. Warm and wet. Delightful. After a few seconds, her tongue flutters against my digit, then her instincts kick in and she begins to suck lightly. She takes enough to satisfy me, and once the minor wound heals, I draw my thumb free with a silent promise to replace it sometime in the near future with something longer, thicker, and more sensitive.

My blood will heal her foot and the bite wound, as well as anything else she's hidden from me. I want her fit and healthy, need her to be both, because feeding from her just signed her future over to me.

Vienna is going nowhere for quite some time.

Vienna

I'm high as fuck right now.

So freaking high, I can't tell what plane of existence I'm on. I'm not sure if I'm physically in my body or simply a myriad of sparkling little stars scattered through the darkness. Whatever I am, I feel… astonishingly *alive.* A thousand energy drinks feed my veins, pumping life into every cell in my body, spurred on by a constant current of stimulating electricity.

Running a marathon? Bitches, I'm sipping margaritas at

the finish line before the rest of the runners make it off the starting post. Climbing Mount Everest? Pffft, I've reached the peak and passed my fellow climbers on the way back down. Lifting weights? Please, I'm juggling motherfucking tanks and dancing an Irish jig.

All the caffeine in the world can't emulate this feeling, and I don't want it to go away. I'm invincible and invulnerable, capable of speeding through brick walls in a shower of dust and rubble. No chains can hold me, no doors can keep me in—or out.

I gasp to myself in the dark, giddy with realization.

I'm the new superhero of Tucson, Arizona.

"For fuck's sake, woman, do you need to think so goddamn loud?"

My superhero instincts flare and I leap from my resting place of soft sheets to land precariously on my feet. "Who goes there, foul being? Announce yourself!"

Material rustles and a heavy masculine sigh fills the darkness. "Stop messing around, Vienna, and get back into bed. There's an hour before the sun sets and I'm not prepared to listen to you wreak havoc while you finish crashing off my blood."

My eyes narrow in suspicion. The voice is familiar to some part of me, but I can't put a face to it. He speaks to me as if he knows me, calls me by name, so who is he? "How do you know my true identity?"

Another sigh, deeper, full of resignation, and then a switch clicks, and soft light illuminates my surroundings. I spin around slowly, assessing the predicament in which I find myself.

"Vienna. Come back to bed and rest. You'll feel more like yourself when you wake, I promise. Some people react to vampire blood differently than others, and you seem to be one of them. You are not a superhero, trust me."

My eyes bug out of my head as it whips to stare at the bare-chested man lounging easily in a massive sleigh bed carved from cherrywood. "*Vampire blood?* Be gone, foul beast!" I shriek loudly, slamming my index fingers together in the sign of the cross and shaking them at him.

He mutters something, rolling his eyes as he shakes his dark head, and simply turns his back to me.

I slap my hand to my heart, feeling his demonic presence sucking my life force from my veins. All my glorious energy seeps away slowly, leaving me weakened and at his mercy. Before he can drain me completely, I flow into motion, bravely pouncing onto the bed with what little stealth I have left.

If he's going to kill me, the least I can do is rid the earth of his evilness with my last breath. I vow silently to do just that, studying the muscled length of his exposed back, pinpointing where his dead heart should be. I don't have a weapon to hand, but Vienna, Protector and Guardian of Tucson, needs no weapon to slay the demon.

I *am* the weapon.

"Jesus, you have one hell of an imagination," my prey grumbles, sitting up slightly to pound his pillow. "I won't tell you a third time, Vienna. Role-playing isn't my kink but I'm happy to demonstrate what a real bad guy does to his captive."

I snarl. A threat? And such a weak one at that. Rather than laughing as I want to, I bare my teeth and launch myself at him like a holy missile. My hands curve into claws and as our bodies collide, I bite into his undead shoulder, growling and savaging his flesh while my nails gouge into his skin.

Victorious!

I know I've wounded him badly, but not enough to save myself. The last of my superhero energy wanes, reverting me back to a simple human, and leaving me to face off with a disgruntled, bleeding vampire.

While my brain downshifts several gears and catapults Vienna the woman back into the driving seat, the man I know as Colt remains deathly still beneath me. My teeth are still in his shoulder, and my hands begin to shake as it dawns on me how dead I'm about to be.

"Are you done now?" he asks calmly.

Oh, shit. This is catastrophically *bad*. I mean, bad with a death knoll on the D. I've opened up a can of worms I never normally would touch, and now there are thousands of the damn things rising up against me in the form of Colt.

My neck throbs once, remembering the punch of his fangs into my jugular, and I slowly disengage my teeth, coughing as I lick my lips and taste an oddly recognizable flavor. It's heavy on my tongue—metallic one moment, and moreish the next.

My pussy betrays me as I shove away from my captor, scrambling off the bed before... nope, not before. I yelp as a strong hand locks around my ankle, dragging me back to the center of the mattress on my back. Colt's show of dominance and utter strength does crazy things to my insides, engaging a flood of slickness to wet my panties.

"Three times I've told you," he tells me in that slow drawl, the heat in his voice lighting up every nerve under my skin, "to come back to bed and rest. Didn't listen, did you? Had to be a bad girl and break my rules." He flips me effortlessly onto my stomach, his fingers gripping the waistband of my shorts. "I was considerate, leaving you dressed, giving you a sense of modesty, and you… you tease me with the scent of this pussy."

"It's not my fault!" I protest, kicking half-heartedly at him. I should really be trying harder to escape this scenario, but if he wants to hurt me, he's had ample opportunity to do so. "I wasn't myself, asshole!"

Colt's nose runs up the back of my calf and along my thigh, making me shiver in awareness. In one quick yank, my shorts are down my legs, and he removes them faster than I can blink. My panties aren't so lucky, ripping apart with a tug of his hands. "Are you yourself now, Vienna? Is my little superhero tucked back in the closet?"

Trick question. I recognize it as such before I open my mouth to answer, which is probably wise and more luck than clear thinking right now. If I say yes, he'll be on me in a heartbeat, doing who knows what to my defenseless body… I grimace as the thought spurs my arousal higher, a goddamn bucking bull scoring prime airtime.

Saying no… well, I'm not in a position to determine my fate if I say no.

"I don't feel like I can leap over the Grand Canyon anymore," I mutter sarcastically, then yelp as fire streaks across my left buttock like vengeance. "What the hell? Oh, you are in for such a—" My right buttock trembles under a matching blow. I bite the sheets to stop my moan escaping —I'm not encouraging his Neanderthal behavior with positive reinforcement.

My hips are jerked up and a cool pillow settles beneath me, keeping my ass raised high for this monster in the bed. I hate it, hate the vulnerability of being at Colt's mercy, but as I struggle to wiggle away, he lights up my ass again.

"I think we'll set some rules in place," he growls, scraping his nails down my thighs to the sensitive hollows at the back of my knees, then shoving my legs wide. "Your life rests in my hands, Vienna. I suggest you listen carefully before you make the decision to disobey me. Are those keen ears of yours engaged?"

I buck angrily in response.

"Good. Rule number one: respect at all times. *Sir* suits me just fine; if you can't wrap your tongue around that, it'll be put to other uses until you learn enough manners to call me by the honorific. You want to sass me, go ahead, but with the same results."

Well, hell. My mouth is going to land me in some serious hot water if I don't find a way to sneak out from under his hawkish gaze.

"Rule number two: crying and lying will get you nowhere with me. I abhor dishonesty and crocodile tears just piss me off. If I ask you a question, you answer it honestly and swiftly."

I scoff. "Or what? You'll put my mouth to other uses?"

When he chuckles, the sound black as night, I ponder the wisdom of mocking him. Yeah, I need to start remembering he's not human, and he's more than capable of doing terrible things to my mortal body for as long as he likes before disposing of me where I'll never be found.

Both his palms slap down on my ass, parting the cheeks. Even as I clench, he just holds them apart, and my most private hole tries to seal itself completely under his hungry gaze. "I deal with liars a little differently than disrespectful subs." A cool finger presses against me, stealing my breath. "I find stretching tiny holes around my cock hammers home the *no lying* rule. Trust me, there won't be any crocodile tears if it comes to that course of action, Vienna. Your tears will be real."

My ass is begging me to behave myself but, unfortunately, I know myself too well. If I can lie to get out of a jam, I'm damn well saying whatever I need to. "I don't cry. I'm not built that way."

"We'll see," he says ominously, releasing my derriere. "Rule number three: as of right now, you're mine. I've taken a liking to you, Vienna, and you pose a challenge. I don't get many challenges to hold my attention these days, so consider yourself lucky. I'll do what I want to you, with you, until this... fascination with you ends. With the way you taste, I wouldn't bet on being a free woman again."

My hands fist in the sheets, clinging tightly to the smooth material so hard, my fingers feel like they're going to snap. I'm pretty sure punching his lights out is a violation of rule number one, and with my ass still exposed, I'm not risking it just yet. "I am a free woman, Colt."

The mattress shifts and Colt's hands land on either side of my head, his body fitting the contours of mine. My back ripples with a quiver as skin touches skin, and there's no stopping myself from raising my hips into the impressive erection rubbing along the crack of my ass.

"Rule number three," he croons in my ear, licking the ticklish shell until I squirm, then nibbling his way down my neck. I stiffen, waiting for the stab of pain, but he just continues down to my shoulder. "By the time I've marked you, every square inch of this delightful vessel, you'll realize the truth."

"Don't dominants respect consent anymore?" I haven't forgotten his little jibe about disrespectful subs; that one sentence summed his attitude up completely and wrapped it in a BDSM bow. "I thought your ilk was all about safe, sane, and consensual?"

He purrs, the sound reverberating into my back. He bites my shoulder, teeth shearing lightly over my flesh. "You think

I'm going to give you a safeword, little one? Perhaps I should. I'm not so much of a monster I can't give you that."

I lose track of the conversation as he works his way down my back, nipping and kissing my skin. Every brush of his lips ignites sparks, overriding my brain and sending my body into rapture. I blame myself for my reaction—too long between bouts of physical intimacy, and I turn into the needy, wanton creature currently making herself known under Colt's skilled caresses.

For all his rough and steamy talk, he's still made no move to hurt me.

I whimper as he eases back. I'm ready to post giant red arrows and directions to my needy pussy if he doesn't hurry up and do something. My prayers are answered a moment later, an implosion of sensation erupting in my veins when his mouth covers my aching sex and his tongue works magic against my clit.

Obviously, however many centuries of being undead haven't been put to waste. This guy is skilled with his hands, his tongue, his voice... seriously, if all vampires are this adept at bringing an orgasm screeching to life in seconds, they'd make a killing—no pun intended—as professional sex workers. Hell, slap a badge on them and call them sex therapists.

He rips a moan from my throat effortlessly, his grip on my hips holding me still as my control goes awry and I flounder in the throes of outrageous pleasure. I mean, I'm fairly sure there's rainbows and stardust shooting from the tips of my fingers and toes.

"Moaning isn't gonna cut it, Vienna," Colt murmurs, nipping his teeth into the back of my thigh. "I want to hear you scream before I fuck you. You've got a sweet voice when you're not cursing me out, but I want to hear it sing."

The bleating blare of a cell phone saves me from trying to reply. I can't, my tongue is tied up in a pretzel knot and totally incapable of doing anything. It proves my point when I slur, "Shouldn't you get that?"

Colt digs his fingers harder into my hips, his nails boring points of fire into my flesh where they break the skin. His tongue slides along my slit leisurely as the phone continues to wail for a long, long minute. When it cuts off, a thick finger penetrates me, pushing deep and drawing a relieved exhale from my body.

This is what I need. *This* will stoke the fires until they incinerate me and set me free.

"Been a while, hasn't it?" he comments, then goes completely still as the phone rings again, this time with a different tone. "Goddamn it. I have to take that." In an instant, he's across the room with the phone in his hand. His tone is dark when he says, "Don't be a smart ass, Vienna. If they know I have someone here, they'll get nosy. They'll want to know where you came from, how we met, why you're here. Your life won't rest in my hands anymore, it'll be in theirs. Trust me when I say I'm the nice one."

Something in his voice tells me he's not trying to persuade me not to use the call as a cry for help from outside sources. He's genuinely warning me my life hangs in the balance as soon as he answers that call.

Between him and the unknown, I'm trusting him.

If he's the *nice* one, I don't want to meet the bad ones.

I nod silently and Colt relaxes slightly as he takes the summons. He turns away as though having his back to me means I can't hear his side of the conversation. While he mutters into the phone, I take the opportunity to inch my way off the bed and find my shorts.

What was about to happen here is now off the table.

There's one thing being caught up in the moment, swept away by crass words and a powerful touch, but I can't deny what he is. I assume he's murdered people, innocent people, and he's definitely involved in some real shady shit with the Russian.

Meals On Wheels for vampires, for Christ's sake. Or maybe that should be Meat On Feet. However I look at it, it's wrong, and not even a body-contorting orgasm justifies me getting tangled up in it all.

I tug my shorts back on, keeping one eye on Colt as he runs his hand through his hair in agitation, trying not to drool as the muscles in his back and arm pop with the movement. Bad girl. Averting lustful eyes... now.

"Antoine, as much as I would love to get you a sample of your order ahead of time, can I just remind you that the *whole* shipment is arriving at the same time? It's not like I keep surplus stock to hand as samples." Colt's voice rises slightly. His body is loose, limber, but when he turns and his dark, tawny eyes land on mine, I see the frustration in them.

I take an involuntary step back when frustration morphs into consideration.

"Actually, Antoine, I think I have the perfect sample after all."

3

olt

IT GALLS me to be put under this kind of pressure. A few decades ago, I was a chilled, laid-back undead guy minding his own business, but I'm unliving proof that too much time in a hostile environment shapes *everything* into something different to what it should be.

Vienna is standing across from me, with the bed between us. She's braced, ready to run, but she should know by now there's nowhere *to* run. I am her world, and I wasn't lying when I said she's mine. Unfortunately, being mine means she's going to have to bleed for me, and from the look in her storm-colored eyes, she's not going to be open to that suggestion.

"You'll bring this sample to me, tonight." Antoine adopts his usual French accent, lacing it with a hint of scorn I can't stand. "I will not pay for subpar product, Colt. If you wish payment to be made upfront, you will bring me a fresh specimen."

I want to grind my teeth but the prick on the other end of the line will hear my irritation. He doesn't know I am aware of his true identity and would likely unleash his attack dogs on me should he be enlightened by the knowledge, but the asshole isn't even French. His great-great-great-great grandparents probably couldn't tell you what the Eiffel fucking Tower looks like.

His real name is Bertram. Fucking Bertram—what self-respecting parents call their son *Bertram?* They evidently didn't take into consideration the fact their son would live *forever* with the hideous name. He doesn't even originate from Europe—our boy Bertie hails from good old Saskatoon, but rules his little domain like one of the long-ago lords.

Heads literally are removed from necks if they even form the thought of nudging one of his ridiculous laws.

Personally, I think Lucius will take Antoine's rusty crown soon enough, putting an end to the puffed-up fool before he brings the true death to us all with his antics.

But, that's not my decision.

My conundrum here is that while being an insufferable tyrant, Antoine is also one of the wealthiest vampires of my acquaintance. He holds court in his spacious mansion, hosts orgies which evolve dangerously fast into slaughters, and his bank account is fat enough to make a sizeable dent in the national debt.

Rhonulls are his newest fascination, and he snapped ten up as soon as he found out I'm Vadim's delivery boy. Ten human heads for the grand sum of fifty million dollars.

As much as I loathe the cocksucker, losing this order will put me in Vadim's crosshairs. Playing nice is getting harder and harder to do; I'd rather gut him and play nice with his entrails while he screams and flails.

I grimace at the image, finding it repulsive yet delightfully appealing. Another example of how unsavory surroundings affect a person—Vadim's crews are full of vampires who revel in doing just that, laughing as they eviscerate one of their own.

While Vienna's gaze remains locked on my every move, I curl my hand around the nape of my neck and squeeze. She's the sweetest thing I've encountered in a long time, she has the most exquisite blood I've ever tasted, and I hate the thought of this faux-French asshole laying a hand on her. "It's going to take time to collect her, Antoine. Retrieving her and getting to you might not be possible tonight—we both know dawn comes early these days."

"Pah!" He dismisses my excuse with a puff of sound. "You have me intrigued, *mon ami*. Tell me, you must have her sequestered away for a reason, yes? Have you claimed one of these Rhonulls for yourself?" The excitement winging down the line is sickening. "Is she divine to taste?"

My mouth waters before I can control it, my fangs extending to their full and visible length. I follow my captive's gaze to where she's eyeing my unfading erection, and I understand if I make one wrong move, she's aiming for the crown jewels. "She is, Antoine, and she is mine. I will bring you your sample this evening. Tell the dogs at your gates to expect me."

Pride flutters in my chest, a rare and unexpected feeling, as I watch Vienna assess the situation, the conclusion of the call, and I almost laugh as she stretches out the muscles in her arms and legs. Gearing up for a fight she can't win.

"I anticipate your arrival, Colt." The call cuts off.

Tossing the phone aside, I fold my arms over my chest

and observe with some curiosity as Vienna continues to warm up. She's no longer semi-naked, much to my disappointment. However, those damn peekaboo shorts don't conceal much, and knowing she's wearing nothing beneath is driving me insane.

When her eyes meet mine, fierce and determined, I lift my finger to my nose and inhale deeply, savoring the scent of that delectable pussy. The sadist in me wants to tattoo my name across what's mine, etched forever in black and red ink just above that pert little clit. "I didn't tell you to leave the bed, Vienna, nor to cover that pussy. Naughty, naughty girl."

A radiant blush rouges her cheeks, but she doesn't simper beneath my hard stare. Her eyes narrow in defiance. "You didn't tell me I couldn't, *Sir*."

Well, she's got me there. "Next time I have you naked, those shorts are being torn into pieces. That tank top will be nothing but rags. The only thing you'll wear are my cuffs around your wrists and neck, and a butt plug shoved so far up your ass, you won't be able to sit down."

She laughs harshly. "You like your threats, don't you, Colt? Promises and threats, the two things you don't follow through on. Letting me go before you get hurt is the smartest thing you could do right now."

For the moment, Antoine is cast from my thoughts. I'll do my job and take him his desired sample in my own time. *Right now*, as my little vixen advises, I'm going to be smart. I grin as the word *vixen* comes to mind. It suits her perfectly —intelligent, stunning, sassy as all hell, and more savage than a riled badger. There are ways and means of taming scrappy little things such as her, and I'm mentally rolling through the plugs in my arsenal, wondering which will make her rue her words most. "You'll find out in due course what I follow through on, Vienna. Letting you go isn't an option; deal with it."

I'm wondering what to do with her while I drive through the night to Phoenix to meet Antoine. I'd take her with me but his guards will scent her in seconds, and I don't trust her not to keep her mouth shut. She's the kind of treasure Antoine loves to hoard... until he grows tired of his toys and sends them to the kennels as entertainment for his dogs and men.

"Deal with it?" she spits at me. "Beheading works just as well as staking with your kind, right? I bet there's something sharp enough around here for me to remove your head. I'm not your puppet, Colt; deal with that!"

Oh, she's growing on me more and more. Every passing second of our acquaintance forges a stronger tie between what's left of the man inside me and the raging spitfire facing me. She's something I never thought I'd find; a woman who remains unflinching in the face of danger. "I'm telling you how it is, little vixen. Unfortunately, I don't have time to argue with you, and although I'd love to continue from where we were so rudely interrupted, bad girls aren't rewarded for foul language, being disobedient, or stomping their feet in tantrums."

For a brief and amusing second, her pretty features are blank. It's in that split fraction of time that I strike, leaping over the bed and tackling her gently to the floor. My intentions of saving her from harm, however, are thwarted by her stubbornness.

Pinning her to the floor as she struggles gives my active imagination far too many fantasies to play out in future and, although I outweigh her considerably, I'm fighting tooth and nail to maintain the upper hand.

"Must you defy me at every turn?" I hear the exasperation in my tone and feel the demon inside me stir lazily as it gets a whiff of confrontation. It loves nothing more than a good fight, and Vienna is offering just what it desires. "I am trying to save your life, you foolish female!"

Six centuries, three decades, and eight years of surviving among mortals should have warned me she wouldn't take that well, but I'm too wrapped up in her scent and the feel of her body cushioning mine.

She's quicker on the attack this time, sneaking in a deft uppercut to my chin that snaps my damn head back before I snag her wrists and smack them against the carpet on either side of her head. "Keep bucking this way, Vienna, and I'll ride you the way you need to be ridden. Hard, fast, and dirty."

"God, why are men such pigs?" Her hands strain for purchase but there's no leeway to gain any. I like my eyes where they are, unbloodied and with full vision. "I swear I'm gonna burn this place down around your ears!"

Quick as a snake, I lean down and claim her lips, stealing a kiss from that savage mouth before Vienna sucks in a shocked breath. The mouth that's cursed me, sassed me, threatened all manner of things, goes soft beneath the forceful pressure of mine.

She makes me hunger in a way no other mortal ever has. It's more than feasting on her blood, drowning myself in a bath of her life essence. I want to strip her down to the skin and beyond. Take her apart piece by piece until I discover what secrets she squirrels away in her heart, dismantle the hard-ass attitude until I pilfer the labyrinth of her soul.

Her eyes are wide, searching mine as I take the kiss deeper, all but leeching the fight from her like the vampire I am. Those tense hands go limp, her fingers twitching, and the fiery ball of energy inside the long, taut body under me quiets.

Hmmm, I've found the key to taming the wildcat.

However, her threat about setting the building on fire isn't something I can ignore. Leaving her unsupervised in my sanctuary is my only course of action while I deal with Antoine, but I'm not happy about it. Nor am I overjoyed at the thought of abandoning her for several hours, bound to my bed. She could hurt herself if she tries something stupid—which, undoubtedly, she will.

God loves a trier; He must adore this woman.

Ending the kiss with a sharp nip to her full bottom lip, I swipe my tongue over the bead of blood forming, savoring it before I shift fluidly to my feet and stare down at the dazed woman sprawled in front of me.

It's roughly a two-hour drive to Phoenix, where Antoine rules his little kingdom, so that's a four-hour round trip alone, not factoring in traffic and the possibility I might be detained in his compound longer than I'd like.

So, Vienna will not be coming with me, and wrapping her wrists up in chains wouldn't be fair. Humans have needs I barely remember—they have to eat every few hours, use the bathroom, be entertained—and she won't have any of those while I'm absent.

My only recourse is compulsion. I imagine she'll be vocal about it when she wakes upon my return, and if we don't go to war over my taking the choice from her, I will be eternally surprised.

Vienna may be my captive, but as her captor, I have responsibilities.

Keeping her safe until I decide what her ultimate fate is going to be is just the tip of the iceberg. I'm really not looking forward to making that choice because, somewhere in my gut, I know death will play a hand in it.

My internal sundial alerts me that the danger is gone, and night is once again my playground. Time to move, to get things set into motion. There's too much to do with consequences too large to miss deadlines.

Vienna blinks at me when I scoop her off the floor, that blissful look fading into a scowl far too quickly for my liking. "You kissed me!"

My lips twitch. "You don't know how happy it makes me to know you didn't miss it. I hate to repeat myself, but considering the repetition means tasting that mouth again, I'll allow it this time."

"First you try to fuck me, then you kiss me. Have you never kidnapped anyone before?"

"Plenty," I deadpan, and give her a moment to process that. "I just wasn't aware there's kidnapping etiquette. The way I see it is, I captured you, I'm keeping you, therefore I can do whatever I wish with you, whenever I choose. Is that not standard kidnapping protocol?"

"No!" The word ends on a squeal as I drop her onto the bed, and she bounces softly. "No, you're supposed to keep me in solitary, feed and water me, and blackmail my parents for money. Not... not this!"

"Huh." I skim my fingertips along her leg and the air sweetens with her natural perfume. "I guess I'll pass your concerns along to the complaints manager of this fine establishment." My head cocks and I nod to myself. "There. He says I can do what the hell I like because I'm the one in control."

I can't stop touching her, my fingers trailing up to the narrow strip of skin revealed between her tank top and shorts. Circling her navel elicits a quiet curse, and a shiver I feel running through me as tantalizingly as it does her. I keep caressing and, little by little, she submits.

It's not enough to quell the stubborn, bratty attitude, but sufficient to lower her guard a fraction so I can slip under her reinforced mental defense into where I need to be.

My eyes lock onto hers as my fingers curl around her throat, squeezing lightly. Visual and physical connection works best for me when it comes to compulsion. I can compel anyone with my gaze alone, but for those a little more strong-willed, I find skin-on-skin contact helps... solidify my commands.

I stare into her eyes until those unique irises are black, eclipsed by the pupils, then I'm sucked into that busy hive of activity she calls a brain. Memories, thoughts, feelings assault me from all sides, but I don't take the time to sift through them.

I did that once before, in my first century, and damn near lost myself in the dull mind of a scullery maid. Nobody warns you how dangerous compulsion can be to the vampire—it's so tempting to peek into those memories, but one leads to another, and another, until you're mired so deep inside the maze, there's no getting out.

"Vienna, are you listening to me?" My voice comes from far away to my own ears. Vocal directives are optional, and I rarely use them, but I want her to understand what's happening.

"Yes."

"Good. I have business to see to which may take several hours. In my absence, you are to stay in bed and sleep. Sleep, Vienna. Understand me?"

The faintest shimmer of iris fights the pupil then capitulates. She has a freakishly strong mind, and I foresee it causing me considerable problems. "Yes."

"Good girl. Take a nap now. I'll see you when I get back."

Breaking the visual bond pains me. I want to study every nuance of emotion in those eyes when they're awake and aware. I need to know if that constant inner bitch gleam softens into something more malleable with the right... stimulus.

Vienna's eyes return to normal as they flutter shut. I brush the hair away from her face, tucking it behind her ears. Satisfied she's asleep—she'd never let me do that if she wasn't—I tuck her under the covers and leave the light on for her.

Dressing to meet Antoine is a complex business. He's been known to take exception to the smallest things, including, if the rumors are true, one of his men's cufflinks. The color of the metal didn't quite go with the color of the suit, apparently, and the poor guy lost his hands as punishment for affronting the Phoenix lord.

In the end, I go with black. Suit and shirt *sans* tie, and definitely no fucking cufflinks. If he takes exception to the lack of color, he can sit on my middle finger and swivel. I'm not losing any body parts to the likes of him.

With a glance at Vienna, I access the door hidden in the shadows at the back of the room and walk through six feet of hallway into the rest of my sanctuary. While the warehouse floor is a decoy, down here is my private area.

My living room takes up a good chunk of floor space, kitted out with a leather couch big enough to seat six people. I'm a tall guy and I like to stretch out in comfort when I get the chance, in those rare moments when I have a few minutes of spare time and the inclination to sit and brood. Maybe it makes me feel like less of a monster and more civilized to have a few home comforts.

The big-ass flat screen television affixed to the wall

doesn't get much use, but it provides company in high definition when required. Not to mention, porn on a screen that size? Prepare to have your eyes opened *wide*.

Passing through, I head for the doors at the far side. One leads to the state-of-the-art bathroom, another to my weapons store. The last one is my destination, and it's one I'd rather Vienna not lay eyes on during her stay.

There are two more rooms hidden on either side of the hallway leading to my bedroom, but they don't get much use. A small kitchen where I mainly store my blood packs for emergency use, and a small safe cell I had installed in case I ever need somewhere secure to store something precious away from attack.

The room I go to is not a torture chamber, per se, and I wouldn't call it a playroom. I've had no need for either, but I do collect... things. Little bits and pieces of things time and civilization have forgotten over the years, cast by the wayside and glossed over with upgrades.

Maybe if Vienna stays with me for any period of time as I'm starting to crave, I'll expand this into a working playroom. See if I can tease the submissive lurking under all that hostility into submitting fully rather than hiding away. Although I might have to consider stashing my treasured Scavenger's Daughter somewhere else.

I've got my eye on a Brazen Bull I really want to add to my collection, but the logistics of getting it down here are not ideal. That's a problem for another day.

The polished wooden sideboard tucked against the wall holds a variety of implements, most of which I use in my career as Vadim's trafficker bitch. I've got drawers full of restraints, needles, syringes, vials... you name it, I've got it somewhere. Everything is disposable, a lot like the humans being ferried onto US soil.

Fifty fucking people. Vadim is getting greedy already, not a positive sign of success. Between the price tag and my own suspicions about the quality of the shipment, the Russian stands a good chance of sinking his venture before it really gets a chance to float.

Although, with Antoine's fifty million in his pocket, Vadim is laughing already. Because it won't be him who takes a stake in the heart if the cargo isn't up to scratch. No, it won't be the smarmy Russian bastard.

It'll be me.

I can't deny I deserve it for my part in those humans' demise. I've done terrible things in six hundred years, earned myself a rep in the early stages of my development I'm not proud of, but I've changed a lot. Obviously not enough.

I take a vial and hospital-grade syringe from a drawer. Antoine wants a sample; I'll give him one. But he's not getting his hands on the source.

She's mine.

IT'S ALMOST midnight by the time I drive up to Antoine's gates, and Vienna's blood is burning a hole in my breast pocket. As usual, a small army of armed guards surrounds the car as one approaches my window and taps his gun on the glass.

It's laughable, really—one small, rich vampire protecting himself with a battalion of security while the King of Tucson has a few of his sired who remain loyal to him. Oh, and his wife, the shifter-vampire hybrid who scares the shit out of most people she meets.

The window purrs open at a press of a button and I'm

greeted by the muzzle of the gun just inches from my forehead. I lift my eyebrow at the guard—one who should know better, considering we've met often. "Oscar, is that necessary?"

Bald as a scalped raccoon, Oscar grins down at me before lowering his weapon to his side. "Had a few pranksters lately. Swapping and changing vehicles, trying to piss us off. Don't know if they're casing us or just doing it for the shits and giggles, but we've been ordered to intimidate anyone who pulls up. Get the word out we're not messing about with our security measures, y'know how it is."

"Can't be too careful," I reply with a sober nod. "You need to search the car, see some ID?" From the corner of my eye, I see several weapons relax from shooting position. Good, I'm not keen on spending the rest of the night pulling wooden bullets from my flesh. "I did tell him to let you know I was coming."

Oscar gestures with one hand and the guards scatter back into formation, leaving the area in front of the hood clear for me to drive through. The gates screech, then glide open without a sound. They need a good oiling. "You're all clear, Colt. Whatever you're bringing him, bring more. He's been different since he spoke to you."

"I'll see what I can do." I tap two fingers to my temple and continue on my way through the gates, onto the cherished grounds of a vampire who thinks himself above the rest of us.

Manicured lawns surround the monstrosity of a mansion, watered constantly overnight by several dozen sprinkler systems. I catch sight of several arcs of water gleaming under the moonlight as they spin. Every tree, bush, and flowerbed are immaculate, not a leaf left untrimmed.

I'm surprised the droplets aren't evaporating the moment they leave the sprinkler heads.

The winding drive looks as though the gravel has been swept into perfection. And it's not just *any* gravel. It's one of Antoine's many boasts. No, the common stuff peasants around the world find satisfactory is not good enough for this jumped-up asshole—the way he tells it, he bought sapphires by the ton and had them crushed just for this purpose.

I roll my eyes at the thought.

No one in their right mind would destroy precious gems in bulk in order to make a road for cars to drive on. But it's a case of hold my tongue or lose it, and calling him a liar won't bode well. It's easier to keep quiet and agree with him.

The drive leads up the small hill, where the mansion sits like a giant mammoth. It doesn't fit into the landscape of this area of Phoenix, and simply screams Antoine's lack of taste and complete disregard for keeping a low profile.

Between the lights shining out of nearly every one of the sixty plus windows, and the water bill for the lawns, I bet his utilities companies dance a jig come payday.

As soon as I come to a stop at the half-dozen white stone steps outside the front doors, Antoine's personal valet rushes to open my door for me. I step out, leaving the engine idling, and the valet goes to work without a word, sliding into the vacated driving seat and driving away before he's even shut the damn door.

If he smashes it off on his way to parking the car…

Taking a deep, bolstering breath, I jog up the steps. Don't need the oxygen, of course, but I find the action is a boost to the system. So much is riding on this meeting, and I can't help but feel like I'm not prepared.

Antoine's right-hand man, Garçon, sweeps open the

massive wooden doors as soon as my foot hits the top step. Like his boss, Garçon is using a fake name, and he's as French as my left foot. A sour-faced vampire with the same outlook on eternal life, he isn't weathering his many years gracefully.

Then again, I might be the same way if my boss insisted on calling me *Boy* for the rest of time. It stinks of disrespect and keeps Garçon in his place, I suspect, but there's only so much disregard even a loyal subject can take.

"He's been waiting for you," he chides with a bitter glare. His muddy brown eyes survey the steps, the grounds beyond, before they meet mine with distinct disapproval. "I was told we'd be expecting you plus one, Colt. Did you leave something in the car?"

The temptation to kick him in the balls is strong, and I wonder if I've inherited some of Vienna's violence through drinking from her. The man irritates me as much as he's helpful—so quite a bit—but I've never had an overwhelming urge to send his testicles on a visit to his throat before. "A change of plan, Garçon, nothing more. I've brought the sample as promised."

He flashes his fangs. "He wanted to see the full product, Colt."

"Well, we all know each product is one of a kind, down to the last fingerprint. What matters is what's flowing through the veins." And I'm fairly sure Antoine won't be thrilled we're having this conversation in the open air. "Either let me in, Garçon, or I'll walk with the sample. I'm not having a pissing match on the damn doorstep."

One side of his mouth spasms, a bit like a rabid dog. After a moment of silence, he eases back and allows me entrance, snicking the doors closed sharply behind me. The click echoes in the huge foyer, bouncing off artwork and sculptures worth millions of dollars. Priceless artifacts that will likely never fall into human hands again.

"Pray your sample is worth its weight in gold," Garçon hisses, and walks away toward what is known as the sunroom, snapping his fingers for me to follow like a good little lapdog. If he's not careful, he'll discover how sharp my teeth can be when put to use. "He wants attractive merchandise. He doesn't enjoy fucking ugly dregs from the bottom of the barrel, says it takes the enjoyment out of draining them. You'll give him the pick of the delivery."

"Since when do you speak for him, Garçon?"

He's almost as tall as me, but luck of genetics means my eyes are a fraction higher than his so he has to look up at me to glare at me. I have height, weight, and skill in my favor, but he has age and strength in his. It will make for an interesting fight if it comes down to it. "Just laying it down in clear terms, Colt. Fifty million dollars buys him the cream."

"He's paying the same as everyone else. Five million a head. Just because he's buying more doesn't mean he gets dibs over my other customers. He'll need to sweeten the deal if he wants special favors."

Something that resembles respect whips into his eyes before his usual dour expression returns. "Antoine might not see it that way, but I can see your reasoning. Perhaps he's in a good enough mood you'll be able to convince him to add a little honey to the deal."

We pass through an open archway into the horribly extravagant sunroom. Everything glimmers and shines, from garishly framed art down to the gold plating between the tiles—tiles I've seen awash with blood and ash more than once.

Classical music drifts serenely from all corners of the room, whispering from speakers set into the wainscoting. A tepid piece with no real tempo, it's filler noise and nothing more. If Antoine enjoys listening to this, his taste in music is as dull as his right-hand man.

The man himself is lounging in a wing-back chair, attired in a formal dressing robe that looks like it's made from velvet: heavy and uncomfortable, especially in the current heat. One foot rests on top of his opposite knee, and his fingers are tapping along to the music.

At his side, a young man with lash marks and burns littering his skin kneels by the chair, hunched over. I see why when I spot the thick black collar around his neck and the short length of chain secured to the leg of Antoine's chair. It's short enough to keep the man's head bowed in constant respect.

"Colt, welcome. I've been anticipating your arrival." Antoine reaches down and grabs the man's thick hair, yanking his head back and almost strangling him with the collar. "Can I offer you a drink?"

"Thank you, but I'm afraid I'll have to be antisocial and pass. I have another meeting in Tucson at four, so we'll have to get straight to business if you don't mind." I lie without a qualm, watching Antoine's meal turn red. His eyes begin to roll back in his head. "Your dinner is about to pass out, Antoine."

With a Gallic grunt, Antoine releases his food and the tortured soul wheezes in a grateful breath, returning his head to a more comfortable position. "He's almost served his purpose, anyway. One more feed, and he'll take his last ride down to the kennels."

Garçon clears his throat. "Apologies, my liege, but I thought you wanted me to make arrangements for this one to be photographed after your usual method of dispatch?"

My stomach turns. I've seen Antoine's collection of postmortem artworks and it's gruesome. If ever an art gallery requires a display of the range of human pain and terror in death, they'll sign the bogus Frenchman instantly.

The man in question looks down at the blond head beside him and then flicks his hand in disgust. "It turns out he's not the subject I thought he was. He doesn't deserve to be preserved throughout eternity. Let the dogs have him. I reward loyalty, not failure."

"As you wish, my liege. I'm sure the men and the hounds will be grateful for your generosity, as always."

"Now, let us discuss our arrangement, Colt. I was hoping you'd bring me a gift, but it seems you have none to give." Ice-cold blue eyes scan my face idly. "Are you hiding your gift, Colt?"

"I have what you asked for, Antoine."

"Hmm. Well then, take a seat. I'm eager to taste the future."

Taking my normal chair, a plainer one than his, I face Antoine and study the smug face I dislike with a passion. A white shock of hair accompanies those killer blues, but the face itself is that of a kindly grandfather. He had the misfortune to be turned in the later stages of his mortal life.

He'll be forever seventy.

"If what you've brought me isn't as described, Colt, you know we're going to have a problem, don't you?" Antoine's tone is easy, conversational, like we're two friends sitting down for a casual chat, but underneath... steel scores his words with dangerous inflection. "Fifty million dollars is quite a substantial sum for ten humans. I could buy tens of thousands of human whores for that amount and dispose of them all in the same way."

I nod soberly. I have no doubt Antoine is responsible for any number of missing mortals scattered over continents.

He has a tendency to watch people, and when he sees what he likes, he takes it. Whether they're willing or not. "You'll like this, Antoine, you have my word. My source assures me the incoming shipment will be just as appealing to your taste."

"Your source, the smug Russian Avtoritet," my companion says knowingly. "Come now, surely you didn't think I'd do business with you without making sure exactly where my money would be going, did you?"

The answer to that is no. There are already rumors circulating that the vampiric Bratva have their fingers in this pie, but not one of my other clients has managed to pinpoint Vadim's connection to it directly. Not yet, anyway. "It makes no difference to me whether you know my source or not, Antoine. Vadim is supplying the merchandise; I'm just distributing it to interested customers in good faith. If there's a problem with the stock, take it up with Vadim."

"Oh," he purrs, "I will."

His response sends a chill down my spine. Antoine has the money and the power to buy quite literally anything he desires. Walking blood bags, human whores, weapons... those are the small things he enjoys toying with. There's speculation that not only are his dogs hellhounds—which is frightening enough, considering their natural-born urges to destroy *everything*—but that Antoine might just have an honest-to-God werewolf chained in one of the many rooms in this hell.

Not a wolf shifter. I'm on speaking terms with a few packs of those around the world. An actual *change into a mindless, slathering beast three times a month* kind of werewolf. The rarest of the rare.

If Antoine finds grievance with Vadim, there is a high possibility of war breaking out between the two. Both powerful men, both rich as sin, and so lacking in morals they'd happily decimate both their cities—nay, countries—in order to rise as victor.

"Will my order be comprised of males or females?" he inquires nonchalantly, and my mind immediately swings in the direction he's travelling.

"I honestly can't say. Until the shipment arrives, I have no idea what I'll be receiving other than fifty Rhonulls ready for dispatch." It's the truth. Vadim sends me what's ready to be harvested. "Vadim is a smart man, Antoine. I'm sure you're aware that Rhonulls can only be bred by pairing one Rhonull with another. Rhonull crossed with any other blood type won't produce the goods."

He lifts his hand to swipe his index finger slowly over his lips. "Yes, I've done my own research. The current number of Rhonulls the world is aware of tallies to a pitiful forty-three individuals. I wonder how many the Russian is hiding from that count?"

I shrug and offer my hands in open denial. "Again, I'm not privy to that side of things. His operation has been running for a long time. Who knows how much breeding stock he's in possession of? But I know one thing, and I'll repeat myself, Vadim is a *smart* man. None of the stock he sends out of Russia will be fertile. Male or female, they'll all be sterilized so no one else can hijack that section of business out from beneath him."

Blue eyes darken, giving me a glimpse of the demon lurking in the shell. That's the primary reason Antoine has spent so much on so many Rhonulls this shipment. He wants to start his own breeding program. But he doesn't vocalize anything other than acknowledgement, leaving me wondering how this is going to backfire on *me*. "I see. That's useful to know."

Deciding now is a good time to veer away from Antoine's plans blowing up in his face, I reach into my shirt pocket and pull out a slim glass vial. I twist it between my fingers, letting the light spark off the glass and the single mouthful of Vienna's blood I stole from her sleeping body earlier.

A plastic vial might have been wiser to transport such precious cargo, but plastic taints blood. Any vampire who has ever fed from a live vein and from a sealed blood donor bag can taste the difference immediately. It... curdles the blood, to an extent.

Glass, however, preserves the original taste immaculately.

Antoine's eyes light up and he extends his hand out for the fragile vessel. "This is from your own specimen?"

I curl my fingers around the glass carefully. One wrong squeeze and this mouthful of glorious blood will go to waste. "Before you taste it, Antoine, know this: the human this blood comes from belongs to *me.* She is not for sale. If anything happens to her, there will be consequences beyond the telling. Are we clear on that?"

"Absolutely," he says cheerfully, fingers wiggling. "Please, may I?"

I lean forward and drop it in his weathered hand. Bad omens niggle at me as soon as it leaves my grasp, but I'm powerless now to do anything but watch as he uncaps the vial and scents the blood as a human might nose a fine vintage of wine.

His eyes gleam red as he sniffs again, harder, deeper, and his hand shakes with excitement. Regardless of bad omens, I know I've hooked him into taking his delivery, no matter whether it fits in with his plans to go head to head with Vadim. He raises the vial to his lips and pours the thick, red liquid onto his tongue and holds it there before washing it around his mouth and swallowing.

Nostrils flaring, he pins me with his gaze and licks his lips. "Outstanding. You're a lucky man, Colt, to have access to a Rhonull of such quality. Simply divine," he sighs lustfully, "like drinking from the golden vein of a goddess."

I nod and purposefully check my watch. "It's to your liking then?"

Antoine closes his eyes, throat rippling as he swallows again. "I feel like a young man again. Vigor in my blood from one sip, life surging through arteries clogged with dust. The money will be deposited in the account when I receive word the shipment is in your hands. Oh, and Colt?"

"Antoine."

"Make it heavy on the females, would you? Attractive, young, and with some stamina. I have a feeling they'll be worked hard while they're here, and I will be feasting often." Those eyes open and land on mine. "I fuck men and women but this... this gives me a yen for sweet, wet pussy while I feed."

Disgust roils in my gut. This vampire's proclivities are not those most vampires will claim to enjoy, but sadly, more and more seem to be following in his depraved footsteps. It's no longer simply about feeding or a clean kill. Torture and misery are a big part of many of my kind's feeding habits. "I'll make sure you get only the best, Antoine. I see this being a profitable relationship for us both."

He nods. "Make sure of it, Colt. There's a little something extra in it for you if you do. Not just money, I'm sure you're not short of that. I bet you'd give quite a bit to rid yourself of your ties to Vadim. I can help you with that, but that's a conversation for another day. See yourself out."

4

ienna

SOMEONE'S in the room with me.

Even though I'm tucked up under nice, warm covers, a sliver of ice shivers down my spine before my eyes open as I hear soft footsteps padding around the room. I already know this isn't my room—even snapping out of sleep so deep I feel like a new woman, my faculties are all in order, and Colt is the first thing that springs to mind.

Damn him.

Something squeaks and I risk opening my eyes a fraction to peer around the dimly lit bedroom. There's nobody lurking in the shadows, but I've got personal experience in just how well that vampire conceals himself in darkness when he wants. I go for all or nothing and sit up slowly, peering into every pool of shadow for a suspicious form.

Nothing.

My gut says it's not *nothing* and I'm inclined to agree with it. Moving like a ninja cat in slow motion, I ease out of the bed that's not mine and sneak toward the nearest wall, using it to guard my back as I inch along it, hoping I don't bump into anything.

Wouldn't that be embarrassing.

My suspicions are vindicated when I catch the low, angry murmur of a masculine voice coming from... somewhere. *Okay, butt monkey, show me where you're hiding*. I close my eyes and focus on the hum breaking the quiet. It sounds far away and yet... my feet move toward the pull of it, drifting over the carpet as though guided by invisible hands.

Colt.

Eyes still closed, I follow his voice. Behind my lids, the cadence glows like Christmas lights, pulsing gently, growing stronger the closer I get. The air around me changes slightly, cooling and less restrictive. I'm no longer in the cocoon of the bedroom.

Nervous, I stumble slightly to my left and brace my back against the doorjamb, groping over the wall and somehow brushing my fingers over a set of switches. Light blossoms across my eyelids and I open my eyes to stare at the room spread out like some men's fashion magazine idea of male simplicity at its finest. Glancing behind me, I can just see the faded glow of the bedroom lamp. Fuck, it's as though I've stepped through the wardrobe into Narnia.

There's a huge couch and a television to rival it in size, and that's it. No artwork, no keepsakes, no personalization whatsoever. Hell, there's not even a rug on the floor to break up the monotony of the silvery-gray carpet.

"Oberon, I won't tell you again. Tonight isn't good for me. I got back not twenty minutes ago from visiting Antoine. I'm tired, hungry, and not in the mood for your simpering right now." Colt's irritation comes from behind a partly open door —one of three across from me. A drawer slams, then the vampire in question storms out and sets the door shuddering on its hinges with the force he uses to shut it. "Antoine is in. That's all you need to know. No. No, Obe, do not—fuck!"

Our eyes lock across the sparsely furnished room. I think mine probably take up most of my face, while Colt's narrow with something I can't quite decipher. Fury and lust, I think, but I'm not willing to hang around and wait for my theory to be confirmed.

Not when he's looking at me the way I eye up a plate of chicken wings.

"Oberon," he says dangerously into the phone pressed against his ear, "if you think I'm going there tonight, you'll be waiting a long time. Whatever's got your panties in a knot will wait until tomorrow. I've got more pressing things to deal with." His fangs extend and the tip of one sinks into the curve of his lower lip, dragging over firm flesh before releasing it. He gives me a feral grin. "You know how I am when I'm ravenous, brother."

I'm not stupid. I know that when faced with a predator, you're really not supposed to run—it triggers their hunting drive, yadda blah, and basically turns all their focus on one thing.

The chase.

The hunt.

The kill.

Those three elements combine into that *one thing*.

But when Colt's nostrils flare and his grin turns triumphant, my sense of self-preservation no longer exists. I'm not brave enough to stand in front of this beast, waving my arms in his face and hollering. What lurks in his eyes is pure devastation and will mow me down to get what it wants.

I bolt.

Maybe it's foolish to believe I can reach the door, shut and lock it before Colt gets his hands on me. It's certainly ridiculous to think a large, thick plank of wood will keep him from what he craves. It's definitely moronic to assume he'll give me a head start in some weirdly thrilling game of cat and mouse.

A strong arm hooks me around the waist before I recover from my first stumbling stride, lifting me off my feet and carrying me not toward the bedroom, but back into the living room—if I can even call it that—to toss me on the couch.

I bounce with a startled grunt and try with difficulty to roll off the soft leather. Jesus, this thing is like a cold black cloud, sucking me down into the cushions. Quicksand drawing me into a trap the more I struggle.

Just when I surface, Colt's big hand lands on my head and shoves me back into my smooth prison. I flail in the cushions, tiring quickly, while my captor simply stands warriorlike over me in a suit fitting his form exceptionally well.

"Tomorrow," he snaps. "Ten o'clock. Leave your whining at home, Oberon."

I swallow audibly as the phone wings across the room, thudding and skipping over the carpet. My body goes very, very still as Colt growls and unbuttons the suit jacket one button... at... a... time.

Fuck, that's hot.

He strips off the jacket, tosses it aside. The pristine black shirt beneath follows, arcing through the air to flutter to the floor in a heap. Man, someone knew what they were doing when they designed him.

For a broad man, he's not brutally muscled. No 'roids for Colt. He radiates strength, sure, but his muscles are in keeping with his frame. Shoulders, arms, chest... all the way down to the subtle vee just visible above his waistband.

He has the most fascinating scatter of dark hair over his upper chest, dusting over his pecs before arrowing into a thin line shooting straight down his subtle six-pack abs and beyond.

I don't recall seeing it before but I'm wondering now how the hell I missed it—oh no, wait. High on superhero brain, that's how. I'd been more interested in vanquishing the foe than submitting to him.

"I trust you slept well," Colt drawls slowly, popping open the button of the pants slicking over his legs like paint. I really wish he'd turn around so I can see whether his ass is as fine as I imagine when hugged by that tight material. "You didn't stir when I came in."

My throat constricts. He isn't making easy conversation; he's leading up to something that's about to snap his leash. I feel it, the tension building around us, and it is moments away from blowing up in my face.

"I'll take that as a yes." The soft whirr of his zipper lowering makes me squirm, but there's no escaping this couch without help. "I'd remind you of rule number two, but in a few minutes, you're not going to remember your name. We'll go over the rules again soon."

He starts to push the pants down, then leaves them clinging to his hips as he tuts quietly and shakes his head. "How rude of me to undress myself before helping you." He reaches down and grasps my tank top between my full, aching breasts, tearing it down the middle without pause.

"Hmmm, and to think I almost let these pretties escape without my attention."

Calloused fingertips grip my nipples, pinching them sharply and rolling them until I squeal in a mixture of pain and rapture. My toes curl, tightening every muscle between my feet and my core, making my pussy clench in delight.

"I'll endeavor to pay them extra special attention," he hums darkly. "No sassy comeback, Vienna? No complaints, no witty remarks? Well, now I know how to quiet that bratty mouth." He releases my nipples, almost blinding me with the throb of pain that follows, then skims a fingertip down my exposed belly to my shorts. "I've been dying to get rid of these. Covering up the pussy that belongs to me. Naughty girl."

He's danced me right back around to where we were rudely interrupted by his phone call earlier in the night, with words and dominance. Wet, wanting, whimpering. A phone call won't save me from myself this time. I think the roof and the warehouse above us could come crashing down on our heads and it still wouldn't deter him from staking his claim.

With a couple of firm tugs of his hands, my shorts are in tatters, just like he promised. I lie before him, quivering under his heated gaze, partly terrified of what he's capable of when he cuts loose, and partly enthralled.

I am in so much trouble.

"Scared yet, vixen?" he asks, and I'm positive his eyes are darkening by the second. He belongs in the dark, this creature that shouldn't exist, and yet… for all his fear tactics and his sexy, seething dominance—scratch that, bad Vienna—his high-handed, obnoxious dominance—yes, that's much better—he isn't ripping me to pieces. "With the games I have in mind, you should be."

"Aw, did someone send baby home from the nursery in a bad mood?" I blink, shocked by my mocking jibe, and squirm helplessly in the cushions. I can't stop the rest of the words spewing out and my ass is already tingling with the consequences. "Want me to get you your pacifier and a blankie, big guy?"

Colt's smile isn't sunshine and lollipops. His lips curve slowly, exposing those freaking fangs again, while his eyes gleam with retribution. "I can think of something much sweeter to suck on, believe me. Several somethings, in fact. Game on, Vienna."

His pants are gone in seconds, thrown aside, out of sight. I suffer a single moment of trepidation as I watch him stroke his hand down the length of his cock, back to the crown, before he's on me. My yelp of alarm ricochets around the room, echoing back at me as he flips me upright and spins me against the rear of the couch.

I hiss between my teeth as my exposed front presses mercilessly against cold leather, the thin sheen of sweat on my skin sticking me to the damn furniture like a fly in a spider's web.

My captor's knees drop between mine on the cushions and he uses his legs to force mine apart, inch by inch, until I feel the head of his cock brush between my legs. Even as I twist to claw at him, any part of him I can reach, his hands capture mine and hold them prisoner on the back of the couch.

My breath erupts in angry, panicked bursts. If my heart beats any faster... oh wait, there it goes, kicking into higher gear when Colt's body surrounds me, smushing me against the soft seat. "You know you're in a very vulnerable position right now, don't you, Colt?"

His laugh ripples through me. It only takes a subtle

move of his hips to have *me* in the most vulnerable position of my life. "Better hope you're wet for me, Vienna, else this is going to sting."

He thrusts hard, wrenching a sharp moan from my throat. It's been a while since I engaged in sex, and my body pays the price. Although I *am* wet for him, goddamn his arrogant ass, this is one well-hung vampire, and he stretches me in all the right places. Deliciously.

The pain between my legs is exquisite, and Colt nurtures it carefully. Slow, hard jerks of his pelvis urge his cock deeper, bit by bit, until I'm keening pitifully and chewing on the couch cushion.

He lets go of my hands, easing back to frame my shuddering body with his own big appendages. They skim down my sides, molding me from shoulders to thighs. Just when I think I can't take anymore, when my pussy reaches maximum capacity and I'm sweating at the idea of being pounded by what's inside me, Colt leans down and tuts softly in my ear.

"Oh no, you don't, vixen. There's another inch of my dick for you to take, and you don't get to give up until you take it." He grips my hips, angling them as he rocks and twists his pelvis. "We'll see who needs the pacifier and a blankie when I'm done with you."

Too much pressure. I'm about to pop and ignite like flammable glitter. My thighs shake with the almost violent need to come, infecting the rest of me with every passing second. My teeth gnaw on leather as I grunt and savage the material, unable to speak when he gets his way and gains the extra inch.

Colt groans, his hands keeping my ass pressed firmly to his groin. I whimper, squeezing my internal muscles around his girth in time with the slow, thick throb of his cock. "Been a while since a tight pussy took all of me, Vienna. Congratulations, you win a prize."

"Do I get to kick you in the balls?" I toss back at him, releasing my mouthful of couch and resting my heated cheek against the cool material. "I'd really like that."

His laugh is low and dangerous. "No, vixen. Emasculating me isn't on the cards, but coming is. Now be gracious," he advises, grinding deep before pulling out until only the tip of him remains inside me, "or I'll make you work for it instead."

My short, witty reply—which effectively boils down to *fuck you, Neanderthal*—is lost in a desperate cry that burns my throat as he surges back to the hilt in my pathetically grateful pussy. I've never been with a man who wields care and rough-handedness in equal measure, who takes everything yet gives just as much back.

We might have skipped foreplay this time, but by all things holy and awesome, it's so freaking worth it.

Things blur a little. Time is meaningless, narrowing down into flesh slapping flesh, hands lighting fires under sweaty skin. Possessive grunts resonate against my back, accompanying each punishing drive of his hips, and drowning out my own breathless moans.

I come apart at the seams, breaking into shattered pieces I have no hope of putting together again in the right order. Body and brain part ways, one blinded by pleasure so acute it is barely remembering to function, while the other twists and writhes in the control of its master.

Colt commands me completely, and he knows it.

"Good girl," he snarls in my ear. *Snarls* it as though I'm a bad girl for taking his cock, a naughty girl for letting him wrench my power away from me. His fingers tighten on my hips, bruising me, adding more frissons of pain to the already overwhelming riot of sensations assaulting me. "Give me more."

There *is* no more. I'm wet cloth in his hands and he's wringing me dry. Only his relentless body is keeping me from sliding into a pile of mush on the couch, drooling and half-comatose. If he wants more… he'll have to take it.

"Again, Vienna. Fucking come again."

Impossible, he's asking the impossible. If he wrecks me with another orgasm like that again, this soon, I'll never be the same. I fear for the safety of my sanity, but Colt has no such concerns—his hand slides around my front, fingers finding where we're joined and then unerringly landing on my clit.

"No!"

His mouth hovers at the side of my neck. Exertion stains his words, but I miss the waft of warm breath over my skin, the heat of a straining body fueling mine. Nevertheless, he's making up for the minor points he lacks in humanity with superior strength and intimidating stamina. "Come now, vixen, or I'll make you. Your body's ready to fly again, so let go and fucking soar."

He pinches my clit sharply, nudging me closer to the edge of the cliff I'm standing on. He pinches again, holding on this time and rolling the swollen nub between his fingertips, squeezing in sync with his quickening thrusts.

A scream slices the air as my precarious footing slips and I tumble off the ledge into the gaping chasm of climax waiting for me. I'm snatched from the dark and catapulted into the sky when his fangs pierce my artery and pleasure becomes tangible.

I barely register the kick of his cock inside me as he forces himself deep. His savage roar sends me reeling, but

I'm fairly sure there's a smile on my face when I pass out beneath him.

Colt

I've been to war a few times but my experiences on the battlefield never left me feeling like this. I'm exhausted, exhilarated, and sated simultaneously.

I finish feeding and seal the wound in Vienna's throat while my body jerks its release one last time. I've never known another like her. Her blood, her sass, her unrelenting fearlessness when taunting me… there isn't another mortal woman in existence who compares to her.

She's limp, unresponsive, but I'm not surprised. I rode her hard, perhaps harder than I should have, considering my size and the mood I was in when I took her. She isn't—wasn't—a virgin, which is some consolation. I can be a bastard when I want to be, but some things I still consider sacred, and virginity, the innocence that comes with it, is something I revere.

Calmer now, I ease from her carefully and settle her trembling body on the couch. Her consciousness may be on a quick vacation but her physical form is still reeling from a proper fucking.

I've bruised her in many places, marking that pristine skin with perfect dark splotches that are already blooming black and purple, the imprints matching my fingertips. While I enjoy being rough—and Vienna responded beautifully—there's a sliver of regret growing inside me for marring this wondrous body.

I shouldn't have claimed her while I was furious with Oberon and Antoine.

But it's done, and now my dominant side is urging me to take action, to nurture and tend my female. Leaving her where she is, I walk naked to the bathroom and gather a warm, damp cloth and a dry towel.

I'd prefer she slept naked beside me, the scent of my cum soaking into her skin to warn others off her, but I don't think she'd appreciate being put to bed with semen slicked down her thighs. Or waking in a wet spot.

My vixen is easy to rile and once she's fired up, she's capable of anything.

Now I've had her, I'm liable to fuck her anytime she uses that smart mouth to give me attitude. I like it, the bratty side of her. She's sharp and witty, feisty and fun. An appealing, entertaining female with a mouth like a sailor and a body built for doing bad, dirty things. I suspect she has the mind to match.

The problem now lies with the fact she's a Rhonull.

Returning to her, I take a moment to admire the long lines and sweet curves of what now belongs to me. I should have known how different she is the instant I first tasted her blood—Golden Blood is addictive, the highest narcotic available to vampires, and so scarce, few of us ever get to feast upon a single drop. Even sweetbloods—humans manipulated by various means to produce sweeter blood pumped full of adrenaline—don't have the same tang as a Rhonull.

Antoine's reaction to the blood in the vial confirmed the seedling theory I'd been growing on the drive to Phoenix, and now I have a quandary on my hands.

Vadim cannot know about her, ever.

Antoine cannot be allowed to find her, ever.

I cannot let her go.

As I see it, I have two merciful options, and two despicable ones. The kindest thing to do for her is to either kill her now while she floats on whatever high she's experiencing, or to turn her. To make her like me. As a vampire, her blood will be useless to everyone and that will render her safe from my boss and my clients. It will make her mine in no uncertain terms—there is no bond like that between a sire and their offspring.

Conversely, if I choose to be callous, to embrace my selfish side, I could call Vadim now and trade her life for my freedom. I don't doubt he would exchange my service for a Rhonull; I would be free, but Vienna would suffer immensely.

Just as she would if I sell her to Antoine.

Shaking my head, I cast aside any notion of handing her over to the Avtoritet or to the mogul. How can I consider it when I know her fate at their hands? Raped over and over, bred until her frail human body is unable to continue the vicious cycle of conception, gestation, and birth. Forced to bring life into the world, only to have it wrenched away and raised for its blood. Her life would end when Vadim either drained her body dry of the last drop of gold, or sold her to the highest bidder for whatever he could get for a worn-out husk of meat.

I'm sure Antoine's plans run along similar lines for whatever Rhonulls he gets his hands on.

As gently as I can manage, I clean up the mess between Vienna's thighs, fiercely tempted to wake her with my mouth on her pussy and an orgasm ringing in her ears. Only the sight of more bruises along her thighs and her red, swollen sex prevents me from doing so. She is going to be sore.

Before I question my motives, my thumb is already bleeding and pushed between her lips onto her tongue. The tiny wound lasts no more than a few seconds, but what she takes in will be enough to undo the damage I wreaked upon her, and perhaps assuage some of my guilt at being too rough.

Not that I'll say a word about that, mind you.

If anything, my little vixen is something of a painslut, and I intend to delve further into those proclivities.

Oberon wishes to meet with me at Club Toxic tomorrow night. It's a bold and daring move for one with so short a spine. The club is owned by the vampire we fear most, and Lucius is in residence there damn near every night, along with his nubile queen, Selene.

To meet right under Lucius's nose...

Oberon must have a death wish.

So must I for even considering his request, but I happen to know there's a secret dungeon beneath the club itself, catering to vampires. A BDSM club with all the trappings and equipment any dominant vampire—male or female—could hope for.

It's the perfect place to give my vixen a proper test drive, as long as I don't draw blood. One whiff of her essence in the heat of the dungeon, and I'll be in a fight to the death with every vampire in there.

It might be wise to find a way to silence Vienna's sharp tongue for a few hours. At least until I get her down into the dungeon... or I could dare to ask a favor of Lucius and stash her there while I handle the meeting with Obe. At least then, the skittish little bastard can't run back to Vadim and tattle to the Russian about my newly acquired toy.

Daring, yes, and probably idiotic, but it's too tempting an opportunity to miss. I want to see her skin rise in perfect welts, watch her writhe under the flogger and the envious eyes of others. I need to hear her cries, those gloriously throaty and arousing noises she makes, rise to a crescendo that drowns out every other sound in that damn room.

She brings out a possessiveness in me I want to flaunt.

She's mine. She'll never be yours.

It's the kind of attitude that will end up with me as a pile of ash, but I don't care. I've been inside her now, and her blood runs in my veins. Mine is combined with hers, pumping through her cells with every delicious *buh-dum* of her heart.

My skin tingles, warning me of approaching dawn. I'm safe down here, we both are, but my bed is calling me to sleep. I don't want to miss a minute of being with her but in this, I have no choice. I'll make it up to her when I wake.

She croons to me when I scoop her up and cradle her to my chest. It's just the softest hum of sound in the depths of her throat, appealing to my protective side. She doesn't stir as I carry her to bed, switching out the lights as I go, but for the first time in a long time, I feel like a man rather than a monster.

I tuck her in beside me, anchoring my arm over her waist and pulling her back against me before drawing the covers over us. I let the warmth of her body and the softness of her skin seep into me as I count her slow, rhythmic breaths, and fall away from the world.

VIENNA

Apparently, my vampire lover is a snuggler.

We're wrapped together, touching from my shoulders down to my feet, with his cock resting along the crack of my ass. That's as far as *that* will be going. When I recall the way he stretched my pussy, he can think again if he thinks he's exploring any other part of my body with that weapon.

I'm feeling good. Real good.

Not quite superhero high but there's an element of it singing through me, and no discomfort. The big softie dosed me with his blood again so I wouldn't be in pain—I'm not sure whether to be grateful, comforted, or annoyed.

Of course, I'm grateful. While there's a satisfaction in waking with twinges and aches after a pounding like the one Colt gave me, it's nice to be able to move without wincing. That he thought of it gives me comfort, and solidifies my opinion that he's not the completely monstrous asshole I assumed he'd be.

But I am annoyed he keeps feeding me blood like I'm some infantile vampire.

Who knows what side effects prolonged exposure to his blood will give me? After all, I've already been a deluded hero attempting to slay the demon. What if suddenly I become the villain, tainted by the thing lurking inside him?

Although, I would make a pretty damn fantastic villain.

But that's not the issue.

If he keeps erasing the effects of hot, rough sex after every bout, I'm never going to learn my limits on what I can take from him. What happened between us was raw and fucking awesome, but he has more locked away in his vault. I know he was holding back; if he unleashes the full force of his desire on me, we're both in trouble.

I stretch lazily and wonder when the hell I accepted being here with Colt as finality. Jesus, is this an effect of his blood? Stockholm syndrome? Or have I finally been given a reason to feel like I belong with someone? With him?

Because, for all my protests, I'm starting to like what I see.

Right now, for instance, I should be sneaking out of bed and trying to find a way out of this bunker he calls a home, or searching out his cellphone like I'm a truffle pig on a mission, but no, I'm humping my ass back on his cock like a desperate, wanton hussy.

Colt is my poison, and I'm literally injecting myself with him.

I'm letting opportunity pass me by when I could be alerting the authorities or calling my parents to let them know I'm still alive but not coming home anytime soon, or... hell, I don't know! My parents won't give a shit as long as I'm having fun and not wasting my trust fund on frivolous things which, evidently, I'm not going to get a chance to do.

Unless... I glance at him over my shoulder and he's out cold, dead to the world. Whatever magic weaves over vampires when daylight is in place has its hold on him and he's lifelike but unresponsive. If I was scientifically minded, he'd be blowing my brains out with a surge of excited curiosity.

He would look *phenomenal* in one of those laboratory cells you see on TV shows with the three white walls and the glass front. Seriously. Naked, cocky, padding around like he owns the fucking joint and fighting the security guards every time they go to pull him out for the scientists...

Maybe I should try screenwriting for porn—I could sell Colt all day long and every day of the week. Build my own fortune and become the next Queen of Porn. Move over, Hugh Heffner.

Well, if Colt's out for the count, I'm going exploring. I'm buzzing, revving, needing something to do. If I find an escape route, I'll figure out what to do with it. What I want to do with it.

If I could just remember where he tossed his

cellphone...

Eyes half-closed, I play back the last moments before Colt's shit flipped and see the phone skip, skip, skipping across the carpet before he distracted me with his peacock display of stripping off his jacket. Which means the phone is in the living room and I can find it if I can maneuver myself back in there without stubbing my damn toe—the asshole shut the damn door this time.

Unfortunately, I'm starving, parched, and in dire need of sustenance. Can pizza delivery trace phone numbers back to their addresses? That would be so handy right now, especially if I can track Colt's wallet down and steal his credit card to pay for it. After all, he's kidnapped me; he should be providing me with food, water, and a safe place to sleep.

I spend ten minutes easing out from beneath his restraining arm before I realize I'm not exactly going to disturb him from his vampiric slumber if I pick up his arm and set it aside.

Today is turning into a serious lesson on how not to look at the bigger picture, and waste enough time to ensure my twenty-ninth birthday is knocking on the door with a bouquet of flowers and a cheap two-dollar box of chocolates.

The bastard.

I huff and disengage myself from Colt. In just a few months, I'll be down to the final year of my twenties, and then I'll hit the adulting years. Joyful. While my parents allow me to fritter away my trust fund to some extent while I'm young and carefree, my thirties may prove different.

Both my parents were forged in their thirties—my grandparents were formidable in their parenting skills—and they were forced to settle down, to stop living off what was given to them, and become productive members of

Chicago society which, obviously, they achieved with great success.

Me?

I don't want to go to work in the family business; I don't have a head for numbers, my editing skills suck, and I am *not* a team player on the best days, let alone when I'm menstruating. One wrong word on those days, and even Colt will be leery about speaking to me the way he does.

Vampires have *nothing* on a PMS-ing woman, trust me.

Naked, I try and find the door back into the other rooms. My inner thigh muscles twinge with every step. Colt riding me into next week really put my body through its paces, and I'm feeling the vaguest echoes of it. Blood doesn't fix everything, apparently. If he and I are continuing on this energetic path, he really needs to feed me.

There isn't a door handle as such. As I feel around the wall for where the door should be, I don't find as much as a seam for what appears to be hours, but I eventually notch a fingertip into what feels like a divot in the wall. It's big enough to hook my finger into and tug open.

Well, that's one way to hide an entrance.

And he's switched off all the lights in here as well. Wonderful. I follow my footsteps from before, down the dark hallway with my hand trailing along the wall, until I reach the living room. I remember where the switch is... sort of.

Hungry I may be, but I'm curious about what secrets my vampire lover is hiding in the rooms straight across from me. Three little rooms and so much time to explore—a kid in a candy store comes to mind. I want to find out what makes my sharp-toothed playmate drool and then use it against him. I want him on his hands and knees while I ride him like a toddler taking her first ride in the mutton bustin'.

Then maybe I'll let him fuck me again, because that man is a demon in the sack.

But no butt stuff. I'm drawing the line at that.

I'm delusional, thinking I can stop him from doing anything he wants to with me, but sometimes there is comfort in delusions. Control in illusions. Colt is the one with my life in his hands and yet I'm willing to go along for the journey because *I* think I can outsmart a centuries-old vampire.

I forget everything but the lure of the doors as I approach. I don't give a shit I'm naked. My palms itch as I reach for the first handle. Dead bodies, treasure and art, an extravagant library? Whatever shall I find beyond the door?

I'm almost dancing with excitement.

I imagine the look on my face is nothing like what I expect when I open the door and light spills into a fully functioning bathroom. And by fully functioning, I obviously mean state of the fucking art bathroom, with a shower big enough to perform magic tricks in, several heads set around the edges for an all-round bathing experience. Not just that, it doubles as a bath, *and* there's an honest-to-God toilet.

I'd started to fear Colt simply pissed around the perimeter of his territory.

Well, what's his is mine now, and I need to pee.

Once I'm done, I wash my hands and debate between taking a long shower or continuing with my explorations. Explorations win and as one door clicks shut, I open the next. Meh, not quite as exciting.

It's like some kind of medieval weapons locker. Wood and metal gleams everywhere. Whether it hangs from the roof, the walls, or is protected behind glass counters, Colt's armory gleams with the shine of care.

The blades look sharp. His guns are freaking deadly and

come in all manner of shapes and sizes. I don't know any of the makes or models and don't want to. If anything, I'd rather be handed a bow and arrow or a sword and shoved into a battlefield than have the muzzle of a gun pressed to my forehead.

Looking around, I see he does actually own both bows and swords. Is he some kind of collector? From the number of weapons I can see without actively searching for more, he's either a collector, or a slightly crazy survivalist who thinks he's going to need all of these vicious implements when Armageddon comes calling.

It might not be in my lifetime, but it could possibly be in his.

The last door is the one Colt emerged from in those calmer moments before his lust went on the rampage last night. It's ajar by the barest crack. Now I'm not so much curious as full of trepidation. The twist in my belly becomes nasty, warning me away from what I hope isn't about to change my opinion of Colt after I've spent so long—see the sarcasm there—formulating a hypothesis that he's not such a bad vampire.

Stepping into the room, I hunt for the light switch, tottering inside on my bare feet as my palm skims the wall. The door drifts shut slowly behind me, eclipsing what little light I've got, and snicks shut with an ominous sound of locks engaging, leaving me in the dark in a strange, claustrophobic room.

Fuck. I've locked myself in.

I'm in the darkness, in a room with a door I can't seem to unlock, with hours to go before my captor, lover, and apparent savior rolled into one delicious specimen wakes from his demon sleep to release me from whatever hell my snooping has brought down on my head.

5

Colt

TRACKING Vienna's scent through my home is easy enough to do. Even if her scent trail had been disturbed, I can follow her angry grunts and curses well enough—they mirror my own. After all, I had expectations for my vixen to be right where I left her when I woke, and she is definitely not there.

Tomorrow, she will be chained into position so that when I wake, I won't need to hound her through my rooms in order to satisfy my urges.

That is, if we're both still alive and not crushed beneath Lucius's foot.

I stomp through the living room and haul open the door to my workroom, intent on snagging my errant vixen by the hair and dragging her back to bed for a quick bang before I get my head in the game for my meeting with Obe. I need the release before we go, especially if I'm taking my prize possession for a spin in Club Toxic as well. I've woken with several sadistic urges, the least of which is flogging Vienna's delectable pussy for all the trouble she's putting me through right this moment.

I think there's a studded flogger in my bag which will make her sit up and sing prettily for the delight of my fellow bloodsuckers.

As it happens, I'm unprepared for Vienna to leap at me like a demented flying squirrel as soon as the way is clear, so focused am I on getting my hands on her and making her suffer in all the best ways. But she tackles me, barely shifting me an inch, and I take in the riot of destruction spread over the floor in the room before I wrap my arms around her and stop her attack dead in its tracks.

"Satisfy your curiosity?" I demand gruffly, noting the myriad of stuff tossed carelessly here and there. "Hope whatever you found is worth it, vixen. It would've been less painful to ask me what you wanted to know."

She's vibrating like an angry hummingbird in the cage of my arms, her bare feet stomping on the tops of mine, to no avail. Whatever bee is crawling under her feathers is riling her up good and proper. "What the hell is all that shit?"

My gaze scans over the mess, separating the medical equipment from the sex toys. "Some of it I use for work, some I use for play. And some, nosy little vixen, I use for both," I whisper in her ear and set off her temper as easily as sparking a fire. "Calm yourself down or I'll be happy to demonstrate the dual-purpose items. We have a busy evening tonight and I don't want to wear you out this early, seeing as you've had such a busy day."

She splutters delightfully. "Busy day! I've been *locked* in this damn room since this morning, starving to death, dehydrating, waiting for you to get your sorry ass out of bed and take care of me! I'm human, Colt, I can't live on fresh air."

Hmm, she may have a point there. I've been neglectful in my duties as her guardian, and I will rectify that before we leave for Club Toxic. It so happens I did remember to call in at a convenience store on my way home from Phoenix and pick up a few edible goodies for my little vixen... I just forgot to bring them in for her. "So you went divining through my cupboards in search of food and water?"

Her beautiful cerulean eyes glower at me. "I was looking for food, asshole. And I found that!" Her arm shoots out, pointing at the room.

I shrug. "I'm a dominant, Vienna, I thought you'd gotten the gist of that. If it hasn't sunk in yet, tonight is gonna be a real eye opener for you." Oh yes, her fierce blush and the quick flare of her arousal tells me she's not prepared for what I have in mind for her... but she's not afraid. "What in particular has you all in a dither, little vixen?"

My hands are already fondling her breasts, cupping their weight as my thumbs feather over her nipples. I think I'll have these bare for the evening, open to my gaze so I can see just what effect the club has on her as the minutes tick past. Right now, those tender buds are peaking, in color and size, and I have an urge to pierce them, adorn them.

Her ribs shudder on a pleasurable inhale and she's losing her snap, crackle, and pop. The angry stance is sliding away with the antsy shift of her hips and the subtle press of her thigh muscles. Vienna knows what I want, and she is not going to let me have my cake for free.

Fine by me.

She hasn't answered my question, but it doesn't matter anymore. We have limited time to take the edge off before I doll her up to the correct specifications for Club Toxic, and

I'm not wasting a moment. Squeezing the root of my cock with one hand, I slide my other around Vienna's nape and twist her hair once around my wrist, pulling her head back until she whimpers softly.

"Get on your knees, Vienna. I want my cock harder than stone and wet with your saliva by the time I fuck you. Do a good job and I'll reconsider fucking your ass here and now, even though," I murmur darkly, using my hold on her head as leverage to sink her to her knees before me, "I want very much to fuck it, plug it, and keep it on display."

Distaste flashes over her face even as her eyes flutter in submission. She's a mess of contradictions, believing she wants one thing while craving others. Denying herself the dirtier things in life she really wants. Well, she's mine now, and she's going to experience her darkest fantasies if I have to sieve them from her vault-like brain by force.

She opens her mouth to speak, no doubt preparing to shoot some attitude my way, and I simply guide my cock through those plump, parted lips with ease. Her splutters are music to my ears, the suction of her mouth around my crown divine.

"Make it good," I warn, releasing my cock and using my fingers to support Vienna's head as she swallows nervously, "or this will get rough, little vixen."

Her lip is dying to curl at me; I see it twitch and direct her aggression with a firm thrust of my hips. I don't need her teeth getting ideas about severing my cock from my body. Eternity without my best friend is a prospect I refuse to consider, and I do not have time for a trip to the ER tonight.

Vienna gamely takes me deeper, uncertainty flashing in her eyes as I take her to the edge of her trust in me. Her throat works, swallowing reflexively as saliva begins to pool in the corners of her mouth. I change my grip, holding her head firmly in both hands now and coaxing her to let me in just… a… little… further.

"Relax and take me in, Vienna." The flat of her tongue works restlessly along the underside of my shaft, fluttering and rolling as I press against the resistance at the opening to her throat. Her warm, wet sucking feels amazing, coaxing cum to rise from my tightening balls. She has a way with her mouth, talented little minx. "Oh, good girl. Don't fight me, V. Deep breath and… oh fuck, you little superstar."

My knees go weak as she all but inhales my dick, pulling me deep and gulping around the sensitive head. A flurry of nonsensical babble erupts from her, coming to life as a maelstrom of angry humming that ripples along my cock and literally yanks my orgasm from my testicles.

I get a hint of *fuck you, Colt* as my hips work against her face, feeding her my cum in a way I find far too sexy for my own good, then stagger back a step. One last lash of semen kicks from my cock, decorating her swollen bottom lip like frosting.

It's quite possibly the most embarrassingly quick orgasm I've ever had, but on the same token, Vienna has pleased me beyond measure, even if she is snarling at me like I've just sprayed her beautiful face with cum instead of leaving a small deposit on her lip.

She jerks her head away as I reach down to rub the offering into her skin, her teeth flashing in warning. Naughty, feisty vixen. In a split second, my fingers twist into her hair and snap her head back with a shake of my own. "Don't be a bitch, Vienna. You pleased me, very much, but that doesn't mean I won't spank the brat if you bring her into play."

She hisses at me, eyes sparking with genuine distress.

"Don't ever come on my face without asking. I hate it." She's not fighting the grip of my hand, but neither is she submitting.

We stand on a tenuous pinnacle.

With my other hand, I cup her cheek gently, smearing my spend over her lower lip as I gaze down into her furious eyes. I incline my head, unwilling to continue on combative ground when things have been so smooth between us. "My apologies, vixen. My intention wasn't to offend."

Vienna blinks slowly, her eyes narrowing. Ah, is she wondering whether she's overreacted? Thoughts flit around her savvy brain as I watch with interest, and I wait for the moment everything clicks into place. It doesn't take long at all, and she sags at my feet, baring her throat as she gives me control of her head.

There's no apology, but her capitulation is enough for me.

I release her slowly so as not to jar her delicate neck, then urge her to rest her cheek against my thigh. She surprises me by obliging my silent request, and the surprises keep on coming as she wraps her arm around my calf and relaxes into me. The only reward I have at hand is the stroke of my fingers through her dark hair, stimulating the pleasure receptors in her scalp, but she accepts it, sighing contentedly.

"I'm not a tyrant, Vienna. I want you to tell me if I do something that upsets you. I can't guarantee I'll change whatever it is you object to, and I might even continue doing so just to keep you on your toes, but communication is important to me. I've never kept a human as a pet before."

Her nails bite into my bare calf as a subtle warning. "I'm not your pet."

"I'm your everything, Vienna. Until I decide what to do

with you, you need to see me as your keeper, your lover, your master. My world is your world until further notice." I roll my shoulders and notice the time. "Go take a shower. I'll get you some food while you do so, then we need to go."

Her face tips up. "Where?"

I can't stop the predatory smile from curving my lips. "Purgatory."

VIENNA

Colt wasn't lying when he said we were going to purgatory. I honestly feel like I'm suspended between heaven and hell right now, not daring to so much as sweat in case the rabid horde of vampires around me scent my fear and come in for the kill. Which is really, really possible considering I'm wearing little more than a pair of boy shorts and a sports bra, and I'm scared shitless.

Colt brought me here in a pair of fur-lined cuffs and a blindfold, leading me along like a hesitant puppy on a leash. I think we crossed a dancefloor, and I know he made conversation with several people before guiding me down some steps. When he removed the blindfold, my wrists were attached by a length of chain to a metal ring set into a bar, and I was told to keep my ass on the barstool until he came to collect me.

Then the fucker gagged me, paid the bartender, and vanished.

Two hours later, here I remain with drool pouring down my chin, saturating the black sports bra, and my wrists chafed from my frantically covert escape attempts.

The bartender lifts an eyebrow at me with a smirk.

Okay, maybe not so covertly.

My jaw aches, my ass is numb, and my skin is crawling with the gaze of a dozen vampires leering at me from around an honest-to-God sex dungeon.

How do I know they're vampires, you ask, and not just ordinary perverts?

I've been in the company of everyday perverts and never have they licked their lips, flashing their fangs at me in a way that makes my pussy curl up in a ball and whimper. The next time I think Colt is a bad, bad man, I'm going to remember this moment and remind myself that he's the lesser of several evils.

"I can't offer you a drink, sweets, as your master hasn't given me permission to remove the gag." The bartender swings my way again as he has all night, and he seems like a nice enough man even if he is a demon in human skin. He's in his mid-twenties, and tattooed from his fingertips all the way up his arms to his shoulders, where the ink disappears beneath his black silk vest, then reappears in the broad gape of material across his chest.

His hair brushes his shoulders, blond and glossy, and he has a range of piercings from nose to ears to nipples. He winks at me with a sharp blue eye.

Such a shame he's gay.

I grunt at him and try again to loosen the cuffs. Colt wasn't stupid enough to leave the buckles accessible. Oh no, Mr. Smartass did something to the clasps which is making it impossible for me to release myself.

"You seem to be in somewhat of a difficult predicament," a smooth British voice murmurs in my ear, making me jerk and scowl. I give the newcomer an earful of unintelligible grunts and mumbling, then lift my hands imploringly. "I'm afraid not, little miss. One of Lucius's primary rules in here is that no one interferes with another dominant's submissive unless the subbie is in danger. You seem quite comfortable, despite your restrictions."

Asshat. I bare my teeth at him around the gag.

"Now I see why he's gone to the lengths he has," the Brit continues with a laugh, moving around me into the light from the bar so I can see him more clearly. "For a submissive, you are delightfully fierce. Although only a brave man would leave his mortal submissive in a dungeon full of hungry vampires." He breathes deeply and I shudder as his intelligent brown eyes begin to glow red. "Brave... or foolish."

An alarmed squeak ripples in my throat as I scramble backward off the stool and almost end up falling onto my ass. I have nowhere to go, and the British vampire is eyeing the artery in my neck like it's a chocolate fountain.

"Rupert," the blond sings out from behind the bar, slapping a towel down on the glossy top. "Do I need to remind you of the rules? She's not your property."

"Yet she's been left so prettily bound," Rupert murmurs seductively, giving me a glimpse of his fangs. He's a fucking peacock, extending his tail feathers into a fan and shaking his ass to gather doting female admirers. "I'm sure her master won't mind me taking a sip."

A hand grasps me by the nape, tightening as I arch up onto my tiptoes. I hate to admit it, but my bladder is on the brink of releasing. My courage flees screaming from the room, leaving me bound and helpless. The gag renders me speechless, but fear blinds me.

"Her master will roast some English balls for breakfast if you so much as brush her skin." Colt's voice comes from behind me and my knees go weak with relief. His tone is cold, his displeasure evident, and I have a horrible feeling he's going to take this unpleasant interlude out on my ass. "Step away, *Rupert*, while I'm still in a civil mood."

A shudder rips down my spine and I burble around the gag as best I can. The quick squeeze of Colt's fingers shuts me up; whatever he's been doing while I've been sitting here like vampire bait hasn't made him happy.

"Shouldn't leave your toys unattended," Rupert mutters, letting his eyes roam all over me. I immediately feel dirty, as though his gaze has fingers and they've just smeared crap over every inch of my bare skin. "Someone else is bound to want to play with them."

The air closes in around the three of us. Behind me, Colt bristles furiously, and I'm sure there's gonna be bloodshed. The way he's growling seems to be a declaration of war because Rupert is puffing himself up, fists clenching, his whole demeanor evolving into something beastly.

Something cracks down onto the bar, and both Rupert and I glance toward the interruption. My throat clicks with a swallow as I take in the baseball bat the bartender smacked onto the oak top in warning, only this isn't any old bat.

This thing is solid wood, riddled with inch-long silver studs.

"First one to spill blood on my bar is going home hurting." The bartender glowers at both Colt and Rupert, his inked hand flexing warningly on the shaft and tapping the spikes gently on the wood. "Rupert, the girl has been attended all evening. She's quite obviously claimed. Back the fuck off, or Lucius will hear about your total lack of club etiquette."

I blink in surprise. This place has etiquette?

The British vampire scoffs but steps away, inclining his head a fraction in deference to Colt. "When you want a master more invested in your wellbeing, little miss, you know where to find me."

Colt snarls and it's a terrible sound. There's a split second where I think he'll ignore the bartender's warning and simply rip his fellow leech's throat out right here and now, but the Brit must know he's overstepped the boundary because he blurs away into the shadows faster than my eyes can follow.

My lover slaps two twenties on the bar. "Fucking asshole wants his hands breaking. He give you much trouble, Austin?"

"Rupert's used to acquiring what takes his fancy," the blond answers with a shrug. He sends me another blazingly blue wink as he plucks the bills off the wood. "Can't say I blame him, Colt; she's a sweet little thing and she's been sat here all night radiating innocence. She was bound to draw some attention."

Two glasses appear in front of me. One fizzes lightly, and I assume it's a coke from the color and the bubbles. The other is Scotch, I think, or some other hard liquor. It's amber in color but there's a darker splotch in the middle, like a shot's been dumped in there. As I stare at that random blob, it dawns on me.

Whisky with a hit of blood.

My mouth curls in distaste.

Colt's fingers nimbly unbind me from the metal ring I'm locked to, releasing the chain enough to slide it through the ring… and through a clip attached to his pants, exchanging one mooring point for another before he lifts his drink and tips it back.

The gag pops free and I spit it out gingerly, moaning as my jaw comprehends just how compromised it's been. My teeth ache, the hinges of my jaws are locked in the open position, and I'm humiliated by the flood of saliva now spilling uncontrollably from my trembling mouth.

"You fucking asshole," I rage at him, livid that he's left me for so long with that damn thing silencing me, but what comes out is more like, "Oooo thucking thassho." I think he's caught my drift though, as he swipes the towel off the bar and patiently cleans up my mortification.

"You all good?" Austin asks. He must read something in Colt's expression because he nods and slides the baseball bat back under the counter. A moment later he glides away, summoned by the hail of someone hidden in the darkness beyond the lights.

More people are gathering here now, and Colt lifts me back onto my stool, crowding me from the rear as he brings the glass of soda to my lips and lets me drink. "Drink, vixen. You need the sugar. I'll make sure you have plenty of water before we play."

I *pffft* at him. There won't be any playing, not after this stunt. I wiggle my jaw gently and am relieved to find there's no permanent damage, just a residual ache and maybe slight muscle strain. "Think again. Two fucking hours you left me here, Colt. Two hours bound and gagged. I want to go home."

He pushes my hair away from my neck and begins nibbling down the side of my throat. His tongue and teeth find all the little erogenous zones between my ear and my shoulder. "I didn't think I was going to be away from you for so long, vixen. My meeting was considerably longer than expected, with absolutely dismal results. A good submissive would want to make her master feel better after such a traumatic meeting."

I hear the laugh in his voice and *pffft* again. But I must admit, now I'm more than a bit curious about his meeting and the topic, and the outcome. Then I sneer at myself, remembering what happens when I let my curiosity rule my head—I end up on my knees sucking cock and taking a shot of cum in the face like a whore.

Fire builds in my belly as the anger kindles again. "Go find yourself a good submissive, then, because you've pissed off your captive one too many times tonight."

Two sharp pinpricks of pressure bite into my shoulder, reminding me just how much pleasure Colt gives me along with the pain. "Not even if I promise you a minimum of three orgasms? I'm in a giving mood tonight, vixen. The gag and restraints were an unfortunate necessity in my absence."

"If you'd asked nicely, maybe I would've stayed of my own accord."

"Doubtful, but not impossible. My concern was more that one of the other monsters in this safe haven would steal you despite the consequences. Even if you wanted to stay with me, every single person in this dungeon is bigger and stronger than you. More than capable of picking you up and hauling you away. Or compelling you to go with them."

Why the hell am I leaning into him? Annoyed by my growing dependence on the idiot, I jerk myself away and continue to sip at the sweet liquid in my glass. "What was your meeting about?"

It's a complete one-eighty away from the subject of sex and the promise of orgasms, and I'd put fifty bucks on him zipping that talented mouth shut if I had fifty bucks to spare. Good job I don't, because he shocks the hell right out of me when he answers promptly—and apparently, honestly.

"A few technical issues we're having with our delivery

system. Oberon's an obsessive worrier sometimes, and likes to hash out every viable possibility that could go wrong."

Movement across the room snags my attention. I freeze in place as people move quickly out of the way of quite possibly the sexiest power couple I've ever laid eyes on. "I don't think you should be worried about the delivery system," I whisper, my mouth easing open, watching the tall, dark, and delicious guy stroll through the crowd with that air of arrogance that says *I own this*, with a sleek and atrociously attractive white-blonde female tucked into his arm. "I think that's who should have you concerned, Colt. That's a man who knows what shit's going down in his town."

"Lucius and his mate, Selene," Colt says tightly. "That's the closest you'll come to vampiric royalty, vixen, so get a good look while you can." He nips at my ear. "But then again, he's your new employer, right? Of course you know who he is."

My mind goes blank for a few deadly seconds before it remembers what our stupid mouth claimed upon capture. Well, hell, trust the smartass to remember my original statement. "Sure. I won't bother him," I retort airily, gesturing with my hand.

"I think maybe we should introduce you properly." Colt chuckles darkly.

I swallow hard, looking over at the gorgeous couple. "You're so sure I won't divulge your little secret? It's a big gamble, Colt."

His hands smooth down my shoulders, along my arms, to my hands. My eyelids flutter as I imagine him following the same route with his mouth, ending with him sucking on my fingers until my toes curl and my pussy weeps. "At this point, Vienna, I don't care. Run to Lucius, tell him everything. Stay here with me and protect my secrets. I trust you to make up your own mind."

Oh wow. I didn't expect this. He's offering me an open door to run through and now that the way is clear, I hesitate. I study his face, essentially ageless and so fucking beautiful he takes my breath away, and search for something that says *stay with me*.

It's written right there on his face, lurking in the shadows of his tawny eyes. Not quite a plea—Colt's far too self-assured for the likes of that—but an edge of vulnerability that lets me know he knows his fate and mine rest in my hands.

My eyes slide back to Lucius and his queen of their own volition; they've moved through the busy dungeon to take their seats on honest to freaking God *thrones* set upon a stage at the other end of the room.

Without warning, I meet the eyes of Selene and blush as a pale eyebrow rises in interest. Shit, I think I may be on her radar. Without expressing panic, I turn back to study the gleaming wooden bar as though there's hieroglyphics inscribed in the surface.

Don't be shy, little one.

A touch of warmth slides over my shoulders as though a hand rubs my back. Fuckity fuck fuck. I'm not imagining that, nor have I conjured the sweet, soothing voice cruising around my mind. I'm most definitely on the she-vampire's radar and she's calling me in.

Why don't you come visit with me? I'd like to make your acquaintance.

That invisible hand strokes the nape of my neck, urging me to turn my head again and seek Selene's gaze. She's waiting for me with a small smile on her lips, leaning over the throne slightly to walk her fingers up her husband's arm as she speaks softly to him.

The Vampire King swings his keen gaze over to me and I shrink into myself. I've gone and done it now. If either of those two can read minds and don't have any personal boundaries when it comes to breaking into people's thoughts, Colt and I won't see the outside of this place again.

Suddenly, protecting Colt is imperative.

I don't even know why.

Squeezing my eyes shut doesn't keep the nice voice from penetrating my thoughts, coaxing and teasing me to go over to the dais where the vampires other vampires fear are sitting, patiently waiting. I dig my nails into the bar, holding on for dear life.

Then the sweetness, the cajoling, is disturbed by one single command.

Come.

"Vienna?"

My feet are moving without conscious thought from me, compelled by the smooth, dark voice directing me across the dungeon. I feel Colt lunge and clutch at my shoulder but there's no stopping the almost euphoric draw of that masculine voice.

Fear pools in my belly with every step I take, the chain leashing me to Colt straining as he stands still in an attempt to anchor me. I shake my head as he grips the fragile links. "Take the cuffs off and run," I murmur, hardly able to form the words. My mind is ringing with the king's command, drowning out everything else. "If they find out your secret, they'll kill you."

I know I'm standing on the wrong side of the moral line. I should be on the side of good, willing to spill every drop of knowledge I have about Colt and his association with the

Russian, with Oberon, and the sick business they're running under Lucius's nose.

Perhaps Lucius has the connections and the manpower to put down the Russian blood-breeder and wipe out his operation, but the thought of losing Colt in the process is digging claws into my heart.

Tawny eyes dart between the dais and me. Jaw tense, Colt removes my cuffs completely, sliding his fingers through mine before I follow the siren's call in my head. "I'm an asshole, V, but I'm not leaving you to fend for yourself against entities you have no knowledge of. We're in this together."

Pain begins to bloom, sharp stabs of pain behind my eyes. Whatever Lucius and Selene are using to draw me to them doesn't like being ignored. I tow Colt along with me through the growing crowd of vampires, almost shoving one out of my path in my haste to obey. "Keep that in mind, Colt."

The lighting in the room flickers, shimmers to red. I don't know who gives the orders around here, but someone hit the goddamn ambience switch. With just a change in light, the dungeon part of Club Toxic becomes less of a pleasant social area, and more like what it's supposed to be.

"Stop right there." A big vampire steps into my path when I'm only a few feet away from my destination. The niggling voice in my head is still coaxing me, and I'm prepared to bulldoze my way through this beast of a man if it means the damn thing will leave me alone. "Where are you going in such a hurry?"

Colt lets me go as I wrench my fingers from his and take a step forward, clenching my fist. Colt's hand swallows it and yanks it down to my side. But before either one of us can speak, the pretty voice from my head beats us to it.

"Maximus, leave the girl alone. I asked her to come play."

The thick body encased in a perfectly fitting black suit—what is *with* these guys and their goddamn suits?—turns slightly toward the thrones. "Do you know these people, Selene?" The guard dog named Maximus uses a respectful tone.

A beautiful smile graces her lips, as terrifying as it is stunning, and her striking gray eyes skim over me with mischief. "Does the poor thing look as though I know her, Maximus? If it makes you feel better, search her. With what she's wearing, I doubt very much she's armed, unless there's something up her—"

"Selene," Lucius growls in warning. "Behave."

My heart is about to collapse under the combination of Maximus's considering gaze and Selene's devilish appreciation. I take a step back, ready to flee without giving a good damn about my dignity. There is no dignity when you're *dead*. Bumping into a hard form at my back, I squeak.

"Do not run," Colt breathes into my ear.

This is some cat and mouse shit right here. I'm the teeny, tiny mouse with both barrels loaded, ready to fire. And around me is a swarm of feline foes whose bite is definitely worse than their meow.

Shit, now I'm mixing metaphors.

"Maximus, let them up. If they're stupid enough to annoy me, you can deal with them." Lucius sets his fingers together in a steeple, tapping the point of his joined fingertips against his lips. "You are new to me, mortal. You," he says to Colt in a cold tone, "are not. Perhaps you'd like to make the introductions, Mr. Dockery."

Colt sighs, his grip on my hand releasing. His move to my hips, holding me in place as I battle between dropping to my knees and praying they kill me quickly, or seeing who can get to the exit first—me or Maximus the mighty.

"Vienna, this is Lucius Frangelico, King of the Tucson vampires, and his mate, Selene." He squeezes my hips gently. "My liege, my queen, this is Vienna."

The respect in Colt's voice astounds me. After all, the first time I heard him talk about the king, he'd been derisive, damn near dismissive. Listening to him now, you'd think he was the royal couple's most loyal and supportive follower.

Lucius doesn't seem impressed. His dark eyes assess me, and I almost feel naked beneath his stare. Not even the ridiculous boy shorts and sports bra Colt found for me can deflect the feeling I'm being X-rayed by an expert. Abruptly, Lucius stands, and with a sharp glance at Colt, orders, "Come with me."

Who, me? Oh fuck, they want to dine *al fresco*.

My feet are planted on the spot despite Colt urging me to follow after Lucius and Selene. Images of being led outside into a dark alley and laid out like a buffet for the masses are dancing in my head. I dig my bare heels into the wooden floor when he tries to push me. It probably isn't helping my panic to find Maximus waiting impatiently, massive arms folded over his broad chest, looking at me as though he's thinking about just snapping my neck and being done with me.

"Relax, vixen. I'm not leaving you."

Oh, that's really comforting. My lover is going to stand by and watch his superiors *eat me*. I don't suppose he has a choice. If he interferes with their dinner plans, they'll probably stake him, and what immortal being would sacrifice their eternal existence for a mere mortal?

The events of the past forty-eight hours catch up to me in my next breath. Somehow, I've conned myself into believing everything would be okay, despite knowing what Colt is. Being bitten by him, the sex, the threats... I've twisted it all into some fanciful fantasy where death by vampire isn't a possibility.

Here and now?

It's a completely different scenario without the fantasy safety net. Reality strikes swiftly, without mercy, and opens my eyes to the fact I'm an idiot, playing with vampires like a kid with a fucking puppy. Only, the puppy is ten times stronger, faster, and meaner than I am.

Fuck it, I am *not* dying here. Not like this.

I take a shaky step forward, shaking off Colt's reassuring hands. I miss his touch immediately, then kick myself for being an absolute moron and trusting him. He's one of them, after all. A couple of porn-quality rolls in the sheets doesn't change that.

Once I'm free of his grasp, I sidestep around Maximus.

"Lucius doesn't like to be kept waiting," he warns ominously.

For the briefest second, I wonder if he knows he looks like a Russell Crowe impersonator. Maximus would fit right in with the cast of *Gladiator*, that's for sure. He'd eat the goddamn lions and shred his opponents with his big, brutal hands.

A scream echoes through the club, high and wild. It draws the attention of everyone toward the sound, including that of Maximus and Colt. While they turn and seek out the screamer, I bolt.

This bitch can make zero to sixty look easy with the right incentive.

My feet barely make a sound on the floor. Running with my weight on the balls rather than the whole soles gives me an advantage in speed and silence. Dodging in and out of club clientele, I aim for the wall nearest to the exit, hoping the shadows will give me some cover.

My heart beats so loudly, I know it will give me away. My breath is whistling, forcing its way through the fist knotted in my throat.

The stairs to the exit are ten feet away.

Eight. Six. Four.

My feet slip as I scramble around a tall, lean woman escorting a young man toward the bar. My knee smashes into the floor, apparently imploding on impact if the pain is anything to go by. There's no time for self-pity—Maximus is wading through the people behind me like a juggernaut.

Fuck, I can't get up. My knee is done. It won't function, and I'm blinded by the pain. Clenching my teeth until I'm sure one cracks under the pressure, I drag myself forward, crawling the distance to freedom.

My fingers are a scant inch away from touching the first step when someone steps around me, in front of me, and plants familiar black boots in my path.

That's it, folks. Game over.

Defeat isn't something I've ever accepted lightly. I think a person should fight until their last breath because who knows when a saving grace might swoop in and change the whims of fate?

But lying here, keening under my breath as agony hacks away at every nerve ending I possess, I've reached my line in the sand. Hell, I've just skidded over it on my face.

"That was impressive," Colt tells me, crouching down to stroke my hair. "I honestly thought you were going to make it. Was it worth wrecking the knee?"

My lip curls in pain. If I open my mouth to speak, it's not words he'll hear, but a keening groan of agony. Unable to bear it anymore, I surrender.

6

olt

My brave little captive is out cold on the floor of Club Toxic.

I can't say I'm surprised. I heard her knee pop when she hit the floor, as did everyone else here. Yet she hasn't made a sound of pain. I must admit, I expected to find her screaming—the link between us, forged by the consumption of each other's blood, is still vibrating with agony and panic.

As footsteps come down the stairs leading from the nightclub above, I sigh and scoop her limp body into my arms. No point getting myself in more shit with Lucius for disturbing his clientele further by causing an accident on the stairs.

From the look in his eyes, he's gunning for me anyway.

I still can't quite believe she had the guts to run in a

room full of predators. Oh, I can understand why. Her thoughts were clearer than the glass bottles lining the back wall of the bar, scrolling over her face, her mesmerizing eyes wide with anxiety.

The vixen finally figured out this isn't a happy ending kind of life.

Maximus is waiting impatiently, his scowl less than pleased. He simply gestures for me to walk ahead of him once Vienna is safely in my arms. "Keep your submissive under control, Colt."

I snarl at him under my breath. "Give the girl a break. She's not the only mortal to freak out at the prospect of being eaten by vampires."

"Which is why we have strict rules about mortals knowing what we are. Lucius's laws are in effect for a reason." Maximus gives me a shove in the back to keep me going. He's pissed with me, which means Lucius is definitely sharpening a blade intended for my neck. "Walk faster if you value your life."

I'm not too concerned for my own wellbeing right now. My focus is on Vienna, completely. I need to fix her knee before she comes around and screams the roof down, and I absolutely cannot allow Lucius to harm her for my mistakes.

We slip into a side room disguised by shadows. Decorated in the style of an old-fashioned drawing room, it radiates warmth and comfort. While Antoine collects the garish and adorns his rooms with symbols of his wealth, Lucius's style is less arrogant.

A pair of matching solid walnut chaise longue love seats take up a great deal of space in the room. The woodwork is intricately carved—French or English, at a guess—and I think they hail from the Victorian era, carefully reupholstered in a regal shade of blue.

They would draw the eye even without the vampire queen seated upon one. She looks imposing, more so than her husband in this moment. The split of her red sheath dress bares an exquisite length of thigh as she crosses one leg over the other. The color makes her hair, pale skin, and keen gaze stand out.

I step into the room, careful not to bash Vienna's head or legs on the jambs. Maximus's presence fills the doorway behind me as he stands guard. Whether or not we walk out of here again rests solely in the hands of the man presently pouring blood into a glass.

"Make sure we're not disturbed, Maximus." Lucius commands without turning. He doesn't need to—his senses are more acute than those of any other of my kind I know.

The door clicks shut, and I wait, praying Vienna doesn't wake.

"Is the female hurt?" he asks after taking a long sip from his beverage. I can smell the O-positive from here, and it doesn't draw my appetite as fiercely as it should.

Why would it when pulses of the best blood available are pumping almost beneath my nose? I clear my throat. "Some damage to her knee. Your guard dog didn't allow me time to check her over."

"Maximus knows the value of keeping my temper under wraps," Lucius replies. He glides over to the love seat, settling himself beside Selene and folding her beneath his arm. With the glass in his hand, he gestures to the one across from them. "See to your female, Colt. My patience is stretched thin enough without adding a wailing mortal to the mix."

"What happened?" Selene asks quietly, and I'm relieved to hear a touch of worry in her voice. There are myths and rumors circulating through the paranormal world about the queen, some of which are laughable, and others... well, others hit close to the truth.

Shifter turned vampire, Selene is the impossible entity.

An abomination to some; the holy grail to others.

In her short time as a leech—as the shifters often call us —she has become legendary for her skills. Many tout her as more bloodthirsty and drawn to death than vampires of 'pure' blood, but they speak from fear.

Selene is sweet and kind-hearted. Loyal to Lucius despite the mission which brought them together in the first place—the mission which should have ended with Lucius as a pile of ash. She is a fierce creature, the perfect blend of what she was and what she became, and her loyalty drives her to violence if she feels threatened.

Basically, don't fuck with her, and you'll live to see another day.

I carry Vienna to the love seat and set her down on the plush curves. "I think she thought you and my liege intended to drink her dry." My hands stroke over her limp form, down to the thigh of her injured leg. Her knee is already swollen to twice its size, boiling with black and purple bruises. "She took off, slipped, landed badly on her knee. Something popped," I mutter, concentrating on the flesh under my fingers as I palpate the joint. "She tried to crawl her way to the stairs, then passed out."

"Who on earth gave her the idea we want to kill her?" Selene's eyes are boring a hole in the back of my head. "Have you been spreading the rumors, Colt?"

"Of course not."

"How much does she know?" Lucius demands, his tone cold as ice.

Shit, this is where everything I've worked towards over the past half-century goes tits up and leaves me dangling over a very dark pit. Assessing Vienna's knee, I don't bite my thumb this time, but sink my fangs into my wrist and shove it against her mouth, prying it open far enough that my blood drips between those luscious lips.

"More than I'd like. She knows about Vadim's operation, Oberon's involvement, and believes me to be a Russian puppet. She has no idea how deep undercover I am for you, or that you and I know each other as well as we do," I tell him as a pink tongue slides out and laps at my wrist.

There's a low growl of displeasure. "So, in essence, you've brought me a clusterfuck. Get rid of her, Colt, before she destroys decades of hard work. Either wipe her mind and set her free, or drain her and dispose of the body." Lucius's temper frays as he shoves to his feet. "The fucking Russian is posing too much of a threat now he's peddling his wares in the US. He's damn well testing my authority by smuggling mortals into my goddamn city."

"Oh, there's more. Antoine has aspirations to become the next big Rhonull breeder. The shipment Vadim is sending on Friday contains fifty head. All supposed Golden Bloods, but he won't send the quality stuff over here." The wound in my wrist closes; I stroke my hand over Vienna's hair, then stand and face Lucius. "Antoine has purchased ten of those fifty. He wasn't pleased when I told him they'll be sterilized so they can't be bred. This could start a war between him and Vadim."

"That's good, isn't it? They can wipe each other off the face of the earth and end this barbaric practice of breeding humans like cattle." Selene frowns.

"No, it would cause a great deal of problems," I tell her as politely as possible. "It opens us to the threat of exposure to humans. Vampires like Vadim have accrued a lot of weapons and manpower over time, and Antoine isn't sitting on all of his wealth—some of it has been funneled into building himself an army. If the two go head to head… there will be casualties."

"Casualties?" Lucius scoffs, shaking his dark head. "Blood will run in the streets and bodies left to turn to ash by sun's first light."

"Phoenix is only two hours from here. My guess is, if things escalate between the two idiots, Vadim will hammer the city with everything he's got. He'll eradicate Antoine and those most loyal to him. Merge those who'd rather live into his own forces. Once Antoine is gone, controlling the Phoenix vampires will be easy. Join or die. From there…"

"The asshole knows what he's doing, sending sub-par product," Lucius muses. "You believe this is his first move toward taking over the US clans?"

I nod soberly. "I honestly do. If he goes to war with Antoine, very few people will give a shit. Everyone hates the faux-Frenchie with a passion. No one will pay attention until he targets someone of more importance, and by that time, it'll be too late. Vadim isn't stupid, and he has a good team of strategists at his back. They'll have told him attacking the likes of you directly, without cause, will be a declaration of war. No room for a sneak attack."

"And we don't have the manpower he does."

"We don't, but even if we did have the numbers, going for him first would be exactly what he wanted: a reason to invade with full force, in supposed self-defense."

"For fuck's sake. Can we not just take Antoine out?"

Oh, yes. I like that idea. The thought of stripping the fucker of his immortality is certainly enticing. Especially now he knows the taste of Vienna. "It's a definite possibility. Vadim might just find another way to snake his way into power."

"What about the people?"

I lift my eyebrow at Selene. "People?"

"The people," she repeats as though I've gone daft in the head. "The fifty people being tagged and loaded into crates, shipped to a foreign country to become meals. What are we going to do with them?"

Lucius and I exchange looks. We both know previous shipments have been delivered to their destinations—a necessary evil to build my rapport with Vadim and prove I'm a trustworthy individual capable of being an asset to his business.

"My dear, don't concern yourself with that." Lucius gives her a smile that doesn't reach his eyes. He, more than anyone, understands how strong his mate is, but perhaps that gives him all the more reason not to test her strength. Just because she can kill a vampire as fast and as inhumanely as some of the eldest and most cruel of our kind, doesn't mean there isn't humanity or compassion inside her. "Colt handles those details."

Selene rises now, graceful and deadly. Her tiny finger pokes into her mate's chest with a quick stab. "Don't *my dear* me, Lucius. Those people are not *details.* Just as Colt's woman is not someone he can just discard."

I smirk because, hell, it's fucking funny to watch Lucius being admonished by a female half his size. Vienna is much like Selene, all attitude and fire, trying to top from the bottom. But my face is serious when I say, "Those people might buy us a few more days to get our plans into motion, Selene. If I don't deliver them, Vadim will catch on to the rat in his midst. As said rat, I'd prefer not to end up on his traitor radar until I'm prepared."

She glares at me. "So, we're willing to sacrifice fifty living beings in the hopes we're not at war this weekend? Have you considered the possibility Antoine might be working *with* the Russian and that time might not be on our side?"

"Selene—"

"Wait." I pause, lifting my hand to stop Lucius from berating his mate. My thoughts go back to my meeting with Antoine, running through the conversation. Fuck. "Antoine is aware Vadim is the head of the Rhonull program. He admitted it, flaunted the information like he wanted to unnerve me. Not just that, he told me he had a proposition, one that would release me from Vadim's control."

Lucius's jaw clenches. "Antoine buys a hefty chunk of faulty merchandise from the Russian, with you as the facilitator. Makes a concerted effort to discover the identity of the main man, and what? Strikes a deal to not have a target on his back when Armageddon comes?"

"Men." Selene's gorgeous gray eyes roll in exasperation. "Frenchie, he's rich?"

"Obscenely."

"He's bought himself a slice of the pie," Selene states simply, shrugging her shoulders. "Buy into the Russian's organization, bargain for added protection, and if he's as much of an asshole as you make him sound, negotiate for a cut of the real Rhonull stock. If he's smart and got any sense of business, he's put together a plan for expanding Vadim's enterprise here in the US without the need to smuggle people in. An offshoot of the mother company, with stipulations that Frenchie runs the stateside operation."

Well, double fuck. That's something I haven't considered, stupidly. I nod slowly, mulling over the different scenarios. It makes sense. Antoine's proposition would likely involve me losing my obligation to Vadim and saddling myself with a new faux-French thorn in my side.

I'd rather dust myself with a dawn greeting.

Vienna stirs, groaning under her breath as she begins to wake. Lucius's gaze arrows toward her, and I step unerringly between them. "Selene could be right," I tell him, hoping to distract his attention from my captive. "Antoine is a dick and not too smart in some respects, but he's rich as fuck, and someone on his payroll keeps the cash coming in. It would be something he'd find profitable, both monetarily and in blood."

"I agree. Very well. Schedule a visit, before Friday. Do some digging, find out what this proposition entails, and whether he's whored himself out to the Russian."

Fabulous. Another evening of listening to the prick preach in that shitty French accent. "And if he incriminates himself?" If Lucius wants me to kill Antoine in his own freaking mansion, I'm going to need assistance getting out with my life.

"If he's guilty of tying himself to the Avtoritet, they can both hang from the same fucking rope in the sun." Lucius's British accent is strong, vibrating with power and death. It chills me to the bone because I've seen Lucius dole out worse punishments and know exactly what he's capable of when he's riled.

Selene, on the other hand, purrs and rubs herself against his side, apparently aroused by her mate's fury. She sure does like living dangerously.

"If you can execute Antoine without putting yourself at risk, do so. If not, we'll lure him out of his bolt hole and put him down," Lucius says.

Edging back an inch toward Vienna, I accept the weight of his command. "I'll request an audience with him tomorrow night."

Seemingly calmer now the topic of treason is off the table, with a resolution in sight, Lucius sits again, pulling

Selene down with him. "Once Antoine is dealt with, we may need to look at relocating vampires we can trust into Phoenix. Someone capable of commanding loyalty and exhibiting leadership skills. It might make Vadim think twice about trying to take the city over as his centerpiece of control."

Vienna starts humming and I can't quite place the tune. I wish she'd shut up, because she's drawing Lucius's attention right back to her, and I need him to forget she's there.

"What do you want me to do with the shipment?" I ask.

His dark eyes close for a moment. When they open again, they're laced with stone. Whatever decision he's come to, I may not like it. "Sit on it, for now. By tomorrow night, we should have some indication of what the score is. How many buyers do you have lined up?"

"Antoine's taken the lion's share, with ten. Twenty more have bought one apiece, and ten have earmarked pairs. Thirty-one buyers in total, if no one backs out at the last minute; some of them were struggling to come up with the five million per head."

"Email me a list of the buyers for this shipment, and the last. I'll have someone check through it, see if anyone else has grand designs on pledging their allegiance across the water. Until then, accept the delivery and lock it down."

Something weird jitters through me. I imagine it's something akin to what humans feel when they're hyped up on an overdose of caffeine. A second later, I curse ripely as Vienna's humming grows louder, and I recognize the theme song to Superman.

Selene's face creases in amusement as she watches with avid eyes whatever antics Vienna's getting up to behind my back. Too late, I recall what happens when she's imbibed my blood. As I turn with the intention of keeping her down, Vienna leaps on my back like a goddamn monkey.

Fucking superhero brain is back.

A slim arm hooks around my neck, throttling me. Strong legs ride my hips, her heels digging into the fronts of my thighs to lock her in place. Her other arm whips forward past my head as though wielding a sword. "Onwards into battle, mighty steed! We shall vanquish evil this night, with naught but our wits and skill!"

"Mighty steed?" Selene snickers.

I grin, unable to stop myself. I love Vienna when she's animated this way. She's high on my blood, but the imagination and energy is all her. "V—"

"Who goes there?" she demands, lowering her arm to point at Selene. "Are you friend or foe?"

Jesus wept, she's going to give Lucius an aneurism if I don't get her out of here. While his mate seems enamored by Vienna, my liege is eyeing her with a hooded gaze, likely weighing up how much of a risk she is and what to do about her.

"If you'll excuse us, my sub and I have a date with a spanking bench."

"Sit, both of you. She's in no condition to participate in anything until she comes down off her high, and you," Lucius gives me the eyebrow of death, "you have some explaining to do, Colt. I want to know the circumstances surrounding this... union."

Hell. The one conversation I want to avoid. Vienna squawks a protest as I obey, sitting on the edge of the love seat with her still perched on my back. Spreading my hands, I brace myself for the interrogation. "I'll answer what I can."

"Who is she?"

"Vienna Mulrooney. An artist from Chicago." I brief him

as quickly as I can, from the moment I realized someone was at the rendezvous point to now... give or take a few minor details. And I'm damn proud of being able to do so while my blissed-out subbie is bouncing up and down on my back, jabbing her heels into my legs as though she's riding a goddamn horse.

Once she's snapped out of it, she'll be riding something much more satisfying as payment for the shit I'm going to have ripped out of me by whoever hears about this. And they will, I have no doubts. Selene's finding it too amusing for her *not* to spread the fun.

Colt the stallion.

Har-de-fucking-har-har.

"If you're not able to wipe her mind, I'll do it," Lucius decides. "I need you focused on the tasks I've set, Colt, and she... as lovely as she is, she's nothing more than a distraction. Particularly in this state. I'm sure you'd find that preferable to a more permanent solution."

Vienna starts nibbling on my neck, summoning my cock to an immediate salute. She hums in delight, completely oblivious to her fate hanging in the balance, and the scent of her arousal begins to permeate the air in the small room. All that riding has morphed crazy high into horny high.

"Can't do it, Lucius. I can't kill her, and I can't turn her loose."

"Maximus can take care of it."

I bare my teeth, my fangs sliding down in a threat of dominance that might just see me dead. "Maximus touches her, the pair of us are gonna hurt by dawn. Vienna is mine, Lucius. I stood by your decision when you took Selene as your mate. I respected your choice."

"You dare imply I don't respect yours?"

"He's not implying, Lucius. He's telling you. And I agree with him," Selene pipes up boldly.

His lip curls, flashing a fang, and I wonder if it's Maximus I'll be fighting with for Vienna's life, or the king himself. Neither appeal, simply because the odds of me surviving are non-existent, but it won't stop me from stepping into the ring and protecting a mortal female I've known less than three days.

"What's so special about her, Colt? There are thousands of women in this city for you to fuck if that's the reason you're courting disobedience. I've known you most of your life and you've never expressed a serious interest in a woman—human, shifter, or vampire. So, why her?"

I dislike being questioned about my feelings and motivations. "I'm assuming for the same reasons you turned a goddamn shifter, Lucius. Not only a shifter, but one who *really* wanted you dead. Is love not a good enough reason?"

"If it's what you truly feel for her, it might be. But there's something else." Lucius's head cocks in speculation. "I'm not trying to judge her. She may be riding one of my most trusted enforcers like a pony on the track, but there's no personal grudge against the girl."

She really is. Grinding her pussy against my lower back as best she can, Vienna is having the time of her life. What I say next has the power to destroy her future irrevocably, but if I don't tell Lucius and war comes, there may be no one else but him I can trust to take care of her.

"She's something both Vadim and Antoine would kill for."

Lucius's gaze sharpens; Selene smiles.

"Vienna is a Rhonull, Lucius. She's a Golden Blood. If I turn her loose, let her go her own way, she'll never be safe. A papercut would give her away to a vampire, and she'll either end up dead, or sold to the highest bidder. I won't allow her to fall into their hands, so she stays with me."

"Rhonull. How fascinating. I didn't expect that. May I?" It isn't a request. His eyes gleam, his curiosity piqued, and unfortunately, we've come to an impasse. We've known each other long enough that he'll tolerate some disobedience, some dodging when it comes to certain things, but on this... if I tell him no, he will kill me.

"Vienna." My tone is low, and I infuse it with a thread of dominance to summon her attention. There are soft little pants mewling in my ear as she hovers on the edge of an orgasm that belongs to *me*. "If you *dare* come, your tight little ass is going to meet my cock."

She giggles, fucking *giggles*.

Silence hangs heavy as I wait to see what consequences she's going to choose. I glance over my shoulder, ignoring the two pairs of eyes boring into me from across the room, and grin wolfishly as her face tightens, her slim neck straining with a silent cry as her head tips back.

Her unsteady breathing is the only noise in the room.

Amused, relishing the idea of sinking my cock into the one hole she's desperate for me *not* to fuck, I bide my time until she calms, her forehead thumping lightly onto my shoulder. "Naughty, naughty sub," I chide, shaking my head. "I hope you aren't planning to sit down anytime soon, V."

"I... what?"

With superior strength and speed, I twist and hook my left arm back around her waist. In an instant, I've peeled her off my back and have her over my knees. My hand lands five stinging blows on her upturned backside, two on each firm cheek, and the last directly on her sensitive pussy. "What. Is. Rule. Number. One?"

Vienna squirms frantically, shouting curses foul enough

that I treat her to another set of five. Rules number one and three have gone out of the window, dropkicked into outer space. She is going to be really unhappy when she realizes she's just added a blowjob to tonight's festivities.

I smirk, raining blows on her bucking bottom until she capitulates, going limp and sniffling. No tears yet, which has me slightly concerned. She should be bawling her eyes out and begging for forgiveness—which she'd receive after a heartfelt apology.

When I shift her to sit on my knee, she bites back a grunt of discomfort and refuses to look me in the eyes. "What is rule number one, Vienna?"

"Respect at all times, Sir," she mumbles.

"You'd have done well to remember that five minutes ago. Once you apologize for your behavior, you can crawl to my liege and his queen and offer a sincere apology to them as well. Lucius would like to meet you." I remember to say *meet* instead of *eat*. Lucius has every intention of sampling Vienna to validate my claim she's a Rhonull, but she doesn't need forewarning—not unless I want a repeat of picking her up off the floor. "When you're ready, Vienna."

Her teeth grind. Her butt is trying to hover an inch above my thigh. I don't miss how she stiffens at the mention of Lucius's name. Her voice is so, so small when she gives in and mutters, "I'm sorry I was rude... Sir."

It's not the lengthiest expression of regret I've ever heard, but she means it. I think I've temporarily beaten the sass out of her. I love her attitude under the right circumstances, so the thought saddens me, but now is not the right time or place for her to be a brat. "Apology accepted, vixen. Now, hands and knees please. We've held Lucius and Selene up for too long already."

She doesn't question my use of their names, fortunately.

Her heartbeat hammers in my ears—part arousal, part fear, and part discomfort. Her body's trying to process what the fuck just happened, straight off a damn good blood high.

Feeling like I'm sending my pet lamb to slaughter, I slide her down onto her knees between my feet and give her a not-so-subtle nudge with my boot.

Head low, she starts to crawl.

Vienna

This is so embarrassing.

One minute I'm flying through the clouds, my body ruthlessly using Colt's as a hands-free stimulator. The next? My ass is as hot as seven suns after the plank of wood he calls a hand collided with it, repeatedly. And then, while I'm still reeling from the harsh sting and slow burn assaulting my innocent bottom, he does *this*.

I'm crawling like a fucking dog on my hands and knees toward the very people I've just tried to escape. I don't have to wonder why my knee isn't howling in pain anymore—the high from drinking Colt's blood hasn't quite dissipated. If I'm not careful, I'll have an addiction not easily broken.

The material of these stupid boy shorts rub over my tender skin, and I'm hissing between my teeth as I shuffle pathetically toward my doom. If I hadn't tripped, I wouldn't be here. I'd been so close to the damn stairs and freedom.

My hair hangs over my face, and I'm so mired in my own misery, I forget to look where I'm going. I bump solidly into something and, as a feminine snort breaks through my thoughts, I glance up into unamused eyes.

Something changes inside me, like I'm handing over the controls of my body and standing behind the driver's seat.

Seeing, hearing, feeling, but with everything feeling... wrong.

"Kneel," Lucius commands, and it's as though I'm tied to multiple strings, all leading back to his governing hand. I rise onto my knees, unable to look away from him, and wait for the light of my life to fade to black. "She is strong, Colt. She fights me for control."

"She is. Fighting seems to be her go-to defense."

Lucius leans forward. I try to lean back, away, as he infringes on my personal space, close enough to run his nose along my collarbone and up the side of my neck. "She bears no noticeably different scent," he observes, sniffing. "Although... perhaps..."

Close your eyes. Blink.

My eyes are frozen open as if still locked on the king's. Whatever compulsion he has over me, I need to break it. He has full control of my body, but as long as my mind belongs to me, I'm not giving up hope.

Lucius eases back and lifts my hand. Long, elegant fingers examine my narrow wrist, his thumb brushing over my tanned skin and the veins beneath. He purses his full lips, and my heart kicks into overtime at the sight of his fangs sliding down to gleam in the low light.

Terror floods me. It's not like I haven't been bitten before —the anticipation of Colt's bite when we have sex makes everything hotter—but Lucius is an unknown entity and far, far stronger than my lover.

Colt isn't exactly a weakling.

"Vienna, it's okay. It will be over in a few seconds." Colt's voice comes from a distance, echoing. Trying to reassure me. I'd kiss him... if I wasn't blaming him for bringing me here and putting me in this situation to begin with.

Fear and fury twine together inside me, and I'm

suddenly pissed not only at Colt and his fucking king, but at the goddamn universe for slamming me with this shit. What the hell have I done to deserve being slurped on like some kind of protein shake?

Nothing.

Something snaps inside me with a small *pop*, and I blink once, twice. My poor eyeballs feel dry, but it's inconsequential. I jerk away from Lucius, yanking my hand from his before he realizes I'm no longer under his thrall.

Selene gasps.

"How fascinating," Lucius murmurs, his eyes almost black when they lock on me again.

Scrambling back, I trip over my own goddamn feet, knocking the breath from my lungs as I hit the deck. My tongue is tied in knots; there's no hope of my razor-sharp wit saving me when I can't speak. Everything inside me shrivels and dies when the vampire stands, shooting his cuffs as he advances.

"Lucius—" I think Colt is on his feet, braced to defend me. His anger is tangible, hot sparks in the air ready to ignite.

The king takes a step forward, then his mate is in front of him, her hands on his chest, peering up into his face. They murmur quietly as time stands still, my fate in the balance.

Taking advantage of their distraction, I inch backwards over soft carpet toward Colt… until one regal hand appears around Selene's slim form and, without Lucius so much as looking at me, jabs a warning finger.

"Stay *exactly* where you are, mortal."

More murmuring, a surprisingly affectionate laugh.

My lungs are heaving, I'm laced with panic sweat, and I don't know whether I should be rooting for Selene or wishing her to hell. Whatever she's saying to the king, he's listening intently. It's evident by the way he focuses on her face, those intense eyes warming slightly.

He glances at me, says something and, with an incline of his head, kisses the slim blonde with gusto. Elegant as ever, he returns to his seat, spreading his arms along the carved back.

Eternally in control.

Selene turns fluidly, her stunning face softening as she observes my pitiful state. If ever I'm going to have face envy, hers would be my obsession. Not that I swing toward girl-on-girl, but if I did... she'd top my bucket list.

"We've gotten off on the wrong foot," she tells me, extending a pale hand. When I don't take it, she lowers into a crouch without retracting the offer of help. "Lucius has a reputation, which means he's truly intimidating to everyone who knows him. And to many who don't. Sometimes he forgets rigid force isn't necessary to gain someone's cooperation—we're used to the darker side of life. He's sorry he's scared you." Her tone changes, hardens just a fraction. "Aren't you, Lucius?"

One sleek eyebrow rises. "My apologies for frightening you, Vienna."

I don't trust either of them, but there's a tiny part of me that *wants* to. No reason, no logic, just a shred of instinct that tells me they could be something other than very deadly enemies.

I squash it.

Kind gray eyes meet mine, but there's a hunter's edge lurking under the sheen of sympathy. "We have no intention of hurting you, Vienna. One of Lucius's set in stone rules is that no human will be harmed in the club. You have additional protection, seeing as you're Colt's. We just need to verify you are what Colt says you are."

I swallow hard. My voice cracks when I speak. "What does he say I am?"

"A Rhonull. One blessed with Golden Blood. The rarest of the rare."

What the fuck? I shake my head in denial. Even if I *was* a freaking Rhonull, I'm not admitting it to vampires who buy, sell, and breed humans. The likelihood of that happening has the same odds as the possibility of a person being a damn Rhonull—damn near nonexistent. "That's ridiculous. I'm not... no."

Her head tilts curiously. "You don't know your blood type?"

"Does *anyone?*"

"Vixen, I've had the honor of tasting you. I was hooked after the first sip. You're a Rhonull, which means you need protecting from the likes of Vadim and Antoine. If they knew you existed, they'd stop at nothing to take you." Colt sounds earnest, I'll give him that. "Lucius and Selene are our best shot at keeping you out of the breeding farms."

I shudder at the term. *Breeding farms.* Does the Russian let the men mount the females naturally, or is he using artificial insemination for a cold and contactless conception? God, why am I even *thinking* about that?

"I know you're probably dead against working with us, Vienna, but we really can help you. All I ask is that you let me take a sip—a sip, that's all—from your wrist," Selene coaxes. Fuck, she's good. The gentle, persuasive tone of her voice eases under my skin, and winds through the network of nerves currently straining with anxiety. "I promise I won't hurt you."

My pulse is calming, and I can finally catch my breath.

While the relief is nice, I know the game she's playing. "Don't use that shit on me." I want to squeeze my eyes shut to stop her from working her weird compulsion crap on me, but I'd rather see what's coming. Can't fight what I can't see. "I'm nothing special so, no, you don't get to bite me."

Selene remains crouched, that hand waiting patiently. "Obviously, Colt has bitten you; I remember the first time his lordship drank from me. That moment when fangs pierce your skin is the worst, isn't it? The pain, that sharp fear of helplessness... it's not what we imagine, is it? It's worse."

Oh, she's changed tactics. Offering woman to woman support, oozing sympathy and connecting us with shared experiences. It's working as well, much to my disgust. As my throat tightens, all I can do is nod.

"But then it becomes pleasurable. Orgasmic, even." Her lips curve into a wicked smile. "What if I told you I can take what I need without the pain, Vienna? Shoot you straight into pleasure without you even feeling the bite?"

My lip quivers. Lucius's impatience is becoming more and more evident, though he's not said a word since his 'apology'. Colt's hands are tied, his loyalty bound to his king. And I get the feeling if I refuse Selene, her mate is going to take what he wants no matter how much Selene wheedles.

"C-Colt? Can she do that?" My voice quavers on the question.

"Selene has many talents, V. She's one of a kind among vampires, and she's not a liar. If she says she can do it, she can."

"I hate the fucking lot of you," I snap, shoving my hand into hers before I change my mind. I'm prolonging my own torture by procrastinating, and I just want this over, one way or another. "If you kill me, I'll haunt you for the rest of your unnatural life."

Selene laughs, a rich sound of delight. "Feisty. No wonder Colt's taken a liking to you." She grips my wrist loosely, then uses the fingers of her free hand to stroke my forearm from wrist to elbow. Back and forth, back and forth, barely brushing my skin. My arm tingles, my thoughts grind to a halt. "That's it, much better. I need you to look into my eyes and tell me what you see, Vienna."

I snort slowly. "Compulsion crap?" But one peek into those gray eyes, and I'm lost. She's so much better at this than Lucius. Rather than being held captive behind the controls of my body, I'm cut loose.

The only way to describe it is like being suspended at the peak of orgasm. Captured at that moment where the body arches with achievement, muscles rippling and spasming, heart pounding with the sheer pleasure that comes with letting go of the reins and spiraling into oblivion.

I'm moaning, probably sounding like a feral alley cat calling all available suitors for a quick orgy behind the bushes, but I don't care.

Even as I watch Selene lift my wrist to her mouth, her head dipping to press her lips to my skin, I feel nothing. Not the pressure of her fingers, the touch of her mouth against me. I'm numb all over, free from pain, as her fangs flash briefly before piercing my flesh.

Floating, floating, as crimson liquid dribbles down my arm.

Floating, floating, as one sip turns into a feast.

Falling, falling, as the world tips and slides away.

7

Colt

THERE ARE few things in my life I regret. Things that really dig deep down into my demon-infused soul and hook their claws into me. Becoming what I am isn't on that list. Living the way I do hasn't made the cut. Playing a part in peddling innocent humans for blood and money almost checks the box.

Trusting Selene to control herself currently glows in neon lights at the top of my *Fuck, I really shouldn't have done that* catalogue of regrets.

I shouldn't blame her. I don't blame her, not really.

She wasn't prepared for the intoxicating punch of Vienna's blood, and she's a newbie vamp. Newbs don't tend to have full control of their reactions until they're at least past the century mark, sometimes not even then. The most conscientious vampire slips every now and then when bloodlust overrides everything but instinct.

It takes both Lucius and me to drag her off Vienna.

The moment she took that first swallow of rich, red blood, I knew we'd fucked up. Well, Lucius fucked up. He was the one who caved and allowed Selene to take control of the situation—a situation designed to sideline me and put me firmly in my place.

As soon as we manage to unclamp Selene's fangs from Vienna's wrist—after she takes a bite out of her mate—I leave Lucius to subdue the vicious creature his sub has become and scoop up my own.

When the door opens to reveal Maximus on full alert, I have no other option but to blur from the room with Selene's frantic snaps and snarls echoing in my ears. I don't stop for anyone or anything, catapulting an unconscious Vienna through the busy dungeon to the private playrooms at the back.

As I skid to a halt outside the furthest room, I can hear the murmurings of interest begin. Vampires picking up the scent of fresh blood... and the aroma of the legendary. Some of my kind believe Rhonulls to be a myth, a delicacy that no longer exists.

They're believers now.

Fuck, I can't get Vienna upstairs. Lucius would have my head if I blurred through the club with an unconscious woman in my arms. Containing exposure would be difficult, mind-wiping multiple humans a pain in the ass, and as fast as I am, I'm not entirely sure I could outrun a horde of vampires willing to kill for a taste of her.

There is *always* someone faster.

I shoulder open the door, relieved it's empty, and drop Vienna on the bed. Kicking the door shut, I drag the heavy spanking bench across the room—thank fuck for top quality equipment—and wedge it beneath the handle. It fits, just barely. The padded leather surface will no doubt bear scars, but I don't give a fuck as long as it holds.

We're as safe as I can make us until Lucius and his sired sort this clusterfuck out. That is, if Maximus, Tiberius, and Augustus don't get caught up in the frenzy as well. Hell, if those three want in here, there won't be a door or blockade strong enough to keep them out.

Jesus wept, what a mess.

There's a riot of voices building on the other side of the door. Dismissing them, praying to a God that's never answered a prayer of mine, I sit beside Vienna and check her pulse.

I'm fairly sure Selene didn't manage to get more than a few strong gulps before we wrenched her free but more blood has spilled from the puncture wounds, so I'm not entirely sure just how much Vienna's lost.

Her pulse throbs beneath my fingertips.

The only saving grace I find in this disaster is that Vienna passed out before she saw Selene's true nature. Not from blood loss, I'm certain of that, but from the sheer overload of pleasure Selene gave her before the vampire's feeding instincts kicked in.

Lifting Vienna's injured arm, I inspect the puncture wounds. Deep, raw. Some jagged edges where the tips of Selene's fangs ripped the soft tissue. Blood dribbles from the holes in slow streams; Vienna's arm is stained with tracks and smears.

Biting hard into the heel of my hand, I rub it over the punctures until the wounds close. She's going to wake up feeling pretty groggy, a combination of compulsion hangover and blood loss, but she's alive.

With infinite care, I lick the blood from her arm. The last thing I need is for her to wake and see herself looking like an extra from *Jaws.* An over exaggeration perhaps, but I've witnessed my fair share of mortals freak out at the sight of their own blood—be it a papercut or a major trauma.

The divine tang sits on my tongue, stirring the beast inside me.

No, I can't blame Selene for her actions.

Not when I could easily drain Vienna dry before she knew what was happening. A sly voice in my head tells me that would be the kindest thing to do. Her heart would stop before her eyes had a chance to open and she'd just slide from sleep into death without pain or fear.

And I could drink every delicious drop from her juicy veins.

Keep it all to myself.

Growling, I silence the voice. I don't need or want the input of the demon, now or ever. Not when it comes to Vienna. I'll always want to do what's best for her, and the demon... well, vampires are selfish bastards.

The rabble outside the door is growing, but above the din of slavering vampires wanting a kill, Tiberius's voice booms, ordering them to back the fuck off and clear the area.

Something slams into the door. The handle won't budge, it's too well jammed into the bench, but if enough bodies work together, they stand a good chance of smashing through the wood. If I'm really un-fucking-lucky, they could shove the bench clear.

Stroking Vienna's hair, I take a moment to second-guess myself. Running out into the club with a bleeding Rhonull is definitely not the highlight of my *Finest decisions ever made* reel, but staying in that room with Selene salivating for more would only have ended in disaster.

Add in Maximus's presence, and I'd have a dead Vienna on my hands.

Our current situation isn't brilliant, but there are some upsides, I guess. Vienna is alive and unaware of the chaos we've just brought down on the dungeon. We're out of Selene's way, so hopefully she'll be able to shake the blood-lust, with a little help from Lucius's heavy hand.

But.

It all comes down to that little three-letter word, doesn't it?

Vienna will never be safe in the company of vampires. It can't be any simpler than that. A nosebleed would incite this reaction among my kind wherever she goes. She'll be hunted, chased down, and terrorized to make her already divine blood sweeter, richer.

We vampires do love our sweetbloods. Fear, adrenaline, orgasms... the methods we've discovered to flavor and enhance our food are numerous, and not all of them are kind. Pain is a particularly popular additive—get the blood screaming through the veins, saturated with endorphins, and hey presto, you've got yourself a gourmet feast with minimal effort.

That's Vienna's future.

It fucking rips the heart right out of my chest.

I sigh, listening to the sound of fighting in the hallway. From the shouts and level of hostility my keen hearing picks up, Lucius's sired are tearing through the rabble with determination. There may be hope we'll escape this mess without Vienna becoming embroiled in the middle of a massacre.

And then?

I honestly don't know. I'm going to go out on a limb and assume Lucius won't be thrilled a mortal has the mental capacity to evade his thrall. Snorting, I shake my head and rub the backs of my fingers over her cheek.

Evade? She fucking broke his compulsion into pieces.

I've never seen anyone—mortal, shifter, or vampire—snap Lucius's hold on them once he has them enthralled. He's a master of the art; he slides them under with barely a glance, maintains exact control for as long as he requires, and releases them without so much as a stray thought in their heads about what they've done.

The fact Vienna shrugs off compulsion as easily as blinking, combined with the potency of her blood and the riots she has the potential to start, means Lucius might deem her a threat.

Lucius eradicates threats.

Vienna's head lolls, rolling slightly to the side. My relief is immense, especially when a muscle in her cheek twitches. Her groggy eyes open to narrow slits for a brief moment before closing again.

"Sleeping beauty wakes," I murmur, cupping her cheek. "Might as well come all the way out, vixen. I've got you. That's a good girl." Encouraging her, I wait until those eyes open again, and this time, focus on me. "Back with me now?"

She gives me a throaty, sleepy grunt.

"How are you feeling?"

Her hand lifts, her movements a bit uncoordinated, to rub at her eyes. She grimaces, moaning her displeasure. "Ugh. Did I get drunk and pass out?"

Well, it's a better explanation than the reality of what happened. I'm tempted to use it, but if—when—she discovers the truth, she'll probably scalp me and dance around with my hair clutched in her fist. “No, you’re perfectly sober. Just take a few minutes to settle.”

Her eyes widen as Augustus’s deep baritone thunders through the door, then something heavy crashes hard into the wood. Hard enough, I note warily, for the door to shake in place and a crack to run down the upper half. “What the fuck is going on?” She looks around the room, and swallows hard. “Did we have sex? I don’t remember having sex.”

I clench my jaw. My cock hears the word *sex* and perks his head up in interest, despite it not being the time or… well, yes, actually this is the place. The fantasy of a blowjob and anal is temporarily shelved for when we get out of here and I know Vienna is safe.

“No sex, vixen. I may be dead, but I prefer my women alive and with their senses intact when I fuck them.” The noise levels outside are dropping, and some of the tension in my shoulders eases off. Maybe Lucius’s triumvirate have more willpower than I gave them credit for. “There was an incident. Things got a little dicey, but Lucius is handling it.”

“Incident?” Vienna glares at me. “What *kind* of incident?”

“We’ll just say you’re definitely a Rhonull, and Lucius knows it. Let’s not get mired in the details.”

Her glare intensifies until her eyes glow with ferocity. Her gaze drops to her wrist where, although I healed her wounds, the faint scars of Selene’s fangs remain, as do the ones on her throat from mine. Her mouth drops open and she looks horrified. “Oh my God. She… she…” Her hand slaps against her neck, her fingertips seeking her pulse. “She went overboard, didn’t she? Am I dead? Did you let her kill me, you asshole?”

Oh boy, Vienna is *pissed*. Well, it’s time she learns that here, submissives don’t have the ruling hand. I yank her hand away from her neck. "You're not dead. Selene drank a little more than promised, but nowhere near enough to do you any harm. It only highlights how tempting you are to vampires, and why I need to keep you safe. And as for the asshole comment," I continue with a wolfish grin, "you might want to keep in mind my cock already has a date with both your mouth and your ass, vixen. You really don't want a flogging before I do sinfully bad things to your body, do you?"

Her eyes go round as the moon as she goggles at me. "What the hell are you talking about?"

Well, that's certainly distracted her from the subject of Selene. Mission accomplished. I rub my chin casually, losing the grin and giving her my best stern-dom look. "You broke the rules, V. You orgasmed without permission, after I asked you to stop humping my back like a sex-starved animal. You showed a lack of respect to me and to my king, and his queen. So, there will be consequences."

I shouldn't find her pathetic show of teeth amusing, but I do. Even when she's backed into a corner with me, she's armed with her sass and her bravado. A shame, really, that neither will change the outcome of her behavior.

Quick as a whip and faster than I'm expecting, Vienna rolls away across the bed and lands on her feet on the other side. Barely, mind you. Her legs buckle the moment she tries to stand, and she grabs the edge of the mattress for support. "My ass is off-limits. *Nothing* goes in there, especially not that!" She jabs a finger toward my crotch.

Severely tempted to tie her down on the bed and prove to her just how wrong she is, I stand slowly. "The matter isn't up for discussion. When I said you were mine, I wasn't bullshitting you. When the time comes, you'll take your punishment like a good girl and all will be forgiven. Hopefully, you'll learn that breaking my rules is something you should avoid."

"You have no idea how much I hate you right now."

"Oh, I'm fairly sure I do. Sit down before you fall down, Vienna."

Someone hammers on the door. Vienna flits across the room, damn near falling on her goddamn face, then presses her back into the corner and holds up her index fingers in the sign of the cross.

Rolling my eyes, I shake my head.

Surely, she should know by now that such things don't have an impact.

"Colt, you'd better fucking be in there," Augustus bellows. "If you are and you're not answering me, you'd best be dead."

"That's a given," I mutter sarcastically. Ninety percent of Toxic's body count are dead, technically. "Give me a second, Augustus."

"And I hope you're not in the middle of fucking that little troublemaker while we're out here saving your sorry ass," he grumbles back.

"I wish," I say as I move forward to shove the spanking bench out of the way.

"He wishes!" Vienna shouts at the same time.

Perfect timing as always, I think sourly, yanking open the door and coming face to face with Augustus. Impeccably clothed in a dark grey suit, pristine white shirt, and black tie, the vampire is the epitome of *dressed to kill*. Judging by the blood spatter across his jacket, Augustus has broken a few noses this evening.

Sharp green eyes land on my face and his lips twitch. "Troublemaker living up to her name, Colt? Never thought I'd see the day when a submissive got you all twisted up."

His nostrils flare, and I come close to doing my own share of nose breaking. "Must admit, I'd let her twist me up for a taste of what she's got in her veins."

Vienna's horrified gasp sets my protective instincts on edge. She's stronger than any female I know, but she's had enough torment tonight. I tell myself I don't count—she knows me well enough now she's comfortable in my company, maybe trusts me just a little—and convince the voice of doubt in my head that she's mine, so I can tease her at will.

"I am *not* submissive, and you are *not* eating me!" She's revved her bravado to the max, firing on all cylinders. "I don't care how fucking big you are. I will—"

Point zero of a second is all it takes me to blur across the room and clamp my hand over her mouth. The sexy, vocal mouth which is going to drop both of us in hotter water than we can stand if she doesn't shut up.

Augustus isn't known for his tolerance of rude subs. If she hits his buttons wrong, he'll plow straight through me and deliver a punishment that makes mine look like a stroll along the fucking beach. His eyebrow is already arching into a questioning curve. "Thought you'd have taught her respect before bringing her into Lucius's domain, Colt. Slacking on the job?"

Hardening my voice to match the steel tone of his, I squeeze Vienna's cheek in warning. A barrage of angry, muffled profanity releases into my palm. "You'll have to excuse her, Augustus. She's had a long night, and she's been under a lot of stress. I'll correct her manners when I get her home."

"Do that," he responds gruffly. "Lucius wants to see you. Both of you. The club's clear so you don't need to worry about being mobbed." He jerks his head toward the main dungeon. "Come on."

With Vienna's back against my chest, I feel her muscles go rigid. She doesn't remember what happened after she passed out, but some part of her *knows*. I wrap my arm around her bare midriff, her stomach sucking in at the contact, and heft her off her feet. For her ears only, I murmur, "Best behavior, V. Lucius isn't going to hurt you." I glance at Augustus. "Selene?"

"With Lucius. Under control, unlike some." With that barb tossed at me, he stalks off back down the hallway.

Releasing Vienna's mouth, I swing her up and slide my free arm under her knees, adjusting my hold around her waist so she feels secure. She's not in a fit state to walk anywhere—I really need to source some food, and something sweet for her to drink—and I'm not risking her attempting a second flight mission.

"You fucking—"

"Do I need to pick up a ball gag before we leave the room?" I interrupt before the full brunt of Hurricane Vienna crashes down on my head. She's a Category Four and rapidly building to a Five. "If you can't hold your tongue, the correct answer should be *Yes, Sir*."

She growls. Actually has the fucking *audacity* to growl at me. Given the circumstances of this evening, I'd thought to give her a reprieve from receiving her punishment, but if she's this feisty, she's going to take every goddamn inch of castigation, and take it *hard*.

Her hand jerks up, flipping me the bird.

In a quick move, I upend her over my shoulder. Her breath whooshes out on a wheeze as her stomach hits my shoulder, then her tiny little fists hammer at my back. Grinning, I bring my palm down on her upturned bottom as though it's painted with a big red bullseye.

"Bad girls don't get treated like princesses," I snap, utilizing my dom voice. The strict, low tone puts a rapid end to her tantrum, but I don't relax. She's probably figuring out how she can rear up and bite my ear off. "They get treated like recalcitrant children until they make amends."

"I'm not saying sorry," she spits.

"Probably not, but by the time I'm done staking a claim on what's mine, you're going to be screaming it."

She bounces lightly in position as I stomp from the room after Augustus. I'm a bit taken aback by the lack of carnage—Tiberius and the crew seem to have dispersed the ravenous crowd without spilling too much blood on the walls.

As promised, the main room is empty, aside from Tiberius, who's prowling around, helping the human bar staff with clean up. It's not in his job description, but I'm betting he'd rather keep his hands busy while he remains on guard duty. Vamps are tenacious, and there's no guarantee that the evicted members won't be struck by a lingering scent of Vienna's blood and decide to come back for another try at getting to her.

He scowls when he sees us, dark brows almost meeting from the fierceness of his expression. "Can't go anywhere without bringing chaos on your heels, Colt?" he calls out. "I should ban your ass from stepping foot in here again."

"You'd miss my pretty face and witty repartee," I retort without slowing my pace. "Could you do me a favor and see if you can rustle up some food and a soda for my sub? I'd appreciate it," I add smoothly, unwilling to ruffle his feathers any more than they already are, "and so would Vienna."

Tiberius levels me with a lethal stare. "Do I look like a servant to you?"

Now I pause, which gives Vienna time to buck and kick as she balances on my shoulder. Smirking, I let her wriggle to the tipping point and then over. She drops headfirst toward the floor before I tighten my grip on her legs and catch her before she's gone more than a few inches.

I sure hope she squeals and squirms just like this when I have her strapped down on her hands and knees, ready to receive her punishment.

"Not at all," I assure him, hooking my hand into the back of Vienna's shorts and hoisting her effortlessly back into position where she belongs. Her heart is racing, her breath puffing in soft little exhales of shocked relief. "As I said, a favor, Tiberius."

He snorts loudly, making Vienna jerk nervously. "Fine, I'll see what I can find. But you owe me, Colt. Make no mistake, I will collect."

The smug bastard is more than likely going to ask me to scrub the damn toilets. He's a bit of a sly one, has a sharp brain and a quick temper, but if Lucius keeps him close, he's trustworthy.

Right now, I need everyone I can trust to get Vienna out of this mess.

"Thank you." My attention veers over toward Augustus as he jerks his thumb toward the small room where disaster has already struck tonight. "You know where we'll be."

Another snort. "It'll be on the bar when you come out... if you come out. I'm not a fucking waiter, Colt." He turns his back, and I roll my eyes. Temperamental asshole.

Vienna trembles as I walk toward Augustus. Through the open doorway beyond him, I can see Lucius seated where he was earlier, but Selene is not sitting by his side. I squeeze past the bouncer and carry my eerily quiet sub back into hell.

She whimpers as the door closes, leaving Augustus standing guard outside.

Selene kneels beside her mate. She doesn't seem happy, but she's quiet and a hell of a lot calmer than the last time I saw her. Maybe it has something to do with the padded cuffs linking her wrists closely together, or the ball gag strapped in her mouth.

She lifts her eyes as I cross to the love seat, and I spot the faintest gleam of bloodlust sparking to life. Lucius slips his hand beneath the sleek fall of her brilliantly white hair, fingers grasping the leather collar around her throat, and gives it a swift but gentle yank.

"Sit," Lucius commands.

Swinging Vienna off my shoulder, I drop her carefully onto the love seat. She sits stiffly, muscles ready for flight if she deems it necessary. I settle beside her, my arm around her shoulders as a reminder I'm there... and she's going nowhere.

"I think it's safe to say Vienna is dangerous," he begins without preamble. "She poses a danger to both our kind and to herself. The smell of her blood alone was enough to drive the vamps here in the club into a feeding frenzy—luckily, the staff were relatively uninjured. As for the effects of feeding off her..." His aristocratic hand strokes over Selene's head tenderly, his fingers gliding through her hair. "Vienna is the sweetest temptation."

My captive's trembling escalates.

Her mouth is clamped shut.

Smart girl. Keep it that way.

"She is," I agree easily, a sinking feeling causing my guts to ache. "But then, so is any sweetblood. Lucius, you know I wouldn't ask you for help if I didn't need it. Hell, I *wouldn't* need it if I wasn't risking my goddamn head so you can take down Vadim. The past fifty years have been engineered for that purpose."

Vienna's head whips around to face me, but I ignore her.

"If I didn't have this shitshow to finish, I'd be gone. A thousand fucking miles away from here, away from anything and everything that could hurt her. Because..." My jaw clenches. What I'm about to say is going to seal my fate and Vienna's. "Because Vienna means as much to me as Selene means to you."

Being studied like a bug trapped between two glass slides doesn't feel comfortable. Lucius's eyes grow darker, almost sinister, as he plays the part of entomologist. "So, you're willing to sacrifice eternal life for the mortal?"

Goddamn it, how did I know it would come down to this?

"Want me to take a knee and offer my neck?"

I really shouldn't provoke my king, but he's starting to piss me off. As he stands, so do I. It seems the bloodshed of the night isn't over. If he wants to fight, I'm going to lose. Older, stronger, faster, Lucius has a trio of aces in his hand, while my draw of the cards is slightly less impressive.

"No!" My brave, fierce, utterly stupid sub lunges to her feet, sidestepping in front of me. The top of her head doesn't even reach my chin, but she's apparently oblivious to the fact she's half Lucius' size and no match at all for the king. "Don't you punish him for protecting me!"

Heavy silence rains down on us.

I grip her shoulders tightly, whirling her around so my body will take the hit if Lucius strikes. Furious with her, I press my mouth to her ear. "Just you wait until we get home, vixen. Don't *ever* step between two vampires again."

The little minx kicks my shin. "You're not sacrificing yourself for me. What the hell am I supposed to do if you have to be vacuumed off the floor?"

Ah, self-preservation instincts at their finest. "Your concern for my welfare melts my heart, V. Put yourself in danger again, and sodomizing this tight ass will be heaven for you compared to what I do to it beforehand. Now stay here and keep quiet."

A slew of profanity erupts from her lips in a mutter as I slap her ass in warning, then turn to face Lucius. My head jerks in surprise when I notice he's no longer standing but sprawled casually back in his seat. He flicks his wrist in a *sit* gesture, and I obey, pulling Vienna down onto my lap.

She glares at me.

I ignore her, focusing on the lethal predator across from us. The bastard has the balls to look amused by the exchange. Well, at least he's not geared up to rip my head off my neck.

"She defends you," he muses, each word slow and measured. "This just gets more and more fascinating. Do you want to keep her? Does she want to be kept?"

"We haven't exactly discussed the future, Lucius." We haven't, but I'm one hundred percent certain about having her in my life. She brings sunshine into my dark existence. "But yes, I want to keep her. She's mine."

"And you, Vienna? What is your wish?"

If I could hold my breath, I would.

~

VIENNA

. . .

PERCHED ON COLT'S KNEES, I blink at the Vampire King. There's a restlessness in me, as though a bad shadow hangs over my shoulder. Part of it has to do with Selene kneeling beside her liege, bound and gagged, and I know in my gut something happened in here while I was squirming in the throes of an orgasm.

"Now my opinion's worth something?" I snipe bitterly.

Lucius has the most impressive chastising expression. It's so effective, he doesn't need to say a word to convey his displeasure. He's probably not used to impertinent women giving him attitude.

My eyes catch Selene's and the primal beast inside her stares back at me.

Yeah, he maybe is used to it.

They're talking about keeping me as though I'm a mangy stray dog they've picked up off the street. And while part of me is seriously aggrieved they see me that way, another part of me is warm and fuzzy at the idea Colt wants me around.

Just as a snack, maybe, but still, it's nice to be wanted.

"Exactly what does being *kept* entail?" Yes, I am considering becoming the world's most idiotic female on record by allowing my hormones enough rein to even contemplate this. "I mean, this is a life or death decision, right? I don't want to be a pet."

"A pet still has claws," Lucius tells me with a smirk, his hand gripping Selene's hair.

"Keeping you as a human pet wouldn't be much different to how we are now. Decisions I make would be for your protection, and your wellbeing would be my primary concern. Ensuring you stay alive." Colt sighs against my shoulder, but there's no flurry of breath over my skin. "Our best option is to turn you, V. You're walking temptation for anything with fangs."

I giggle stupidly, then clap my hand over my mouth to stop the ridiculous sound. Now is not the time for my nerves to make themselves known. Vampires smell fear, right? Even a bloodsucker with anosmia could smell the turmoil inside me. Hell, I can smell it myself.

All I can think right this second is...

If I ever catch those fucking punk ass bitches who stole my car, I'm going to beat them until they're bloody and whimpering, then toss them to the vampires of Club Toxic as midnight snacks.

My parents won't miss me... too much. I guess that's a blessing. As long as I send them a postcard or drop them an email every few months, I can hold them off. My trust fund will keep me going; maybe I can find ways to stretch it out and multiply it enough to make undead living comfortable.

My career as an artist... well, I guess I'll have ample time to perfect my technique, right? Centuries of time to dabble in the mediums I want to try, and hone the skills I have already.

I snort, realizing that time as I know it is about to come screeching to a halt, to be replaced by concepts I never imagined. Decades will be like minutes, centuries morphing into days and weeks. Millenia passing faster than the seasons.

At what cost?

My hand presses to my heart. It beats quickly in my chest, blood pulsing through my veins and warming my flesh. I wonder what it's like to live in silence, as Colt does. To wake every night without that one vital sign of life. Never feeling it kick in joy or grief or fear.

Humanity is the heart of us.

If that heart stops, what do we become?

From those I've met so far—Lucius and Selene and Colt as my prime examples—there seems to be some small iota of humanity in them still. Yes, there's an edge to them —that predatory aura that immediately kicks my brain into prey mode—but they haven't really been cruel or hostile.

Not in the way I expect soulless demons to be.

But can *I* willingly become what they are? It's a heavy question. I mean, in most books I've read, the vampires were either turned by trickery against their will, or they begged their sire to do the deed and initiate them into the elite.

I don't believe Colt would use deceit to get his way. I really don't. I can't see him feeding off me and taking it too far in an *ooops* moment, then turning me as a way to 'rectify' his mistake. I don't know him as well as I should, but I'll lay my soul on the line here and say it's not his style.

And as for begging… I'm not above it, not at all. One of the greatest sexual moments of my experience was begging quite dramatically for harder, faster, fucking *deeper*, and receiving all three with enthusiasm.

There's only one thing that could persuade me to beg for death, and that's being in so much pain my body can't physically handle it. It's the only scenario I can envision where I would actively beg for someone to end my life.

Fingers crossed, it never happens.

Fingers crossed, but the way my life is going, anything might happen.

"Take her home, Colt. She's in no right mind to make a choice tonight. However, I will expect one by the time you report to me after your Friday meeting with Antoine. If this is our chance to eradicate Vadim and Antoine, I cannot allow a mortal loose thread to threaten our chances of success."

Colt stiffens in displeasure, and instinctively, I lean back to offer support. My head rests on his shoulder. Somehow, I feel as though it belongs there, just as the rest of me is at home on his lap. "I understand the stakes here, Lucius."

"Good. A pleasure to make your acquaintance, Vienna. If you feel you're in any danger, you are welcome with us." Lucius's hard gaze brushes over me. "We really must figure out how you broke my thrall, but for now, it's late and you can see yourselves out. Until Friday, Colt."

Oh, we've been dismissed. Politely, but ever so firmly, the king is setting his foot on our asses and shoving us out of his place of business. I don't think I've ever been so nicely booted from a nightclub, especially while sober.

The whole *breaking my thrall* parting comment sounds a lot like a threat to me, and I think Colt hears it the same way, as we're suddenly no longer in the little room, but in another world altogether.

My body and my brain don't feel quite right. My senses are picking up the scents of alcohol, sweat, and desperation while my eyes take in the neon lights and the humdrum of a mass of people in drunken abandon, but my body is convinced it's still with Lucius and Selene.

My stomach is threatening to revolt.

"The nausea will pass," Colt reassures me as he strides across the dance floor, exuding an aura of *fuck off* as hands grab at us and try to pull us into the merriment. "Moving at speed is disconcerting until you get used to it."

Moving at speed? Is he freaking joking? There's moving at speed and then there's blipping from one part of a building to another so quickly, your brain can't register it. "Maybe next time you could slow it down a few knots? My internal organs are still limping up the stairs."

"Sorry, vixen. It's not something I give thought to anymore." Lights flash and dance over Colt's pretty face in a disturbing array of colors.

I really want to nibble along that firm jawline. Maybe run my tongue up that cord in his neck...

We jolt as someone crashes into us, laughing like a loon, and I feel a snarl rumbling in my savior's chest as the intoxicated idiot whoops and hollers before staggering on his way.

"I could do with some of whatever he's been on," I state casually. A bottle of Jack Daniels would sure go down smooth after the night I've had. Some mental oblivion with alcoholic help would be a welcome break.

Somewhere, in the last few hours, my death warrant has been signed.

I just can't pinpoint the exact moment.

"You know, if you're going to eat me, I would appreciate a heads-up beforehand. There are a few mortal things I'd like to do before vampirism steals them away from me."

"Like what?" Colt's tone is absent-minded, and I can't blame him. Getting through the throng of revelry is akin to dancing on landmines. It's a bit like being a boat on a stormy sea with a hurricane swirling around us—no matter which way we turn, we're still getting bumped and battered by the waves.

I wave my hand in the air. "Oh, I don't know. Get drunk, watch a sunrise. Eat a last meal—I really, really want a damn fine pepperoni pizza. I'd like to interact with people, normal people, one last time before I start eyeing them up as snacks. I want to feel alive before I die."

"This is the wrong place to discuss this," he mutters.

"I think this is exactly the right place," I argue quietly, lowering my voice until the pounding music drowns it out. Colt will hear me, his hearing is just that good. "Considering this is likely where I'll kick the bucket."

He sighs. "You don't have to die, V. It's an option, that's all."

"The other two options aren't so appealing. Live like a prisoner, chained to you for the rest of my days so I don't get taken and bred until my ovaries crumble to dust," I snipe with just the smallest smidgen of bitterness. "Or spend years looking over my shoulder, being hunted for my blood, waiting for someone to toss a black bag over my head and shove me into a cargo van with a sliding side door. Wouldn't that be the worst cliché?"

"Being a... being different, the way I am, isn't a bad life, Vienna. Yeah, it has its hardships, and it sucks sometimes, but show me a mortal who can't say that about their existence. There are dietary restrictions, obviously, but there are also benefits." Colt dodges a couple making out—lucky fuckers—and twists sideways to squeeze us through a small gap in dancers.

A few strides later and the dry, overheated air of Tucson hits us like a hot palm. A different heat and humidity to what's inside the club, it sucks the breath from my lungs in an instant.

Have I said how much I hate the fucking heat here?

"Can you feel the heat? Do you get cold?" Stupid, inane questions, but suddenly the most important ones I can think of.

"Well, my cock appreciates the heat of your pussy. Does that count?"

I flush. We're outside, and anyone can hear him if they have their ears in working order. I wiggle in these ridiculous clothes, well aware I'm barely wearing anything, and all Colt has to do is yank down these miniscule boy shorts to gain access to all my warm, wet bits. "I ask you a serious question, and you have to turn everything around to sex."

He grins down at me. "Sex *is* serious when my cock gets involved, V."

8

Colt

SHIT, that was corny.

Sex is serious when my cock gets involved, V.

If my hands weren't full of lush female, I'd punch myself. Not my proudest comeback line in six hundred and thirty-eight years, that's for damn sure. But it certainly has reawakened some of my more prurient urges from earlier in the evening, before Selene turned Vienna into a human Slurpee and things went to hell on all fronts.

A quick glance at the sky confirms my suspicions—Club Toxic has played its magic fingers over time itself and the night has once again passed by. This leaves us with two options—racing back to the warehouse and betting against the sun, or going back inside and begging sanctuary from Lucius for the day.

Somehow, I doubt I'll feel safe enough to sleep here

after the mass riot we incited downstairs. Although the club will be locked up and secured for the day, my security is so much better than Lucius's.

My plans for sex and domination may have been completely fucked tonight—unlike my pretty little captive—but that doesn't mean she's getting away without punishment. I think she can sleep with a training aid today. With my Friday deadline looming in only a couple days, I'm not wasting any time with her.

Vadim's shipment will be arriving on Friday night. Once I've culled the most promising specimens, I'll deliver them personally to Antoine, and have myself another meeting with the faux French bastard—this time, with specific questions at the ready.

It's risky, I know it is, and so does Lucius. But in order to end this fucking disaster before it digs its claws in so deep we'll feel the ramifications for centuries to come, some sacrifices will have to be made.

Vienna will not be one of them.

It's a rare thing for a vampire to admit they're in love. We become stupid if we hold onto the emotions that made us human. We are not human, period. We look like them, talk like them, fuck like them. But we are not one of them. Love is a reminder of what we were, once upon a time.

Still, it doesn't stop some of us from being eternal idiots and dragging mortals into our world. Dangling them into danger, drinking their pleasure, and all the while conning ourselves into believing that life could be that fucking cliché of two point five children, the family dog, wedding bands, and the quintessential white picket fence.

Hah. It's like something out of a sitcom. Chances are, I'd get hungry, snack on the kiddies, eat the dog out of boredom, and then that unbroken circle of gold would flash dangerously in the sunlight when Vienna tossed me out into the brightly lit yard. I'd either burn to death under the sun, or stagger and fall into the picket fence, one of those freshly painted wooden spikes driving through my back and kissing my heart.

That's all a damn joke. I can't produce children, dogs hate me with a passion that can only be derived from their aversion to demons, and I'm positive Vienna would rather eat a bullet than marry me.

Two slim fingers appear in my vision and snap loudly. I blink, lowering my gaze to concerned blue-gray eyes. "You in there, Colt, or has your cock short-circuited your brain?"

"You like my cock," I remind her, then head in the direction of my car. The subtle hum of electricity that preempts dawn is already starting to fizzle on the air.

I'm working out the minutes in my head as I stride along at a faster pace than normal. If it wasn't quite this close to dawn, I'd consider blurring, but there's no way of knowing who is up and on the street at this time. There are too many shift workers making their way home or to their jobs.

"We're cutting it kinda close, aren't we?" There's no judgement in her tone, just that uneasy concern, as though she's realized we could end up in a predicament.

"I've got time, sweetheart. We just need to hurry."

"Well, do your zipping thing then," she says in exasperation. "Forget the car and just run all the way home."

She's just phenomenal, isn't she? Despite the fact I almost made her throw up in my haste to get her away from my king, she's prepared to let me do it all over again to save my ass from crisping like fried chicken.

One might think my vixen loves me.

Bad choice, Vienna. Don't ever love the bad guy.

"Somehow, I think Lucius will be even more displeased

with me if I did that and someone caught sight of us." My boots pound the sidewalk in a fast rhythm, much like Vienna's heartbeat. It's gratifying to know she's anxious for my safety. After all, if I turn to ash here and now, she's free. "Five minutes to the car, and then I can put my foot on the gas and get us home. Fuck the speeding tickets and the fines."

"You have a license?"

I laugh, picking up my pace as the hairs on my arms begin to rise. "Don't be ridiculous. This handsome face on government records? Please. If I have an interaction with a cop—a rarity in itself, I might add, as they'd have to catch me first—they don't remember any of it afterward."

That beautiful face is slack with shock. "Oh, my God. You eat the police?"

She really does bring light into my life. After so long in the dark, I'm enjoying the reprieve she offers. "Ugh, no. We don't eat law enforcement, V. Uniforms taste disgusting."

That mouth of hers is tempting, all cute and delectable in that O of disbelief. I have all manner of depraved ideas in mind for her. "What do uniforms taste like?"

Absolutely straight-faced, I reply, "Overcooked Brussel sprouts."

Vienna makes a gagging sound. "Ick."

I kiss the top of her head. "Such a gullible mortal, vixen. Clothes don't flavor the blood. Hormones, pheromones, natural chemicals and DNA all contribute to a person's taste. What they eat, drink, smoke… everything seasons blood."

"Like barbeque?"

"Same principle, I guess. If there's enough of a substance in a body, it's similar to marinating a piece of beef. The taste comes through in the eating."

"I should be totally grossed out by that imagery, but I'm a sucker for barbeque." Vienna kicks her legs gaily as I stride along as fast as I dare. The catch with blurring is that it's so easy to cross the line from a believable human gait to exposing my kind to all of humanity.

A small but deadly line.

Before I can answer, I finally spot my car less than fifty feet away. Either I've walked faster than I thought, or it's not where I parked it several hours ago. I sniff the air. My nose isn't as refined as a wolf's, but it's never let me down yet.

Oberon's been here. I can smell the potency of his sweat and sickly cologne still hanging in the hot night. It's faded somewhat, so he left a while ago, but this has something to do with him. There's another scent… no, two. Both carry the faintest whiff of death, the telltale mark of my kind.

Torn between setting Vienna down and examining my vehicle, or handcuffing her to me, I approach cautiously. I don't want her in a position where she could be ripped away from me in an instant. I don't want her in danger.

The warning tingle of my sun radar is screaming, starting to burn along my skin. The edges of the horizon are brightening, and the haze of darkness is lifting. Dawn approaches fast, and I might be running out of time.

"Colt? Did we park here?"

"No," I say tersely without looking at her. No, we definitely did not, and I have no idea why Oberon would move my car and then do this to it.

The driver's side window is smashed. Glass glitters on the road, but the majority will be inside the car. The windshield is splintered with giant cracks. Someone's pried open the trunk, and all the doors are caved in.

All four tires are slashed.

I'm surprised the engine isn't in pieces on the street.

For whatever reason, my vehicle has been disabled.

Fuck.

"Hold on tight, Vienna. Close your eyes and turn your face in to me." My voice is laced with fury. I couldn't give a shit about the car, but the ramifications are disastrous. "Don't open them again until I tell you to."

To my mind, Oberon has discovered one of two things. He either knows about Vienna, or he's uncovered my allegiance to Lucius. Both have dire consequences; unfortunately, I have a feeling I know which secret he's unearthed. Losing five decades of undercover work would be disastrous, but I've been so careful for so long. My guess is the little fucker scented Vienna on me.

I scan the area again. It's risky, me being out here with the minutes ticking by, but if there's an ambush about to happen, that means I'm not the only one with a high chance of finally meeting my maker. As much as I'd like to call them out and play chicken with the assholes who've destroyed my ride, Vienna is stuck in the middle. If Oberon wants to take her and hand her over to Vadim like some grand trophy, he'll need the element of surprise.

He knows me well enough to understand I'll kill him for stabbing me in the back.

"Change of plan, V." I set her on her feet, then turn my back to her. "Hop on, hold on, and pray."

It takes a second before she jumps onto my back, her arms locked around my neck and her legs curling around my hips. Clinging like a limpet, she doesn't utter a word of complaint or question. Perhaps she trusts me more than I originally thought, or maybe she just understands my absolute urgency to get her away from here as fast as possible.

"Don't let go for anything," I warn her, and take off running, Lucius's wrath be damned.

The route back to the warehouse is fairly straightforward, but I have no way of knowing whether Oberon has located my home. If he has, and he's planned this so I take the direct path back to my safe haven, then he'll have traps in place along the way.

Taking a longer route might cost me several layers of skin, or more. Taking the short route could cost Vienna her freedom and her life. There's no comparison between the two—one life is vital, one life is not.

I blur down the street, sensing movement behind me. Someone comes out of hiding, no doubt with the intent to drive me headlong into an interception. Well, if they think they can push me into plunging headlong into a trap, Obe doesn't understand the way I think. I veer right without warning, hearing Vienna squeak in my ear, and bolt down an alleyway toward an eight-foot chain link fence blocking my path.

One leap and my fingers grip the top of the fence, my boots finding the barest purchase against the links. Vienna's weight is barely noticeable, not affecting me in the slightest, but her body clinging to my back makes me more aware of how I move, conscious that one wrong move might dislodge her. "Still with me, vixen?"

I expect a sick whimper, some pained response, but really, I should learn not to underestimate my little mortal. Dangerous situations don't affect her the way they should; quite the opposite, in fact. She's bouncing on me faster than the balls in a ping-pong tournament. "Can you go faster or do I need to get the spurs out?"

What a firecracker. I laugh in disbelief as my boots thud onto the ground on the other side of the fence, amazed by her nonchalance. She's not stupid, she's aware of what awaits her if she falls into hands other than mine. She just doesn't let things bother her until they come into being. It's a hell of a way to live, if I'm honest. "Just make sure those arms stay right where they are, V."

I'm not looking back. I don't have the time to. Moving forward is the only way, and if someone's hunting us through the streets of Tucson, he'd better be bringing an army.

I probably shouldn't joke about that, I remind myself as I skid around the corner at the end of the alley, and swing left. Not when two men I'm about to make enemies of do, indeed, have armies at their disposal.

No reason to tempt fate and all that, is there?

The sky is lightening at a rapid rate, and we're only two-thirds of the way back by the time I'm weaving my way through back alleys to avoid human exposure. I think I've lost the tail but my sense of smell is impaired by the stink of garbage. The hot humidity amplifies the stench by a thousand, seriously offending my nose, and it's the same rancid smell in every single alley we pass through—fleeting but lasting.

"Colt, you need to dump me and get to shelter. The sun's coming up." Vienna's voice is strained in my ear.

I don't need her to tell me what my body is screaming. My internal sun alarm is bleating like a strangled goat, my skin tingling and starting to feel tight. It's only going to get worse the longer I'm exposed, and not even the shadows are providing any decent cover.

I'm a rat in a trap with no way out.

Cutting down another alley, I ignore Vienna's plea and blur for home like a baseball player heading for the plate. Digging deep, literally yanking the last of my strength from the soles of my feet and every ounce of speed from my body, I switch off and just *run*.

This is the closest I've been to the sun in centuries.

Dawn kisses the tops of the highest buildings, glinting off glass, settling over the city like a blanket of death.

Somehow, I get my girl home. It's nothing short of a goddamn miracle, but it might be short lived. I know my time is down to seconds as I streak across the parking lot, damn near stumbling under the weight of Vienna on my back, my strength sucked dry. I barely have the energy left to unlock my own security measures and fall through the door.

And by fall through the door, I do mean literally.

"Colt!" Vienna sounds concerned, which is nice when I think about it. How many captives would seriously be worried about the welfare of their captor if they were in the same position? Phenomenal fucking or not, I guarantee the answer is zero. "Colt, you need to get up. You need to get downstairs."

My face smarts from connecting with the concrete floor. I smell my own blood, and wince. I'm more anxious about the rest of me, truth be told. With blurry vision, I watch smoke curl from my hands, understanding the hardened shell my body has become is just moments away from combusting. A few more seconds out there, and...

"Shut the door," I croak and feel her unlock her grip from around my neck. At least I broke her fall—concrete wouldn't have been kind to her skin. Her presence scrambles away and a second later, the heavy metal clangs shut. "Enter the code... to lock the door. Twenty-one... zero-two... sixty-five."

The numbers beep as she keys in the code, then the system responds with a sharp buzz of acknowledgement. All security measures are back on alert, and I have a feeling deep in my gut we're going to need them. Smashing the car up, not taking advantage of the precarious position they put me in... I think Oberon just tried to locate my sanctuary.

Sprawled on the cool concrete, I hope I've done enough to lose whatever tracker he had following us. Has to be human or wolf, but Obe has no human minions that I know of, and certainly hasn't alluded to any ties with the shifter clans. The clans I'm friendly with have never indicated they talk with the likes of him, probably because they're bloody pernickety about who they associate with. It took me sixty years to build a formal working relationship with them, so I have firsthand experience of what it takes to earn their trust.

Oberon is too skittish, too fearful, to con the shifters into believing he's worthy of their attention.

Given what we learned tonight, the conspiracies thrown around for our consideration, I wonder which of the two big bads my partner is working for. As far as I know, Oberon is scared shitless of Antoine and Vadim equally, with good reason. Neither will tolerate spinelessness in their midst—a vampire without a backbone is a weak point in the hierarchy, capable of bringing the whole fucking operation down—and both reward cowardice the same way they do betrayal.

Excruciatingly complete eradication.

That's my fate if Lucius can't pull me out of my undercover duties in time. There will not be a hole I can hide in without the Russians dropping a smoke bomb down it and flushing me out, or the faux-French sending in the hounds. I have faith in my king's abilities, of course, but if it comes down to the wire, if the choice is whittled down to saving our species as a whole, or saving my life, Lucius already made it deadly clear that, all heroics aside, my life is forfeit.

"Colt, please, you have to stand up. I can't carry you downstairs and if you're planning on playing dead until dusk, you're going to be vulnerable."

I'm quite prepared to swear Vienna's boot is nudging me in the ribs.

"I hate it when you play dead. Get your ass up, and drag yourself to bed."

"Demanding little vixen, aren't you?" I groan, snarling under my breath against the pain. The sun's done a number on me, eroding my muscles. There's going to be no dragging myself anywhere, bed or otherwise. "Go downstairs, to the kitchenette... blood packets in the refrigerator. Bring two."

"You want to eat? *Now?*"

"Kinda imperative that I do." The curls of smoke are subsiding slowly, reducing to gentle wisps the longer I lie here. I think as long as I stay out of the harmful light for a while, there's no chance of me igniting and blazing like an effigy on Guy Fawkes' night. "Have to heal, V. Need to drink to heal."

"Oh, for God's sake, of course you do." Exasperation laces her tone, then a slim wrist is shoved in my face, her pulse surging through the deliciously plump vein sitting just below the heel of her hand. "Don't argue," she preempts, shoving her exposed flesh against my lips. It isn't the firmness of her breasts I've been dreaming about, but there's no doubt she's tasty all the way through. "Just do the fang thing and get it over with. I don't like being up here like this if someone's got it in for us."

Us. One of the smallest words in the English language, yet so indicative. She's accepted her place here, which is surprising but certainly refreshing. Some captives never wrap their minds around being held hostage to our kind, too scared and intimidated to open themselves to the inevitability of their demise. Even Stockholm Syndrome can't help them.

Vienna isn't under the influence of my thrall or a

syndrome, and she's come to terms with our solidarity. She and I, charging headlong into whatever shitstorm Oberon is gathering above our heads. I can't see a victimless victory in our future, but I can hope, can't I?

"Colt, stop being a jackass and bite me." That delectable limb scrubs hard over my lips until her fragrant skin rubs over my teeth. She hisses between hers as my fangs descend quickly, the sharpened points catching her delicate flesh and scratching the surface. The first crimson drops hit my tongue, inspiring an urge to feed that blows my mind.

I know I'm in a sorry state, my energy and body depleted by exposure to the dawn light. In most cases, I'm ashamed to say, a vampire would fully drain a human or two in order to correct the imbalances brought about by UV light. While our blood is a miraculous cure to humans, able to cure wounds down to the most grievous injuries, mortal blood doesn't have those same instantaneous properties for us. Feeding for healing takes a large quantity of blood... depending on how far gone the vampire is.

My tongue licks the tiny wound, fluffing the vein. Vienna knows what's coming, I can tell by the sudden increase in her heart rate, the surge of her pulse. Her trepidation tastes exquisite in the single drop I lap from her skin before my fangs snap down into her flesh. I barely hear her cry of distress as Golden Blood floods my mouth, but I taste it. That tart edge of pain and shock so delightful on my palate.

I drink deep, savoring her blood as it loses the tart edge and mellows into the smooth flavor of arousal.

Such a little masochist, my vixen.

The warmth of her offering fills my belly, spreading through my own veins like the best kind of poison. The allure of the Rhonull is unmistakable. If ever the general vampiric population get a sample of Vienna or any of her kind, there will be war waged. Too many vamps, not enough Rhonulls to keep them all happy, and the majority of my breed is stupid enough to slaughter everything to get more.

I feel invigorated. Alive. Disengaging my fangs, I clean up the precious dribbles of blood trickling down her wrist, then lick my lips with an appreciative smack. I'm on my feet in an instant, dragging Vienna to hers as I go. She sways a little but seems otherwise unaffected by the amount of blood I've imbibed. My mouth brushes over hers, curving as I whisper, "Thank you, vixen."

She waves my gratitude away, her waxy cheeks flushing prettily. "Do you think we can get away from the doors now? When you go down like a felled redwood, I'd rather you already be horizontal so I don't break my back trying to get you comfortable."

"Horizontal sounds like a damn good idea." I shake my hair out of my eyes, reminding myself to have it cut shorter next time, and cast my gaze over the security system. The light gleams red, indicating the system is live and on alert. All exits and entrances are secured correctly. "You need to explain this playing dead idea to me, Vienna. I'm intrigued."

Her arm trembles in my grasp as I lead her toward the hidden entrance to downstairs. The viciousness of her reaction reminds me she never got the refreshments Tiberius arranged for her at the club, which means I need to feed and water her before she crashes. "When dawn comes, you go into this catatonic state, like you're dead. It's kinda creepy. The sun comes up and you... well, there's no one home."

Hmmm. If I was intrigued before, now I'm fascinated. "What makes you think that?"

"Maybe the fact you literally look like the dead man you are?" she asks as though I'm stupid.

I mull over my reply as I access the door and usher her

down into the bowels of the warehouse. Our footsteps sound loud and clunky on the metal steps taking us down into my bedroom. The door shuts behind us, the locks snicking into place, and both Vienna and I relax with the knowledge we're as safe as I can make us.

"I'm not comatose when I sleep, little vixen. If you need me, just wake me. I've always been a heavy sleeper, but that's about as catatonic as it gets." I snap the lights on so Vienna can descend the stairs without falling and breaking her neck. Sleep is the furthest thing from my mind, watching her ass sway in front of me. "When the sun rises, it's like it sucks all the energy out of the air. I can fight it if I have to..." Like now, for instance, when I have a punishment to take care of. "But if there's no reason to fight it, I don't."

"So, you don't just switch off wherever you are? No," she answers herself with a sigh as she realizes if that was true, I'd be sleeping like a statue upstairs, "you don't. Huh, the things you learn, I guess."

My fingers snag the back of her boy shorts before she escapes the long arm of my law. I pull up and back, wedging the material into the tender cleft of her pussy if her pained yelp is anything to go by. "The things, indeed. Did you enjoy the orgasm you stole earlier, little vixen? I know Lucius and Selene certainly got a kick out of watching you come all over my back."

"I was under the influence!" she howls.

"Is that a valid excuse for disobeying me?" I muse rhetorically, pursing my lips as she tries to twist away. "I think not." Curling my arm around her waist, I barely dodge the quick snap of her head as she uses it as a weapon. I grin, already gearing up for a fight we both know she won't win. "Well now, that's no way to show you're sorry, is it, vixen?" I release the waistband and slide my hand inside the shorts, feeling her cheeks clench hard to keep me out.

She jerks and moans quietly when I dip between her thighs instead, driving two fingers up inside her. The sound of a wet cunt submitting to my penetration is almost as gratifying as feeling the heat clamp around my digits. Tight and hot, just the way I like her. I toy with her, stroking the ridges of her vaginal wall until she ripples around me, slicking my hand with liquid sex.

"You were told what the rules were," I murmur in her ear, adding an octave of dark warning to my tone. "You were given ample opportunity to abide by them, were you not?"

Her breathing is erratic, thick and uneven, her stomach shuddering under the rope of my arm. "Under. The. Influence," she bites off the words in little staccato beats. "You know what your blood does to me, Colt. I can't be held responsible for what ingesting your blood does, especially when I didn't drink it by choice."

She does have a point. Thoughtfully, I drum my fingers inside her pussy as I consider where she's coming from. Her sex responds delightfully, clamping down as I tap on her favorite spot. "Very well, we can agree that not *all* your actions were your own tonight. Because I'm a really nice guy, I'll halve your punishments from two to one."

Vienna snorts. "Nice, my ass."

My fangs scrape gently over the top of her shoulder, followed by a sweep of my tongue. She's still resisting, still relying on her bravado. I'm pretty confident her snarky remarks and sarcasm will soon be nothing but yelps and noises born of both pleasure and pain.

I don't know who is coming for us, or when. It could be today, tonight. My guess is tonight, when Oberon can gather whatever hidden forces he's amassed behind my back for a dedicated and strategized attack, rather than the half-assed one he put together this morning. I need to beg an audience with Antoine, remove him from the equation, but it might be more difficult than I anticipated. Oberon's twisted fingers might have already dabbled in that pie, or worse, be commanded by the frog.

If today is all we have left… we may as well go out with a bang.

Slipping my fingers out from between her swollen labia, I hum throatily and tease the plump lips. My vixen is smart enough to know which of her punishments she *won't* be enduring, yet she isn't begging me to change my mind. Is she hoping the temptation of her pussy is enough to distract me from claiming what I truly want?

"Take off your top," I order, nibbling across her nape to elicit the shivers she gives so freely. She's so sensitive there, it's delightful. "Then push your shorts down over your hips and kick them away. I want you naked, vixen."

She mumbles under her breath, wisely not forming the words well enough for me to catch anything that might make her reprimand worse than it already is. The thin material keeping her breasts from the sight of unwelcome eyes is dragged over her head and tossed aside. Her ass wiggles seductively as she dutifully obeys my command.

Such a good girl.

She's naked now, and my cock is a fucking divining rod in my pants. She uses her foot to launch the shorts across the room, then stands with her back ramrod straight and her thighs pressed firmly together with my hand trapped between them. Clever little minx.

I gently wedge my boot between her feet, nudging them apart in the smallest increments she'll allow. She's fighting me, subtly, but it won't make a difference. My fingers tease her again, circling that entrance to her pussy, drawing the wetness out. Quick as a whip, I drag my hand back, using the heel of my hand to part her cheeks before she can squeeze them tight.

"Shit," she hisses.

"Shush, Vienna. Don't tremble so. Has no one ever taken this tiny little hole of yours?" I know the answer. Anal virgins are just so much fun to torture, and she gave away how innocent her ass is from the start. When you're an ass man, a connoisseur of the nether hole, an unplundered pucker is the holy grail of sex.

She tries to wrench out of my hold. "Just do whatever you're going to, Colt."

"If it distresses you," I tell her quietly, pulling her closer to me, "say so." I find the slight indent of her hole, press my wet fingertip against it. She stiffens and growls threateningly, as though it's going to make a difference to my intentions. Feisty vixen. "If something hurts, tell me."

"I hope," she grinds out, "you're not planning on sleeping anytime soon, Colt. I'm going to stake you so many times, you're going to wish—"

Her threat cuts off sharply, words evaporating into a guttural grunt as I breach the tight hole, sliding my finger deep. Her head falls back onto my shoulder, body trembling, hands gripping my arm around her waist. My voice is low, soothing, and dominant as fuck when I whisper, "Mind what you say, vixen. I don't have any plans to hurt you, but I suggest you think twice about finishing that sentence."

Neither of us is prepared to back down… or so I believe, until Vienna does the unthinkable and capitulates quietly. Her body goes loose, her muscles losing their tautness. She's breathing harshly through her nose, her heart bouncing against her ribs. The little spasms of her ass around my finger as it accustoms itself to my intrusion are wonderfully erotic.

Tightening my arm, I lift her and carry her effortlessly to the foot of the bed, setting her down and encouraging her to fold herself over the rounded end of the footboard. The cherrywood is smooth and cool, which might help her to calm that fiery spirit for a moment or two. It just needs dampening to take the bite out of it, not be extinguished completely. "Do you trust me, Vienna?"

"I'd trust you a lot more if you didn't have your finger up my butt." She's pressed her face into the bedspread, trying to hide, so her reply is muffled and distorted. But oh, that sass. I love her sass.

Carefully, I withdraw from her, rubbing my palms gently over her upturned bottom. I leave her there for a moment, stripping as I walk to the bedside table. By the time I make my way back to her, naked, lube in hand, my vixen has the bedspread clutched in her fingers, her knuckles white. Not a single word of fear or pleading has passed her lips.

Leaning over her, I trail my fingers down her spine from nape to ass, caressing the curve of her form. Her skin twitches beneath my touch. "A punishment doesn't necessarily mean pain, Vienna. Penance is doing something you might not like or enjoy." I click the bottle open, pour a pool of clear liquid into my cupped palm. "You fear this, for whatever reason, so this will be your penance." A groan strains my throat as I slicken my shaft, making damn sure every inch is covered. "Would you like me to make you a promise, Vienna?"

Her gulp is audible, poor thing.

"Ah, vampire's got your tongue. Completely understandable." The bottle cap snaps shut, making her jump, and I toss it on the bed. My fingers return to her dainty rosebud, tracing a circle around her anus before I push two inside her, bringing her up onto her toes with a sharp cry. "I promise you it won't hurt as much as you're dreading, vixen. Might be you even come to find pleasure."

She snorts dubiously; I twist and scissor my fingers slowly, coaxing open the shy ring of muscle strangling my digits.

"My advice is to relax." I have an insane urge to be inside her, to join us together in what—throughout centuries past—has always been a taboo act. A sinful use of the human body, forbidden for years. It remains a touchy subject for many, but for me… well, we'll just say the female derriere is a beautiful thing, one women shouldn't be ashamed to share.

I understand why they are reluctant to do so. Pain is a great deterrent as well as a magnificent motivator. For a long time, I was a dealer in pain. Pain, blood, death. In my early days, when the bloodlust overpowered everything but my need to destroy, men and women alike felt the agony of my bite as I fucked them. I was an angry vessel, driven by my demon, and living by the rules of my time.

Newbies of the present day don't seem to inherit that anger, that loss of control. Perhaps it's because civilization has evolved, multiplied, and the demons we are cannot flaunt ourselves so readily as we once did. But there are still those—human or otherwise—who are careless when taking a lover, who damage their partners.

There are still sadists in sheep's clothing.

Me? I'm an asshole, sure, but a sheep I will never be. I don't hide what I am.

The ring of muscle squeezing my fingers flutters and eases a fraction. I stroke her flank as a reward and remove them, grasping my cock just behind the head. A familiar zip of excitement rips up my spine as I press against her, my free hand gripping her hip and flexing lightly in reassurance. "Take a deep breath in for me, Vienna. That's it, that's my good girl. And out again, nice and slow." I coach her quietly, pleased she's not stubborn enough to ignore my help. "In... and out again. There now, isn't that better? Once more, vixen, big inhale... now breathe out and bear down."

Caught up in the rhythm of my voice, Vienna obeys before she understands what I'm asking. A hard roll of my hips, a few long seconds of constant pressure, and my vixen's dark star surrenders. This moment is the one I love most of all, those few seconds of resistance before my lover graciously submits.

Vienna, however? Yeah, *gracious* and *submit* are two words not walking hand in hand with her right now.

She keens softly, breathing hard. "Fucking get on with it, will you?"

Ever the fighter. I roll my eyes and come to the conclusion I'll probably come before she relaxes enough for me to move deeper. Shaking my head at her pigheadedness, I set my hands on either side of her spine, above her pert buttocks, admiring their curves. Using only the heels of my palms, I caress up to her shoulders, drag them back down. Up, down, up, down. "There's no reason and no point in hurting you, V. Focus on your breathing and just relax."

Her laugh is bitter, biting. "Go to hell, Colt. I'm not in the mood."

Up, down, up, down. My cock is throbbing, the need to fuck dire, but she's not ready yet.

Her body turns against her mind. I can feel it beneath my hands, softening, accepting. The keening lessens to quiet mewls, her hands relax in the bedspread. Sliding my hands beneath her, I curl my fingers over her slim shoulders and kiss across the blades. Skim my lips over warm, fragrant skin until the mewling becomes an urgent moan.

Gotcha.

Striking at the point she relents, I lift her upright, letting her weight finish what I started. The sensation of her channel sliding down my cock, the velvet heat enclosing me like a tight fist, is the best dream come true. She chokes on a warbled cry, scrabbling at my arms, but she's already fully impaled, taking my length and girth without too much discomfort.

Patience is the key. When hunting and killing is what you're designed for, patience is second nature.

Her head falls back, thumping lightly against my shoulder. She's quivering, finally accepting who the boss is in this scenario, and I'm just a little in love with her submission. Her ass tightens around my cock, squeeze and release, squeeze and release, until I have no choice but to fuck her or let her do all the work, ending our time together far too soon for my liking. An ass like this is designed for fucking, and I don't intend to let it down.

"How are we doing?" I murmur, biting carefully along her shoulder. My fangs pierce her skin a few inches apart as I move my mouth over the soft curve, pressing the tips into the muscle so only the points break the skin, making the smallest marks and bringing tiny droplets of crimson to the surface.

"Sleep with one eye open, you bast—" The rest of her sentence peters away, dying into a keening moan. It's beautiful and haunting all at once, a sweet serenade of pain and pleasure rolling into an honest melody. "Holy water in your coffee. Stakes in your bed and, oh, *fuck*."

The tirade of threats stutters to a halt when I grip her hips and let her fall forwards onto the bed. Doggy style is one of my preferred positions, particularly for anal sex. There are so many different and wonderful angles to exploit when a woman is pinned face down on a bed, her ass up and ready to be hammered into.

Lucky Vienna, getting to try them all today...

9

*ienna*

THREE TIMES, I've tried crawling out of this bed and away from Colt's amorous intentions.

I'm contemplating a fourth attempt, only I'm not sure my stealth skill is as well developed as his stamina. The fucking vampire has rutted me into unconsciousness twice, made me orgasm until my vagina poked a white flag of surrender into the air, and is apparently planning on seducing my exhausted body yet again.

"No," I mumble into the sheets. "Colt, you'll fuck me into an early grave."

"I wouldn't do that," he protests as though I've offended him, but damn him, he's hard to read when he's this playful. For an undead guy, he sure does have a firm grip on his emotions. Playful like a little kid, stricter than a Supreme Court judge. Whatever mood he thinks is right for the occasion, he pulls it out of his magic hat like a fluffy white bunny rabbit. "And you, my feisty little fox cub, are a long way from dying."

Fox cub. Vixen. Anyone would think Colt has a fascination with the species. To my knowledge, I look nothing like a fox, but then I suppose these things are in the eye of the beholder. How Colt sees me is down to him, and I'm not sticking my oar in that creek. As for dying, well, that's closer than he'll have me believe.

He and Lucius have plans for me they're not willing to share—my heart ceasing beating is part of those plans.

I get the feeling the decision has been made, whether or not I'm on board with it. I'll be honest, if that's the way of it, I don't want to know when they've scheduled my demise—not the day, not the time, not *anything*. Seriously. I know it sounds ridiculous and I'm probably not going to make a dent in my bucket list, but I don't want to see it coming. Still, there are two stipulations I need to discuss with my randy lover when it comes to my death, and neither is negotiable.

One: the only vampire snuffing my mortality out like a candle is Colt. Lucius may be royalty when it comes to vampires, but he scares the ever-lovin' shit out of me, and I don't want to be afraid when I die. Death's scary enough without adding his lordship into the mix. Colt is my executioner, no exceptions.

Two: they don't tell me when it's going to happen. I don't want a hint, I don't want subtle little clues. Sympathetic, pitying glances? Don't want 'em, don't need 'em. Colt can fuck me into oblivion and drink me dry, that's fine by me. Wait until I'm asleep and siphon my blood from a vein until I fade away, that'll suit me just dandy. Painless, quick, and clean is all I ask.

Firm fingers cup my pussy, my swollen flesh setting off

alarms in my head that are akin to tornado sirens. My body has been twisted, contorted, hammered, pounded… you name it, Colt has done it in the last few hours. Insatiable. He's an unstoppable, insatiable, inexhaustible powerhouse of sexual prowess, and he's got me locked in his sights.

"I need a bathroom break." It's the first thing that comes to mind that has the power to save me. "I need water and food, a shower, and several hours of sleep. If you make any attempt to breach the sanctity of the pussy, I swear to God she's building a fortress with a freaking moat full of alligators. Drawbridge access only, Colt, and that fucking bridge won't be coming down for anything."

The smug asshole has the audacity to laugh. I give a vague thought to rolling onto my back and slapping the amusement off his devilishly good-looking face, but I don't have the energy. The last fragments of it dissolved sometime around when my feet were by my ears, and Colt's cock was introducing itself to my lungs.

"I've ridden my pretty vixen too hard, haven't I?" Fingertips pet my labia as though that's going to make everything okay. Colt's voice is warm and smooth like heated molasses, crooning as softly as one of the jackasses on late-night radio duty urging all his fans to come hither and listen to him—only I'm the one listening to him, and listening is not listening in the traditional sense.

"Understatement of the century," I snipe. I should see if I can find his *off* switch and give it a good smack before he decides to while away the afternoon making my body pay even more. "I don't know what the hell has gotten into you, *Sir*, but for God's sake and mine, cool your sex jets."

"Sex jets, huh?" Colt's voice is low, strumming over my exposed nerves and seducing my system. He has the most wonderful voice when he uses it for good. When he's pissed, really livid, his tone is sharp enough to carve sculptures out of a block of ice, but when he's relaxed and amiable, he makes everything melt into warm… wet… puddles. "I guess I could arrange for a short intermission."

My body flops over at the behest of his hands, rolling onto my back so I sprawl uselessly on the damp, sweaty sheets. I consider myself lucky I've got any fluids left in me —hours of carnal activity have drained me of everything, just about. I mean, I don't have much use for my breasts half the time, but usually I can at least claim they're perky and firm. Not today. Now they seem content to sort of droop limply to either side, as exhausted as the rest of me.

Colt drags a fingertip down my center line, from throat to clit. "Go get a shower, vixen. I'll see what I can rustle up by way of food for you, and then I think we need to talk."

We need to talk. Quite possibly the worst four words in the English language when linked together in that order. The warm softness of sated bliss ekes out of my soles, replaced by dread. Groaning, I murmur, "This is my come to Jesus talk, isn't it? Where you tell me how I should consider what's going to happen over the course of the next couple of days, and how it's going to affect me."

"That's pretty damn close to my scheduled speech, yes." Colt swipes at the lock of dark hair dangling over his eyebrow. Naked—he should always be naked, in my opinion —and looking no worse for wear after dicking me into the mattress all damn morning, he almost looks regretful. "Something bad's aiming for us, V. I feel it in my gut. There's no turning it back, and no diverting it around us. Whatever's coming, we're going to hit it head-on."

I guess we're talking about this now. Not the best idea when my eyelids are like lead weights, determined to slip shut. This probably sums up my life to its current point—

most important conversation *ever* and I'm almost sleeping my way through it. "I get it. Life as we know it is dwindling to a halt, we might not see past tomorrow night, blah blah." I yawn through the *blah*s. I barely register the words falling out of my mouth. "If you believe turning me into Fangtasia is the right thing, do it. You've got my blessing, Colt, or whatever you need."

"I... huh." Aw, he looks so freaking cute when he's baffled. "Just like that?"

Stretching, I try to find a cool part of the bed to wiggle onto. My skin's too warm, pumping out post-coitus heat in waves. My shoulders lift in a shrug as I watch him through the slits my eyes have become. "You've had days to hurt me, Colt. I think the worst you've done is scare me, although... put your cock near my ass again and it's history, buddy." That last part is a warning simply because I don't want him to take my poor abused booty for granted. Anal sex? Not exactly the hideous, excruciating experience I was expecting. "So yeah, just like that. As long as you promise it will be you who turns me and you don't tell me when, go for it. Who says romance is dead?"

Colt sits beside me, his hand resting on my thigh. "There's a bit more to it than—"

"You bite me, you drain all the blood from my body, and then you feed me some of yours. Vienna the mortal dies quietly in the arms of her vampire lover and wakes again as Vienna the vampire. Gotta love the alliteration," I say with a huff of laughter, ending it with a soft snuffle. Conversation be damned, I'm tired and I want to sleep. "Vienna the vampire. Superhero... or supervillain?"

The last thing I see is Colt still looking perplexed, shaking his head at me, before I finally succumb to sleep.

When I wake, everything's changed.

Literally.

Bedsheets? Clean.

Me? Clean, and smelling rather delicious.

I recognize the scent on my skin. No longer sex, sweat, and Colt, but the addictive scent of his body wash. Lifting my hand, I trail my fingers through my hair and find it slightly damp and tangled. The sappy bastard gave me a shower while I was sleeping, which tells me the vampire is soft on me—or his delicate nose couldn't stand the smell of me for a moment more. I don't know how keen his sense of smell is, but I imagine it's fairly precise.

I ask my legs to move, pleased they're still in working order. The muscles in my thighs and my hips are screaming at me, obviously worked past their limits, but I'm relieved to feel the ache. Colt means well when he feeds me his blood, I know he does. I just don't want to become someone who feels like she's invincible when she isn't. That way lies danger, especially if Colt isn't around to make my claim a truth.

My head rolls to the side and my lips curve at the sight of *actual freaking food* sitting on a plate beside me on the bedside table. Nothing gourmet, just a cheese sandwich, some chips, and a handful of double chocolate chip cookies. Not gourmet, no, but it looks like the meal of a queen to my eyes. My stomach agrees wholeheartedly.

Colt's bedroom is quiet and empty. I take advantage of the peace and push myself into a sitting position with the pillows plumped against my back, then balance the loaded plate on my raised knees. I'm drooling before the sandwich is within biting range. Within a few minutes, the plate is empty, my belly is full, and I'm dozing quietly, bobbing along on the tide of contentment.

I assume Colt is on the other side of the basement, dealing with whatever he needs to get wrapped up before night falls, so I'm shocked when I hear the door leading to the warehouse snick open and feet patter confidently down the metal steps. They're too confident to be an intruder. It can only be Colt, but what the hell has he been doing up there?

"Oh good, you're awake. Just in time."

"Just in time for—what the fuck did you do?" Staring is so, so rude but I can't help myself. The figure descending the final step moves and sounds like the lover I remember. He sure as hell doesn't look like him.

His hair is drastically different, no longer brushing his shoulders. I've never been a girl who likes long hair on a man, yet Colt pulls it off easily. *Pulled* it off, I should say. Right now, I want to dig my fingers into all that short, spiky hair and feel it prickle my palms.

The lean face I love so much carries a killer edge to it now without the longer locks to soften it. His eyes are brown and gold, so tawny and alive. He's become every inch the predator, and I think I know why. "It's after dark, isn't it?"

The last time he met with Antoine, one of the bad guys involved with the Rhonull trafficking, Colt wore a suit. Not tonight. If his plan is to meet with him again, Colt's decked out ready for motherfucking war. If my body didn't feel like I'd gone ten rounds with a bucking bull this morning, I'd be ready to saddle up and ride that bad boy into battle with a sword in my hand.

He's wearing heavy black boots, the kind with the thick soles and steel-lined toes. Shit-kickers. The ideal footwear for a warrior on a mission. These are topped by black jeans, form-fitting, and just tight enough to enhance every muscle below his waist. He's also wearing a utility belt and a leather jacket, adding a dangerous aura to the ensemble, especially when his black shirt is buttoned all the way up to the collar.

Black suits the beast.

"Are we going on a reconnaissance mission?" I ask quietly, licking my lips. The world may be on the verge of imploding around my ears, but I'm going to appreciate the hell out of the man trying his best to avert disaster.

Colt rubs his hand over his chin. "I've got a meeting set up with Antoine tonight. I'd thought to confront him tomorrow when the shipment comes in, use the delivery as cover, but I've spoken to Lucius again and we've tweaked the plan. I can't make the kill and a clean escape if I'm worrying about the humans. It seems Selene has put her foot down over the treatment of the shipment, and employing them as bait or leaving them as snacks is not sitting well with her."

"I have to agree with her. You know, what with me being one of the ones destined to become a breeding snack."

"That's not going to happen. I'm taking you to stay with Lucius and Selene. They'll look after you during the transformation until I return from Phoenix."

"The transformation… ah." So, tonight *is* the night, then. Now I wish I'd taken my time with the sandwich and cookies; savored the chips. I would have done, had I known it was literally my last meal. "What… happens during the… transforming process, exactly?"

Colt sighs and perches on the edge of the bed. His hand is cool when he takes mine, and I wonder if—when I'm like him—he'll feel warm to the touch, or remain on the colder side. "You hit the nail on the head earlier, Vienna. Exsanguination followed by an appropriate exchange of my blood. You'll lose consciousness before any of that takes place.

There can be complications; sometimes the process doesn't work. If it does, you'll be pain free for the duration, and feel like a new woman when you rise."

"And if it doesn't?"

His expression is so forlorn, it brings tears to my eyes and squeezes my throat closed. Knock me down with a feather, he actually cares. "Lucius will ask you to fill in a form when we get to Club Toxic. He and Selene will escort you from there to his home—we can't go there in case we're being tailed. If the siring fails, he will return your body to wherever, whomever you state on the form. It's not something we usually do as a species, mainly because Lucius frowns upon unauthorized turnings, but I've asked him to do this as a favor. I figure you'll want to go home if things go wrong."

Home is the last place I want to be. I love my parents, and I'm sure if they ever lift their heads from their laptops and spreadsheets, they think of me fondly. Should this go wrong, as Colt so eloquently puts it, they'll grieve. They'll bury my body in the family crypt in Chicago, another useless headstone to go with the rest of the dusty shit being forgotten with the passage of time, and they'll go right back to business.

My fingers pluck at the sheets. "I don't want to go back to Chicago, Colt. If this gets fucked up—and the way my life's been going recently, it *will* get fucked up—please don't send me home. There's nothing for me there, no one who's going to remember me. I'd rather be buried here, or burned and scattered in the desert."

It should be hitting my morbid buttons, discussing my preferences for body disposal. It's definitely surreal, knowing I'm making contingency plans in case my attempt at becoming a shadow in the dark side fails. We're taught as children that monsters exist in the dark, and as we grow older, we're schooled into believing the monsters aren't lore and legend but human predators. Murderers, pedophiles, the dredges of humanity.

Despite everything I've seen in the few days since meeting Colt, there's the smallest sliver inside me doubting the vampire. Maybe this has all been some wacky hallucination arising from the weed smoke I inhaled, courtesy of the little carjacking bastards. Maybe I'm still lying on the side of the road, so high I'm out of orbit and dreaming about hot vampires, a global human trafficking ring, and sacrificing myself to keep my body from falling into bad hands.

"Little vixen, your wish is my command. Whatever you want me to do, I will, but we're not going to fuck up. Lucius is the most experienced vampire I know when it comes to siring newbies. I wouldn't leave you in his hands if I didn't know he's the only one who can bring you through this whole."

Whole and dead. Well, walking, talking dead, hopefully, otherwise just plain *dead*. "And you're off on an assassination mission while I'm vegetating and evolving from an omnivore into a full-fledged carnivore? What course of action do we take if you end up being the one assassinated?" It hurts more deeply than I imagined possible, thinking about Colt being gone.

"That, we're not worrying about. It's a quick in and out job. I'll be back in Tucson before you know it."

"Colt, don't treat me like an idiot. You have a plan."

"Fine. If I die, Lucius will raise you. He and Selene will become your family and teach you what you need to know to survive. You're not stupid. Far from it. The world will be at your beck and call, but my king and his queen will always take you under their wing if you need it." Colt lifts my hand to his lips, then his forehead. "If tonight doesn't go to plan and war becomes imminent, stay with Lucius. He's the right side in all of this, he's the one trying to stop Vadim's operation. Maybe he's the only one who can."

"The Russian is afraid of him."

"He pretends not to be, but yeah, Lucius is the thorn in Vadim's side. There are a lot of vampires in the world with money—you'd have to be dirt stupid or a fucking gambling addict to get to Lucius's age without amassing some kind of fortune. Vadim has gathered himself an army because he knows he's going to need one if he wants to take over the US. What he doesn't understand is that while Lucius has no use for an army, it doesn't mean he can't assemble one faster than Vadim can think about landing his soldiers on American soil. And not just vampires. Lucius has his fingers in many supernatural pies, and there's a whole host of sect leaders who'll toss their hats into the ring on the king's behalf. If Vadim and Antoine want war, they'll get what they want tenfold."

That's just too frightening to think about. War in itself strikes fear in the hearts of most civilians. Not just the fact it has the capability of changing life as we know it, but the loss of life, the threat of bombs dropping and soldiers storming the streets with automatic weapons... not knowing whom we'll lose or when... wondering whether dying will be better than living through whatever comes if the enemy wins.

But war between the supernaturals? Vampires and shifters and whatever fucking else is out there, at loggerheads? It wouldn't just be ash littering the streets on D-Day. The blood of the innocent would choke the gutters and run in rivers of red. I have no idea what *supernatural* really encompasses in the grand scheme of things. Vampires are obviously real, and there's been mention of shifters, so I have to assume they're on the, 'Yes, ma'am, we're real as real can be' list of entities, but there has to be more, right?

"What kinds of sects?" I ask hesitantly, not entirely wanting to know what else lives alongside an oblivious mortal society. If Colt so much as mentions crazy giant spider people or any variation of over-proportioned exoskeletal beings, I'm out. I cannot continue to exist in this world, knowing there are giant bug people roaming around.

"Hmm. I don't have access to Lucius's contacts. Most sects prefer to remain the stuff of legend and lore, keep that air of mystery around them. If I recall..." Colt's eyes narrow in thought, and he looks pretty damn cute with the little furrow in his brow. "The Djinn don't really have a base, they're all about being one with the universe. Vampires and shifters are worldwide, as you know. I'm not sure the leprechauns will fight; they can be ornery little fuckers, and stubborn as hell. Lucius would really have to strong arm them into going to war."

"Leprechauns are Irish," I remind him with a raised brow. "They live in Ireland, where everything is green and wet."

"Not all of them. There was some big family falling out a couple of centuries ago, a disagreement over who lost the pot of gold at the end of one rainbow or another." He shrugs off their history with ease. "Long story short, half of them emigrated to New York, land of the Irish bar, and whiskey. Swore they wouldn't return to the homeland until the gold was found, and as far as I know, it's still unaccounted for."

I can't help the snort of laughter, even though I try my best to swallow it. "The leprechauns got pissed off and left?"

"Yeah. Apparently, you fuck with their gold, they get their tiny panties all tied up in a knot." He grins wickedly and we share a moment of amusement. "There is a small congregation of Reapers up in Ohio beholden to Lucius, and I seem to remember a small colony of fae residing in Florida, but I could be wrong. The world is a supernatural oyster, little vixen, and every pearl is different. Don't discount something because of what you've been raised to believe."

Seriously? After the last few days, if he tells me fucking dragons are alive and well in Montana, or there's been a sudden breeding surge among pixies, I can guarantee I'm not dismissing his claims. I feel lost and not a little alone when he sets my hand down and looks far too serious for my liking as he checks his watch.

"It's going to be okay," he reassures me. "We're going to get through this, both of us."

I exhale softly and close my eyes. He doesn't have to say the words, but I do. "That's a subtle way of telling me to get my ass out of bed and moving, Colt. Not to burst the bubble, but I don't have any clothes, and we don't have a car. I am not going to stand in front of vampiric royalty naked, whether you blur us to the club or not."

"Nakedness doesn't bother Lucius. However, I made a few phone calls while you were playing Sleeping Beauty so well. There are new clothes in the wardrobe, clean underwear in the drawers—although I'd prefer you not wear any—and we have an old but working car at our disposal." My lover strokes my forehead, using a lone finger to brush an errant strand of hair away from my eyes. "I did a bad thing, dragging you into this. Understanding that, accepting it, I would still do it all over again just to have you here."

"I'm pretty sure I'd let you." Resigning myself to crawling out of my comfy nest, I toss back the covers and swing my legs over the edge of the bed. Even in the bowels of the warehouse, the killer heatwave is making itself known.

There's no chill against my warm skin, just the overheated kiss mirroring whatever hellish temperatures wait for us upstairs. "I'm no fashion queen, Colt, but please tell me I'm not dying tonight in some flowery dress or—"

He laughs morosely. Not quite the tone I was aiming for when I cracked the joke, but it's something. "Didn't figure you for flowery or frilly. Personally, I think you're going to look completely kick-ass. But then, I'm biased. I'd be inclined to fuck you if you wore a string of paperclips slotted together."

Well, now I'm intrigued. That visual certainly appeals to the artist in me, I must admit. I barely take notice of Colt as he walks away; I'm too busy trying to arrange the paperclip chain over my metaphorical body. Maybe I'm procrastinating, drawing my last minutes or hours out just a few seconds longer. The way the timeline is running in my head, I figure Colt will strike shortly after we arrive at the club.

He has a long drive to Phoenix, and a short window of time to accomplish his goal for the evening if he's going to make it back to Tucson before dawn. I'm thinking murdering a vampire shouldn't take long—there won't be a body to dispose of or a crime scene to wipe down. But as last night proved, people and fate are conspiring against us.

It's unnerving when I realize I'll be dead when Colt's off playing assassin. Dead, and my physical form undergoing changes I have no real concept of other than: *Grrrr, I vant to drink your blood.* I'm kind of hoping I may grow an extra inch or two, but I can't see that happening. Pretty sure vampirism isn't some kind of woo-woo fertilizer.

Soft weight lands on my bare lap, the small pile of clothing appearing soundlessly, just like Colt. His fingers stroke over my head as he asks, "Second thoughts?"

I shake my head slowly, mulling over the question. Is

that what this is? Me, discovering cold feet in the peak of a freak heatwave? It's possible, I guess. I know the reason behind letting Colt use me like a Slushie and irrevocably altering my biological structure, and I agree with the steps we're taking. I have zero desire to end up strapped down on some breeding bench with my feet in stirrups, waiting for a Rhonull bull to mount me, impregnate me, and keep the Russian's breeding program running.

As much as I like to think I'd fight and give the assholes hell if I was captured, they'd break me in the end. It might take months or years to do it, but they would. Rape, pregnancy, and labor on a rinse and repeat cycle would be enough to shatter the strongest soul if done often enough. To birth a child and watch it be taken away, understanding it would serve one of two purposes? The thought is enough to make my fists clench and my temper flare.

Imagine what I'd be like if my thoughts became reality.

"Musing," I tell Colt, setting the clothes on the bed. There's no bra, no panties. The halter top is pretty damn cool. Bright red, it has the ties at the back and the nape for easy release—it's easy to guess why he's chosen this particular top. I'm not too impressed by the slimline black jeans he's picked, they're gonna cling to my legs with sweat after a few minutes, but it's a small issue in the big picture. At least I'll look hot on my deathbed. "Just musing."

His fingers work into my hair, massaging my scalp. "No one's gonna blame you for not wanting to die, V. We were all human once, we know what you're giving up. You can say no."

"My options are limited. Live as a human and be bred constantly, tortured by dead Russian men who only want my blood, until I'm useless—that's not really what I had in mind for my future, y'know? At least this way, I control what happens, to some degree. Not many people get to choose when they die," I point out with a nervous laugh as I shake out the jeans.

His fingers tighten into a fist in my hair, yanking my head back in a dominant move that takes my breath away. Not just with the pain element. He grips my hair with purpose, yet it feels like he's almost cupping my skull tenderly. The contrast between the two is just perfect. "I could get you out of the country. I have friends in England who'd take you in, keep you safe until we clean house. No passport, no problem," he adds quickly when I open my mouth. "We can outfit a cargo box, make you comfy, and ship you to England."

"That's inventive. I appreciate the thought. But I've made my choice and I'm staying with it. I don't want to fly all the way to England in a packing crate to be with strangers while you fight for the world. Not to mention it doesn't solve the whole, 'I have golden blood pumping through my veins' thing. I either change my blood type or I die, it's that simple."

"I get it. I didn't think you'd take me up on it." His kiss is savage; I wonder if he's regretting his agreement to be The One. I wish I was brave enough, strong enough, to waive the stipulation and let him step aside. Lucius is probably very good at draining potential new vampires, but it's not his blood I want fueling my undead body. If I'm to be born again, rise again as something *more*, I need Colt to forge that link. My blood is in him, just as his is in me.

By the laws of logic, our blood no longer belongs to us as individuals.

I am him; he is me.

Shit, now I want that tattooed on my wrist.

"I'm not leaving you, Colt. But if I don't get dressed, the

whole damn mess is going to swell into a clusterfuck. Deadlines to meet," I remind him, pressing my fingertips to my slightly swollen lips. "So let me speed up the timeline before we fall so far behind, we can't salvage anything."

He paces away, agitation beginning to creep into his movements. I know his body language now, well enough to spot his tells. Rubbing his jaw, fisting his hands. His powerful body seems to quiver in the dim light as I stand and wiggle into the tight jeans.

Is he nervous about killing me?

God, I hope not. A quick twist of my own nerves has me pressing my hand to my stomach. An anxious vampire makes mistakes; I can't afford for Colt to be the least bit unsure about doing this. My life literally rests in his hands, and I have to trust in his ability to take it and give it back. I mean, if I *die*-die, I won't lose much. I've had a good few years really. I haven't known true hunger or real pain. I have no memory of being ill-treated or unloved. It's been a better life than some people in this world experience.

I button the jeans and slide into the halter top, making sure the ties are fastened. Wouldn't want to make a *faux pas* in front of the king by releasing my breasts into the open at an inopportune time, would I? Absolutely not. My toes dig into the carpet, and I realize Colt hasn't given me any socks or footwear. "Am I to be barefoot this evening, Sir?"

"What?" Colt turns, his expression odd. I feel like I've interrupted him in the middle of some deep thinking. Perhaps it's not me who's having second thoughts. "Feet, right. You need something on your feet." He still looks blank, as though he's lost. "Of course." He strides off without another word, leaving me baffled and somewhat taken aback.

Performance anxiety? It can't be easy to kill someone in

front of your boss. Maybe there's an etiquette to turning someone into a bloodless husk. Do they get extra points for not spilling any? Points knocked off if the human screams? A pat on the back for sharing the spoils?

Ugh, bad Vienna. Not the best time to freak myself out over the logistics of dying in a vampire den.

My captor returns a moment later, a balled-up pair of cotton socks in one hand and a pair of shiny black boots like his in the other. Thankfully, he seems to be more in tune with himself. This Colt has regained his confidence in the few minutes he's been absent, he's more like the dominant, cocky bastard I fell in love with somewhere on this crazy fucking trip. "Here you go. Not the ideal footwear for the weather but I find heavy weight on my feet comforting. If we run into trouble, I know you'll have adequate protection on these perfect toes. Go for the balls," he advises with a lazy grin. "Steel toes are the ideal weapon against testicles."

It's ridiculous, but the visuals are enough to make me snort a laugh through my nose. About as elegantly and as ladylike as a hippo in ballet shoes shooting cocaine through a straw, I might add. Behold how classy I am when taken by surprise, but who wouldn't find the image of steel toes playing ping-pong with a pair of testes amusing?

I catch the socks when he throws them at me, unravelling them and running the soft, cool cotton through my fingers. If I do this again tomorrow, will they still feel the same? Does soft *feel* soft when you're undead? Do things smell the same? I keep asking myself these questions without getting the same answers. I stop myself from asking more as I cover my feet, then accept the boots from Colt's outstretched hand.

Yeah, they're weighty, all right. Good, solid boots. Much more appropriate than the shitty flip-flops I was wearing when I met him, the ones thin enough to make walking the bane of a woman's existence. Hopefully, they're suffering in the pits of hell... or in a dump somewhere, rotting away into nothingness. I should have burned the sadistic little freaks of nature.

But the boots fit onto my feet as though they were handmade for me. The leather squeaks a bit as I roll my ankles and test the snugness. The laces are supple and a good length. I hate boots with laces where they're so short, you can barely tie the damn things. Straightening, I walk a couple of steps, adjusting myself to having to put more effort into lifting my damn feet.

I guess it's time. I'm dressed to impress. My carriage awaits, and my driver is watching me with his arms crossed over his chest. A few days ago, I hated him. I feared him, too, almost as much as I hated him, for opening my eyes to what really lies outside the perimeter of humanity's belief that we are the apex predators in this world. We shake in our boots at the thought of nuclear bombs, war, outbreaks of disease, and natural phenomena like the weather and earthquakes. Yet there is this whole other dimension to the world, apex predators—*true* apex predators—which make humans look like ants in comparison, beings who can devour us before we're ever aware of their presence among us.

Hell, I smashed Colt in the nuts *and* the face with a tire iron. Partly to save myself, partly to give him back some of what I was sure he was planning to give me, and partly because I wanted so badly to take him apart, limb from limb, for bringing my nice, peaceful world crashing down around my ears.

"Well, I think I look pretty damn hot," I say with a wink. It doesn't have an impact on my vampire lover, there's not even a quirk of his lips in response. His somberness settles on my shoulders, hard and unforgiving, but I'm not giving up. I'm trying not to see this as the night I end up in a casket, swallowed whole by fire until nothing remains of me but ash. I'm looking at it with my glass half full, an optimistic outlook on my fate. Tonight is the night we do a good thing. The night I become more than what my blood means in monetary value. "Biteable, wouldn't you say?"

"Completely edible," Colt agrees, his arms relaxing by his sides now. Oh good, the somber man is melting, inch by tentative inch. "Ready?"

Strangely, I am. My hand reaches toward him without displaying a single nerve. No shaking, no trembling, no doubts. I'm rather proud of myself for standing here, spine on full display, showing him that he is the man I trust to get me through the shadow of the valley of death, and out onto the other side. "How far behind schedule are we?"

Now his mouth quirks in a rueful smile. "Far enough that Lucius may feel it necessary to hang me by my toes for tardiness. It's fine," he assures me when I scowl, outraged on his behalf. "Lucius isn't an idiot, and he's not unfeeling. He knows what's at stake here, what you're sacrificing. He'll have allocated extra time in case of the event of major procrastination."

"Technically," I remind him as he grasps my hand and squeezes, "I was asleep. Not procrastinating so much as, you know, dreaming."

Colt leads me up the stairs, switching off the lights as we make our entrance from basement to warehouse, then slamming the hidden door closed and locking it. He spends his life concealed. His sanctuary is locked away from prying eyes. From what I've gathered from the snippets he lets slip every now and then, he keeps his head down and himself to himself because he has to. Being a servant to the Russian, being an ally to the Frenchman, he needs to protect what belongs to him.

Lucius doesn't have to hide. Many vampires live in the open, in houses and apartments. They have their safe areas, their sleeping areas, sure, but I think Colt's double life requires him to be a ghost. I mean, look at his security. There are human facilities that don't require half the measures he has in place to protect himself.

I feel bad for him. He's spent fifty years alone. *Fifty years*. That's more than half of a person's natural lifespan. Alone. Pretending to be someone he isn't to fit in with the bad guys. Going along with their schemes, unable to help the people trapped in the deadly web, and fighting to keep his own morals on the straight and narrow. How much effort does that require? Peer pressure can't be limited only to human beings.

He's waded through the shit, been up to his neck in death and Christ only knows what, to bring the Russian to an end. Who knows if the operation will even come to a complete stop if Colt cuts off the head of the snake in charge? Organizations of global magnitude usually have contingency plans in case of disasters. I imagine Lucius and Colt—and whoever else is privy to the existence of Vadim's criminal order—will have a plan to eradicate the rest of the Russian's life's work if killing the asshole doesn't shut it down immediately.

I hope Lucius intends to cut Colt loose after this. Murdering the Frenchman and the Russian will take solid balls—which I can attest he has, those nuts of his are solid fucking steel—and he deserves a break from being the villain. Five decades is surely enough penance to do. I understand that he'll be a hero to some, a huge part of the movement that brings down a psychotic Russian trafficker and saves however many people like me, but he's also going to have a huge fucking target on his back directing the rest of the evil bastards right at him.

I'm open to relocating. Once heads have rolled and the banes of our existence are dust once again, I'm all for packing our shit up—okay, packing Colt's shit up—and getting the fuck out of Arizona. Away from city life and vampire kings asking favors that last for decades. Alone time, me and him, in the middle of some godforsaken wilderness where we can do whatever vampires do. Humping like rabbits all day long sounds appealing.

Our boots thud on the concrete floor as we head for the exit. I think about how I can convince Colt that leaving town for a while might be beneficial for us both, deciding a strip-tease and some girl-on-top might be enough to persuade him. My lips curve slyly as I feel myself getting wet, then I walk smack into my lover. "Ooops!"

He's stopped at the door, swinging around in front of me, and in my giddy haze of arousal, I'm oblivious. After I walk into him, he lifts an eyebrow. "We don't have time for sex, Vienna. Much to my regret. Once this door opens, I don't know what's going to happen. If Oberon trailed us back here this morning, he could be waiting out there."

A frisson of unease skitters down my spine before I straighten it and roll my shoulders. "Well, then, I guess he'll have a fight on his hands, won't he? Y'know, my tire iron would come in useful right about now."

10

C *olt*

I'M BEGINNING to believe my vixen has no sense of self-preservation. Every so often, I catch a whiff of fear, so I know she's not completely oblivious to the threat hanging over our heads like a bloody guillotine blade, but other than those brief wisps of scent, she's not afraid. Not of me and what I'll do to her in about thirty minutes. Not of losing her mortality and becoming a monster like me. Not even Vadim and Antoine seem to do more than pluck lightly at her fear response, which is most concerning.

For all her bravado, she's human, she's female, and she is breakable. I'm not sure she's grasping just what those two vampires—or the thousands more who would literally decimate each other to get their dirty claws on my girl—are capable of doing to her fragile mortal body. The pain they can wreak on her... they've had centuries to practice taking humans apart, body and mind. Centuries to perfect their techniques.

Vienna wants me to laugh at her little throwback moment to when I released her from the trunk of my car and got an iron rod shoved into my cock as a thank you. I wish I could give her what she's fishing for. Truth is, she needs a weapon. If she's taken, she needs to be able to defend herself—I just don't think she'll get the chance to fight back. "Do not let go of my hand, V. If anything happens, you get in the damn car and lock all the doors. Put the key in the ignition, and fucking floor it out of here. Don't stop for anyone or anything." I pull the keys from my pocket and shove them into her free hand. "I will find you after."

She weighs the keys in her palm. "What if I don't want to run away?"

"This time, I don't care what you want. Keeping you safe is my priority, above and beyond taking out the trafficking ring. It sounds fucking stupid, tossing aside years of work to save one human, but *I don't care*. You're my human, the beating part of a heart that died six hundred and thirty odd years ago. You make me feel alive, you make me feel like a goddamn man, and I love you more than life itself, so no, I couldn't give a shit if you don't want to run away. It's what you'll do."

Those blue-gray eyes narrow at me, deadly little arrows of stubbornness. "No."

"For God's sake, woman, it's not like I'm telling you you're not allowed ice cream after dinner." I grind my teeth as I turn and unlock the main door. The car is parked not twenty feet away, and I know for a fact it is precisely where I instructed it be left: beneath a streetlight, the doors locked, and the alarm set. If anyone so much as tries to lift a hubcap, that bitch is gonna sing like the world's loudest, most annoying canary. "Disobey me and your ass is gonna be so sore, V."

My spunky little fox cub has the audacity to roll those eyes at me now. Shame I don't have time to give her a quick taste of what happens when she goes against my word—she seems to require a refresher course. "Yes, mighty master of all he surveys. Dawn will come before we get out of here if you don't quit lecturing me."

"You've been warned." Tempted to make the sign of the cross, I tighten my hold on her hand and inch the door open, peering out into the darkness and watching the shadows. Nothing moves, no vampires rush the door. I may be overthinking things, giving Obe credit for more brains than he actually has, but my gut has been restless for hours. It jerks as I step out and tug Vienna with me, closing and locking the door behind us while keeping her between my arms. My back will take the full force of whatever comes, but she must be protected at all costs. "Stay close."

I can hear her heart beating in the quiet. Traffic around this area is minimal at night, but I can hear the distant noise of cars and voices whispering on the air. Her heart is strong enough to drown it all out. A steady, uncomplicated rhythm. "Should've put the handcuffs on, Sir. What?" she asks with a cheeky flash of her tongue between her lips. "I've seen some of what you've got in your arsenal."

"Now is not the time," I mutter as I drag her across the parking lot, every hair on my body standing up on alert. I don't like the fact no one's shown their face yet. All that drama this morning, the destruction of my car, the brief chase… maybe Oberon is trying to throw me off my game. I hate to admit it, but he could be doing a damn good job of it. "Almost there, V. Stay alert."

I must be losing my touch—or my mind, I think as we

make it to the banged-up Ford without interference. I hate feeling this paranoid, waiting for the damn piano to fall off the cliff and splatter my brains in every direction. I can't tell myself I'm being foolish when I know something is already in motion. Vienna and I are walking into a trap—I just don't know where or when or how. Every step I take with her in tow puts her in danger, yet I can't stop moving forward. Standing still means death.

I guard her as she disarms the alarm and slips the key into the lock. The moment I hear the tumbler turn, I reach around her and yank the door open, bundling her into the aged vehicle that smells disgustingly of old cigarette smoke and sweat. With a terse order for her to climb over into the passenger seat, I keep watch over the faded red roof before sliding into the vacated driver's seat.

The shadows are quiet and empty for now.

Vienna dangles the keys out for me, saying nothing as I snatch them from her fingers and ram the key into the ignition. The engine rolls over and chokes, twice, before it catches and gives a wheezy roar of exertion. A swelling cloud of black smoke billows from the exhaust, and I curse. My contact assured me this would run smoothly and get us where we need to go without any hassle, but the way this fucking thing is shuddering, we'll be lucky to get halfway to Club Toxic before something breaks on the dilapidated piece of junk.

"Get your seat belt on," I command, slamming the car into gear and my foot on the gas. The car responds with an audible *fuck you* in the form of a hard whine, then broncs forward like a demented rodeo bull. I feel a bit better when I hear her belt snick into place as we peel out of the lot and onto the road. "Tiberius and Augustus will be waiting for us at the club. When I stop the car, you get out and you go directly to them. I'll be right behind you. No vampire in their right mind is going to barge into Lucius's club, not even for you."

I'm driving without headlights, relying on my keen night vision to guide the hurtling rusted tin can along a labyrinth route, completely deviating from the usual direction. It's going to take a few minutes longer, but I'm willing to lose the time. I'm breaking speed limits, the tires are squealing around every corner, and we're leaving a thick trail of black exhaust fumes in our wake. I honestly don't care about anything other than getting Vienna to safety.

"What are you going to do with Oberon?"

Good question. Well presented. "Oberon's made his bed with the wrong people. He'll lie in it and he'll die in it, just as soon as I find out which fuckwit he's kissing ass with. He's got information, and I'm gonna squeeze every last drop of data from his throat before I rip it out." I'm growling, so furious with the vampire who's been by my side for decades. I saved his bitch ass from being torn asunder, and *this* is how he repays me? Well, he's going to find out just whom he's pissed off. "In about five minutes, he won't be a concern anymore."

The car weaves around other road users, the steering wheel shivering under my hands as we take another corner too fast. The incessant gnaw of anxiety at the base of my spine is multiplying quickly, growing sharp teeth. There are only a couple of streets to go and then Vienna will finally be out of Vadim's reach, away from Antoine's greedy clutches. Dying changes everything.

My side of the car caves in without warning, the metal ripping and screaming under an immense force. We spin, out of control, while I wrestle with the wheel and try to bring us to a halt, but it's too late. Glass shatters, the windshield explodes in a riot of cracks. Hitting the brakes does nothing; the steering wheel is useless. We're picking up speed and the rusted wreck is falling apart at the seams. I can feel it start to tilt, gravity and momentum forcing us to flip.

I don't know what the fuck has hit us. There were no headlights, nothing to suggest another vehicle on the road. We've been ambushed, expertly, and I don't know how. I told no one the route we were taking, and only Vienna and I know what the plan for tonight is, aside from Lucius and Selene. I can't see either of them breaking confidence.

Vienna grunts, tossing F-bombs under her breath like grenades as the car skids sideways then loses all traction and sends us airborne. She's drowned out by the sound of more metal crunching and grinding along the asphalt, the remaining windows exploding on the first hard roll.

I hit the roof, literally. Connect with it hard enough to feel my collarbone snap with a sensation similar to a gunshot. Short and sharp. My body tumbles with the car, bouncing and being thrown around. Searing pain stabs into my side, just beneath my ribs. It's the kind of injury that would render a mortal dead before the car stops. *Glass*, I think. A shard of glass from the driver's window shoving deep into me, for God's sake, and I've no way of pulling it loose while we're still skipping down the street like a stone on a still pond. I hear bones break but there's no corresponding surge of pain in my body. Vienna's cry of agony hangs in the air as the Ford slows, tipping halfway before rocking back to rest on its tires. Thank Christ for that.

There's blood all over the interior—mine, I think. I hope. I can smell it for the briefest moment before the scent of gas masks it. I hurt, but my collarbone is already healing.

The wound in my gut can't until the glass shard is removed. That's going to pose a problem.

Groaning, I try to figure out what kind of contortion I've ended up in, where my limbs are, and where Vienna is. I work out I'm mangled and twisted, but she's still strapped in safely.

There's a gash on her forehead, but it's nothing serious unless the perpetrators of this crash are vampires. I can't reach her to give her my blood or clean the wound. Her arm's draped across her midsection at an odd, ugly angle. My vixen is out cold.

Metal screams as her door is ripped off what's left of its hinges. I catch a glimpse of a knife as it slides through her safety belt like butter, then hands reach in and drag her out. Not human. No human could pull a heavy car door off so easily, especially not when the car itself is little more than a flattened pancake of scrap metal.

This is not happening on my watch. They're not taking her. I crawl over the seat toward the open door, dragging myself with one hand while fighting for purchase on the blood-slicked glass in my side with the other. "Vienna!"

"The whore has a name." Fingers fist in my jacket, and haul me unceremoniously out of the wreck. Oberon has finally shown his weasel face. "Antoine won't care, of course, and neither will Vadim. She'll be nothing but a number when she's shoved into a crate and loaded onto the plane to Russia."

Both of them. Son of a bitch, he works for both of them. I play dumb, lacing my voice with as much confusion as I can muster. "What the hell are you on about, Oberon? Why would Antoine or Vadim be interested in the measly little human I'm fucking?"

"They're not pleased with you, Colt. It's not wise for you

to play dumb right now. Vadim knows he hasn't sent you a Rhonull, and the sample you gave Antoine was pure. It didn't take a genius to realize you had access to a Golden Blood; I smelled the female on you last night. One of my men was in Lucius's club when you went bolting through with your little fuck buddy bleeding everywhere and causing a riot. Orchestrating things from there was simple enough, and this is going to be one fuck-off feather in my cap. Vadim wants the girl; Antoine wants you. Lucky me, I get to deliver both and reap the rewards."

He always was a mouthy bastard. Likes to say too many words when only a handful would do. My lips peel back in a snarl as I wrench the glass from my flesh, the scent of more blood blossoming. "They're working together, then. With you as their lackey. What the hell did I waste the last fifty years for?"

"You were a means to an end, Colt. There were plans to bring you deeper into the fold, *all* the way in, but you blew it by meeting with his lordship, King Lucius of the high and fucking mighty. Did you think it would go unnoticed, you being summoned into the back room by the royal couple with their guard dogs on display? There are eyes and ears *everywhere*. Vadim takes no chances, and we knew there was a rat in the works."

I lunge to my feet as Oberon's minions haul Vienna's limp body away from the wreckage toward a small black van with tinted windows. The odds of me finding her if they get her in that vehicle are slim to none. "Bullshit, Obe. You've been trying to undermine me since the day I saved your worthless life and ended up enslaved to that fuckwit! You want to be the big man? You want to be Vadim's right-hand bitch like I've been for the past fifty years? Go right the fuck ahead. Take my place, see what I've gone through *for you*, and have a good life. Just give me back the girl, and I'll gladly walk away from the whole sordid mess."

"That's not my call to make. Antoine wants a word with you. Vadim already has a stud lined up to knock up your pretty little slut and deliver the next generation of blood bags. So, say goodbye to your whore. I'm sure you'll see each other again in hell in the near future."

I hear the rumble of the van door sliding open and make my choice. The palm of my hand slams into Oberon's nose with a crack, blood spurting in crimson arcs. If bone fragments haven't penetrated his brain, I'll be surprised. He staggers back, goes down, and I take off as best I can. Blood loss affects us as harshly as it does humans, and I've bled out enough of the good stuff to make my legs weak. It's only the thought of Vienna being flown off to some creepy science lab, strapped down and raped by a stranger for Vadim's profit that keeps me upright as I propel myself toward the two assholes manhandling her like a bag of trash.

My body crashes into the taller of the two, hammering him into the side of the van hard enough to leave a man-sized dent in the metalwork. Pain rips through my healing side, more blood seeping through already sodden clothes. He grunts in surprise and drops Vienna's feet with a thud, turning to face me as I batter his kidney with all the strength I have left.

There are sirens in the distance, which bodes badly for all of us. Someone's obviously heard or seen the collision and done the civil thing, but I can't explain how I'm covered in so much blood when the wound is still knitting itself back together slowly. The kidnapping attempt will come to an end if the police show up, but only if I can hold Oberon and his goons off until they arrive.

The second thug drags Vienna into the van as I wrestle

with his partner, then he hops out and joins the melee. Fists flying, I'm giving as much as I get until one of them drives his fist directly into the closing wound in my side. I roar, doubling over and taking a blow to my shoulders. Beyond enraged, I swing up and out, digging my fingers into the soft flesh around the shorter man's windpipe and crushing it in my fist. As he wheezes and claws at my wrist, I rip out the offending piece of flesh and toss it aside, rounding back on the taller one with the intent to do the same to him.

A faint whine is my only warning before I'm hit in the back by a pair of prongs with enough kick to down a fucking elephant. Fifty thousand volts of electricity stream through me, frying every circuit in my brain in a split second. My body becomes a puppet, the strings in the control of the motherfucking Taser, dancing dementedly even when I'm flat on my face. Groaning, I try to push up, but a foot lands on the back of my neck and pins me down.

"Go, before the bastard cops show up," Oberon snaps. "I've got Colt. Message me when you're clear at the rendezvous point. I'll deliver the goods to Antoine and meet you before dawn. Don't stop for anyone. We're all dead if anyone but Vadim takes possession of the Rhonull. Call me immediately if you have any problems. This needs to go smoothly."

Goddamn it, I can't lose her.

The body of the man I've just ripped the throat out of is lifted into the van. He was one of Oberon's human minions from the smell of his blood—he won't rise again. The van door smacks shut, and the driver's door opens and closes. The vehicle purrs to life as Oberon drags me by my feet in the opposite direction. My body limp, my heart breaking into fucking pieces, I'm helpless to do anything but watch the van peel off with the screech of rubber on asphalt, taking my vixen with it.

Now it's not just my blood I'm covered in. I'm wearing the essence of the mortal hapless enough to get caught up in Oberon's stupidity, and it's making me mad. My clothes take the brunt of the burn from being dragged over the street, but my hands and face are certainly starting to feel the abrasions. My limbs are twitching, jerking back to life as I will myself to man up and beat the crap out of this piece of shit, but I'm still wiped clean by the electric shock. "Kill... you.... dead."

Oberon snorts loudly, but it's still barely audible over the scream of sirens drawing nearer. They're only a minute away. "Had your chance and failed, old man. Phoenix is your last stop, Colt. We both know how your life is going to end. I'm just sorry I won't be there to see you die. Antoine is apparently quite the artist when it comes to torture. The things I could learn from a master such as him."

Ugh. The adoration in his voice is sickening. If Antoine is the kind of vamp Oberon aspires to become, I hope to God he gets a stronger stomach in the coming years. The boy pukes if he sees the barest glimpse of internal organs. "He'll eat you... alive."

I'm picked up by my belt and the collar of my shirt, and tossed into the back of a truck. I hit ridged metal, bounce and roll until my shoulders collide with a steel wall. I'm in a custom-made transporting cage in the back of Oberon's pride and joy. No windows, no bars, no grills. Once the door closes, it's going to be pitch black and stifling hot. No doubt he's going to drive like a dick and hit every pothole he can find to make the journey as unpleasant as possible.

No worries. I've got two hours to heal—a slow process, without blood to speed it up, but manageable—and by the time we get to Phoenix, Oberon is going to wish his sire had never laid eyes on him all those years ago.

It's going to be a busy night. Two vampires to kill, however many more to exterminate if they decide to interfere, and I need to gather information on where Vienna is being taken. All before dawn.

My clothes are stuck to my skin with blood... by the time dawn rises, the streets of Phoenix will run with it.

~

VIENNA

GRENADES EXPLODING INSIDE SKULL... check.

Body feeling like a steak under the tenderizing hammer... check.

Sick feeling of dread... check.

Broken arm...

Double fuck, that hurts so bad. Even though I'm experiencing an almost out of body sensation and the pain is muted to a degree, I still want to scream until my throat bleeds at the agony ripping from my fingertips to my elbow, and the slow, nauseating pulse accompanying my heartbeat. But I choke back the vomit and the screams until I can figure out where the hell I am, and what happened.

Because everything seems a little hazy, and I don't like not knowing what's going on.

There are more than a few questions spinning in my head and I want answers to all of them. Like, now. Questions such as: where is Colt? Is he alive? How badly is he hurt? Is he here? Where am I? Who smashed into us? So many damn questions, I can't keep them all straight in my fuzzy brain. Somehow, it's imperative I try. If I don't keep my head, there's a good chance I'm gonna lose it.

Flat on my back, eyes barely open to slits, I force myself to take in as much of my surroundings as I can. It's dim, there's barely any light at all. My eyes are adjusting to the darkness, enough that I can make out a shadowy form beside me. It smells… wrong. It doesn't smell like Colt at all, and the longer I stare at it, the more I realize it's not him. Too short, too bulky. Plus there's the whole dead thing.

I'm stuck in a black hole with a really dead guy who isn't coming back to life.

I add *anxiety attack* to my checklist.

Do not lose your head over this, Vienna. Do not lose your shit. Now is not the time!

Honestly, I really think now is the perfect time to lose my shit. Alone with a dead body in a small, dark space. My vampire is nowhere in sight, no one aware is of where I am or how to save me. I have a pretty good idea who's put all this in motion, and it doesn't look like I'm the girl in a romance book who gets her happily ever fucking after. I'm the one who ends up with a body dilapidated and exhausted from abuse, her mind in tatters, and her life snuffed out without ever seeing sunlight again.

Drained dry, veins sucked flat, corpse dumped in a Russian ditch covered in snow.

Yeah, I'm seeing sunshine and roses in my future… not.

"Oberon, where the hell are you? I've been sitting here for nearly five hours. The damn van is starting to smell like a murder scene. Answer your goddamn phone." The harsh male voice hums in the confines of the metal van, angry and frustrated. Is that a touch of fear I can hear? "If you don't contact me in the next twenty minutes, I'm dumping the body and taking the girl to Vadim. I can't give her any more damn drugs, and I'm not handing over an overdosed shipment. Twenty minutes."

The jolt of shock I feel at hearing I've been out for five hours is painful, but understanding it wasn't due to some major brain injury is slightly relieving. At least I don't have a bleed on the brain or gray matter leaking out of my ears. Both would just be messy, and right now, with a dead guy stinking up my holding cell, I can't deal with messy.

So, I need to think ahead. Twenty minutes before things start moving and shaking again, and I need to be ready. The broken arm is going to be a complete hindrance, but I can bear the pain. There's no other choice. Pain versus living? Hands down, I'm fighting like hell, no matter how much it hurts.

Aside from the broken arm and the burning gash across my forehead, I don't think I'm injured, per se. Bruised and aching, sure, but I can motivate myself enough to get out of this situation.

Clenching my teeth, I roll onto my side, away from my dead companion. Funny, now the invisible man has mentioned it, I can smell death. The copper scent of blood cooking in heat is enough to sour my stomach, but add the almost sweet odor of a body breaking down, along with the expulsion of all those bodily fluids leaking from cavities... shit, I knew I shouldn't have watched those crime documentaries. We're in the middle of the greatest heatwave in Arizona history, and I'm trapped with a body.

My luck is seriously running low.

Everything goes white when I move. I swear my eyeballs turn into supernovas. I need to make a support for my arm, but there's nothing in this godforsaken metal box. The impulse to just lie down and let another five hours pass me by is strong—so strong, I'm tempted to give in. Pain wears a person down, and God knows, I'm hurting.

Up. Get up.

My boots scrape on the metal floor as I struggle to dig them in for leverage. I have a horrible feeling I'm sliding around in Mr. Dead Guy's blood. Yuck. I brace my broken limb against my belly and press my free hand against the wall, dragging myself up into a standing position that's more hunched than human. My stomach twists once, sharply, and I deposit its meagre contents onto the floor unapologetically.

Wiping my mouth with the back of my hand, I hobble as quietly as I can manage to the side door, spotting the handle that leads to freedom. There's no way I can get out of the vehicle without being spotted by the driver, but I might be able to leave a clue, or at least *try* to escape. Who knows, I might be able to schlock him with a rock and stagger my way to civilization.

Colt won't give up on me. I'm not giving up on myself.

I step over the corpse gingerly, reaching for the handle. If that sucker sits up and grabs my leg now, the air horn on a freight ship won't hold a candle to the volume of my screams. Vampires, werewolves, whatever, I've got my head wrapped around the concept of their existence. After a few days of being immersed in this world, they've become a normality.

Freaking zombies? Nada. Nope. Not happening.

My fingers touch warm metal, curling around the mechanism before sliding off. My hand is too damn sweaty for stealth. The second attempt is successful, after I wipe my palm on my jeans. The lock clunks, far too loudly for my liking, and there's no way of pushing the door open without the telltale rumble giving me away. Looks like I'll have to be inventive.

I ease the door back, an inch at a time, letting more heat whisper into the already overheated coffin I'm in. Still, anything is better than this godawful smell. I don't dare pop my head out of the gap—if the driver sees me in the side mirror, my goose is well and truly cooked. I keep nudging the door open as smoothly as I can until the gap is big enough for me to slip out of unnoticed.

I set my boot on the runner, holding the door open, and manage to awkwardly sit myself down without landing hard on my butt, moving my feet onto solid ground. It's now or never. My legs are visible, which means I'm vulnerable. God, I hate that word.

From the front of the van, a phone rings. My ears perk up as the driver answers with a terse, "Reynolds."

I pause, wanting to make sure the phone call will last more than two seconds.

"Oberon, where the fuck are you? I'm sat in the creepiest fucking rest area known to man with my dead associate stinking up the works. The girl? She's fine, out cold. Should be out for another half hour or so with the last dose I gave her. No, no, she's still breathing. My life hangs in the balance of getting her to Vadim alive as much as yours does. You're not my boss any more than Ralph was—we *all* answer to the Russian. So you'd better be here in the next ten minutes, or I'm taking the girl and claiming the credit."

It's all I need to hear. It sounds as though Reynolds is winding up for a fight with the vampire, which gives me a couple extra minutes to get as far away from this death trap on wheels as I can. I'm not taking a single moment to wonder what's happening to Colt right now, but I do send a quick prayer to whoever is listening that he's okay, and he finds a way out of whatever mess Oberon has dropped him in.

I reach back and grab the dead man's rubbery hand, tugging him as best I can over to where I'm sitting, enough to wedge his fingers under the door to hold it open—I can't risk it sliding closed and giving me away. The distance I drag him is only a few inches but, shit, does my body know about it. My muscles flare with pain, my arm spikes as it jostles. But it's worth every moment of discomfort if it gives me time.

Deep breath in, long breath out.

Run. Colt's voice hisses in my ear as though he's crouched behind me. I can almost feel the pressure of his big hands on my shoulders, holding me steady as I stand up slowly. *Run like the fucking hounds of hell are on your heels, little vixen. The devil is coming, and he wants you. Run!*

One foot in front of the other in the darkness. Slowly at first, tripping and stumbling. I think we're out in the desert, back where this shitshow began. The ground feels grainy, dusty beneath my boots. I can make out the shape of boulders and cacti. I hope fervently I don't run into one of those spiky bastards, I'll be yelping like a scalded cat. Not good for a ninja escape plan.

My body hates me so much in this moment, and I don't blame it. We're beyond our limits, exhausted and in pain, and I'm so damn thirsty I could drink a camel under the table. I remind myself, sternly, that survival means going above and beyond physical limitations. It means endurance, even when your body wants to roll over and die. It means perseverance, pushing muscles past the point of obliteration. My ungraceful stumbling turns into more of a hobbling jog, reducing my arm into a mewling limb of fire.

I really want to be sick again.

I don't know where I'm going, I just hope I'm going in a straight line. From somewhere behind me, I hear a massive bang, and a curse loud enough to shake coconuts from the trees... if they had any coconut trees out here in this massive fucking wilderness. I giggle to myself, thinking of monkeys swinging from branches, pelting each other with the hard, brown shells. My jog slows to an ungainly shuffle, but I can't stop.

Somehow, I make it onto the smooth blacktop of a road. Left or right? Right or left? Which way leads to salvation, and which way will have me skipping like a guileless lamb to the slaughter? Who knows which way is what? Not me, that's for sure. My head is too muddled to make sense of anything. I'm walking through molasses, damn near dragging my sorry ass. I turn left and trudge along, every step taking me further away from the van of death and its reaper.

A car flies past, kicking up dust along with a breeze as it passes. Oh, that feels so nice. Something to stir the dead air sucking the life from my lungs. I don't even have the energy to raise my hand to hitchhike. Just keep putting one foot in front of the other. Have to get to Lucius. Have to tell him... something. Need to find Colt, and bring him home.

More cars pass, ignoring me.

I'm blinded by headlights, stopping in my tracks as a rumbling SUV pulls off the road a bit and pinpoints me in the glare of its high beams. Weakly, swaying on the spot, I lift my hand to shield my face as the truck door opens. I hear footsteps approaching and can just make out the faintest shadow of a figure behind the halo of light, but whoever it is doesn't say a word.

Not until he steps in front of the truck and blocks out one of the paralyzing beams. "You okay there, miss? Bad stretch of road for you to be walking on at this time of night. You broke down or something? Need help with your car?"

"K-kidnapped," I blurt, my mouth feeling like I've just eaten a sandbox full of cat litter. "Find... Lucius."

"Oh, honey," the man drawls sympathetically. I'm too fatigued to note the hard edge in his voice until it's too late. "Good King Lucius can't help you now. No one can. I know, I know. You're harboring some wild fantasy that Colt is gonna come riding to your rescue anytime about now, right? I'm going to burst that sweet little bubble and tell you he's not going to save anyone today. I left Phoenix a couple hours ago, and he was well and truly... preoccupied."

It's a jagged barb digging just under my heart. "Don't underestimate him, jackass."

Low laughter sends ice down my spine. "He's definitely a tenacious fucker, I'll give him that. But I doubt even Colt is enough of a hero to escape heavy silver chains around his ankles, wrists, and neck. Add on the fact half his guts were hanging loose from his body, and Antoine was taking great delight in drilling a hole into his brain—no, I don't think Colt will be leaving Phoenix in one piece."

The sheer glee in his tone sums up what kind of monster I'm dealing with; I pray this fucker is lying to me, exaggerating my lover's fate to make me falter. Colt might be an asshole, he might have kidnapped me and made me his sex slave, but the man I'm in love with—the fucking vampire I gave my heart to—is one of a kind, it seems. Somewhere along the path of his many years walking this earth, he retained his humanity. There's a huge piece of him still clinging to who he was.

This freak? He fell off the sanity train and embraced his demon a long time ago. His humanity is erased, consumed by the evil inside him, and I'll be damned if I let myself be tainted by the ugliness he exudes.

"Please, stop," I whisper, swallowing hard for a touch of moisture to strengthen my voice. When Oberon—it can only be Oberon, I recognize the slight whine—chuckles darkly, obviously thinking he's cowed me with his graphicness, I lift my head and smile at him. "I'm loving all these ideas you're giving me on how to make your death so painful, you'll beg me to turn you into ash. They're making me horny, and you won't like me when I'm pissed off and turned on. I get really creative."

He takes the most subtle step back. One blink and I'd have missed it. It's enough to tell me he's not sure he knows exactly who he's dealing with. Good. I dislike being underestimated. I may be banged up and broken, but I've still got fight in me. If he tries to take me again, we're both going to end up in a world of pain the likes of which we've never experienced before.

"See, I'm thinking no one's really told you anything about me, because no one knows who I am." Aside from Colt, he's had the full force of me for days, but I don't volunteer that information. "They haven't told you how much I object to being thrown about like a dead animal, having my bones broken, stolen away from a life I was beginning to like. They won't have told you I'm the kind of woman who will kick a guy in the dick for fucking with me, or that I'm more than happy to gouge his eyes out for looking at me the wrong way." I take a step forward; Oberon retreats a half-step. It's a perverse dance of sorts—I can't get cocky and presume to know all the moves. That's how people trip themselves up. "Do you like your dick, Oberon? I bet you spend a lot of time with it. Stroking it, playing with it, wishing there's a pussy in the universe that would let you put it in..."

His face darkens to a rather unattractive shade of bloody murder. "Fucking cunt."

"Well, that's rude." *Try not to rile the bad man, Vienna,* I tell myself as he puffs himself up into as scary a figure as he can manage. He pulls it off, just. He looms over me, straightening his shoulders and glowering at me. "It's a simple question. How attached are you to your dick? Not in the literal sense, obviously. I'd just like to know, given the circumstances."

"The circumstances?"

I let a slow, malicious smile curve my lips as my expression hardens. "The circumstances of how you're going to end up a eunuch if you don't take me to Colt right now. Because, trust me, if you don't, I will leave you in a bloody heap on the ground with your precious dick in your hand." It's a bold claim. I have no weapons and I look like shit, no doubt. A toddler could probably take me down at this point, but I stick to my guns and show no more weakness than what he can already see. "Think I'm bluffing? Try me."

Oberon weighs me up silently. With the lights where they are, it's hard to see his eyes, his expression in general. I can see the side of his face where his color is still angrily flushed, but his features are shrouded in darkness. His laughter booms after a few seconds, and I know I've lost the smack-talk portion of this round. He's gonna call my bluff, and now we're both going to hurt. Goddamn him.

"You're really quite delightful. I understand why Colt has been so secretive and kept you hidden away from the rest of us. Unfortunately for you, you have a prior engagement to keep. I can offer you something for that broken arm if you like." *Oh, look at him being all nice and genial.* "I remember what a broken bone feels like, vaguely." He rubs his nose. "It's not pleasant. Vadim will be displeased if you arrive in less than pristine condition."

I scoff loudly. "From what I've heard, he intends for me to live the rest of my life in less than pristine condition. Somehow, I doubt my physical wellbeing is of much concern to the likes of him." I cradle my arm closer, wincing and biting back a cry of pain. "Besides, if you take me to him, you'll have to kill me first. I won't be a broodmare for the next thirty years."

"Then you and I have a problem. If I need to use brute force, I will."

Oberon lunges for me before I have time to reply, blurring forward and snatching my arm, wrenching it away from the support of my body and twisting the broken bone. Red fills my vision, black spots dancing in front of my eyes as I scream blue murder and drop to my knees in the dirt. The pain is outstanding, a physical entity strangling me from head to toe. I retch uncontrollably, what little is left in my stomach hurtling up and over his shoes, his pants.

With a disgusted grunt, he releases me and growls. "Filthy fucking human." He fists his hand in my hair, hauling me up to my feet, but they don't work. Won't work. Pain has eradicated all my capability of functioning like a normal person, so he just drags me along the ground toward the rear of his truck. "I cannot wait for the day Vadim takes control of your pitiful species. All of you shackled and chained, kept in your rightful place beneath the heel of the vampire."

I'm sorry, what? My scalp is on fire, the hairs ripping out by their roots as Oberon continues his assault. Such a big man, manhandling the little female. I'm still screaming as my injured arm bumps and grinds over the rough terrain, pretty sure I lose consciousness every couple of steps for the briefest second. It's too much, the agony breaking me apart, separating mind from body.

"Reynolds. I'm on the highway. Burn the damn van with the body in it. I've got the girl. If you're not here by the time I've got her loaded, I'll assume you're finding a rock to hide under in the hopes Vadim won't track you down." Oberon chuckles darkly as he drops me in a heap. "Excuses, excuses. Drugged, you said, bordering on an overdose. Not so drugged she couldn't slip out from under your dumb ass and make a fucking break for it. What the hell were you thinking?"

As he waits for the answer, Oberon kicks me onto my back and crouches down, biting into his wrist deeply and shoving it against my mouth. I taste sweat—*ick*—and press my lips firmly together, but he just holds the phone between his ear and his shoulder, using his fingers to force my lips apart. Blood pools over my teeth, some of it leaking into my mouth while the rest dribbles down my cheeks. Oberon huffs and sets his thumb on my windpipe until I gasp for air, choking on his blood.

"You're a dead man one way or another, Reynolds. The Russian is not known for tolerating mistakes. You can face a quick, clean death if you come back with me, or meet with a drastically agonizing end if you run. I'll leave the decision up to you." Oberon pauses, glaring down at me as I attempt to throw his blood back up into his face. No one has the right to feed me blood but Colt, and the weight of it in my belly is the epitome of betrayal. "Well, good luck to you. No doubt I'll see you in a day or so. I'd tidy your affairs before I find you, Reynolds."

The flow of blood into my mouth dwindles, much to my relief. As Oberon's wrist lifts, I spit out what I can, but I've already imbibed enough to feel the effects of it working through my system. I grunt as he scoops me up and dumps me in the back of his truck, into yet another small, airless box several times smaller than the back of the van. This is going to mess with my head and open up the gates to claustrophobia hell.

"Make yourself comfortable," he advises. "It'll be your last chance to rest for quite some time."

The door slams shut, leaving me in pain, in the dark, alone.

Fuck.

11

olt

THIS WASN'T how this evening was supposed to go.

If things had gone to plan, Vienna would be sleeping away her mortality right about now while I disposed of Oberon and Antoine. But no. Nothing ever goes according to plan, does it? If it did, I would not be hanging from the ceiling of Antoine's kill-slash-torture playroom by my wrists and neck. It's damned uncomfortable. The silver chains bite deep into my flesh, blood trickling down my throat in what I imagine looks like some morbid horror-type necklace, with matching bracelets around my wrists.

My stomach, chest, arms and thighs are adorned with deep gashes from the almost playful swipes of the French frog's sharpest knives.

Apparently, Antoine has been just *dying* to string me up this way, and Oberon offered him the perfect excuse with the tale he's woven of betrayal and disloyalty to the cause. To be honest, ninety percent of the story he told Antoine is true, I can't deny that with a clear conscience, but the other ten percent? Pure and utter bullshit designed to rile the faux-French asshole into a sadistic frenzy of tearing me into shreds and scattering my remains around his estate like ashen confetti.

Oberon and I will be having some serious words when I get out of this predicament.

"Tell me again, my friend, what you think I want to hear. Oberon puts forward an interesting rundown of events, but I am curious. Vadim would offer you the world once this deal was done. Any woman you desire would've been at your feet, bound to you for as long as you wished. Yet you stab him in the back—me, as well—and range yourself beside the one who calls himself *King*." The tip of Antoine's newest weapon digs into the hollow of my throat and scores a line downwards, splitting my skin like silk. Blood-stained silk. "You've kept quiet, not once defending yourself from Oberon's accusations. If you do not speak, I have to assume you are guilty."

The wound is superficial in the scheme of things. Stings like a bitch, sure, but even after however many hours I've been chained like a dog in this hellhole, Antoine still hasn't actually done anything that I'd constitute as detrimental to my health. He's waiting for something, whether it's for me to profess my innocence or confess, but I know damn well he's holding back. Most of his intended victims die in here before twenty minutes pass, if they're lucky.

"Already decided, haven't you? You were happy to throw away years of our acquaintance on the word of a vampire who used to be my friend. If you didn't believe him, I wouldn't be in chains. We'd be upstairs, discussing this bullshit like civilized people," I spit.

"Oberon provided a very convincing argument." Antoine shuffles his bulk from foot to foot, his stupid velvet dressing gown covered by a see-through rain mac. Wouldn't want to stain the velvet with blood. The edge of the scalpel follows the faint center line of my abs, all the way to my navel. "Come now, Colt, my boy. You have to admit, it does look suspicious. We both know Vadim isn't sending any of the good stuff out to his buyers. The deliveries are comprised of the useless half-bred cast-offs he has no use for."

"Yet you were going to pay for ten of them."

"Not at all. The ten coming into my possession tomorrow night are part of the payment agreed between Vadim and me. What's that quaint term you Americans use? Ah, yes. *Freebies*. They hold very little monetary value in this world, so Vadim gifted them to me for my part in this little exercise. I was to be awkward, yes? Give you some difficulty and see how hard you worked to make the sale. This, you passed quite admirably. I was impressed with your tenacity." The scalpel jabs in a circle around my navel, making me growl between my teeth. "They will entertain me for a short time, then keep my dogs and my men amused for a while after that. It is all they are good for."

It is all they are good for. He's talking about people—living, breathing people—as though they're nothing but brown paper bags scrunched up and tossed into the trash. It's the mindset of many of my kind, and it's unfair to humans. Without the mortals, we would be forced to live on pig's blood. Believe me when I say feeding from a live pig is an experience you don't want to try more than once. My first and only attempt happened when I was newly turned, and I was starving.

That fat bastard took me for a ride over three fields, through a beck, and halfway through a forest before I drank enough to slow it down.

"When did you buy into the organization?" I ask between clenched teeth. It's only a suspicion, but the opportunity to pry into their business dealings is too good. Antoine is a blabbermouth at the best of times, and now shouldn't be any exception if he thinks he's killing me tonight. "I'm presuming Vadim sweetened the deal for you there, too?"

"Smart boy. Very smart boy. I really do hope this turns out to be a misunderstanding, Colt. That sharp brain of yours would be most beneficial to me. Yes, I am now a small partner in Vadim's Rhonull production, and have been for around six months. I did my homework, you see, and saw the potential to expand my bank account as well as have access to the rarest blood available." Thoughtfully, Antoine inscribes my flesh with a random swirly pattern as he speaks. My fangs elongate as I resist the pain. Once that shit worms inside you, it's far too easy to let it shatter you. "I get a healthy chunk of monetary profit, which has already paid for the buy-in fee, and I use my contacts around the world to bring in more custom for Vadim. Not to mention an unlimited monthly shipment of Rhonull rejects to play with."

"I'm disappointed in you, Antoine. A man of your stature, beholden to the likes of Vadim? The man is the Avtoritet. He's the Russian mafia. Why are you hanging on his coattails rather than forging ahead with something similar yourself?" I'm pushing buttons, hoping to find the right one. I haven't forgotten Vienna, far from it, but I have to concentrate on myself so I can finish my job here, and hunt her down. "You've got the financial means to buy properties big enough for research labs and holding cells. You've certainly got the manpower to hunt down Golden Bloods of your own. Start an empire of your own, built on your own foundations."

It's a good job I don't need to breathe. The links of the chain are digging deeply enough into my throat to alter my tone, making me sound strangled. If I needed oxygen, I'd have crossed the living-slash-dead line hours ago. I bite off a sharp, bitter curse as Antoine jams the scalpel through skin and muscle, sliding the wicked blade expertly between my ribs. I've said something that doesn't please him, evidently.

"And where do you suppose I could find one of these magical creatures, Colt? Vadim has scoured the earth and found the majority of them, leaving no stone unturned. Are you volunteering yours, perhaps? Donating her for scientific purposes?" The blade cuts the muscle between my ribs, bringing a snarl to my lips. "That was a bad thing you did, Colt. Hiding that sweet temptation from me, taunting me with just a vial of heavenly elixir."

Antoine's eyelids flutter rapturously, remembering Vienna's taste. I want to smash his fangs from his mouth and pound his face into bloody mush, before I take him apart limb from limb. If he doesn't butcher me in the meantime, that is.

"As I warned you at the time, Antoine, the girl is mine."

"No longer, she is not. Vadim is expecting her arrival in Russia. Oberon has been tasked with retrieving and delivering her to Phoenix, holding her for safekeeping until tomorrow night," he continues nonchalantly, yanking the scalpel free and jabbing me lightly in the stomach, "when she will be taken to Phoenix Sky Harbor International airport, where she will be crated and flown to Russia. Vadim has promised me her final moments when the time comes."

Do not get angry. Rising to his bait is what he wants. Negative reactions equal betrayal. Prove you're loyal.

I'm already on the precipice of ripping the elderly vamp's head off his shoulders. No one touches Vienna, especially not this sadistic fuck. Her life won't end at his hands; I won't allow it. She's not being packed into a crate like a dog and smuggled through customs. "That's between you and Vadim, Antoine. I've worked for the Russian for five decades. I know what he's like, what his business practices are. He'll screw you over, and I like you too much to watch him sink you." The lie is oh-so fucking bitter on my tongue.

"This is not what Oberon tells me, Colt. He tells me you fake your friendship with me." The scalpel clatters onto the tiled floor, rattling into the filtered drain below me. "Apparently, your opinion of me is less than likeable."

I roll my eyes in plain view. "Huh, you mean the way Obe faked his friendship with me? I saved his life after he fucked up, have been paying penance to Vadim for Oberon's sins ever since, and he repays me by screwing up my life so irrevocably, I'll be lucky to see another night? I've been faithful to you, Antoine, and to Vadim. I've had a hand in building one of the world's most intricate mortal trafficking rings. Yet *I'm* the one swinging by my neck, being sliced into ribbons, on the word of a serial liar?"

Antoine sweeps regally across the playroom. I say playroom lightly—this space was designed and built for one thing only: killing things messily with minimal cleaning afterward. Eighty percent of the room is tiled, including the floor, which has several handy drains set here and there. There are cupboards and drawers full of implements of torture, and an untold amount of restraints hanging from the dark walls.

There are ghosts in this room, hundreds of them

crawling around me. I can feel them—hell, I can scent their anguish. Trapped souls locked in a room built on blood and pain. I'll burn it down to the ground before I'm done.

"This leaves me with a conundrum, doesn't it? Should I believe you, my trusted friend, or the tales spun to me by a concerned member of Vadim's crew?" He picks something up and makes his way back to me. My stomach drops into my numb feet when I see the drill in his hand.

"I'm guessing Oberon gained a promotion recently?" I throw it out as a lifeline.

"He did, yes. Vadim promised him your position within the organization in return for his good work capturing the mole. I see where you are coming from, yes, I do." Antoine taps a fat finger against his lips contemplatively. "If the boy is lying, Colt, why do my sources confirm your presence last night at that club the Tucson vampire owns?"

I'm lying for my life now. This has to be believable or it's all done, game over. When the drill comes out to play, there's no going back with Antoine. That particular instrument of torture unleashes his creative side. "Club Toxic? I'm sure you've heard what lies beneath the nightclub?"

The drill whirrs into action. "Enlighten me, Colt."

"Carnal pleasures. Lucius runs a BDSM club exclusively for our kind below the busy dance floor. A haven for vampires, dominant and submissive alike. The girl is submissive; I took her there to experiment with her. I don't have the equipment Lucius does for a proper scene. Plus, I'd heard rumors the king was aware of the trafficking ring and several key members. I wanted to show my face there under the guise of playing with my submissive, see if I could pick up any new data."

"Hmm. Plausible. What conclusion did you reach?"

"Before or after I was escorted into the back room by

those fuckwits he calls security guards? He knows nothing of the operation. There was no spark of recognition. If he knew I was involved with the trafficking operation, I wouldn't have walked out of there alive." I do my best not to flinch as the drill bit skims over my cheekbone, just beneath my right eye. "Vadim and you are safe from the Tucson vampires, Antoine. You have my word."

"No recognition, you say. Then why were you asked into the back room, into his company, at all?"

I chuckle crudely, raising my eyes to meet his pale ones. "Lucius's bitch took a liking to my submissive. Summoned her across the dungeon and invited her into the back room for an... informal introduction." I let the implication of just what that introduction entailed hang in the air. "There was an incident, Selene drank from my submissive and, in the way of newbies, got carried away. I removed the girl from the room, almost inciting a riot in the process, then returned to the back room once things were under control for an apology from Lucius and his mate. When we left and returned to my vehicle, close to dawn, I discovered Oberon had destroyed my car and left me in the precarious position of being caught in daylight."

"Oh really? An underhanded tactic," Antoine murmurs, letting the drill fall away from my face with a disappointed sigh. "Why do you not call this female by name? The Rhonull."

"A dalliance requires no name," I respond without hesitation. I hate myself for distancing myself from Vienna this way, but I can't let Antoine hear the affection in my voice if I say her name. "Whatever lies Oberon has been feeding you have come from his own imagination, and his desire to take my position. Though he's as old as I am, the boy is still immature in so many respects. He will frame whoever he needs to in order to rise to higher standing, Antoine. He has ambition, admirable ambition, but he goes about it the wrong way, burning bridges he shouldn't."

"Yes, it would appear so." Muttering to himself, Antoine walks away again, ringing a bell with a tug on a plaited gold rope. He tosses the drill onto the counter, obviously pissed off he hasn't had a chance to bore holes in several nasty places on my person, then waves his hand at me as two of the security team who hauled me down here rush into the room. "Take Mr. Dockery down from his restraints and see him cleaned up and dressed. Escort him to the sunroom when he's ready. There will be a meal waiting for us."

In truth, I'm stunned when he glides out of the room without a backward glance, as though the last few hours of torture never happened. There are fresh scars on my body already healed, and the newest wounds are struggling to repair themselves, but I still have my head.

It's more than can be said for most who set foot inside here.

I hear the slow metallic thunk of a winch, and almost cheer as the chains around my neck loosen. I may have a permanent imprint of the links in my skin for the rest of eternity; those silver chains have certainly left a bloody mark. I swallow hard, wincing as the metal peels out of my flesh, sticking to the blood. A moment later, my wrists follow suit as one of the guards wraps his arm around my legs and guides me safely to the cool tiles.

"Must have given him a damn good argument, Colt," he murmurs softly as I finally relax. My muscles are tense and cramping, pinned in one position too long, poisoned by the silver. "You're the only person to my knowledge who's crossing the threshold in both directions."

My groan is long and heartfelt. "Touch and go there,

Alex. Thought he was going to shishkabob me." The other guard, Ryan, hurries across and starts unfastening the chains. "What's he like to work for on a daily basis? Does everyone like him?"

"Why, he offer you a job?" Ryan snickers.

"Something like that." My hand shakes as I rub at the marks on my wrists. They're almost black with bruising, and crusted with dried blood. "The best way to weigh up a potential employer is to ask his staff."

"Run, and don't look back," is Ryan's swift advice.

Alex sighs heavily and scrubs his hand over his face. "Colt needs some fresh clothes, Ryan, his others are wrecked. Why don't you go see if we've got a spare uniform anywhere? Can't let the poor bastard walk around naked." He hooks his arm around my waist as Ryan bolts away, and drags me to a spectator chair in the corner of the room. "I'm surprised he left your cock unscathed; it's usually the first appendage he goes for. Got a four-leafed clover up your ass, Colt? Luck's your lady tonight."

"She's something," I agree, sinking into the chair with a grimace. I feel fucking old. I've known Alex a long time now. I class him more as a friend than an acquaintance; I'll trust his opinion on whatever he's about to tell me. "You like working here?"

"If you have a choice in the matter, take Ryan's words to heart and run. Once you're in Antoine's employ, the only way you're leaving is by the true death." He keeps his voice low, his eyes on the door. "Oberon was here earlier, smug little asshole. He has something of yours?"

"Yeah, he does. I'm figuring on getting it back."

Alex nods slowly. "There's been a lot of shit going on around here lately. Shit I want no part of. The old man is insane, Colt; that insanity is spreading like a fever among the crew. Phoenix vampires aren't abiding by the rules of survival anymore. They're flaunting their presence in the city, killing recklessly and needlessly. I know your... associations in Tucson. Are they planning on dealing with this clusterfuck anytime soon?"

My lips twitch. "Sooner than you think."

"When it's over, would you put a word in with Lucius for me, if I'm still alive? I want out of here while I still can. Tucson seems to be receptive to vampires if Lucius gives his approval. If the world is really going to hell, I'd rather be on the winning team when the gates open."

I don't see the harm in putting in a recommendation. "Sure, I'll ask him. Final decision falls to him, and if he says no, I can't help you. But I'm willing to put myself on the line."

"Thanks, I appreciate it. Look, Oberon was shooting his mouth off to one of the other guards, bragging about the hot piece he was taking to the Russian. He's planning on getting her out of Tucson tonight, bringing her here to Phoenix, ready for the flight out tomorrow night." Alex bites his lip, then reels off the address of a shady hotel that I know from personal experience is where many of our brethren hit up the drug addicts and prostitutes for a quick feed. "That's where she'll be."

Triumph fills my veins, overpowering pain and exhaustion. As much as I hate the thought of feeding from one of Antoine's beleaguered slaves, I don't have much choice. My body is failing, struggling with the injuries I've obtained in the last twelve hours, and it needs blood to replenish what I've lost so I can heal. As soon as I've fed and I'm back to fighting strength, Antoine will die, along with anyone else who wants tonight to be their last night.

Then Oberon is going to have a nasty surprise waiting for him in his hotel room.

"Why didn't he bring her when he drove my sorry ass all the way out here? Doesn't make sense to make two trips to the same place. There's a reason," I mutter to myself.

"My guess? If she's special and Antoine wants her, Oberon wouldn't risk having her on the property while he delivered you. Antoine would think nothing of removing her from another vampire's possession, especially if that vampire is beneath him on the hierarchy."

Yeah, that makes sense. Better to make two trips than give the Frenchman a chance to pilfer Vienna from under Obe's nose. A mistake like that would give Vadim the perfect reason to terminate Oberon… permanently.

Ryan struts back in with an armful of black clothing. I think I'd rather go naked than wear that shitty uniform. He looks me over and glares at Alex. "You could have at least gotten him washed off. Antoine will be getting impatient; you know how he gets when he's been playing with a—oooh, the scalpel was his weapon of choice tonight, huh? Ouch."

"Yeah, not my favorite," I mutter. "Look, just point me in the direction of a shower. I'll get cleaned up, dressed, and join Antoine in ten. No sense in keeping him waiting."

No sense at all. He has an appointment with the reaper tonight; I'd hate to delay his departure from this world.

Vienna

The darkness is choking me. All I keep imagining is long tendrils of the damn stuff slithering down my throat and worming into my lungs until I can't breathe. I keep thinking

I can smell Colt in the small space, just the faintest wisp of his presence. Somehow, it stops me from freaking out completely.

The small box is secure. There are no weapons, no tire iron handily stashed in a secret compartment under the floor. Hell, the freaking floor is just one sheet of metal, riveted down. The whole space is an oven, slowly cooking me from the inside out, wringing every last drop of sweat from my body. Rivulets stream from my pores, stinging my eyes.

I don't know how much time passed before I fell asleep, curled in an awkward ball, blinded by pain, but when I woke, my arm was almost back to normal. Now it just feels weak, despite the flexing and twisting I've been doing to try and strengthen the limb. Vampire blood cures all, it seems, even down to broken bones. I'm just relieved the fucking pain has gone and I can think clearly again.

Think about how to get off this crazy train and find Colt. How to survive the sheer hell barreling toward me like an avalanche of death and chaos. I figure I can take Oberon. It was a mistake on his part to heal me.

Reynolds did not meet him at the designated point, so I reckon he has a death sentence hanging over his head now. Not that it's any of my business. He deserves everything coming to him, as far as I'm concerned. But with his absence, Oberon is all by his lonesome. That little bitch is mine as soon as he opens the damn door.

I wish I'd asked Colt to turn me sooner. At home, in the warehouse, rather than waiting until we got to the club. I could have pushed for it. This could all have been so easily avoided if we'd taken a different approach. It is what it is now. The path is set, and my feet will follow it until there's a fork in the road.

Patiently, I sit and wait in the darkness, closing my eyes and enveloping myself in a blanket of my own shadows. My darkness is different to the one surrounding me. I can control it and, in doing so, keep the claustrophobic panic in check. I think of Colt and our future, what the next fifty, hundred, thousand years of living with him will be like.

Lost in daydreams, I almost don't register the silence.

The engine has stopped.

Ears pricked, I wait for the thud of the driver's door closing, and scoot closer to the back door, leaning back on my hands and bringing my knees up to my chest. I may not have a tire iron at my disposal, but Colt armed me with a pair of heavy boots for a reason.

As soon as the door opens and Oberon's figure fills the space, I plant both thick treads of the boots square in his face with as much force as I can muster. His blood hasn't given me the illusion of superhero ideals like Colt's does, but I feel strong and fit. Even more so as I feel his nose burst under the pressure, the thrill of violence feeding my confidence.

The vampire staggers back with a howl; I shift into a crouch and grab hold of the sides of the door, launching myself out after him. My boots hit asphalt and I charge at him, leading with my shoulder. Connecting with his gut and catching him off-guard, I send him sprawling on his back.

Arms wrap around me like steel bands, lifting me clean off my feet. Enraged, shocked, I throw my head back and smack my skull into a steel wall of a chest. Dazed, I hammer my heels against my captor's legs with everything I've got in me, desperate to get free.

"Well, someone has spirit. I look forward to seeing her put that much energy into her breeding session on Saturday." The accent is thick with Russia, and makes my blood run cold. "Ivan, go with Boris. Accompany our new female to the room and make sure she does not go anywhere. We will join you momentarily."

Fuckity fuck fuck. The Russian cheese is here in all his smarmy glory. This was not on my approved list of expectations, and it's thrown the biggest wrench in my escape plans. I can already hear the gears starting to strain, the gaskets popping. Plan A is in dire need of a rapid overhaul.

The arms around me don't loosen as I'm literally carried off the street and through a pair of double glass doors on the verge of exploding from the spiderweb of cracks running through the dirty, spray painted glass. The hallway stinks of cigarettes, sex, and urine, but my chauffeur doesn't seem too bothered by the stench.

They chatter away to each other in Russian so I can't understand them. Rude bastards. Ivan and Boris, yeah, someone was real creative when it came to naming their kids. If they don't scream *Russian*, I don't know what does.

I try every trick in the book to get the massive vampire to let me go. Twisting, writhing, wriggling. Biting, kicking, clawing. The dead man walking is made out of Teflon, I think. Completely non-stick. I don't even know which goon has me pinned, but the other one wants a kick in the teeth for smirking and running his tongue around his lips in a most lascivious manner.

We trail up two flights of stairs to get to our destination, and it seems the higher we go, the heavier the graffiti and the vandalism becomes. There's artwork and obscene graphics on the walls, sexual invitations and phone numbers scratched into the moldy plaster. The walls are thin enough I can hear the sounds of rough, unattractive sex going on in what should have been private circumstances.

No one wants to hear a woman begging to be fucked

harder, harder, harder. If he's not doing it hard enough the first time she asks, he ain't gonna make the effort on the second and third requests.

Colt does not have that issue. He goes in hard, fast, deep, and continues until I'm a boneless, lifeless mess in the middle of the mattress. He's a very generous lover, and I have every intention of fucking his brains out several times once we've survived this. I'll be damned if I'm dying without feeling that body pressing into mine again.

The first Russian checks a door number against a key in his hand, then unlocks it and shoves it wide open. I snarl and swear as brute two hauls me inside and tosses me onto the double bed in the center of the room. Skin crawling at the idea of what creepy-crawlies are already possessing my body from the sheets, I scramble off the far side of the bed and press my back against the wall.

The vampires don't make a move to stop me.

The room is a shithole. Bed, dresser, bedside tables. Nothing on the walls but mold and grime. The carpet might once have had a hint of color but now it's a dingy brown, almost black from the passage of numerous feet. There's not even a freaking window I can climb out of, for God's sake. It's a room designed for fucking. Pay by the hour, no housekeeping, no hygiene standards.

I imagine the bathroom is... no, not even going there.

How are you going to get yourself out of this mess in one piece, Vienna?

I haven't got a clue.

The Russians are both big men. The one who carried me up here is considerably larger than the other. Shaven heads, scruffy beards, cold eyes. There won't be any negotiating with these two—nor, I suspect, with the man who's walking through the door with a bloody-faced Oberon by his side.

Three Russians and one cry baby.

Not the best odds.

"We have not been introduced properly. My name is Vadim Chernov. I am the Avtoritet of the Russian mafia, and your new master. You have been chosen for my breeding program because you are special, yes? Your blood is golden."

God, he loves to thicken the accent as an intimidation tactic, doesn't he? No matter. If he wants to think he's a big, strong man in charge of this situation, let him hold that thought close. Hell, he can sleep with it like a freaking teddy bear for all I care. Suck his thumb and cuddle his macho bullshit in bed. Whatever works for him; it honestly doesn't make a difference to how this is going to end.

"My blood is red," I correct with a sneer. "Just like his," I add with a jerk of my chin toward Oberon. "If you'd like, I can demonstrate how red yours is when I redecorate this shit room with it. And if you believe I can't take all four of you down, bring it on, bud." I lift my fists into a boxing stance. "What you are doesn't scare me, *Vadim*." I make sure to put a huge amount of disdain into his name.

"It should," he snarls back, flashing me those killer incisors. "I am no ordinary vampire. I can drain you to the last drop and wait for you to fill back up again. Over and over, in all manner of painful ways. You should learn respect for your master before you arrive in Russia. In Russia, there is no one to stand in my way if I decide to kill you in the street. I can do whatever I wish with you, wherever I choose, and no one will lift a finger to help you."

"Yadda yadda blah." Rolling my eyes at his pomp and bluster, I flex the muscles in my shoulders. The two vampires Vadim brought with him are subtly shifting, their body language changing from relaxed to on guard. They're awaiting orders. "You made several horrible mistakes,

Vadim. One, you went into human trafficking. Bad idea. Two, you brought it not only to America, but you dragged the sorry mess into Lucius's territory. Three, you and your henchmen picked the wrong fucking woman to kidnap. Four, you haven't killed me yet. I could go on," I tell him nonchalantly, "but the gist is, the prize for the biggest moron goes to you."

Now, it might be wise to ask myself if igniting a fire of pure rage under a vampire is a good idea at this point in time. After Vadim's threats, I'd say the answer is *no*, but I honestly can't help myself. I have no idea if or when Colt will be able to find me, save me, or even if he's still walking this beautiful earth. My future comes down to what happens in this room tonight—I can feel it as surely as I feel my heart thumping erratically in my chest.

Studying the short Russian Avtoritet with assessing eyes, I don't give myself a high survival rate. He's got the build of a man who lets others do the hard work for him. He lifts a hand, they jump to action. It shows in the portly pudge around his waist, the thickness of his jowls. There's no muscle beneath the perfect fit of his suit, it's all fat. If I poke my finger into his midriff, I bet he wobbles like a dish of jello.

He's immaculately presented, I must admit. Not a crinkle in the material of his dark gray suit, no spots or marks on his pristine white shirt. His hair is black, cut as short as Colt's is now, and slicked back. He's a salt-and-pepper vampire, silver scattered through the short dark strands. Clean shaven—I envision him sitting in a chair with a towel around his neck like a bib, with one of his lackeys stropping an old-fashioned razor blade before painstakingly scraping away any errant stubble that dares grow on that face.

But it's his eyes that hold all the power.

Ice blue, so faded they're almost transparent. They hold a wealth of hostility and violence in their depths, a contempt for mortals—for *me*—even as he weighs my worth as a Rhonull against snapping my neck here and now. For the top dog in the Russian mafia, he has an incredibly easy-to-read face, and I want to put this book down and burn it.

He really wants to kill me.

"Restrain her," he orders softly, murder in his voice. "Do not be gentle. Normally, I wouldn't care for the merchandise to be harmed before transport, but a few bruises might open her eyes to the reality of what waits for her. Gag her if she makes too much noise. I doubt screams will be taken note of here, but we take no chances. If she behaves, she can be fed and watered. If not... let her starve."

Here we go, I think to myself and bounce on my toes. I'm betting on Oberon not stepping in to help unless he has to. The little bitch has already had a taste of me, and he's not keen on taking a second helping. Which leaves me with Boris and Ivan. Both formidable, both a hell of a lot bigger than I am, and both trained to obey orders.

They size me up as quickly as I do them. Looking for weak points, vulnerabilities. I know mine. Female, on the small and light side. Mortal, which comes down heavily on the unfair advantage part of the scales.

Though the situation is dire, I find it amusing not one of us has moved yet. They're waiting for me to make a break for it, to bolt across the room. They need a prey reaction to trigger the hunt. Me? I'm nobody's fucking rabbit. "So, before I royally fuck the pair of you up, which is which? You're Boris, right?" I address the taller baldy first. "You look like a Boris. Numb, dumb, and full of—"

He growls in a way I've never heard before: deep, throaty, as though his demon summons it from the pits of hell. Now *that's* what I call intimidation. The sound reaches into my lungs and squeezes the last drop of air from them in a fierce grip. Apparently, Boris isn't as dumb as he appears. He snaps at me like a damn German Shepherd. "I, Ivan," he tells me in what is possibly the strongest Russian accent I've ever listened to. "You dead."

"Come on then, jackass. I'm tired of everyone threatening to kill me."

They move as one unit, splitting apart to come at me from two directions. As they move, so do I, sliding back into the corner and shutting down their strategy before they can touch me. I don't need to worry about one grabbing me from behind while I fend off the other. I'm restricting my own movements, but it's worth it to have two solid walls at my back.

Surprisingly, it's Boris who comes at me first. Straight in for the kill, reaching for my throat. Their orders aren't to kill me, and I know neither of them will go that far. Not against the word of their boss. I'm too valuable. But, as Vadim stated, bruises are allowed and they want their dollar's worth of fun from me, I have no doubt.

I smack his hands aside, left then right, and lash out with my foot. The steel toe of my boot hits its target perfectly, and I almost wince as I feel something soft squish on impact. I can kick like a goddamn mule when I'm pissed, and I'm not holding back my temper now. I'm sure vampires can recover from a ruptured testicle.

Boris makes an incredibly high-pitched noise, his eyes bulging wide as he grabs his crotch. Dropping to his knees in slow motion, deflating like a balloon, he has no defense against the fist I plant into his nose. Blood splatters, then smears as I belt him again across the jaw. I'm not usually this strong, but thanks to Oberon's blood donation, I have an added edge.

I give him a nudge with my foot to help him to the floor, then lift my eyebrow at Ivan. "Bobo's not feeling so good. Maybe you should go get another room and make him feel better." I wiggle my eyebrows suggestively. "Bet it's not the first time you've kissed his dick, right? You two make a really sweet couple."

It's like that 'science' experiment where someone drops mints into a bottle of coke and shakes it up. It takes a couple of seconds for the elements to react to one another and then, *boom*. Massive explosion of minty froth that shoots about six feet high.

Ivan's temper is that fountain of froth.

He throws his head back and *roars*. I'm pretty sure the participants of every carnal sin taking place in this hellhole of a building just stopped in unison to listen to the utterly primal sound of rage. He bends and picks up his comrade by the front of his jacket, then tosses the limp, groaning form onto the bed beside us without taking his beady little eyes off me.

Shit. I'm no match for this beast.

Ivan's hand closes around my throat, squeezing so hard, he cuts my air off immediately. There's no chance to suck in a quick snatch of oxygen. Again, I go for the nut shot, but he's wise to it, using his thick thigh to block my foot, then my knee. Pounding on his chest is ineffectual, my fists bouncing off pecs so muscular, I could bounce quarters off them all day long. This guy is a world apart from his boss in terms of physical fitness.

My chest wants to implode, my lungs screaming for air. Lightheaded and floating, I hear Oberon cheering Ivan on, hear Vadim encouraging his good little dog to get the job done. I barely have the energy left to lift my arms, but I force myself to lift, lift, lift until my hands reach his face. It seems so far away, swimming in close, then drifting out of focus.

He won't kill you, but you're going to wish he had when you wake up bound and gagged. You have to break his hold. You have to get free before you pass out. Colt can't save you. Do something!

I hope I'm not as purple as I feel. I feel purple. My head feels heavy and twice its size, to the point where I can't physically hold it up anymore. Beneath my fingers, I feel skin. Cold skin. Cheekbones. I dig my fingertips into those firm cheeks, scoring my nails into flesh until they bite and hold. With my thumbs, I find the rounded softness of Ivan's eyeballs and, with barely any regrets for the ickiness of what I'm about to do, push in hard.

I hold on for dear life as the vampire tries to bat me away. He's too close to do much damage, and the only way he can fend me off is to let me go. I'm weakening by the second, putting everything I've got into driving my thumbs into his eyes.

There's a scream, pained and distraught, as something pops beneath my right thumb and fluid gushes over my hand, running down my wrist. I'm half gone, floating, detached from my body as my lungs heave, and I register a surge of oxygen to my brain.

Just in time to feel a heavy thud connect with my temple and switch the lights off.

12

Colt

No wonder Antoine's guards look so fucking miserable whenever I see them. This uniform sucks. The material is stiff and unyielding, and I'm a few seconds away from scratching the top layer of skin off my body. With the money at Antoine's disposal, the penny-pinching bastard could at least supply his security team with comfortable clothing.

Seated in the sunroom in my usual chair, I try not to fidget too much. My wounds are taking too long to heal, and any move I make tugs them open again. The clock in my head is ticking down toward dawn. I have no more than an hour to get this job done and head to the slum where Oberon is taking my vixen. I need to get there before dawn, take cover in those stinking walls, and find my girl.

Antoine, of course, is being ridiculously choosy in his meal selection.

By selection, I mean the row of bedraggled humans lined up in front of our chairs. Six individuals who look as though being eaten might be the best thing that's happened to them all year. Three female, three male. None of them older than their early twenties. All manacled by the wrists, the chains leading down to iron rings set in the floor.

Two females and one of the males are fair-haired and blue-eyed. Antoine seems to like them light. The other female has black hair and hazel eyes, her expression defiant and reminding me so much of my vixen, it hurts. The last two males have brown hair. I don't know what color their eyes are; they don't lift their gazes from the rings they're attached to.

There's not an ounce of fight between the six of them.

The two brown-haired boys have a scrap of material covering their loins, but the other four in the line wear the skimpy clothing Antoine demands of his housekeeping staff. His slaves. He must be running low on stock if he's using his slaves as a food source. Either that, or these poor creatures have finally outlived their purpose for him.

"Humans are such a disappointment," Antoine muses, rubbing his fat finger over his lips as he regards his choices. "They burn out so quickly compared to our kind. These have only been with me for a few months, and already they're ready for the slaughter. Failing their duties to my house, and to me."

Failing their duties. What a crock. I can see evidence of savage beatings on all six frail bodies. They haven't been fed or cared for properly. They carry the scent of poverty, smelling like the peasants I used to pick off one by one from grimy alleyways in my younger years. I remember it well, and it's sickening to think that humans are kept in these conditions so many centuries on.

Beneath it, the odor of semen is strong. Human and canine. More than one of these has been subjected to a period of time in the kennels. Used and abused, beaten and broken. Reduced to nothing but bags of meat for Antoine's pleasure and entertainment.

Swallowing back bile, I imagine all the ways I could make him suffer for his crimes against humanity. Imagining is all I can do. With the minutes passing by, I don't have time to delve into my creativity and disassemble the fat, fake French pig as painfully as I would love to. Feeding him his own intestines would be a perfectly rational place to start, in my opinion.

Antoine snaps his fingers together and points at a small blonde wearing little more than a string thong and bra. There are bruises in the shape of fingers on the insides of her thighs, yellowy-green smudges on her cheek and down her neck. Dried semen flakes on her legs, and her eyes… her pretty blue eyes, no doubt once alive with laughter and life, are dead down to the soul. "That one will do. She's useless, can't even polish the silver."

Garçon steps forward from the shadows behind the six, keys in hand. He rounds the end of the line and strolls down to the unlucky girl, deftly releasing her cuffs and yanking her away from the others. She flinches, huddling into herself, keeping her head down. "Excellent choice, monsieur," he comments, kissing faux-French ass exquisitely.

"Colt? Have you chosen?" Antoine waves at the remaining slaves as if saying, *look at what I've provided.*

My initial choice is the black-haired girl. The one who resembles Vienna. But once Antoine is no more, things are going to fall apart here. I'm hoping Alex and Ryan will be able to smuggle out what humans they can before Antoine's empire collapses, get as many to safety as they can manage. I might have to insist on it, a favor for a favor.

She has a chance. If they can get her back into the free world, she can be put under thrall and the memories of her time here suppressed. I don't see the point of smothering what's left of her spark when I'm bringing this hell to an end in less than an hour.

I gesture to the other blonde girl, my conscience fighting the choice I'm making. This feels wrong on so many levels, but it's a necessity. If I'm going to see my mission through to the very end, I need to feed. "That one looks appetizing."

Dutifully, Garçon removes her cuffs and shoves her forward to stand beside her friend. Without another word, he unfastens the chains of the four unlucky ones from the rings, gathering them in his hand and dragging them from the room to horrors unknown, leaving us to eat in peace.

"Come here, girl." I hear the unmistakable thrum of thrall in Antoine's command and watch as his meal stumbles forward hesitantly to stand in front of him. As he hauls her against him, his hand dropping down to work between her thighs, I look away in disgust, but it's not enough to block out her cry of distress.

Soon enough, those pitiful cries of pain are drowned out by the noisy slurps of an animal feeding on his prey.

The blonde I picked looks scared shitless. No surprise, considering what she can see. I snap my fingers, drawing her attention away from the monstrosity and onto me. I crook my finger at her and silently order her to come to me. She walks toward me, trembling like a leaf, her hands gripping each other tightly. When she's close enough, I coax her to sit on my lap, hushing her softly. "It's okay, little one. I promise I'm not going to hurt you. I know you've had a rough time; I'm going to make it better, all right?"

There's nothing to her. The bones of her ass dig into my thigh, her almost skeletal body rigid with fear. I stroke my hand up and down her back, the vertebrae of her spine bumping against my palm. This is probably the first kind touch she's felt in too long to count. Unfortunately, it's also going to be her last.

"What's your name, little one?" I murmur.

Her narrow face is tight, her expression petrified. "Erica."

"Good girl. That's a lovely name, Erica. I want you to close your eyes and breathe for me, okay? Nothing bad is going to happen, I just want you to relax. You don't have to be afraid of me."

"Are you... are you going to kill me?"

"No, little one." The lie is smooth and seamless. "Just do as I say, and everything will be just fine."

Bless her, she obeys with a little shudder. Body and mind are ready for release. It's a mercy I can give her. Although I prefer eye contact when sliding into a mortal mind, I can't bear to look into those pitifully haunted eyes. Instead, I murmur to her, holding her gently as I delve into her mind and take a firsthand glimpse of her life with Antoine.

Brutality and horror around every corner. Beatings, rapes, sick mind games and punishments.

Despising my host with every fiber of my being, I wipe away every memory I come across of her time here until I reach the good memories she's hidden away of her previous existence. I dig through them until I find a happy one. One filled with what I assume is her family. Mother, father, sister.

She has her arm hooked around the waist of a tall, lanky man with green eyes who's looking down at her, so full of love, I feel my own love for Vienna rise in response.

On my lap, Erica's body relaxes into the memory, falling into and flying away on the beauty of it.

Fangs extended, I adjust her on my thighs so her back is to me and tilt her head to the side. My bite is gentle but firm, hitting the jugular on the first strike. Blood spurts into my mouth, a hot jet of sustenance that makes me moan, then I suck hard on the wound, drawing more into my mouth in time with her heartbeat.

Until that beat stutters and fades... and dies.

When I raise my head, I can sense the difference already. The fresh intake of blood has rebooted my system, and the injuries Antoine gave me are closing up faster than they were before. The taste of Erica remains in my mouth, bitter and acrid from months of maltreatment, but I'm grateful to her. Without her, what comes next wouldn't be possible.

Antoine has already discarded his meal, tossing her aside like trash. I bristle at the sight of the poor girl sprawled on the floor, her limbs twisted and bent where she's landed awkwardly. It doesn't matter that she's dead—her body should at least be treated with respect. "Garçon will be along in a moment to clear this mess away. Just cast that aside," he tells me with a dismissive wave of his hand toward Erica's body. "No need to hold onto it."

Somehow, I can't follow through with the pretense. Guilt ravages me. It hasn't been so long since I took a mortal life, but it rips at me every time. A reminder of what a monster I used to be, and could be again if I don't keep myself under control. I stand, carefully lifting the body in my arms and walking over to the door, setting her down gently, reverently.

I touch my fingertips to her forehead and hope she's found her way to a place where she can find peace.

It's now or never.

I take my time returning to my seat, using one of the linen napkins to wipe my mouth. I don't sit.

"For a beast with your reputation of killing, you express an affection for your meals, Colt," Antoine observes, slouching in his chair with all the carelessness of a man sated and full. He folds his plump hands over the swell of his paunch and gives it a little pat. "There are still tales bandied through the ranks of the newbies of Colt the Barbaric, leaving heaps of human bodies in the streets. How time changes us, eh?"

"Yeah, you could say that." I wander around the room, pretending to admire the artwork and furnishings. All ill-gotten, all attained by killing and stealing. Even the ones bought by money are stained with blood. "Working with Vadim has taught me a lot about who I want to be and how to achieve it." I circle around behind Antoine. "Working with Lucius has shown me that, no matter how much of a beast I was, I don't have to become it again."

"I—what?" Antoine struggles to rise.

I lunge forward, slamming my hands onto his shoulders and pinning him in place. "I hope you enjoyed your last meal, Antoine. I warned you: Vienna is mine. You and Vadim conspired to take her from me, and you're going to pay for it. As will Vadim and Oberon. The trafficking ring will fall. I've spent fifty years helping Lucius make sure of it. I wanted your death to be hard and cruel, the way each of your victims has died, but I don't have the time. Things to do, people to kill. You understand."

His fingernails claw at my hands as he tries to get up.

He's too fat and cumbersome to succeed. "Traitor! Guards! *Guards!*"

"Shush now." My right hand smacks against the side of his skull, hard enough to stun him. Taking his head in both hands, I twist it as the door opens and Alex steps in, Garçon on his heels. "Alex, shut the door. Keep the butler quiet."

But to my surprise, Garçon seems calm and controlled. He stalks over to stand in front of Antoine, his eyes intent on his master's face. His voice is flat and cold. "The butler would like to watch the tyrant meet his end. I could sell tickets to this."

Alex shuts the door. "Been a long time coming. You ready to run?"

With brute force, I twist Antoine's head until his neck snaps. The sharp crack is most satisfying, but I keep going, forcing the spinal cord to do unnatural things. Muscles and cartilage tear, and I'm staring into dead eyes I've wished to hell for so long, I can't remember precisely when my hatred for him started. Another twist, a sharp pull, and blood splatters. I hold Antoine's head in my hands for only the briefest moment before it disintegrates into ash, his body following suit.

"Ding dong, the fucker's dead," Garçon states gleefully. This is quite possibly the happiest I've seen him in all the time I've known him. "Christ, it feels like I can breathe again."

I dust the remains of Antoine from my clothes and nod at Alex. "I need to go; I'm running out of time. I'm claiming this estate in the name of Lucius. Kill any vampire who stands loyal to Antoine or Vadim. All humans are to be kept safe. Feed and water them, clothe them. They're now guests of Lucius's house, understand me? These bodies need to be dropped off where someone will find them. They need to be returned to their families. I'll be back to handle matters when—after I deal with the rest of it."

"Yes, sir." Alex damn near salutes me, then tosses me a set of keys. "There's a BMW with tinted windows parked by the front steps. Sun treated. You'll be safe in there if you get caught by the dawn."

I snatch the keys out of the air and run from the room. The only good part about this uniform is that they didn't have any boots to fit me so Alex returned my own, and they're pounding the tiles as I bolt for the front of the house. Through the doors, down the steps into sticky heat, and the prickly itch of imminent dawn.

The car is exactly where Alex promised. A press on the hob in my hand and the lights flash, signaling locks disengaged. I yank open the door and slide into a butter-soft, tan leather seat. The engine roars to life with a turn of the key and I remember to shut the door as I slam the car into gear and floor it down the opulent drive. The stupid gravel kicks up behind me in twin arcs from beneath the tires, pinging off the paintwork and the underside of the vehicle.

My only thought now is Vienna.

I need to call Lucius, ask for back up and apprise him of the situation here. He might not be pleased he's just acquired a mansion in Phoenix and all the hassle it's going to bring him, but it's too late to change things now. Phoenix needs a competent leader to bring it back to rights, and I can't think of a better vampire to take charge.

I slam on the brakes before I get to the security gates, the bumper almost kissing the metalwork. A guard steps out, sees it's me, and hits the button to open the gates. I lower the window. "Hey, got an emergency here. You got a cell phone I can borrow?"

He glances across to his fellow guard, then back at me.

"Sure, I guess." He reaches into his pocket and pulls it out, offering it to me. "I—"

I don't give him chance to say anything else. As the gates open wide enough for me to squeeze the BMW through, I hit the gas again and take off, ignoring his cry of outrage. He can get a new phone. From memory, I dial Lucius's number and blink as the dashboard offers to connect the call through the car's speaker system. I toss the phone on the seat beside me and focus on driving as the call buzzes through the sound system.

"Who the fuck is this?" Lucius demands without preamble.

"Colt," I snap back, barely slowing my speed as the car careens off the short drive connecting the main road to the security gates. The BMW skews sideways, tires screeching in protest when they hit asphalt, spinning before gripping and launching me back in my seat. "Oberon has Vienna. He ambushed us last night a few blocks away from the club, smashed into us from the side."

"Fuck, that was you? We heard there was a collision; the scouting team I sent out to find you when you didn't show reported back that the car involved was totaled. A lot of blood—human and vampire—on scene, but no bodies. The cops are looking for the occupants of both vehicles."

"Well, they're not gonna find any of us. Oberon took me to Antoine, and handed Vienna to one of his goons, Vadim-bound. He bragged to Antoine's men that he was delivering her to the Russian. Driving her from Tucson to a fleabag hotel in Phoenix, then a cargo flight to Russia tonight. I'm heading to the hotel now."

"You're still in Phoenix?"

I downshift, pushing the horsepower for additional speed. "I'm not leaving until Vienna's beside me, Lucius.

Antoine is dead. No resistance from his security team or the butler, but I'll get you up to speed on that when I have time. The Frenchman's base has been claimed as yours, so good luck with that. You'll need to get someone over there tonight, before all hell breaks loose." My boot presses the accelerator all the way down to the floor. "Antoine bought into the trafficking ring. Has been a partner for around six months. This shipment was a test of my loyalty to Vadim. I was passing with flying colors, by the way," I add with a smirk, "until Oberon grassed me up."

"Is Vadim in Phoenix?"

"No one has mentioned it. I can't discount the possibility, we both know he likes his fingers in all the pies, and he's a slippery fuck."

Lucius hums thoughtfully. "I need you to hold off, Colt. A solo mission at dawn is too risky. If Oberon is holed up in a hotel for the day, Vienna will be safe until dusk. I can't allow you to put yourself in danger for the girl without knowing what numbers you're up against. I have some connections in Phoenix who can be in place at the airport before the sun sets, and I'll mobilize a team from Tucson to travel through the day to be there. Just sit tight for the day, rest, and prepare for a battle. I'm sure Antoine was his usual gracious self."

I slam my hand against the wheel. "Don't ask that of me, Lucius. You wouldn't sit back and leave Selene to fend for herself. Vienna is still mortal, she's no match for Oberon or his goons."

"I would if I was confident she'd come to no real harm. I'm not asking you to step back, Colt; I'm making it a goddamn order. Vienna will be fine. She's a strong, resourceful young woman with more guts than any mortal

I've ever met. Give me the address of the hotel; I'll ask some friends of mine to keep watch."

I growl. If I refuse to obey his command, Lucius might just decide not to send reinforcements. Then I really will be screwed, and Vienna will be on a one-way flight to Russia. Not that I won't raze Russia to the fucking ground to find her, because I will, but I'm more concerned about what will be done to her in the time it takes me to infiltrate Vadim's complex. Grudgingly, I hand over the location of the hotel, and confirm the airport where Oberon plans on flying her out of the country.

"You've done all you can do for now. Get yourself to safety, Colt. Fifty years of hard work and your personal sacrifices are coming to a close. Tonight, we'll get your Vienna back and take a massive step forward in shutting Vadim down." The line goes dead.

As I hurtle into Phoenix, easing off the gas just enough to abide by the speed limits—getting pulled over by the cops in daylight is pretty much suicide—and navigating my way toward the hotel, I know I'm not going to be cozied up in a room somewhere, waiting for the sun to die. If Alex is right and this car is sun-proof, the UV rays unable to reach me, I'm parking this sucker right outside the front door and watching the exit like a fucking hawk.

I can't wait to get my hands on Oberon.

Luckily for me, I'll have all the time in the world to dispense of his sorry ass once Vienna is back where she belongs.

Lucky, lucky me.

~

VIENNA

. . .

I DID NOT GET FED, I was not given water.

When I come around, my head is throbbing, and my throat is on fire. My body is stretched out on the contaminated bedspread—double ick—with my limbs restrained to all four corners. Fabulous. And if that isn't bad enough, I'm stripped down to the skin. Not a stitch of clothing left on me.

Oberon is sulking in a chair to my left, scrolling through his phone like a petulant teenager. I hope he knows how hard Colt is going to murder him in the near future. My vampire is fiercely protective of me, and this scenario is the catalyst to kicking off World War V. There's a part of me *dying* to watch my man take the little shit apart, piece by agonizing piece.

Bloodthirsty, right? I like the rush.

Boris is nowhere to be seen. Maybe he's curled up in the bathtub, soaking his crushed testicles in cold water. I bet those suckers are swollen and bruised. Serves him right. I know vamps can't reproduce, what with being dead and all, but if he'd been human… I take a great deal of pride in knowing his stupidity genes would no longer be viable for breeding more idiots.

Ivan, however, is staring at me with pure hatred—out of one eye, of course. His left eye is covered by a makeshift patch. I'm assuming he lost it, considering the pop I felt and the amount of viscous fluid that followed. The way he's looking at me tells me he's just biding his time for an opportunity to pay me back.

The Russian will give him one, I'm sure. An eye for an eye and all that bull. I'm kind of surprised I haven't woken up missing my sight and my tongue, if I'm honest. I'm sure eyeballs and tongues aren't a requirement for breeding, not in Vadim's twisted little mind.

Then there's the devil himself, standing at the foot of the bed, studying his newest acquisition like a thoroughbred breeder at a horse auction. I wonder if my conformation meets his standards, then come to the conclusion that my physical attributes aren't vital to his operation. I could be limbless, brain dead, and bluer than the fucking sky, it wouldn't matter to him. It's not the package, it's the contents, and my veins are bursting with rich Rhesus-negative blood.

Those lifeless eyes meet mine, and the fucker grins like a shark. All teeth, no emotion. "Ah, the warrior wakes, finally. It might have been more convenient for you to remain sleeping while we transfer you to the plane, but no matter. There is no fun in this." He strokes his chin thoughtfully, then shrugs and checks his watch. "This time tomorrow, you will be settled into your new home, patiently waiting for the stud I have handpicked for your mating to fuck you. This is exciting, yes?"

"Wow," I croak, my voice cracking sharply as my muscles strain, "you could give a girl a chance to at least make the place feel like home."

"Such wit. Such fire. A shame both of these qualities will be extinguished." Vadim sets his hands on the bed on either side of my hips, obviously undeterred by the germs lurking in the fabric. Then again, what do dead guys have to fear from germs and bacteria? "You will be taken from the plane to my testing facility. You will undergo medical tests, fertility tests, and be injected with a tracker. Just in case you decide escaping is a viable option. It is not," he warns darkly.

"It is not," I mimic, rolling my eyes. I jerk my chin at him as he leans further over me. "Ever hear of personal space? Because you're encroaching on mine right now, and I don't appreciate it."

He narrows his eyes at me. "Bold, you are bold, yes? And unwise with the use of your tongue."

I bare my teeth at him in challenge. "I also bite, asshole. Wanna see?"

Laughing, Vadim braces himself on one hand and uses the other to fondle between my legs, tracing my labia and flicking my clit. His touch is cold and impersonal; it does nothing for me. Colt is the only one who inspires my body to rise to the occasion. One brush of his fingertip over my earlobe can make me come like a geyser, hot and wet. Compared to him, Vadim is little more than an abrasive annoyance who has his finger on my bitch switch. "You will not be given the opportunity to do so."

"There's always an opportunity," I purr sweetly, clenching my teeth together so tightly, I swear I hear one crack. He's getting more handsy now, those horrible fingers playing with my pussy as though he has every right to touch it. "Take your fat-fingered hand off me, you bloodsucking fuckwit, before I make you eat it."

Ivan steps forward, fists at the ready. Oh yeah, he wants revenge. "You want I should teach lesson, boss?"

"Calm yourself, Ivan. This little kitten has claws, yes? But so useless they are." Vadim lifts his hand to his mouth, wetting his fingers. "She thinks she is fearless, she is strong and powerful female." His tone is mocking; I want to rip his tongue out and wrap it around his neck like a bow tie. "But what is one thing all women fear? It is not dying, no. These creatures will die to defend the ones they love, so no, it is not fear of losing life." Shit, his accent is getting thicker by the word. "They fear the unwelcome touch. Being reduced to what they are—nothing but worthless cunts, used as they are meant to be used, as sheaths for the cock."

My situation is precarious, balancing on a very fine line

between life and death. Anything I say or do could result in losing non-vital parts of my anatomy. So what does my crazy brain order my mouth to do? Does it tell it to behave, to keep *shtum*? No, it does not. It fires the laughter cannons at full force. I can hardly breathe, I'm laughing so damn hard. "What freaking century were you turned in? *Sheaths for the cock*," I repeat with a howl of mirth. "Jesus, I'm a human being, you idiot, not a freaking fleshlight."

His expression turns thunderous. "No longer are you *human being*," Vadim snarls, the sound vibrating in his throat as though he's a rabid dog. I guess he's just that, a rabid Rottweiler off its chain, causing carnage. "No longer are you *woman*. You are nameless, faceless, *number*." His fingers shove into me, through the dryness, causing pain unlike anything I've ever felt before. It's worse than any broken bone or open gash in my skin. "This cunt belongs to me now. I choose what goes in it. What comes out is mine."

"Colt will kill you if I don't," I choke the words out on a wheezing sob. For the first time, my fearlessness wavers, straddling the line between collapsing in a violated heap, and gathering itself for a reckoning Vadim has no chance of withstanding. Somehow, I wasn't prepared for this, and now I'm paying the price for my naivety.

Still, even as I quail against the age-old terror the thought of rape brings to mind, I refuse to beg for mercy. I'll beg for nothing from this vampire, not even my life. There is nothing I can't survive if I'm strong enough. I have to tell myself that over and over as cold, dead fingers assault my insides. Breathing harshly through my teeth, I say, "And just in case you didn't know, *cunt* is a horrible and demeaning word. It's very offensive, y'know?"

His fingernails scrape along the sensitive tissues of my pussy, using sex as punishment. I squirm, trying to twist my hips to escape. "Your opinion means little. And as for your lover, you can forget about seeing him again. Traitors in my midst are removed with force. I hope you have something to remember him by, yes? Now that his ashes are all that remain of him."

It's the second time one of these monkeys has suggested Colt is dead, and the second arrow strikes my heart just as swiftly as the first. Barbs digging deep. Part of me believes what they say; I can't help it. Colt's been gone so long, it seems, without a word, without a sign. I hate how easily that part of me believes them. Yet the other half of me, the larger and more volatile side of me, stands up and hammers her fists on her chest and screams in protest at the lies they feed me.

Closing my eyes, I banish everything from my mind.

This will end soon. Nothing lasts forever, however long it drags on for. Be strong, stand firm, do not back down from your beliefs. Colt will come, sooner or later, and he will gut this spineless asshole if you don't get a chance to do so before he swoops in. Come on, Vienna, we've got this. You've already broken a nose, blinded one vampire, and kicked another so hard in the balls, he'll feel them every time he swallows for the next week.

They needed to tie me down to control me. Tie me down so I can't fight back, because they know I can hurt them every bit as much as they hurt me. Four vampires against one mortal woman, and the undead are scared. Oh, they can claim they're the superior breed, the unequalled sex, but I've proved I can take what they give me and bounce back.

My eyes pop open.

I am not a victim. I am not a ready-made meal. I sure as hell am not some breeding bitch to be used at Vadim's leisure.

The restraints on my wrists are thin leather bands, connected to the bed by sleek silver chains. I don't think I can snap the chains, the links are too well made, without any sign of weakness. But the leather bands... they may provide me with a get-out clause I wasn't expecting.

Ignoring the fire burning inside me—not the good kind —I focus on those strips of cowhide, concentrate on what I'm going to do when my hands are free. Unleashing the torrent of rage throttling me, I yank against the restraints, using the full range of motion the short lengths of chain offer me. More pain, self-inflicted this time, as the bands dig into my skin, ripping into me as I try my damnedest to snap the leather and free my hands.

As if controlled by the manic movements of my hands, my feet join in, kicking and lashing out. My entire body is alive, dancing in the hold of the chains, and Vadim doesn't know what the fuck to do with me. I free my voice, letting loose with a scream that claws at my throat with acid-tipped talons, deafening everyone in the room.

Oh yeah, I'm just that good.

There's an insane sense of relief when I feel Vadim withdraw from my sore pussy, even if the imprint of his goddamn fingers is etched into my vagina. Dismissing that for now, I suck in a breath to repeat my eardrum-shattering performance, and instead sink my teeth viciously into the meaty hand that slams over my mouth.

It tastes of salt and something disgustingly acrid. I want to vomit as the taste hits my tongue. Rather than hurling, I savage the hand mercilessly, chomping down several times in quick succession and shaking it in the way a terrier would a rat. Blood fills my mouth from the wounds I inflict, but I refuse to let go.

Ivan howls.

Oh, I'm on his shit list now, that's for damn sure.

"Enough!" Vadim bellows, his face turning an intriguing shade of reddish purple as he almost hops from foot to foot in temper. He looks like a very angry, substantially vindictive Russian gnome. He just needs the long beard and the stupid pointy hat to complete the illusion. "Ivan, get her ready to transport. The sun is dying, it's time to move. If she gives you trouble, knock her the fuck out. I'll deal with her when we arrive in Moscow."

Ivan pulls his hand away from my mouth, hissing as my teeth give him a farewell kiss. "My pleasure."

Oberon stands when the Russian snaps his fingers at him, his eyes wide and uncertain. He's probably wondering if bringing me to Vadim was such a good idea after all the trouble I'm causing. I want him to die for being an asshole and betraying Colt, for subjecting me to this pantomime of cruelty, but I don't want Vadim or Ivan to have the satisfaction of ending his miserable existence.

That's for me to do, and I already have ideas formulated as to how I can make it beautifully bloody.

"Oberon, get Boris down to the van. Make calls to the airport and check the plane is ready to take off upon our arrival. The moment she is secured in the hold, we fly." Vadim clenches his hand into a fist, then shoves it in his pocket. "Keep your eye out for any signs of the Tucson vampires. They should not know of our plans, but I take no chances. Kill anyone you recognize."

"Yes, sir." Without argument, the cowardly little weasel scurries toward the bathroom, disappearing inside and emerging with a dazed Russian minion in tow. Hell, I must really have rattled his balls if he still hasn't recovered from that kick. Vampire healing should have patched up his booboos already. "Time to go home, Boris."

They leave the room, leaving me alone with Ivan and Vadim, my two least favorite vampires in the whole fucking world. I glare at them both, baring bloodied teeth at them.

"Might want to kill me now. I'm really much more hassle than I'm worth. This? This has just been a taste of what I'm capable of, Vadim. I haven't even broken out the top weapons in my arsenal yet."

Ivan pounces.

13

Colt

If I remember correctly, humans revere Fridays. Fridays are the day of the week everyone wants to come around sooner than all the rest. It's the gateway to the weekend, to two nights of drinking and debauchery without worrying about going to work the next day with a hangover the size of Texas. It's the day of the short work hours, after-work drinks, and hitting the town with a paycheck in your pocket.

For me, this Friday has been the longest day of my goddamn life.

Stuck in the damn BMW as the sun rose higher in the sky and the heat grew to levels even I found uncomfortable. Praying fervently that whatever the car is treated with didn't suddenly dissipate and leave me sitting in the driver's seat as a pile of ash. Wanting so badly to charge across the street and kick in every door until I find Vienna.

I know she's close; I can sense her. A tingling down my spine, a little quiver of acknowledgement telling me she's almost within touching distance. I've caught myself gripping the door handle several times throughout the course of this excruciatingly long day.

The tedium has been broken up by a barrage of phone calls between myself and Lucius. True to his word, he's summoned help from whoever his contact is here, and I spotted three non-vampiric individuals in place before eight a.m. I think they're shifters; they carry themselves with the innate grace and athleticism I always associate with the feline kind. Whoever—whatever—they are, they haven't moved from their position since their arrival.

Lucius and Selene are already in the city. They arrived just after lunch with a small contingent of vampires from Lucius's territory. God knows what strings he's had to pull to get them to venture out into daylight—even with the protection of UV-resistant tinted windows in their vehicles, like the BMW possesses—but all that matters is that they're here and they're already in position around the airport. For security purposes and to avoid being spotted by anyone on Vadim's payroll, they're stationed close to the entrances and exits, ready to move in when we've identified the vehicle Oberon is using to ferry my girl around.

Thanks to my keen eyesight and boredom, I've already earmarked a truck parked in the lot around the side of the hotel as one of interest. From my position across from the front of the rundown building, I can just see the tail end of the truck. I'd lay money on the table that it's the same damn vehicle that brought me here.

The phone rings again as the sun tips down, sinking behind the buildings. It's almost showtime, and I'm more than ready to start. I answer curtly, keeping my eyes on the cracked glass doors. "Everything ready?"

"Eager to begin, Colt?"

"I could have had this over and done with hours ago," I point out, keeping the worst of my bark to a minimum. No reason to strike out at Lucius when he's bent over backwards today to not only provide me with support, but to travel to Phoenix to see this through himself. "I'm sick of waiting, sitting on my hands and feeling useless."

"I know. We're ready to go as soon as you give us the signal. The team has orders to capture Oberon if possible. I want more information, and he may have kissed enough ass to get a few details you couldn't. After that, he's all yours. I called in a favor with my contact. He's got connections of his own at the airport. The plane scheduled to leave for Russia is supposed to take off at nine p.m. It's been unexpectedly delayed by thirty minutes, forty if he can push it that far. If something goes wrong, we're on our own."

What he means is, if they get past us and load Vienna onto the plane once the delay runs out, we're fucked. The aircraft can take off without any more interference. We'll have to take the fight to Russia, onto Vadim's turf, where Lucius doesn't have the contacts we need. "It won't go wrong. I'll kill Oberon and every last lackey he's got with him if I have to. Vienna is not getting on that plane."

Movement catches my eye—the glass door swings out as the last of the sun's rays fade. A familiar and unwelcome face peers around the door, searching the surrounding area. Oberon's gaze skips over the BMW; I don't move. The tinted windows should keep me from view, but I'm not taking any chances. Not at this stage of the game. "Lucius, I have a visual on Oberon."

"You're sure it's him?"

"Positive I.D.," I confirm, narrowing my eyes as my former friend steps onto the sidewalk, dragging a short figure behind him. Male, forties, at a guess. Bald. I relay the information to Lucius as Oberon leads the man around to the parking lot. "They're heading for the vehicle. The unknown subject appears injured. Looks like someone's used his genitals for football practice."

"At a guess, I'd say your girl has handled herself well," Lucius comments.

Yeah, Vienna's trademark is written all over the pained waddle. I don't take my eyes off them as they round the corner of the building. Lucius is talking to someone on the other end of the line, so I ignore him for the moment. This is where it all begins.

Oberon's truck pulls out of the lot and swings around to the front of the hotel. I get a clearer look at it now than I did last night. "Lucius, Oberon is driving a black Dodge double cab pickup truck with a canopy bed. Solid canopy, no windows. There's a steel cage in the back. No sign of the companion he came out with, he might be in the backseat."

I fidget in my seat as Oberon exits the truck and heads back into the slummy hotel. I'm tempted to run over there and give the little shit the shock of his life. Minutes pass, with Lucius giving orders to the rest of the Tucson team. A quick glance shows me that the Phoenix support has vanished. I don't know if they've switched positions, or been called away completely now night has fallen. I suspect the latter.

My fangs lengthen in anticipation when Oberon walks out again, holding the door open. My heart tumbles down to my feet when Vadim steps out behind him, strolling nonchalantly to the truck and climbing into the passenger seat without a care in the world. "Fuck. The motherfucking Russian is here, Lucius. He's been here all goddamn day." Visions of what he's done to my vixen while I've sat twiddling my thumbs out here shred me.

"Keep ahold of yourself, Colt. Whatever's been done, we know he won't have harmed her too badly. She's too valuable for him to kill. Have you seen her yet?" The king is ruthlessly calm.

"No, I—she's there." My hands fist on the wheel as a man the size of a small mountain exits the building with a small form draped over one broad shoulder. Vienna isn't moving. Her legs are pinned by the guy's huge arm but as he strides to the rear of the truck, I see her arms swaying limply down his back. "She's out cold. They don't seem concerned about being seen with an unconscious woman in public. She's wearing the same clothes I last saw her in."

"Do not do anything rash. She'll be safely back in your care within the hour, but you need to keep your head in the game, and don't do anything stupid. Give them a slight head start then follow them at a safe distance. When they get to the airport, we'll have them surrounded. Just exhibit some of that renowned patience you're famous for."

Giant baldy dumps my girl in the cage and slams the door shut. I battle back the urge to smash his head against the sidewalk. He's in no rush as he wanders to the rear passenger door and climbs in, squeezing his bulk into the cab. No sooner than he closes the door, Oberon is settled in the driver's seat, and the truck pulls away smoothly.

The BMW purrs to life and I swing it in an illegal U-turn, cutting off a couple of cars that protest with a quick blast of their horns and a flipped bird or two out of the windows. Whatever; I don't care. My only goal now is staying on the heels of the truck. "Get ready, Lucius. ETA twenty minutes. I'll call you if they change direction."

"We're waiting," he replies. "It'll be over soon enough, Colt."

Not soon enough, I think as I end the call. It's difficult to abide by the rules of the road when I want to floor the gas and sit on Oberon's tail all the way to the airport. Drawing attention to myself that way would seriously fuck everything up, as would being pulled over by the cops, or doing something moronic like hitting a pedestrian or causing an RTA.

So I cruise along, keeping a dozen cars between the BMW and the Dodge as we join heavier traffic. I weave in and out, flowing with the humans going about their daily lives, not realizing blood-trafficking vampires are in their midst.

My hands flex on the wheel. I feel like I'm about to explode. All I can think about is Vienna in that fucking box, being shipped from pillar to post, alone. Has Vadim touched her? Is she hurt, in pain, scared? It doesn't matter that I saw her unconscious. She might have come to now, she might be awake and bewildered, wondering where she is and why I haven't come for her yet.

Worse, she could be grieving. Who knows what that arrogant little fuck has told her. Oberon uses everything and anything at his disposal to get things to go his way. That he might lie to Vienna, crushing her world, isn't far-fetched. I know he would take great delight in telling her I'm dead. Fuck, he probably believes I am. He dropped me off at Antoine's mansion with the specific intention, and the knowledge that the Frenchman had designs on my life.

I'm almost beside myself by the time the truck bypasses the turn-off to the airport parking lot, winding its way around to the private runway at the back reserved for the holier-than-thous of flying. It means Vadim can skip the usual customs frustrations and load Vienna straight onto the plane. He pays those in his pocket a lot of money for this privilege, and he's smuggled a lot of people in and out of the US this way. It wouldn't surprise me if he's lined the wallets of a few senators and lower ranking politicians to keep this stage of his operation quiet.

I hang back for a moment, giving Oberon time to pull ahead and stop beside the aircraft waiting on the tarmac. As the occupants of the Dodge disembark, I gun the engine and charge down onto the runway with a screech of tires and the smell of rubber burning, noting with relief the two butch SUVs following me. I hit the brakes, veering to a halt ten feet in front of the nose of the plane, and throw myself from the car.

"What the fuck are you doing here?" Oberon demands. His pale complexion is almost transparent when he sees exactly who it is interrupting their schedule. He backs away several steps, attempting to shield himself with the giant bald guy who manhandled my woman. "I left you with Antoine! You should be fucking dead!"

I cock my head. "Should be. Obviously, I'm not."

Lucius and Selene climb out of the first SUV, flanked by another four vampires. Tiberius and Augustus are two of the faces I know best. The others, including another five sliding out of the second SUV, are vaguely familiar. It makes the good guy total a substantial twelve against Vadim's four.

I like those odds.

The Russian stands behind the wall comprised of Oberon and the other two. The expression he's wearing does not bode well for Obe. "Ivan, get the girl. You know where she goes."

I quiver, stepping forward with blood in my eye. The

waddling goon, not quite as incapacitated as when I last saw him, struts toward me with the cockiness I've come to expect from Vadim's choice of manual labor. He likes them dumb, capable of taking orders, but he never hires a vampire smarter than he is. Not unless he has something to hold over their head to use as control.

"Tell Ivan to leave Vienna where she is, Vadim. Tiberius will get her from the truck." My voice is calm, surprisingly, but my tone is straight from the arctic. "You signed your own death warrant with this stunt. Oberon's, as well. Antoine, well, he paid the price for his part this morning when I twisted his head clean off his shoulders. Don't think I won't do the same, and worse, to you."

"Traitor. Years I train you down drain." Oh, he's losing his temper. He drops words and thickens the accent when his emotions get the best of him. It must be a Russian thing. "Boris, deal with annoyance. We have plane to catch."

I curl my lip at Boris in challenge. I'm ready to shed blood, and he's just moved to the top of my list. I let him land the first blow, a stunning uppercut under my jaw that sets me back a step. Wiggling my jaw, nodding in appreciation of the strength he put behind the punch, I grin at him. "My turn, Boris."

None of the vampires at my back have made a move to interfere. Lucius will want to get his hands on Vadim and Oberon, but this little shit and the taller version of him edging around to the rear of the truck, are what I class as expendable.

I crack my fist into his soft jaw, spinning Boris in a half-circle. Like an animal, I leap and land on his back, wrapping my arm around his neck and choking him. Driving him down to his knees, I switch my grip. He's off-balance, struggling to gain his feet again and regain the upper hand. In two quick moves, I snap his neck, thrilled by the sharp crunch of vertebrae. My muscles bunch as I behead my second vampire of the day.

"Vienna will be handed over to us, and you're going to surrender to Lucius. You're old news, Vadim. You're outnumbered. This little cloud hopper of yours won't be jetting off into the sky, so give me my girl."

Vadim lifts his hand in the air. "Outnumbered? I think not, boy. My men on US soil are loyal to me. Take look around, yes? Many vampires wanting taste of Colt blood for his traitorous actions."

Fuck. I didn't foresee this. From the hangar behind us, I count eight vamps. That evens the score a bit. Already half of our team are peeling off, heading to intercept the new arrivals. "Eight or eighty, you're not taking Vienna." I reach out and grab the front of Oberon's shirt, tossing him behind me to land at Lucius's feet.

It's the sign we've been waiting for.

Tiberius beelines for the truck; I go for Vadim. As bodies clash and collide, I stalk the Russian like a wolf. He bolts into the plane, blurring up the steps. I chase him, determined to collar him and bring him to justice. I hate leaving Vienna in another vampire's care, but if she's not on the plane, stuffed into a tiny crate, she's safe.

The craft is opulent, mirroring Vadim's garish taste.

He's trying to lock himself in the cabin. Does he have his pilot's license? In all the time I've known him, he's never driven or flown himself anywhere. That's what people like me are for—to cater to his every whim. People to drive him, fly him, sail him wherever he wishes. Girls to kiss his shoes and suck his cock. Men to throw themselves in harm's way to protect the Russian Avtoritet.

Vadim lives for others to serve him, or so he believes.

Amped up on the thrill of the chase, I throw my head back and roar. Part warning, part elation, it should tell the Russian I'm not in the mood to fuck around. I'm going to take the greatest pleasure in beating his ass until he's broken and bruised and bloody, even if I have to hand his worthless carcass over to Lucius for interrogation when I'm done. I'm kinda hoping I've proved my loyalty to my king enough that he'll let me do the honors and dust the bastard.

But first, I have to get him out of the cockpit.

Rearing back, I slam my boot against the door, testing it. Decent thickness, strong lock. It shakes and rattles under the pressure, but holds. *Not for long*, I think grimly, baring my teeth. If Vadim thinks a sheet of wood will stop me, he's underestimated my intense loathing for him. I kick again, hearing the wood crack. Again, again, until my foot forces a crack to open almost from top to bottom.

"Always knew you were a coward, Vadim. Cornered yourself good and proper this time. Should've made a run for it across the tarmac, you'd have had better odds of getting away." My tone is conversational as I smash through the broken door and cross the threshold into the cockpit. Then I laugh and raise my eyebrow. "Go ahead and shoot me. It'll hurt like a motherfucker, but it won't stop what's already in motion."

"You! You ruin *everything*," he spits, pointing a shiny revolver at my chest. Sometimes I wonder if he forgets that the people he works with, tortures, kills, aren't always human. A bullet to the chest would indeed sting like a motherfucker, but even if the bullets are silver, they're not going to kill me. "Years upon years of research and energy have gone into this business, and you... you traitor with your lies, you bring all crashing down."

"Not yet, but I will. Tell me, Vadim, how many humans

do you hold captive? How many undeserving creatures are tormented and experimented on, bred like animals so you can make your millions? No point in evading the question," I tell him, ignoring the gun as though it doesn't exist. "It's about damn time I got some answers."

"Answers!" he harrumphs. "The traitor wants answers. Fine. I have five thousand, eight-hundred and seventy-six humans in the breeding program. Five of them are true Rhonulls. One female, four male. Two females now I have this one you call Vienna."

"How many have you kidnapped, believing they're Rhonulls?"

He shrugs. "Who knows. We try breeding them but pregnancies unviable. We try cloning, but they die. Has become more profitable marketing the useless curs as Rhonulls and selling them to vampires like Antoine. Many do not know difference between Golden Blood and what we provide. Others so desperate to believe they have the finest of food, they do not question. More still are too scared to offer query."

Jesus Christ, it's something out of a science fiction movie. Cloning, breeding, and all the while, it's the vampire world's biggest con. Five Rhonulls—six with Vienna—and the rest are nothing but normal mortals. Sold in a tight fist of fear, pulling in more money than several countries' economies combined, and the whole fucking thing is a lie. "You'll tell Lucius everything. We're going to systemically rip your organization out by the roots and burn the sordid mess to the ground, Vadim."

He grins at me. "You think so, tough guy?"

I hear the whine of the plane door closing, and freeze. There's a battle going on beyond the walls of the plane, vampire fighting vampire, and I have no way of knowing who's winning. My money is on Lucius and the Tucson vampires. They do, after all, have a secret weapon in the form of Selene. She loves to fight, and taking prisoners is not her *modus operandi*. So who the fuck is on the plane with us?

I don't dare risk a glance. One wrong move and Vadim will switch our positions faster than I can blink.

"Ivan, good boy. Has she woken yet?"

My blood turns cold. It's not possible. It's not. Tiberius is a fucking beast, there's not a chance he got his ass handed to him by the big bald goon wearing an amateurish eye patch. I'm already moving, spinning in place to discover that, yes, it is actually possible. What the hell am I supposed to do now? I can deal with two-on-one odds, but not when Vienna is collateral damage in the middle of the most epic clusterfuck I've ever faced.

She's alive. I can see her chest rise and fall as Ivan holds her in his arms. There are bruises and ligature marks on her pale skin, but no sign of the broken arm she had when I last saw her. Oberon fed her his blood. It's the only explanation. Yet another reason to cave his head in.

"No, boss. Out cold."

Not quite. My little vixen isn't as unconscious as she'd like him to think. There's the subtle twitch of her finger, a slight movement of her eyelid. Damn, she's good. "What did you do to Tiberius?"

One dead eye fixes on me, and the vampire smirks. "Nothing at all. Pussy ran off."

I growl, my hands fisting by my sides. There's got to be more to the story, this asshole is just winding me up, but I swear on everything unholy, if Tiberius left her undefended and landed me in this position, he and I are going to go several rounds. I trusted him with her, to get her away from this mess, and instead, she's right in here with me.

Vadim laughs. "Careful laid plan go awry, Colt? Shame."

"Oh for fuck's sake, man, you're Russian with an excellent grasp of the English language," I snap, whirling back to face him. I'm ready to blow, clinging onto control with my fingertips. I just need Vienna out of my fucking way so she doesn't get sucked into the bloodshed. "Either talk like an educated vampire or shut the fuck up."

My former boss struts up to me, braver now he has his minion to hand. In a swift strike, he smashes the butt of the revolver into my face, cracking my cheekbone. Blood fills my mouth as the inside of my cheek splits. "You have never given me orders, Colt. Do not presume to start now."

I chuckle and spit an arc of vibrant red onto the immaculate cream carpet of his plane. "I had to kiss your ass for fifty years, Vadim. No more. I know exactly what you're capable of, but do you have any idea of what *I'm* going to do to you before tonight's over?" I spit again, inwardly cursing him. "You've had the lapdog at your disposal; now meet the wolf."

He backs off slightly, studying me. "One bullet, and your woman's life comes to an end, Colt. Is that what you want? Don't worry, I wouldn't waste all that precious blood that way," he assures me with a cold smile. "But I'd be happy to drink every last drop while you watch."

Staring into his unemotional eyes, understanding he thinks he's won, I say the only thing I can. The honest thing. "I'll kill her myself before I let you have her, Vadim. I'd rather see her dead than live a day knowing she's trapped with you and your ilk."

The barrel of the gun jabs sharply into the flesh beneath my chin. "This is good. You won't live to see another day. Ivan, strap the girl in and get us off the ground before the Tucson King attempts to board. I'll handle Mr. Dockery. Turn around and walk to the rear of the plane, Colt."

"You fire that thing in here, you're gonna put a hole in the plane," I advise him, lifting my hands as he digs the barrel deeper into my jaw. If he presses the trigger now, I might not die, but I sure as hell am going to be messed up for the rest of eternity.

Hands behind my head, I wait for him to lower the gun. Vadim does, glaring at me and gesturing for me to obey. I follow the order because it's all I can do at the moment. He'd put a bullet in Vienna to teach me a lesson. Not a lethal wound, but one to cause her pain and incapacitate me. Slowly, I turn around and wait as the one-eyed baldy tightens the safety harness around Vienna.

Ivan grunts with satisfaction, then shoves past me to get to the cockpit. Our shoulders connect, and I deliberately let myself get knocked off balance, stumbling forward with my hands leaving my head to keep me from falling flat on my face. A foot kicks me in the ass, a warning to get moving. I take a moment, acting as though I hit my head and I'm dazed.

Taking the gun out of the equation is the priority. It poses too much danger to everyone, and Vadim is a wild card. If I can disarm him, I can take him down and then go for Ivan, but I need to work quickly. Once the plane is off the ground, we're screwed. I can't fly a plane, and I'm fairly sure Vienna can't either. I'd have to use the gun to force Ivan to land us safely.

The engines whine and rumble to life just as I hear people banging on the door. Lucius can't help us now, and I've got only a couple of minutes before the goon sets the plane in motion. The BMW is parked right in front of us, but he'll find a way around it, I'm sure.

Trudging down the narrow aisle, I pause before I reach the small area at the back where the toilet and a small bedroom are located. Frowning thoughtfully, I face Vadim again, noting the position of the gun and how eager his finger is on the trigger. "How are you going to smuggle Vienna into Russia if she's inside the plane rather than stashed in the hold? I doubt they'll just let you waltz into Moscow with an American woman who hasn't got a passport in her possession."

He shrugs. "Money buys people."

I nod slowly. "Yeah, I'm beginning to understand that. Everything comes down to money for you, doesn't it?"

"Why spend an eternity living in the gutter when living like a king is much more preferable?"

It's got to be now. The plane is shuddering, building up power as the engines grow stronger. I can't hold off any longer. I nod slowly, as though processing the bullshit Vadim keeps spewing from his mouth, then rub the back of my hand under my nose. "I guess we spend our time building our future on the pain of someone else. I wonder what I can build on yours."

Vadim's eyes widen and he lifts his weapon, trying to aim for my face. I bat it aside, one hand grabbing the gun, trying to twist it from his hold as my other snatches the front of his shirt and yanks him forward. I slam my forehead into his face sharply, and wrestle the gun free.

From the front of the plane comes a warbling battle cry, female and pissed. I haven't even seen Vienna get up from her chair, but she's causing chaos in the cockpit. There's a lot of shouting, both hers and Ivan's, but I've got my own enraged vampire to deal with.

I've never seen Vadim in a fight. He's not the brawling type, or so I thought. Too fat, too slow, too absorbed in his own greed to keep fit. Apparently that's not going to stop him from attempting to kick my ass from one end of the plane to the other.

We exchange a flurry of blows that leave us both bloody. I have the advantage of being fit, strong, experienced. Vadim is counting on his need to survive to see him through as victor. Luck might fall on his side—he lands a trio of jabs that leave me reeling and bruised, blood dripping down my chin where my fangs cut my lip.

Undeterred, I plow my fist into his sternum, following with a right hook that's slightly off the mark. There's no fucking room to move freely in this damn aisle. He staggers back, then gathers himself and charges, using his compact body as a battering ram to force me back. The impact takes me off my feet for a moment and sends me skidding, but I'm up again in seconds and diving straight back into the fray.

Livid doesn't come close to what I'm feeling. Anger surges through my veins as I look into his beady, colorless eyes and allow myself to think—for the briefest moment—what he's done to Vienna in the short time he had her in his possession. I know how he treats captives, how he sees the slaves he takes. They're nothing to him, and he thinks he can do what he wants to them.

I know he did something to my vixen.

Blood blossoms across my knuckles as I ram my fist into his face, over and over. My fury blurs my vision, smearing red over his features until there's nothing left but blood.

Vienna screams.

~

Vienna

Playing dead is actually really exhausting. Apparently, the human body has a way of reacting to things, and it takes a lot of energy to quell those natural urges so you don't give yourself away before it's time. Breathing, for example. Keeping your lungs working slowly, rhythmically, is really freaking difficult when you're trying not to have a panic attack.

I don't know if I made the right choice pretending to be still KO'd when the one-eyed jackass scooped me out of the small dark box, but I made it nonetheless. I could have let him drag me out kicking and screaming, but the likelihood is, he'd have just knocked me out again and I'd have remained useless for another period of time.

This way, I have the element of surprise.

I know I'm on a plane when I squint my eyes open. Colt's presence is a big fluffy blanket around my shoulders, and all I want to do is hug him close when I sense him passing by me with the Russian freak behind him. The urge to help him is strong, but he can take care of himself. I don't want him worrying about me while he deals with the big bad boss.

My concern is the fact the plane is alive and preparing for takeoff. Somehow, I know it's imperative this bird doesn't take wing, and while I can't fly a plane to save my life—no pun intended—I am an expert at devolving situations into absolute carnage. Buying time is probably the only thing I can do. I should open the doors and let Lucius and his crew on board, but I don't have time to waste figuring how to open them, not to mention it's a dead giveaway that I'm not strapped in my seat like a good little hostage.

I creep forward toward the cockpit, noting the smashed door. I'm pleased I'm not naked, even if being dressed means Ivan and company had their fat, dirty hands on my body again. When this is over, I'm showering for a week minimum to eradicate their touch off my skin. My pussy may need to be bleached and disinfected to get rid of the haunting sensation of Vadim's fingers inside me.

That's a trauma for another day.

Ivan sits in the pilot's chair, flicking switches and doing whatever is needed to set the plane into motion. There's an angry voice coming over the radio, telling him he doesn't have permission for takeoff, there are delays, and ordering him to shut down the engines.

I suck in a breath and, with a battle cry that should land me a part in the next big fantasy action film, launch myself at the asshole I hate with every beat of my heart. I lead with my hands, fingers curled into claws, and attack his face like I'm the titular character from *Edward Scissorhands*. Skin rips under my nails, blood running down Ivan's face before he manages to get his big hands wrapped around my wrists. I lunge forward, sinking my teeth into his neck.

See how you like it, bloodsucker.

He howls and throws me back against the console. Buttons and levers slam into my back, almost crippling me as my pain receptors go crazy. Alarm bells start to ring; Ivan curses. There's not a lot of room to maneuver in here. My head smacks sharply into the window opposite him as he hauls me away from the console and tosses me aside.

Dazed, I watch him try to fix whatever we just broke as I catch my breath. I'm sprawled in the co-pilot's seat, blurred vision raking over the buttons and screens. Might as well make things harder for him, right? I lean forward and start hitting every button I can see, flipping switches and spinning dials.

Ivan shouts in Russian, backhanding me.

I collapse back into the seat. The whole damn dashboard is lit up with warning lights. I lean back and lift my foot, my trusty boot ready to send Ivan's tiny brain into fits of anarchy. Grinning, tasting blood on my tongue, I batter my heel into the control center in front of me, smashing the screens, cracking plastic. I kick at the steering column, the joystick, whatever it's called, bending it at a weird angle.

Something hisses nastily, smoke beginning to plume from within the control panel.

Mission accomplished.

The vampire stands, face alive with fury. Beneath his skin, something writhes, distorting his features. Maybe I'm imagining it, but I don't think so. He bares his fangs, snarling harshly as his remaining eye glows red. I've really pissed him off. I have an instant to wonder if Colt looks this way, if his demon surfaces when he's so mad he can't contain himself, before Ivan snatches me up by the throat.

Smoke isn't just pluming now. It's billowing, filling the cockpit and stealing oxygen I need to breathe. Whatever I did, I fucked things up big time. Maybe I overloaded something, blew the electrics, I don't know. I'm not a freaking aircraft electrician.

Coughing, my voice strangled by his fingers, I blow Ivan a kiss. "Colt's going to kill you, by the way."

Glass shatters as Ivan quite literally shoves me through the window. There's a huge *what the fuck* moment as I feel material and flesh slice open, cut to ribbons by the jagged edges of what remains of the glass. I have a second to admire his strength—these windows are designed to withstand being hit by birds and shit while flying along in the sky—before the pain envelopes me.

I don't know if I scream.

I know I'm falling.

I barely feel it when I hit the ground.

When I die, my last thought is of Colt.

14

Colt

Leaving Vadim in a bloody heap on the floor, I leap over his prone form and run toward the cockpit. Smoke fills the small space and drifts into the main cabin, carrying the unpleasant odor of electrical burning. I don't know what the hell Vienna has done now, but she's set the goddamn plane on fire.

The banging on the door has stopped. I don't pause for even the few seconds it would take to open it.

That scream was unlike anything I've heard from my vixen. It reverberates in my head, sharp and shrill, and there's a sick sense of dread in my gut telling me my world's just gone to shit in ways I can't fathom.

A figure lurches from the cockpit, parting the smoke. Too big, too broad to be Vienna, it can only be Ivan. I meet him in the smoke, not hesitating to make the first move. He grunts, shocked, as I drive my stiffened fingers into the soft spot beneath his sternum, pouring every ounce of strength into it. I punch through cloth, through skin and muscle, delving deep enough to locate his unbeating heart.

Merciless, I wrap my fingers around it and rip it free, brandishing it in front of him. "Where's Vienna?"

He blinks at me stupidly. We can survive without a heart; we don't need it, after all, but it must be a shock to see his own organ in my hand. The blood dripping down my arm is no longer his—centuries of drinking from humans means the blood we hold in our veins is far from original. His eye is wide, stunned, darting from my face to the heart and back again. "The fuck did you do?"

"Where's Vienna?" I repeat, aware of the smoke deepening around us. There are sirens whirring to life; there'll be a fire truck here in minutes to contain the plane before it bursts into flames. "Last chance, cyclops."

He wets his lips and offers a pained grunt, lifting his hand to the gaping wound in his chest. "Bitch took a header out the window."

Window? What window? Oh, Christ. The window in the cockpit?

Frantic, I shove past him, diving into the dense smoke, shouting her name. Some of the smoke is exiting through the smashed sheet of glass to my left; there's blood everywhere. I can smell it, smell *her,* even through the stink of burning circuits. I hear shouts from below, a cacophony of noise that makes me want to throw up. So much urgency in those voices, until one voice rises above them all.

Silence follows suit.

I slam the heart in my hand onto a sharp splinter of wood on the broken door. It crumbles to ash, and I barrel through Ivan as the rest of his body disintegrates. I'm numb, horribly numb from the head down as I stagger and fall against the outer door, fumbling with the locking system. It pushes out, swings aside, allowing a wash of hot air to sweep inside the smoke-choked cabin, then I'm clattering down the steps and running toward the crowd at the front of the plane.

The scent of her blood is stronger here. Crisp, fresh, even with the smell of fuel and exhaust fumes in the air.

I shove through the wall of vampires, only for someone to catch my arm and stop me in my tracks. I snarl loudly enough to turn heads, but Lucius doesn't relinquish his grip. He shakes his head slowly, his expression somber. Sorrowful. "Colt."

"Get out of my way, Lucius."

He sighs heavily, lifts his hands clear. "For what it's worth, I'm sorry." Stepping aside, he begins giving orders.

The world dies. It's the only way I can describe it. Every last ray of light is sucked into the darkness. Color loses its sheen and becomes shadow. My mind is a rabbit warren of silence. Thought, reasoning, comprehension… all gone.

My vixen lies on the tarmac, body twisted and bloodied. A pool of blood, the very thing we've been fighting to save, surrounds her. Deep gashes bisect her legs, her back, her arms. I can heal them, I know I can. I'll give her every last drop of blood in my veins to fix this.

Dropping to my knees beside her, I gather her gently into my arms. "I'm here, V. I'm here. I'm gonna make this all better, I promise. Just stay with me, okay?" I stroke my thumb over her cheek. Those beautiful, sassy blue-gray eyes are wide open, blank. Already clouding over. "I can fix this."

"Colt, honey. I'm sorry. I'm so sorry." Selene's tiny hand rests on my wrist, squeezing gently. "The authorities are coming. We have to go. Let me take her."

"No! There's still time." But there's not, and I know it, deep down inside. The sirens are screaming, mirroring what's inside me as I realize Vienna is at the point of no return. "There's still time to turn her."

There's movement all around me. Vehicle doors opening and slamming shut. The damn airplane engines are still rumbling away, labored and grinding now. The smoke is thick and harsh, but I don't give a damn. Let the fucking thing blow us all to kingdom come.

"Selene, get in the car. Tiberius, Augustus, bring Colt. No arguments, Colt," Lucius shuts me down efficiently. "We need to move now before we all get arrested. I can try my best to turn her, but the head wound is severe. She may not come back as the Vienna you know and love, if at all. But we'll have to do it on the move."

I growl as he tries to take her body. "She's mine. I'll turn her."

Strong arms bind me, pin me as Lucius plucks Vienna from my lap and walks off with her toward one of the hulking SUVs. I go into a blind rage, fighting two of Lucius's eldest sired with everything I've got, but I'm no match for them, even fueled by grief. They drag me effortlessly to the SUV, and shove me in beside Lucius.

Augustus folds himself into the driver's seat as Tiberius takes the passenger side. Selene is perched behind her mate, looking devastated. The engine revs, then we peel away from the runway with the second SUV on our tail.

"There's only a minute left in your window of opportunity. I can tell you the odds are greater for success if you allow me to try, but it's your call. Take into account what damage the fall may have done to her brain, Colt. The change cannot heal something as complex as the brain if it's too badly damaged." Lucius lays my broken girl back in my arms, and for the first time, I can see the head injury as we pass beneath the lights flashing by. Her skull took the brunt of the fall. "Give her as much blood as you can spare. She'll need it."

I stroke her hair as memories filter back into my brain. It hasn't even been a fucking week of knowing her, and she's woven herself into the threads of my life so tightly, there's only one option left for me if this doesn't work. I've spent six hundred years and change being a bad man, trying to redeem myself. Six hundred and plus years of being alone.

Until Vienna.

I don't want to spend an eternity alone, not now I know what I'll be missing. I can't get through every day, thinking of her, missing her, loving her until I bleed from the wounds in my heart.

I kiss her forehead, her nose, her lips. Raising my wrist to my mouth, I sink my fangs in deep, bringing blood to the wounds. Praying with my last shred of hope, I press my wrist to her mouth, tipping her head back so my blood goes down her throat. "If this doesn't bring her back, or it brings her back wrong, I'm done, Lucius. I played my part for you, the trafficking ring can be shut down with the information Vadim gives you. If this goes wrong, I want you to promise you won't stop me."

My friend regards me with hard eyes. I can see his thoughts spinning all the angles, foreseeing the ramifications of agreeing. Then his eyes soften, and he nods once. "In your place, I don't know if my life would be worth living either. I give you my word, Colt."

"Lucius!" Selene protests sharply.

"Shush. This is Colt's decision to make, Selene. I'll honor it, whatever happens."

For the next hour, as Lucius makes phone calls and

argues with Selene in a low voice, I repeatedly bite my wrist, opening the wounds over and over again. I feed Vienna my blood, willing it to speed through her veins and bring her back to life. Over and over again, until my eyelids grow heavy and I can barely keep my arm raised.

Some would say I've given her too much. I say I haven't given her enough. If needs be, I'll wring myself dry to offer her the best chance of coming back to me healthy and whole.

"Lucius?" I mumble.

"Colt."

"Did you figure out how she broke your thrall?"

He hums thoughtfully. "Not officially, no. My best guess is she's an exception to most mortals. I have a theory that her blood type may have something to do with it. I've been researching Rhesus-negative blood, and there are some theories that Rhonulls aren't of this world. In my opinion, I don't think she's an alien, but I think there's a possibility that those with her blood aren't strictly human either. What they are, or were, is something decidedly powerful. Without studying others, I can't see how we'll get a definitive answer."

I laugh, but it comes out as more of a hum-slash-grunt. "Told you my girl's special." I have to enunciate the words one by one because my tongue feels oddly thick. Vienna still isn't moving, so I force my wrist to my mouth again, but then I'm baffled as it's pulled away gently. "What?"

"Enough is enough, Colt. You've fed her more blood than you can afford to lose. All we can do now is wait and see if Vienna will survive." Lucius sets my arm down, draping it over Vienna's body. There's a shadow of doubt in his eyes. "It takes time for the changes to take effect. There's a lot of damage to heal, on top of the transformation itself.

Realistically, I don't know if we can give her the odds she needs."

I don't want him to talk anymore. His words stab at me when I'm already at my lowest point. If he doesn't speak, my greatest fear won't come to life. In the silence of the SUV, I can con myself into believing Vienna is only resting in my arms, beginning the ascension from mortal to vampire. Shedding her humanity to blossom into an immortal.

Becoming what I am so she can spend forever with me.

I know the odds. As much as I deny it, I know there's only a slim chance she'll wake up. Her body is stiff and cold, I can't sense even a trace of what makes Vienna the woman she is. Her essence is gone, her spark snuffed out. Surely, if my blood was working, I'd be able to feel her... some part of her.

What's worse is that I cut her odds considerably. I'm starting to hate that word. *Odds*. Where there are odds, there should be evens. I destroyed her shot at an even by refusing Lucius's offer to help, by turning down the most experienced sire of my acquaintance. I don't know what I was thinking. I honestly don't.

The SUV is as quiet as a hearse for the remainder of the journey back to Tucson. My eyes are closed, my brain on hiatus. My energy levels are zero, my heart feels as though it's trapped in the spiked jaws of an Iron Maiden, and my arms refuse to relinquish their hold on my girl for even a second. It's like if I shift my grip an inch, she'll know, and think I'm letting her go.

I've killed three vampires tonight with my bare hands—beheaded two, and ripped the heart from the chest of the third. My hands are covered in blood, my clothes are soaked with it. After tonight, my reputation will either lurk in the toilet, or be raised high on a pedestal. It's inconsequential now. The life I had in mind for after we took Vadim down is evaporating by the second.

I think I'm dozing when the vehicle slows, idles. Lucius issues orders quietly, barely more than a murmur.

"Selene, my dear, why don't you go with Tiberius and check Colt's room is ready? He needs to feed and then rest. Augustus and I will be right behind you." It's not a request, hardly anything is with Lucius, but it continues to amaze me how gentle he is with his mate. "It's been a long night and it's not over yet."

I shake my head, realizing my friend has brought us back to his home. Few people come here as guests, so I guess I should be honored, but I need to take Vienna *home*. She needs to be in our bed, wrapped in the covers we've spent so much time rolling in, on, and under. When she wakes, I want her to have the scent of us in her nose, and familiar surroundings in view. "Take us home, Lucius. Please."

"No. If there's trouble, I'd like to be at hand. Vienna lost her life through mistakes we made. She should never have been put in that position. It doesn't detract from her bravery or her sacrifice. Staying close by is the least I can do for her." Lucius shifts in his seat, facing me directly as Selene slips out of the vehicle, with Tiberius sticking to her side.

My lip curls slightly. Sure, the fucker can glue himself to his queen, but when I need him to protect my vixen, he's nowhere to be seen. I haven't forgotten he's part of the catalyst that led us to where we are now. If he'd done as I'd asked and retrieved Vienna from Oberon's truck, she wouldn't have been on the plane. Her frail human body wouldn't have been slammed through a window two inches thick and left to plummet twenty feet to the unforgiving tarmac below.

No, she'd be sitting here with me, telling me all about her adventures and how she kicked vampire ass. She'd be laughing and vibrant and *alive.*

"Tiberius followed *my* order, Colt," Lucius says. "Before you blame him for this, you should know the choice was taken out of his hands. Selene was pinned between four of Vadim's men. After you vanished into the plane on Vadim's heels, more Russian scum came out of the hangars, and we were outnumbered. They got Selene on the ground and were trying to drag her off. I was too far away to help. Tiberius went to her aid, at the cost of abandoning Vienna. It wasn't his fault."

Bullshit. Selene is one of the most formidable females I've ever encountered. In a fight, she is phenomenal. Even four vampires would pose little issue to her. But I'm too tired to argue. The tiny flames of fury are easily extinguished, pathetically so. I suppose the truth is, I'm not mad at anyone but myself.

I did this. I dragged Vienna into this mess, kidnapped her into a world she had no right being in, and failed her.

"I don't want to talk about this, Lucius. I can't even think about it. You have Oberon, you have Vadim. I'm done with this shit. My job is done. Vadim has five true Rhonulls, and thousands of failed breeding experiments that need rehabilitating. It's down to you now." *Because I don't give a fuck about anything anymore.*

My door opens, courtesy of Augustus. The expressionless vampire waits patiently for further orders.

"We'll talk once you've taken the time to eat and rest. Let Augustus take Vienna, Colt. You're in no fit state to carry her, and there's no point dropping her, is there? He'll take care of her until we get inside. You know him," Lucius reminds me firmly. "None of us are the enemy here, and no one is going to take her away."

I look down at her. She doesn't look like Vienna anymore, not with the pallor of her skin, the almost rubbery texture of her face. Death might be beautiful, but only when it's fresh. In those first few minutes where the body provides the illusion of still being connected to the world, death is glorious. I like to imagine those minutes as the transition, that period of time when a person walks into the light, or relives their best memories.

I hope I was among Vienna's last memories.

Augustus reaches in slowly, sliding his hands under Vienna's body, pausing when my fangs flash at him. When I don't rip his face off, he continues, lifting her with more care than I expect from a vampire his size. He treats her as though she's made of glass. For a long second, Vienna is stuck to me. A copious amount of dried blood acts as a bonding agent between her clothes and mine.

"She should have a bath." It's the most inane thought, but suddenly it's the most important thing on my list of to-dos.

No one wants to be reborn covered in the blood of their old life.

"Of course. I'll see to it. Do you think you can stand, Colt?"

I swing my legs out of the car, set my feet on the ground. I haven't felt this goddamn weak since I rose from my grave wearing my burial clothes and spitting out cemetery dirt. Standing proves difficult, my knees giving out so abruptly, I have to grab the door for support.

Lucius is beside me in an instant, his arm around my lower back. I'm so damn grateful he hasn't decided carrying me is a less troublesome option. He guides me toward the house, slower than a snail. I really need something to eat before I do something stupid, like pass out. I poured everything I am into bringing Vienna back, now I'm paying the price.

One foot in front of the other. Sounds easy enough. A moron could do it.

Not three steps away from the SUV, I go down like a ton of bricks, out cold.

~

REALITY HASN'T IMPROVED by the time I open my eyes.

I'm flat on my back in bed, my chest bare and clean. Someone's gone out of their way to wash me and apparently dress me—that's an affirmative, I confirm, peering under the light blanket covering me from the waist down—in silk lounging pajama bottoms. Lucius's, obviously. I can't think of anyone else who would wear these damn things.

Selene is sitting prettily at the end of the bed, her long white hair braided. The fiercest of watch dogs on duty.

Looking around the room, it appears I've been stashed away in one of the guest bedrooms. Expertly furnished, the room says welcome in that annoyingly British accent of Lucius's. Mahogany furniture, black-out blinds, widescreen TV... every home comfort a vampire requires.

But no Vienna.

Noticing I'm awake, Selene doesn't say a word, just rises and walks to the door. Poking her head out, she murmurs something, then returns to sit beside me. Further up the bed this time, closer to my hip. Her hand rests atop mine. "Back with the undead," she murmurs. "What you did was foolish, Colt. Surrendering so much blood. We had you on an IV drip for nearly twelve hours to replenish what you gave Vienna."

My heart splinters at the mention of her name. "Twelve hours?"

She nods slowly. "Augustus is bringing you something to drink. You'll need to feed every couple of hours to build yourself back up to full strength, but you'll live. I know you were probably hoping Vienna would be here right now, but..." She clears her throat. "Colt, she hasn't revived. There are no signs of regeneration, her wounds aren't healing. Lucius hasn't left her side since we got home, until now. He mentioned you felt it necessary Vienna be washed clean, so I took care of it. I bathed her myself, made her look presentable. I'll take you to her after you've eaten."

Made her look presentable. I shake my head as the words ping inside my head like it's a pinball machine, hitting the alarm bells and racking up points by the second. Selene doesn't think Vienna will come back to me; she doesn't want to say it directly, but I know she's given up hope.

I nudge Selene off the bed and toss the covers back. Yeah, I've definitely knocked myself off kilter with my over-enthusiastic blood donation. It was totally worth it, regardless of the outcome. If Vienna stays dead—the mortal version of dead—I can at least meet dawn with the knowledge I tried to keep her here with me. "Take me now, Selene."

"Colt—"

"Whether she lives or dies, she's not doing it alone. Take me to her, or I'll rip this place apart until I find her." A brave statement, considering I can barely stand up unassisted. There are two things that weaken us to the point of destruction—sunlight, and severe blood loss. The latter won't kill us, but it can make us slow and stupid.

Selene sets her hands on her hips as I sway, regarding me with regal eyes. Lucius chose well with her; I can't imagine him spending eternity with anyone else. After a long moment, she reaches out and jabs me sharply in the chest, nodding in satisfaction as I topple back onto the bed. "Make sure you're in a fit state to follow through when you threaten me, Colt. I'll escort you to Vienna when you've eaten," she repeats in a firm tone. "She hasn't been alone since we brought her home—Lucius has been sitting with her all day."

"I should've been with her."

"She needed to be kept quiet. Lucius swears a chaotic environment disrupts the process and affects a newborn in more ways than we realize. Augustus and I have been bustling around, swapping blood bags, taking care of you. We haven't been loud and obnoxious, but it hasn't been quiet. Lucius didn't want things to go down this way," she continues. "He feels guilty, and he's not a man who allows himself to be ruled by his emotions."

Neither was I, once upon a time. Now look at me. Brought to my knees by a brown-haired, blue-eyed angel with the mouth of a sailor and a heart bigger than freaking Idaho.

"Lucius gave Tiberius orders to protect the love of his life. Tiberius obeyed his sire. Everything that happened last night... it's a cliché, but it happened for a reason. The way I see it, either Vienna is meant to die... or you were meant to live."

"The mysteries of the universe. You know, there's a cell downstairs with restraints and a very nice bed. I've begged Lucius to reconsider his promise if Vienna doesn't pull through. He won't, but that doesn't mean I won't take you hostage and keep you down there until you rid yourself of this idiotic notion of killing yourself." She calls out a soft, "Come in" when someone taps on the door.

Augustus whispers into the room, moving stealthily for a man of his stature. There's a glass in his hand—I can smell the O-positive from here. It holds no appeal. There's nothing in this world that compares to the taste of Vienna's blood, fresh from the vein. "Colt, glad to see you up and about."

Snorting, I flop back on the sheets and close my eyes, gathering myself for another fruitless attempt at rising.

"Thanks, Augustus. Could you tell Lucius we'll be down shortly to see Vienna?" Selene murmurs. I can tell she's not pleased with me, but what's she going to do?

"We're going now." Grinding my teeth, I force myself up again. Something sharp twists my guts, and I get the sense I have to be somewhere urgently. "I need to go now."

"Not until you've—"

Cursing, I snatch the glass from Augustus's hand and gulp the whole thing in a handful of long swallows. I barely taste the thick liquid, but my body insists I need it. Shoving the empty vessel back into the guard dog's hand, I stagger toward the door in my bare feet. I wish fervently for the comforting weight of my boots, my jeans. "Are you coming, Selene?"

"What is it with men and their pigheadedness?" she says with a sigh.

I like to think regular Colt isn't as pigheaded as most of my gender, but grieving Colt is a walking disaster. He's ready to walk through walls and bend steel bars to get to Vienna. I feel as though I've tagged along on the ride, trying to rein in the craziness and keep all the disturbed parts of me traveling in the same direction.

I leave the room and turn left. I can't say why I go that

way; I don't know. It feels like there's a hand on the back of my neck, gripping my nape and steering me toward an unknown destination. The only thing I'm certain of is that Vienna is waiting for me at the end.

Shuffling down the hallway, I pause outside every door I pass and listen before moving toward the next. My world narrows down to the placement of my feet, taking me one step nearer to my little vixen. Five doors along, I stop and wait, and the hairs on the back of my neck stand up. Without hesitation, I push into the room without knocking.

My liege stands as I enter, and we look at each other as if seeing ourselves for the first time. God knows what I look like, but I suspect it's similar to Lucius. The king looks tired, contemplative. Babysitting a corpse, hoping beyond hope that it will come back to life, takes its toll. Mulling over what could go wrong, predicting how a risen newbie will react in their first moments of rebirth... it's enough to drive a person insane, thinking of all the variables.

Creating a vampire isn't as plain and simple as the books and movies make it out to be. From what I understand, the intended newbie stands a better chance of successfully turning if the blood exchange between the human and their potential sire occurs more than once. A slow, thorough infiltration of the vampire virus into the host body before the main event.

That's not something I need to worry about. Vienna carries more of my blood in her than I do. The virus should be commandeering her nervous system, but there are situations—take this, for example—where the human body isn't receptive to the virus and refuses to comply. Sometimes, the damage to the frail shell is too compounded for the virus to heal.

"Selene, Augustus, wait outside," Lucius murmurs, then

gestures to the chair beside the bed he's just vacated. "Take a seat, Colt. I'll leave you with her now. There's been no improvement, no healing. I'm sorry, but I believe now is the time to say goodbye."

I don't sit. I'm not going to distance myself from her even those couple of feet, not if this is goodbye. I cross to the bed and kick the chair away hard enough to smash it—literally—into the wall. "I'd appreciate it if you'd leave now, Lucius."

His hand hovers over my shoulder, then drops without touching me. He doesn't say anything else before he leaves the room and closes the door behind him, leaving me with Vienna.

My beautiful V.

She's so unnaturally quiet, none of her usual sass or blatant attitude are present. Selene has made her more than presentable; she's made her radiant, even in death. Vienna's pale skin is clean, I can't see or smell a trace of blood on her. She looks serene, her eyes closed and her expression slack. The covers are pulled up over her breasts, leaving her shoulders exposed.

Suddenly my throat is viciously tight, burning with unshed emotions.

Selene has brushed Vienna's hair so it's soft and shiny—it feels like silk between my fingers as I lift a lock and rub it gently between thumb and forefinger.

Crawling under the covers, I pull my vixen tight, ignoring the lifelessness of the form I hold. I search deep for some sign she's hibernating somewhere, poised to wake and shatter this nightmare with a peal of unmistakable laughter, but there's nothing. My last threads of hope unravel and flutter away.

"I had such plans for us, V. Less than a week in your company, and you spun my world around. I thought I'd be kissing Vadim's ass for the rest of eternity, plotting to take down his empire without ever succeeding. Then there was you, my vixen in the shadows, eavesdropping where you shouldn't. Kicking my ass, giving me shit, and lighting up the dark like a supernova." I stroke her head, my fingers brushing over the broken area of skull where her head met runway. It's still open and raw. "Bravest mortal I know. I guess you understand by now what's happened. You're probably mouthing off to the angel on gate duty up there, demanding answers. I lost you, V. Somewhere along the way, I did something wrong, I fucked up, and you died for my mistake."

They'll come for her soon. Lucius and Augustus. They'll come and take her away from me, dispose of her body however they see fit. I don't know the proper etiquette for burying a failed attempt at creating an immortal being. Vienna has family, she has people who love her outside of this cuckoo existence. People who will miss her and want to claim her body, but she doesn't want to go back to Chicago.

I'll ask Lucius to pull some strings, find out where her family is and get in touch. Let them know, somehow, that she won't be going home. Then I'll lay my beautiful girl to rest where she belongs, and hope we find each other again on a plane of reality where we can be together. Not as shadows in the dark, not as monsters scared to step foot into daylight, but as man and woman.

"From the moment I met you, I knew you were different. God, you haven't been scared of me this entire time. Do you know how rare it is to find a mortal unafraid of the demon? It's like finding hen's teeth, V—it just doesn't happen. Lucius thinks you're something pretty fucking special. Apparently, some people believe Rhonulls aren't from this world. I don't really put faith in there being aliens walking among us, but hey, I'm a vampire, so who am I to judge what's possible or not?" I frown as a thought strikes me. "What if Lucius is right? What if Rhonulls *aren't* completely human? Not alien but... subhuman. Part human, part... fae, maybe? That would explain how you broke his thrall, wouldn't it? And why you have such a strong reaction to my blood. Fuck."

I'm clutching at straws without proof, but the more I toss ideas around in my head, the more I like how they fit. She looks human. Aside from her potent blood and ability to throw off Lucius's control, she acts human. Death hasn't stripped her down to her most basic form like it does with some supernaturals, which tells me that, at the heart of her, she is indeed human. She's just got a splash of something else in her genetic makeup.

I sit up quickly, thinking hard. What if we're all wrong? If Vienna is mortal, then yes, we're right in assuming the change has failed. But what if that little extra genetic something is altering our concept of the *usual* when it comes to evolving into a vampire? Maybe she just needs more time, a longer hibernation period, so to speak. Or a higher intake of blood.

It could just be the desperation of a man in mourning, but I'm willing to gamble another few liters of my blood on a hunch. Hell, maybe it'll take a Latin incantation and cutting the head off a green chicken to get things rolling, but I don't know Latin and haven't got the faintest idea where to find a green chicken. I can only work with what I've got; blood and time are at my disposal.

Excitement thrums in my veins as I decide to bypass using my wrist as a donation point. I need to use blood from closer to my heart; I'm tempted to rip it out and wring it dry. Instead, I grit my teeth and dig my nails into my flesh directly above the quiet organ. Blood seeps from the wound but not as fast as I need it to. Groaning low in my throat, I delve deeper until the trickle becomes a stream.

Keeping my fingers in the wound, I scoop my other arm under Vienna's stiff shoulders and raise her up, using my hand to brace her head as my arm supports her upper body. It's awkward, but I manage to press her face to my chest, moving my fingers so her lips touch the wound. Hoping this ridiculous position is going to work, I hunch over her so my blood flows over those pale lips and into her mouth.

"This has to do the trick, V. I don't know what else to do if it doesn't." There's blood dribbling from the corners of her lips. Not much, which means there's a lot going into her system. Whatever she is, she's taken enough of my blood to turn a small army of mortals. "It's not too late, Vienna. You can pull through this if you want to. Find the strength, baby. My vixen doesn't give up."

"Oh my fucking God, Colt. Are you insane?"

Caught in the act, there's nothing I can give as an answer. Does desperation make me insane? Probably. Am I right in doing this, going this far? Well, that's in the eye of the beholder, isn't it? To my mind, yes, I am perfectly within my rights to do everything I can to bring Vienna back to me. Including pouring my life essence into her for a second time. "Back off, Selene. I'll explain when I'm finished."

"You're finished now. We didn't spend all fucking day nursing you back to health so you can drag your sorry ass to the brink of death again. Vienna's gone. It's tragic and it is heartbreaking, but there's nothing else to be done." She stomps across to the bed and attempts to tug V away from me. "I'm fairly sure this counts as desecrating her body. Why don't you set her down gently and we can figure out how to put her to rest?"

My teeth snap together in warning as I shift my grip on

Vienna, pulling her in closer, tighter, protecting her as a lion guards its kill. Blatantly ignoring Selene's request, I jab my fingers back into my chest, reopening the hole and deepening it. Releasing more blood in a fresh wave. "I figured it out. We haven't given her enough time or enough fuel for her body to make the change. An engine can't run without gas, Selene."

She rubs her hands over her face. "You got off the train at Crazytown, didn't you?"

"I assure you, I'm fully *compos mentis.*"

"Yeah, sure you are. Put her down, Colt, or I'll have to go get the boys."

A figure darkens the doorway. "My dear, would you give Colt and me a few moments to talk? It seems we have an issue or two to discuss." The king glides into the room, his expression concerned. "I think another beverage might not go amiss." He strokes his hand over her arm as she huffs and stomps past him, pulling the door almost closed as she goes. He doesn't look happy when he looks at me again. "Grief does terrible things to mortals, Colt. It hits vampires worse. I think because we understand death in a more detailed fashion, it strikes us harder. This is an extension of your grief. Understandable but futile."

"It's not futile!"

"No? Explain it to me." Lucius stalks over to the bed and sits, propping his ankle on his opposite knee. "I'd like to hear the reasoning behind this. You've already given her enough blood to resurrect fifty vampires. How does bleeding yourself dry help?"

In a calm, controlled voice, I explain my theory to him as concisely as possible. I'm aware he thinks I've lost my marbles, but I go through it all step by step. So far, he's not pulling rank or looking as though he's going to use excessive force to remove Vienna from my grasp. By the time I've covered everything I can think of, my chest wound is almost healed, the skin pink and brand new.

Lucius reaches out and takes Vienna's hand in his, flipping it over to expose her wrist. With a slash of a fingernail, he slices a gash into the rubbery flesh. There's no reaction from her, nothing to suggest my theory is working. There's no blood, no healing.

My shoulders sag in defeat.

"I admire your tenacity, Colt. Loving a person, particularly a human, is one of the greatest tests for our kind. I like to think of our species as a fifty-fifty ratio. Half of us are monsters, immune to the lure of humans being anything but food. Incapable of emotional attachments, killing without mercy. The other half is like you and me. We don't see them as food, but as people. We work with them, live with them. Appreciate what they have to offer even though it's short lived. Some of them reach in and grab hold of us, just like your Vienna, and we're helpless against them. They make us feel alive, human again. They make us believe we can have more."

"She lit up my world, Lucius. I've been in the dark for so long. Decades of pandering to Vadim and his ilk have taken their toll on me. I've changed in ways I hate, I don't see the joy in this life anymore. I live in a fucking warehouse basement, for Christ's sake. It was all for a worthy cause, don't get me wrong, but it's rotted the core of me and left me hollow." I sigh heavily and study Vienna's face. "She was turning that around, just by being who she is. Snarky, sassy, feisty, and so fucking fearless. Now I'm in the dark again, and I don't want to be here."

Lucius presses his fingertips to his lips. "I have a proposition in mind for you. I wasn't going to discuss it right now, but maybe it will give you some hope for a brighter future. I can't take over Antoine's place in Phoenix. I just haven't got the time or the manpower to set another city to rights at the moment. I've spoken with Maximus, Tiberius, and Augustus, and none of them want to relocate. Which means I either force one of them to go against their will, or forfeit the claim you staked on the city, leaving it open for someone else like Antoine or Vadim to take control. Both options leave a sour taste in my mouth."

"You want me to go."

"I do. I believe it would be good for you to get away from Tucson, have a fresh start. No more living in a warehouse, and you can socialize a bit more, wean yourself away from what you hate so much about what you think you've become." He smiles carefully, his lips curving but his eyes guarded. "I'd pay, of course, for the renovations to that eyesore Antoine paraded as his home. Fuck, knock the whole sordid place to the ground, burn it, and rebuild for all I care. Just go and be happy, Colt. Learn to be happy again."

It's so wrong, talking about fresh starts and finding happiness, when the woman I love is dead in my arms. Lucius is offering me an opportunity to walk away from this, from the last fifty years of hell, and reinvent my life. Only problem is, I've already made my mind up as to what the next stage of my existence is, and it involves walking out into the bright light of day for the final time.

But talking is dragging out the time, so I'll go along with him for now. "Why the hell would you want me to take over Phoenix? I've spent too long taking orders to remember how to give them. I'm unknown, I won't garner the respect I need to rule a city of unruly vampires who have been allowed to get away with shit for years. I'm not you, Lucius."

"You don't need to be. You command respect, Colt. You

walk into a room, and all eyes are on you. You exude authority, whether you realize it or not, and you don't have to exercise violence for people to understand you take control. Your moral compass is strong, which is a quality that city is in dire need of."

I nod slowly. Maybe it's the blood loss, but I feel fucking weird. In the pit of my belly, something tugs sharply, almost painfully. It remains aching, a constant pull. "I guess I'm flattered. It's not every day I get a city entrusted to me. But six hundred and thirty eight years is enough for me. Without Vienna, there doesn't seem to be much to carry on for. I've played my part, and played it well. It's time for me to bow out gracefully."

"Colt."

"No, I don't want you to talk me out of it, Lucius. Respect me enough for that. You promised you would stand by the decision I made, and this is it." I grimace as the pull grows stronger, growing to the size of a fist. "But thanks for thinking of me."

"Shut up, Colt, and *look*."

Lucius all but shoves Vienna's wrist in my face. He strokes his thumb over the cut he made not five minutes earlier, smearing the beads of blood over her skin. My stomach cramps; the superficial wound closes quickly, leaving no trace.

I blink in surprise, elation surging through me. *It worked.* Quickly, I shift Vienna in my arms, sitting her up and leaning her forward so I can inspect the gaping head wound. I barely stifle a victorious cry when I see the fractured skull has healed and the scalp is regenerating as I watch. It seems like the faster Vienna recovers, the more painful my stomach becomes, but I can't bring myself to care.

Something flipped the switch.

"I'll be damned," Lucius murmurs, astonished.

Color, the faintest flush of it, flourishes under her skin. Bit by bit, the stiffness death brings to all creatures dissipates, and Vienna is soft and pliable. Stunned, I look at Lucius. "What the hell did I do?"

"I'll go out on a limb," he says slowly, hesitantly, "and put faith in your theory. It looks like she needed one hell of a meal to push her through the transformation. I've never heard of anything like this in a thousand years. It's... fascinating. Truly fascinating."

Fascinating isn't the word I'd use, but hey, each to his own. I cup my hand against her cheek, willing her to open her eyes. "Vienna. Come on, vixen, wake up now. Don't make me wait any longer to see those beautiful eyes."

Everything happens within seconds.

Blue-gray eyes flash open and lock onto mine. Lucius barks out a sharp warning, already in motion as he drags Vienna away from me. The stomach cramps intensify, then Vienna rears up and forward, slipping out of Lucius's grasp, and her fangs find their home in my throat.

Goddamn her, she's as fucking feisty as ever.

15

ienna

#MINDBLOWN

That's my social media hashtag from now on, I decide as I ride the hum of energy coursing through me. My body feels as though I've downed a dozen energy drinks, several shots of narcotics, and stuck my finger into an electrical socket. Buzzed isn't the word. Complete mental overload comes to mind.

Everything is amplified. Hearing, touch, smell, taste, vision. All five senses are out of this fucking world *amazing*.

I feel like I've been sleeping for years and been given a rude awakening, shocked from my slumber into a world where I am invincible beyond measure. Invincible, and unstoppable. There's a craving, a dark craving gnawing at me. It's followed me out of dreamland, a slathering beast stalking me from the shadows, and before I have a chance to assess my surroundings, it pounces.

My gums ache. My tongue caresses the tips of my new extra-long, extra-pointy canines before they unerringly bury themselves into flesh. I get a quick taste of salt, then blood spurts into my mouth, thick and coppery. *Delicious.* I suck more of the heavenly substance from the source, moaning as it slips down my throat.

My hands grip a firm skull, fingers fisting in short soft hair, forcing it to tilt and expose the vein just a little more. The scent of my victim is as familiar to me as my own, and acts like a match to gas fumes. My pussy goes up in flames, frantic to be filled, wet and wanton.

"Newbies are so eager when they first rise." I recognize the voice, laced with amusement and that classy touch of an English accent. Almost as elegant as the whiff of expensive cologne beneath my nose as his arm hooks around my throat and squeezes until my fangs disengage. "As her sire, she'll need to drink from you until she learns control. Once her base instincts have been tamed, you can wean her onto human blood, but for now… teach her some manners."

I manage to drag my eyes from the masculine neck I've just marked, away from the perfect pair of puncture wounds and the small trickles of blood going to waste. My tongue swipes over my lips, catching the points of my fangs. The arm around my neck means nothing to me; I want that blood in my mouth.

Lucius hauls me backward, dragging my naked body off the bed and away from Colt. He's strong, powerful, his age offering advantages my feral little brain can't even comprehend right now, but he's putting himself between my insatiable hunger and my meal. For an old vampire, surely he should know better?

I'm primed for a fight and don't know why. Curling up in bed with Colt sounds much nicer than causing chaos and destruction, but the beast inside me is howling for more. It wants death and mayhem, blood, and loud, snotty tears. This thing in me has a purpose and it is not going to be denied, not by the king, not by me.

"This will all feel very strange, Vienna. Being a vampire is nothing like you've ever imagined, but the urges you have now will pass. Colt is your sire, your maker. Listen to him, obey him, and he will keep you on the right path. Are you calm enough for me to release you?"

I wait for the arm to relax. Quick as a snake, I slip out from Lucius's hold and launch myself back at Colt. My body is a coiled spring. Every movement is so well oiled, I'm a fucking machine. If I wanted to scale a ten-story building? Pretty sure it wouldn't be an issue. Run from here—wherever *here* is—to the state line and back again? Done in a matter of seconds. I can bend the motherfucking world between my hands and shape it however I want.

Colt blurs from the bed a split second before I land on him, my fangs already bared and ready to strike. Part of me is dying from mortification; why am I acting like this? This isn't *me*. It seems like I'm split into two halves, and the vampire half is definitely more dominant. For now. I won't be a monster. I remember what happened before my lights went out, so I know whatever occurred after I went splat must have been bad.

Colt wouldn't have allowed himself to turn me if he knew I'd emerge as a psychotic, demonic lunatic.

I crash into the mattress, already twisting and preparing myself to leap again. Hands grab my ankles firmly, towing me down the bed until my hips rest on the edge. Firm thighs press against mine, pinning my legs, and a long-fingered hand grasps me by the nape, forcing my face into the sheets.

There's an automatic response to kick and flail, my brain telling me I need to *breathe*, but my lungs are still and quiet in my chest. An eerie silence keeps my head cushioned, no frantic pulse of blood in my ears or dramatic thump of my heart knocking into my ribs in panic. My body might be a powerhouse, but it runs on a frighteningly different system to what I'm used to.

"Vienna. Stop fighting me, and calm yourself. You cannot beat me, you'll only tire yourself out. Colt, go get something to eat. You're slow and sluggish, your reactions can't keep up with her." Lucius doles out his orders with a zing of dominance. "I'll get her restrained until you return. You'll have to feed often and well if she's going to use you as her sole source of nutrition."

"Are you sure?"

I almost cry at the sound of his voice. My Colt. My heart believes it's been years since I last heard that damn voice, listening to his tongue stroking over words the same way it does to my clit. My pussy flutters in response, more than ready to cast aside thoughts of violence and jump straight into the fucking portion of our reunion.

Those fingers tighten warningly on my neck. "Newborns are strong, but I haven't met one yet who's managed to best me, Colt."

Oh, that is so a challenge. Seriously, one would think he's goading me into kicking his ass. If he doesn't watch his step, he's going to press my super bitch button, and somehow, I think vampire Vienna's super bitch button is far more impressive than mortal Vienna's could ever hope to be.

Don't do it, don't rise to the bait. You're dead, you heal fast. If he wants to annihilate you into the ground, he can. He can do virtually anything to you, and the evidence will be gone before the sun rises. Lucius demands respect, so we'll give it to him. We won't give him any reason to go Master Vampire on our ass, because that would be stupid and—

"I can handle one naked newbie."

I'm not ashamed of my nudity, and I seem to have lost my modesty. I honestly don't give a shit that all my goodies are on full display for all and sundry to ogle at their leisure—something I would have hated as a human. But Lucius's taunt enrages my apparently proud demon, inciting a riot. Naked or not, I am not someone to mess with.

Clothes do not make a warrior.

I shove my hands against the mattress and push up, testing Lucius's grip on my neck. I wrench my head to the side, finally able to see. I know his game—keep me pinned, demonstrate his strength and his authority, and keep me cowed and obedient. "Get the fuck off me."

"Ah, she speaks." Lucius actually sounds pleased. "Nice of you to join us again, Vienna. Behave, and I'll let you loose. If not, you'll be restrained until I'm sure you don't pose a threat to Colt while he recovers. Damn fool almost drained himself dry twice to get you to this point, so I won't allow you to do something you'll regret when the emotional purge ebbs."

I snarl, taking great delight in showing him my fangs.

"Um, the damn fool is standing *right here*." Colt waves his hand nonchalantly. "And I'm not going anywhere. Lucius, would you mind giving Vienna and me some time alone? I'm not going to let her take me down; I'm not that far gone. Besides, if she gives me any shit, I'll blister her ass seven ways to Sunday."

Lucius *hmmms* thoughtfully. From the corner of my eye, I can see him weighing up whatever he needs to before he answers. He releases my neck and steps away from me, waiting to see how I react. "Augustus will remain outside. If he hears any signs of a disturbance, he *will* intervene. My plans for you go beyond this, Colt," he says pointedly, and I get the feeling there's a whole other conversation in play here, "and being mauled by your protégée is not among them."

My lover stands taller, straightens his shoulders. Now the bloodlust has eased slightly, I can see he looks tired and worn. Harsh emotions line his face since I saw him last—on the plane, having a standoff with Vadim the Russian fuckwit—and he looks like he's been in a cage fight with a hell-hound. "Oh, she'll mind her manners with me," he says ominously, sending a shiver down my spine. "She knows the consequences for disobeying me."

Smirking, I roll onto my back and spread my legs, fanning my fingers over my pussy in an attempt at seductive concealment. I blow Colt an air kiss, over-exaggerating the purse of my lips. "Big Daddy likes butt stuff. Come on, Colt, get naked with me. No one warned me being a vampire would make me so freaking *horny*. Or hungry," I add with a pout. "Hungry, horny Vienna likes to make mischief."

"That's my cue to exit." Lucius clears his throat pointedly. "If you find yourself in a romantic position, Colt, don't concern yourself with how much noise she makes. We're used to noisy submissives around here."

I purr throatily, stroking myself. "Me? I'm quiet compared to the lion over there." Running the tip of my tongue over my top lip, I lift my hand, fingers curled into pretend claws, and swipe at the air as I give them my best *grrrr*.

"Yes, well… good luck, Colt. You'll need it." Lucius strides away as I wiggle my fingers at him in farewell.

The door closes behind the king, and I'm finally alone with my sire. How exciting. I've fallen down the rabbit hole into freaking Wonderland, and it's quite possibly the best thing that's ever happened to me. There's no grinning cat or psychotic queens shouting, "Off with their heads!", but it's amazing to think I'm part of a secret world where death isn't the end.

It's only the beginning.

"So, you did it. I guess I should thank you for not giving up on me…" Fuck, how sultry does my voice sound? Turning into a vampire obviously wiped out my inhibitions and released my inner sex bunny. I giggle to myself, picturing a sleek white rabbit in a thong, padded cuffs, and collar. It turns and wiggles its fluffy butt, showing off the puffy cottontail, then glances over its shoulder to flash a fang as it winks.

Colt stalks closer, and I'm torn between lunging for his throat again, or tearing off those ridiculous pants and getting a taste of something just as appetizing. Decisions, decisions. He takes the choice out of my hands, leaning over the bed and scooping me up, holding me so tightly my ribs are on the verge of snapping like popsicle sticks. "Goddamn it, V. Goddamn it."

His touch soothes the raging insanity inside me. This is what I wished for in those last seconds before the asphalt broke my fall: to feel Colt's arms around me, wrapping me up tight in love. I think I died the instant my skull cracked onto the tarmac, I can't recall anything after that split second of impact, but I know I wanted Colt to love me one last time before I died. "Rough ride, huh?"

He kisses my hair. "You have no fucking idea. The

moment I knew you were gone, my world fell apart at the seams. It felt like nothing would ever be right again. I gave you enough blood to feed the club, and it wasn't enough. Nothing seemed to be enough to bring you back. Lucius told me the damage might be too much for your body to heal, even with my blood giving it a boost. There was no guarantee you would come back with all your faculties."

Now we're touching, our hands can't stop running over bare skin. Our bodies run at the same temperature, which makes it easier for my brain to believe he's warm. It's a small thing, but it's reassuring. Rest assured, all my faculties are exactly where they should be, as are my hands, clutching his hair.

"You know, now I'm a vampire," boy, that sounds really weird when I say it aloud, "you don't have to hold back. I'm not a teeny..." I nip at his jaw, "tiny..." at his lips, "fragile..." my mouth teases his with a soft kiss, "human anymore, Colt. I bruise, I heal. Something tears, it fixes right up. I know you haven't shown me what you're capable of, but there's no need to hide it. You can be who you are, you can fuck me as hard as you want, and I'll take it. Every... beautiful... inch."

His jaw clenches, his eyes fire into tawny embers. I love watching him resist me. Denying himself, his urges, his primal physical desires. "We have more important things to do before we go at it like rabid sex fiends, little vixen. There are going to be residual emotions, issues arising from the violence of your turning. The manner in which a vampire *becomes* often has an impact on how they will mature. We need to be firm with you from the start, before those issues begin undermining your control."

I roll my eyes and kiss him again, more insistent this time. I will get what I want, one way or another. I kiss him until he relaxes, his muscles softening their brutal grip on me. The man has some serious fucking biceps. My moan when he finally kisses me back, too sweetly for my liking, is low and needy. "My control is just fine, Colt. My pussy, however, needs a strict lesson in discipline. She's been a very bad girl."

Immediately, he stiffens and draws me away to arm's distance, bending slightly to peer into my eyes. "Vadim. What did he do to you, Vienna?"

Shit, this wasn't the direction I was aiming for. My memories dredge up the nauseating sensation of the vampire's fingers inside me. I brush it off, banish the recollection as I shrug carelessly. "The fucker made his point. It doesn't matter; he didn't get what he wanted in the end. I'm not strapped down to a table in Russia, waiting for some poor schmuck to get his quota of breeding bitches in for the week. I'm assuming you took care of the Russian prick for me?"

"Define *made his point.*"

Oh, I do like that dangerous tone. "What do you want me to tell you, Colt? It's only going to make you furious, and there's nothing you could have done then or now that can change it. I'm safe, I'm alive—to a degree, and I made damn sure two of his minions paid a hefty price for what he did." I give Colt a winning smile, but there's a darkness lurking in those tawny eyes that won't be swayed by whatever I say. "One of them lost a testicle, and the other one misplaced his eyeball. I had a very busy night."

"Vienna." *Mmmn*, that dom voice does the best things to my insides. Makes them all squishy and receptive. "I know you have miraculous powers of recovery, a source of inner strength so deep it must have roots in the fucking earth itself, but I am not playing games with you. If he touched you, you tell me, right now."

I shrug again, then squeak as Colt's fingers curl around my throat and lift me onto my tiptoes. It's a violent gesture any way you look at it. An observer would probably raise the alarm. But I'm not concerned, and not just because I trust this man with my extended existence. An observer wouldn't see that his grip is loose enough I can wrench away without any effort at all. An observer can't see what I see in his eyes —a wealth of worry so rich, swirling with the instinctive need to protect and exact revenge. This is love. Our kind of love.

I sigh in exasperation and link myself to him, gently squeezing the wrist connected to the hand around my throat. "He tied me down, made some threats. Got in a good feel. That's it, I promise. It was unpleasant, sure, but it hasn't scarred me, not in the way he hoped it would. The asshole wanted to intimidate me, terrify me into compliance, and it didn't work. All he did was seriously piss me off."

In one fluid movement, Colt releases me, runs his fingertips over my cheek, and spins away to head for the door. The muscles in his back and arms are rigid with tension, and I'm so in tune with him, I can smell the murderous vibes he's releasing. It's an unsettling odor, one unlike anything I've ever smelled. Bitter and coppery, almost smokey, as though it's burning in the hottest pits of hell.

"He's dead, right? He can't hurt anyone again, Colt. Just let it be."

"Lucius has him in interrogation, along with Oberon," he grinds out without looking at me. Only a few more feet, and he'll reach the door. "He'll wish I'd killed him on the fucking plane by the time I've finished cutting his cock off an inch at a time, then his fingers, one by one."

Oh shit. I have an instant to make the choice, and before I realize I've made it, I'm blurring across the pretty guestroom at a speed that brings tears to my eyes. It is so freaking *cool.* I launch myself onto Colt's back as he yanks the door open, sending us crashing into it as my weight pushes him forward. Everything I do, every move I make, is super springy, extra fast. "If he's still alive, Lucius needs him. Personal vendettas can wait until Vadim has outlived his use."

"He already has." Colt twists, trying to dislodge me, but I wrap my limbs around him and cling like a vine. "Nobody touches you like that. Especially not that fucker!" he all but roars, slamming his fist into the wall and crumbling plaster into dust.

I feel like I've downed a bottle of scotch and climbed naked onto a mechanical bull. Some demented idiot has the remote control and is sending the bull cavorting and bucking beneath me. It's anyone's guess how long I can stick with the wild ride, but I'm digging my heels in for the long haul. "Colt, you could be putting all this manic energy into something far more productive, like fucking me," I suggest brightly as he spins sharply; I dig my nails into his chest for balance. "That's sounds much more fun, doesn't it, Sir?"

"Vienna," he growls.

"Colt," I mimic, running my tongue along the side of his neck. "Don't make me do something naughty."

"Goddamn it, V, I need to do this."

"And you can, as soon as Lucius is done with him. Hell, I'll stand there in a thong, waving cheerleader pom-poms, cheering you on. But right now, you need to calm down and think about the repercussions." I should learn to take my own advice. I'm about to do something that will have repercussions that last for days. "I'm hungry, so I'll just have a snack while you have a paddy and throw things, okay?"

"Don't you dare, Vienna. You need to learn manners before you—ow, fuck! That's *it*."

Already latched onto the vein in his throat, I hum in agreement as blood fills my mouth and soothes the gnawing hunger in my belly. No one told me I'd be starving after the change. I could stay here for the next hour, drinking my fill.

Colt's hand reaches back and hooks onto my nape. We spin again as I swallow greedily, then he throws his torso forward, pulling me over his shoulder with a garbled squeal. I slam onto the bed on my back, hastily gulping down the blood in my mouth. I stare at Colt's livid face, smiling sheepishly and wiping away the evidence of my misdemeanor with the back of my hand. "Hi there, handsome."

My attempt at levity doesn't go far. He flips me over, and uses my thigh to drag me around so my ass hangs off the edge of the bed. His palm cracks heavily on the curve of one ass cheek, then the other. It's hard enough to sting like a bitch, but my startled cry doesn't deter him in the slightest. If anything, my sounds of distress only spur him on to a faster, more concentrated spanking.

"Feeding does not mean you steal. It does not mean you can revert to being an animal and just take what you want. There is an etiquette, there are rules. Especially when you're using me as your banquet. Do you understand, vixen?" His hand is lighting up my ass like fireworks in the sky on Independence Day. "Hunger is not an excuse to be rude."

Jesus, he's going to smack my ass cheeks into next week. They already feel swollen and tight, hot from the incessant introduction of his palm. I wriggle, trying to inch my way further onto the bed, but he just redirects his attention to the backs of my thighs. Oh God, that's so much worse.

Tears spring to my eyes, borne of guilt and pain. The only solace I have is knowing that he's going to be so busy blistering my butt, he won't have time to go hunt down Vadim and his cowardly sidekick. "I can't help it if I'm hungry!"

His hand lands between my thighs, directly on my needy pussy, with a wet squelch. He hasn't pulled his blow, and pain spikes through my clit and assaults my nerve endings, bringing me to the edge of orgasm. My hips jerk and buck, riding the high he brings with every punishing strike. "Manners, vixen. *Please* and *thank you*. I'm not raising you to be a monster."

Fuck me! The shrill plea echoes in my head frantically. "*Please*, Sir."

I howl, my eyes rolling back in my head with the thrust of two thick fingers in my slick passage. I clamp down on them, welcoming them into the wet haven between my legs. There's a quick flash of memory, of Vadim's face in my head, then Colt's voice smashes the image into pieces.

"Such a little pain slut, Vienna. So fucking greedy, sucking on my fingers." The glorious fullness retreats, and I moan in protest. The moan turns into a happy yelp as Colt flips me over again, hands lifting my legs and spreading them wide. "You want me to do something fun and productive, V? Have it your way."

The silk bottoms are already gone, my captor well prepared. The thick length of his cock stands proud in my line of sight for a moment before he takes it in hand and notches the plump head against me. I brace myself for what's coming, but I'm still not ready for the sheer force of his thrust, his hips driving the crown deep, the veiny ridges on his shaft stimulating the sensitive nerves in my pussy.

I scream in equal parts shock and pleasure, taking his cock to the hilt on that one stroke.

Colt doesn't give me a chance to gather my wits. I've

unleashed the beast and now I've got to deal with him. It might not be as big a hardship as expected, not when his restraint has completely disintegrated, and his body is teaching mine exactly who the fucking boss is.

Soft, whimpering mewls escape my lips, inaudible over the rapid smacks of flesh on flesh. This is just what I wanted, what he needs. An outlet for the hell he's been living in while I floated in the dark, oblivious to everything going on around me.

The orgasm rears up and rips into me with sharp teeth, savaging me from core to mind. I arch, shudder, scream, simultaneously. There's no room for thoughts in my head; the brutal pounding rocking me up the bed shakes everything loose until there's only me and Colt, connected as deeply as two people can be, chasing pleasure and pain down a slippery slope.

His hands clamp down on my shoulders, yanking me down onto his cock as he rams inside me, his face a study of fury and desperate passion. A bad combination for some, but for me, for us, this is perfect. As a mortal, I couldn't have taken him this way and come out whole. Not without walking funny for a month. I can already sense the bruising starting, muscles crying even through the sweet ripple of the aftershocks.

Aftershocks that are rapidly building into a second orgasm.

"Colt," I choke around the drool forming in my open mouth.

"Again. You damn well come again, Vienna." His eyes burn into mine fiercely. He leans over me, grinding his length deep, and claims my mouth. Tongue plunging inside, battling with mine. "Fucking come on my cock, V. I want what's mine."

Yeah, this is our kind of love. If this is the precedent we're setting for the centuries to come, I'll welcome it with open arms. Love isn't always sweetness and soft touches. It's hard and fast, filled so full of emotions, the heart and the mind overflow with them all. Passion is *this*. It's being claimed as though the world is ending, the sky is falling, and there are only minutes left before the world implodes.

My nails gouge strips down his back, his shoulders. Toes curling, muscles shrieking, I throw my head back and scream again, feeling the orgasm shred me into nothingness. My vision turns white, stark white, for a precious few seconds, but I hear Colt's pained grunts as his own climax tears through him. My pussy ripples around him, squeezing and releasing of its own volition, milking every last drop of cum from his shaft.

He collapses on top of me with a quiet *oomph*.

Knocked for six, I stare at the ceiling and wonder what the hell I ever did to deserve him.

Colt

Letting Vienna goad me into fucking her was a bad idea. A really bad idea of the best kind.

I've been rough with her, too rough. Her screams are still ringing in my ears, her pussy hugging my cock as though the force of my thrusts have fused us together. I'll move as soon as I get an ounce of energy back into my body. At this moment in time, I don't think I can feel anything but Vienna beneath me, limp and sated.

I miss the sound of her heartbeat, the labored lift of her breathing. I loved the sound of her pants, but the silence we're floating in now is just as nice. The woman I love is part of me, and I am part of her. My blood fuels her veins.

I think this might be an unfortunate way to start an eternity together, but any doubts I have are erased the second I look at her face. She's smiling, damn near grinning, with her eyes hazy and blurred. She's one satisfied woman, and that makes me ridiculously relieved. I hate to think I've hurt her, but she doesn't seem to be in distress. Quite the opposite, thank God.

"Vienna. Are you okay?" I shift slightly, freezing when she makes a low sound in her throat. Her eyes flutter, that smile turning wicked at the edges. As a human, Vienna was stunning. There are few humans who go down in my history books as memorable, but she definitely tops the list.

As an immortal, however, she is divine. Alluring.

Magnificent.

"Rocked. My. World." She stretches and mewls, beckoning to my half-hard cock with a sultry crook of a finger. "Just give me a minute, and we're good to go again."

If she can recover that quickly, I've obviously created a monster. I can't recall ever being able to bounce back from a hard knock as fast as Vienna apparently can, not even in my heyday. She's a walking fricking miracle, and she's all mine. "Have you learned your lesson?"

She peeks at me from beneath her lashes, wiggling her eyebrows. "Yeah, yeah. Whenever I want a spanking, all I need to do is bite you. That lesson is thoroughly embedded in my ass, Sir. I appreciate you taking the time to teach me the error of my ways." Her giggle is infectious, goddamn her.

"That was totally not the point of the exercise." I groan theatrically, then drop my forehead to hers. "God, I missed you. Twenty-four hours without your mouth sassing me, and I had withdrawal symptoms."

"Aw, such a softie."

No one's ever accused me of that before. Soft isn't something I've ever been. Before my period of servitude under Vadim, I wasn't exactly a keeper of the peace. I'd calmed down after my violent past as a vicious killer, but the urges still remained, even though I had them under control. Being Vadim's good little servant effectively collared me with a choke chain and kept me on a short leash.

No more. It's so fucking good to think that. No more groveling to the prick, no more hiding my true self to fit into his regime, no more twisting my morals to belong to his agenda. For the first time in decades, I'm free. My time is my own. Not that I want to revert back to a murdering cliché, but it is a weight off my shoulders knowing this chapter of my life is almost over with.

Just as soon as Oberon and Vadim are dust.

"So, what do we do now, Colt? I'm hoping the trafficking crisis is in hand if Vadim is in Lucius's custody. That means you're essentially out of a job, right? I myself am currently ranked among the unemployed undead." Her hand smooths over my shoulder, my neck, to play with the short hair at my nape. "I'm voting for a year-long vacation in the Bahamas. Sun, sea, and sex."

"Mmmn-hmm. That vacation would last all of about thirty seconds, vixen." I nuzzle at her throat. "But speaking of the future, Lucius did in fact offer me an opportunity." One designed to distract me from my plan of self-termination at dawn, but I'm not mentioning that depressing fact. Why spoil the mood? "How would you like to rule Phoenix by my side?"

She eases her head away slowly, narrowing her eyes at me. There's the slightest tinge of red in those eyes, a subtle sign of what she's become. It's my indicator of her emotions, and I'll need it over the next few months when she finds her cagey side. There will come a point where she's ashamed of what she is, where she will try to hide her hunger. It's my job to keep her on the narrow path and stop her from going on a killing rampage. "Rule Phoenix? As in the city?"

"Yeah. I killed Antoine and left the city without a ruling authority the vampires will obey. By rights, Lucius should take the reins, but he has enough to deal with handling the aftermath of the trafficking ring, and governing Tucson. It's going to be difficult, bringing the Phoenix vamps under control and getting order back, but I think you and I between us can accomplish what needs to be done."

Vienna arches her hips into mine, making us both hiss between our teeth. Things are just a mite sensitive down there. "So, we're abandoning our cozy love nest in the warehouse and..."

"Moving into a mansion, of course. After it's been demolished, salted, exorcised, and rebuilt to our specifications. God knows how many ghosts are in that place. We could even move the house a few hundred feet in any other direction; downsize it." I like the idea. We don't need the grandeur Antoine demanded in his surroundings. We certainly don't have to tempt the ghosts of his hundreds of victims. "That is, if you want to. I've done everything Lucius has asked of me, V. This is my time now, and I want to spend it with you, all of it, for the rest of my life. If you don't want to go to Phoenix, I will say no to him."

There's no hesitation. Vienna isn't a woman who hesitates when she's made up her mind. She jumps in with both feet, regardless of whether the water is two inches deep or two hundred feet. "Are we getting a title for this relocation? Because if we are, I've always wanted to be a Countess.

Countess Vienna," she says dreamily, grinning to herself. "Has a ring to it."

I may as well go all in. Twenty-four hours without her was enough to show me I'm not half the man I was before I met her a fucking week ago. Hell, it's not even been a week. Days. It's taken days for her to corrupt me so badly, my life turns into a big black sink hole when she's not in it. "Is a ring something you'd be interested in, vixen?"

"That depends. Does it come with a marriage proposal?"

I laugh. Quick off the mark, this one. "Well, that might pose a problem. Creatures of darkness don't usually tie the knot. I'm not sure a marriage ceremony would be legally binding for us." My mouth skims over her jaw to find her lips. "Lucius may be able to perform some sort of ceremony, even if it only holds meaning for us. Forever is a long time," I remind her. "If I slide a ring on your finger, V, it's never coming off."

Her tongue flicks out over my lip, followed by the sharp scrape of her fangs. "I think we've proved love isn't an entirely human concept, Colt. If you'd asked me when I was mortal, I'd have taken some time to consider it. Growing old while you stay young and fit.. I'd be terrified some gorgeous vampire woman had the potential to walk in and steal you away. This way is better. I love you. Ring or no ring, I want to face the future with you."

The kiss is long and sweet, building into something more as I harden fully. I grin, amused by the knowledge Augustus might not be able to look us in the eye for a while.

We both need to feed soon to keep up our strength if we're going to fuck the night away. Vienna's on a tighter schedule than I am, her system demanding a consistent supply of blood. As her donor, I'll have to make sure she takes what she has to when her body asks for it, otherwise... well, I don't relish the idea of a hangry Vienna.

As I pin her hands over her head, I stare into her eyes and find myself captivated. She's still my Vienna, still my fierce and feisty girl. Those stony blue eyes are alive with lust and mischievousness, a potent combination, and I'm suddenly struck by a thought that amuses me, given our current situation.

She was never my captive, but I'll always be hers.

EPILOGUE

ienna

Night is finally upon us, and tonight is what I've been waiting for.

A month has passed since I traded humanity for an eternity with Colt. Four long weeks of stress, internal struggles, and a gut-deep desire to rend two bad men into bite-sized pieces. Not that I'd eat either of them—I have much more discerning taste when it comes to my meals—but I wouldn't hesitate to feed Oberon and Vadim to the sharks, if I could find some in the middle of Arizona.

Lucius has taken his sweet fucking time getting whatever data he needed from the Russian, and I think he's enjoyed the acquiring process. I can't blame him—Vadim has caused ripples of unease to spread over the world as the extent of his experimentation and breeding programs have come to light. Tales of unending torture, reports of multiple suicides within the walls of his facility, eyewitness accounts from those who have been systematically abused by him and his researchers... it's enough to make even a vampire with a cast iron stomach feel ill.

There are still a few loose ends to snip. People stolen from their lives have been returned to where they came from. Those born inside the facility have been... rehabilitated. Strings pulled by Lucius and Colt brought in help from powerful vampires around the world: men and women of vampire blood, with the same moral compass as my fiancé and his king. Working as an unorthodox force of nature, they have almost eradicated the threat Vadim posed to us as a species.

I find it unbearably sad to think that more than a third of the humans set free from the shackles of Vadim's cruelty couldn't hack life once the chains were broken. An epidemic of suicides occurred a week after the destruction of the underground mountain laboratories. The loss of so many people they'd tried to help devastated both Lucius and Colt.

Tonight, Vadim and Oberon face their punishment for their crimes.

I pace the grounds of the Phoenix property Colt *inherited* after Antoine's death. There are still guards at the gate, but the house itself is gone. I've only seen pictures of the mammoth mansion—Colt refused to let me anywhere near it while it still stood, haunted by the souls who lost their lives at Antoine's hands. There's nothing left of it now.

The wrecking ball took care of the structure above ground, slamming through walls until nothing but rubble was left.

A considerable quantity of C4 explosives eradicated the torture chambers hidden below.

Across the way, what Colt tells me used to be the kennels

is flattened. Crews removed every last brick before Colt ordered half a dozen Palo Verde trees to be planted over the area. I approve of the idea. Too much death happened here and, while we are agents of death, it's a balm to the soul to be able to balance the scales and offer life.

Our new house is already underway, a quarter mile west of where I'm standing. The estate is huge, big enough that we decided not to build our fresh start on top of haunted ground. The ghosts here, those who remain, deserve peace. Once the crater where the mansion stood is filled in properly and more trees are planted, this place won't be disturbed again. We're closing it off, letting this part of the estate go back to nature.

Headlights swing up the drive, two pairs.

Folding my arms across my chest, I let my fangs drop and wait for the SUVs to pull up and the engines to switch off.

Tiberius exits the driver's side of the first black SUV, followed by Lucius and Selene from the rear, with Vadim sandwiched between them. The Russian does not look like the same vampire I met a month ago. Without access to unlimited quantities of blood and his wealth, the man who violated me is almost skinny in comparison to his former bulk. He looks old, showing his age, but those evil eyes are burning with hatred.

There's no fear yet, but there will be.

Lucius promised Colt he could take care of Vadim when it came to his execution. I think Colt demanded it, actually, but the promise was made and kept. It won't be an easy death, not when Colt's temper has been acting up like Mount Vesuvius for weeks.

Augustus departs the second truck, slamming the door

closed. The rear passenger door flies open and Oberon is tossed out headfirst into the dirt, Colt on his heels. My dom reaches down and grabs his ex-friend by the scruff of the neck, dragging his sorry ass over to join us.

"Brought you an anniversary present, vixen." Colt drops Oberon in front of me, slamming his boot into the back of his knee when Oberon tries to scramble to his feet. "Stay on your knees, Oberon. My girl loves a chase, and she's a hell of a lot faster than you are."

Lucius forces Vadim into a similar position before he and Selene move to stand beside me. Colt shifts to my other side, so we present a wall of four. Augustus and Tiberius take their positions behind the offenders, ready to detain them if they move.

"Thank you," I murmur to Colt, sliding my hand into his and squeezing his fingers. "I do love presents."

"Vadim, Oberon," Lucius addresses them coldly, every inch the king his reputation states. "Both of you are sentenced to death for your crimes. Your actions put our survival as a species in jeopardy, threatened to expose us to the humans. Is there anything you wish to say before your sentences are executed?"

"You will all die screaming," Vadim snaps out, curling his lip at us. "The full force of my army will rain down on you, bringing blood and destruction in its wake. Killing me will not stop this. It will only come sooner with my death."

Lucius rolls his eyes. "Your army was disbanded ten days ago, you idiot. Exterminated like brainwashed vermin. There's nothing left of your army, your empire, or your legacy. Everything you've worked for has been eradicated, the damage you wreaked is already being repaired. In six months, your name will mean fuck all. The Russian mafia seems oddly relieved to have you out of their hair, *Avtoritet.* You were a liability, and they know it." He flicks his fingers toward the kneeling vampire. "Colt. He's all yours."

Colt's fingers slip from mine, and he brushes a kiss over my temple before he steps forward. Pulling a flask from his pocket, he grips Vadim's jaw and puts pressure on the joints until the Russian is forced to open his mouth wide. "I've thought long and hard about how to do this. Antoine was a sick fuck, he deserved to have his head twisted around until it popped off his neck. But you… you laid hands on my girl, you asshole." He snaps the lid off the flask and takes a deep sniff of the contents, recoiling slightly. "Oh yeah, that's the stuff. I want you to burn, Vadim. I want you to die screaming in agony."

Clear fluid glugs from the flask into Vadim's open maw, dribbling over his chin and down the front of his tattered shirt. His translucent blue eyes go wide and he chokes, clawing at his throat and Colt's hand. A second later, Augustus snatches his arms and pins them at the small of Vadim's back.

The smell of gasoline fills the air.

"Fuck," Lucius murmurs softly, taking Selene and me by the elbows and hauling us back ten feet as Tiberius tugs Oberon away from the line of fire.

"Make sure you drink every last drop." Colt tips the flask higher, going so far as to shake the vessel to ensure there's no more left. "Bet that's doing some weird shit to your body right about now, huh? Your veins feel like they're filled with acid, your stomach is being eaten away. It won't kill you; it's only gasoline, and you're not human enough for it to end your sorry existence." He digs into his pocket again and comes out with a slim red stick topped by what looks like a piece of string. "This, however, will."

Colt slams the firecracker into Vadim's open mouth and snaps his jaw closed over the little explosive, leaving the fuse poking out between his lips. The Russian is making some interesting noises, but my lover really isn't taking prisoners today. He tugs out a lighter and sparks the flame, holding it a scant inch from the fuse. "There's one thing, Vadim: at least you'll go out with a bang."

He sets the fuse alight and both he and Augustus hold onto the writhing, screaming prisoner until the very last second. My anxiety levels hit the roof as the fuse sizzles down toward Vadim's white-rimmed lips. If they time this wrong, it won't just be Vadim meeting his maker in a few seconds.

At some unspoken signal, Colt and Augustus release their hold on Vadim's jaw, his arms, and blur to safety. Before the Russian can spit the firecracker out, there's a sharp crack as the explosive ignites, and half of his face is gone in an instant. I grimace as blood splatters, Vadim's scream of agony echoing in the still night before the flame takes hold of the gasoline lining his throat.

The Russian combusts into a fireball, dissolving into flaming ash in seconds.

Colt casually dusts off his hands, slapping them together as though ridding himself of any remnants of Vadim. "That was actually incredibly satisfying. Not as much as ripping his heart out of his chest or his head from his neck, but still… satisfying."

"You're fucking insane," I hiss at him as his arms come around my waist. "You could have gone up in flames with him!"

"Some of us are organized and work out the timings before we go ahead with a plan." He nips my earlobe.

"Insane," I repeat flatly, then turn my attention back to

Oberon as Tiberius kicks him forward. Oh, goody. My turn. Now, I'm not as creative as the pyrotechnics master behind me, but I'm not as old as he is. I've maimed before, but I've never taken a life, undead or not.

Oberon throws himself face down at Lucius's feet. "Please, I don't want to die. Give me a chance, please. I'll do anything."

God, have some dignity. The sentence has been passed for weeks now; he should be resigned to the idea of dying. The only reason he hasn't been dealt with yet is because Lucius wanted to make sure we'd been given all the information stored in that sick brain.

"What would you have me do? You conspired with Vadim, kidnapped Vienna, engaged in trafficking. Your sentence is just." Lucius shakes his head in dismissal and gestures to me. "Are you sure you want to be the one to do this, Vienna?"

"Oh yeah. I've been dreaming of this night." Giving Colt's arm a pat, I strut forward, my eyes catching Oberon's and holding them. "You never answered my question, Oberon. How attached to your dick are you?"

He swallows hard. "Wait. Wait! Lucius, look, I fucked up. Let me fight for my life. If I win, I'll serve you for the rest of eternity. I'll leave Tucson, you'll never hear from me again, I swear. Whatever you want, I'll do it."

"You assume you'll win. Whom do you propose you fight? Tiberius, Augustus, Colt?" Lucius spreads his hands wide. "You may be fighting for your life, Oberon, but all three of these men are more than you can take. Revenge versus survival aren't the best odds."

Oh hell, no. If this weaselly little fucker thinks he can squirrel out of me kicking his ass and pulverizing him into dust, he hasn't thought this through at all. But I suppose desperate times call for moronic measures. "He's fighting me. I called dibs on his sorry ass, and I've waited too long to just hand him over to one of the guys. If he wants to fight, he takes me on."

"V—"

"Shut up, Colt. You've had your fun, now let me have mine." I grin wickedly at Oberon and bare my fangs at him, pleased when he almost swallows his tongue in fear. "You didn't scare me when I was mortal, Oberon. I'm stronger, faster than I was then. Still fancy your odds at walking away from this in one piece?"

I shrug out of my leather jacket, stretching my arms out to the sides. The epic heatwave that held Tucson in its grasp broke a week ago, but Phoenix is still unseasonably warm. Not that I feel the heat the same way, but I'm literally dressed to kill, never dreaming I'd be gearing up for a fight. The tank top doesn't offer much protection; my trusty boots, however, will come in handy.

"When you're ready then," Lucius says as Tiberius moves back.

Oberon is on his feet in an instant, charging at me mindlessly. There's no planning, no strategy, just sheer brute force. I take a fist to the gut, then the face, before he slams into me hard enough to send me flying into the dirt. He's on top of me a moment later, using his fists like hammers to pummel my face, sending shards of pain shearing through my skull.

So, this is how he wants to play.

I thrust my hand up, striking his nose with the heel of my palm. Cartilage crunches nastily on impact, and I'm showered with blood. He yelps loudly, batting my hand away and reaching for my throat, but I snag his hand first in both of mine, bending it backwards until I hear bones snap. He rears away, cradling his broken wrist and whimpering as though he can't understand what the fuck just happened.

I pull my legs from between his, leaving him straddling the ground as I draw my knees up to my chest and let loose with a kick that connects with his chest, propelling him back with enough force, he tumbles twice before coming to a stop. Scrambling to my feet, taking a running step and swinging with my right foot, I boot him in the stomach and flip him onto his back.

My ears are ringing; I can taste my own blood in my mouth.

Stalking him as he crawls away, I grab hold of his injured wrist and twist, feeling the bones grind against each other. Let's see how he likes someone manipulating his broken bones, shall we? There's a viciousness growing inside me, fueled by bloodlust and loathing. I want to pull his arm off and batter him with it.

"V, don't lose yourself. Just finish it." Colt's voice grounds me, sucks me out of the spiraling need to annihilate.

"Vienna, you don't have to kill me," Oberon cajoles, his voice nothing like Colt's. It's whiny and abrasive, scraping over my nerves. "We can both walk away from this."

My boot plants itself between his legs before I realize I've moved. His words die off into a high, girlish scream which deflates on a wheeze. I kick him again, and then a third time. Apparently, I have an anger issue when it comes to him. He caused the accident which broke my arm, he caused me pain. He handed me over to Vadim without a thought because he was going to profit from my capture.

Yeah, I really do need to kill him.

My weapon is coiled in the back pocket of my jeans and I pull it out, taking my time stretching it taut between my hands. It's not as creative as Colt's method of dispatch, but it's painful enough to sate my need to dole out agony. I bend down and roll Oberon onto his stomach, dropping onto my knees on his shoulders to pin him.

"Should've been a lot nicer to me when you had the chance, asshole," I tell him as I slip the thin piece of wire under his neck, then cross the ends and pull. He bucks and kicks, his feet smacking the ground as I tighten the garotte inch by inch. "Maybe you wouldn't be losing your head."

Blood pools beneath him as the wire bites through his skin, slicing through muscle. He can't speak, he's reduced to nasty gurgles, and I don't hesitate to yank the wire until it cleaves through his neck completely, severing his head with a nasty jerk.

He disappears beneath me, his body returning to the earth, and I'm... drained.

I drop the wire and scrub my hands over my bruised face. By morning, the tenderness will be gone, but right now, I'm feeling the blows with crystal clear clarity. I'm not sure I'll recover from the emotional impact of this quite as easily. Killing someone, even if it's killing a sick excuse of a vampire, has rocked me to the core.

I sit and stare at my hands.

"Vienna, you did good. Can you look at me?"

I thought killing Oberon would make me feel better. It's supposed to be my nature, right? Death is part of who I am now, but I think maybe something went wrong when I got lost in the change. He needed to die, to pay the price for what he did, but maybe I should have listened to Colt and let someone else do the deed.

No. I'm not thinking like this. I made the choice, now I have to own it. I lift my eyes to Colt's and see the concern in them. I cup his jaw and sigh. "I'm okay. It's done and it's over. We got rid of the bad guys. Everything smells like roses." Well, that's kind of a lie. All I can smell is the tart odor of gasoline. "We can move on now, right? Build the house, move to Phoenix, and just... chill out for a while."

"Yeah, vixen, we can move on. You gonna be okay?"

It's a good question, and I won't know the answer until I've thought it over. But as I sit in the ashes of a man I didn't really know but whom I've come to abhor with every fiber of my being, I'm guessing the answer will eventually be *yes*. When I think of what he was involved in, the horrors he took part in and bestowed upon innocent people, I know the world is a safer place without the likes of him and Vadim taking up valuable space.

If I'm ever in this position again, I'm not going to let my emotions get in the way of thinking with a straight head. It'll be a stake to the heart, and that's it. I've spent the past month learning how not to be a monster, teaching myself with Colt's help how to tame the brutal urges and deal with them in a calm, collected manner.

I lost my shit tonight, and I'm not proud of it.

But I can get it back.

Colt helps me to my feet, pulling me against him. He bares his throat for me, somehow knowing what I need. "Go ahead, V. You'll feel more settled once you've fed."

I sag against him, my mouth latching onto his skin. My tongue laps at the vein before my fangs pierce it as gently as I can manage. Another thing Colt's taught me—how to feed without causing pain or discomfort. It takes patience and control, and I need to reclaim both right now.

His hand cradles my head as I drink slowly. "I've never been prouder of you, Vienna."

Lifting my head, I blink at him. "For turning into a raging bitch?"

"No, vixen. You lost control because he caught you off guard. We can teach you how to deal with that, in time. I'm proud of you because you didn't go on a rampage once he was dust." Colt jerks his chin. "There are five of us here you could have focused your rage on, but you didn't. You're improving. It takes most newbies years to find the control you have, myself included."

I smile. "I must be a prodigy, huh?"

"Oh, you're definitely something. This is the end of the chapter that brought us together, V. Are you ready for what comes next?"

I look at the vampire who spun my world on its axis and sent it spiraling into an alternate universe. He's the love of my life, no doubt. We've had high points and low points, learning curves to face, and challenges that would destroy most people. Yet here we stand in a circle of friends, in the place where we plan to spend eternity if all goes to plan.

Colt is all the family I have now. My parents didn't take the news of my engagement well, especially since it derailed their carefully laid out guidelines for my life after thirty. They are currently refusing to talk to me. It's okay, they'll come around eventually, but I don't need them. Not when I have Colt to fill all the roles in my life.

I slip my hand into his as we fall into step with Lucius and Selene, walking toward the SUVs. We'll go back to Tucson until the house is ready and we can take over the running of Phoenix. We're both looking forward to it, to tackling the issues Antoine left behind. We can make a safe haven here for those who need one, and live our lives together.

It's pretty damn perfect.

"Yes, Sir. With you, I'm ready for anything."

Bring it on.

The End

WANT MORE MIDNIGHT DOMS?

Click here to sign up for news!

Read the whole series for more of your favorite vampire BDSM club:

Alpha's Blood by Renee Rose & Lee Savino

Her Vampire Master by Maren Smith

Her Vampire Prince by Ines Johnson

Her Vampire Hero by Nicolina Martin

Her Vampire Bad Boy by Brenda Trim

Her Vampire Rebel by Zara Zenia

Her Vampire Obsession by Tymber Dalton, writing as Lesli Richardson

Her Vampire Temptation by Alexis Alvarez

Her Vampire Addiction by Tabitha Black

Her Vampire Lord by Ines Johnson

Her Vampire Suspect by Brenda Trim

His Captive Mortal by Renee Rose & Lee Savino

All Soul's Night: A Halloween Anthology

The Vampire's Captive by Kay Elle Parker

The Vampire's Prey by Vivian Murdoch

ALSO BY KAY ELLE PARKER

Hangman's Haunt Series:

Wild - Book 1

Nocturnal - Book 2

Eclipsed - Book 3

Destined - Novella

The Shadowcrown Duet:

King Of Shadows - Book 1

Queen Of Shadows - Book 2

Club Avalon Series:

Dance For Me - Book 1

Standalones:

Speechless

Monsters & Guardians (Trigger Warning!)

Black Light: Branded

Anthologies:

Black Light: Roulette War

Loves Bites

ABOUT THE AUTHOR

Kay Elle Parker is an International Bestselling author living in the wilds of Yorkshire.

She has an eclectic taste in music, reads anything when she has the time, and loves Fell ponies and Border Collies. Her sense of humor is wicked and often misunderstood, downright dirty and infectious.

Writing romance is the dream, and Kay has books in dark, BDSM, and paranormal romance. Just recently, she released her first Western BDSM romance, Black Light: Branded.

She loves writing all things vampire and shifter.

She loves to chat to readers!

Editor: Tabitha Black

Made in the USA
Middletown, DE
23 September 2023